HER WICKED HUSBAND

NADIA LEE

Her Wicked Husband

www.nadialee.net

1

FIONA

The guests hear "Here Comes the Bride," but "Dies irae" from Verdi's Requiem Mass plays in my head. Of course, the only thing they see is a gorgeous groom at the other end of the aisle—someone who should make my heart flutter and my pulse race.

My pulse is racing, all right. But all that's shaking are my legs as I make my way, alone, up the aisle to the man I'm about to marry. It's everything I can do to not turn around and run someplace nobody will ever find me.

Jude Morven is a wolf in sheep's clothing. Lucifer in Gabriel's garb. From his carefully styled golden hair to his crinkling baby-blue eyes and full, cherubic lips, he shines with a beauty that's an unholy cross between arresting masculinity and boyish innocence. But his soul? It stinks, absolutely the worst of the worst. If his appearance reflected his heart, he'd be stooped over, skin pitted, wiry hair growing out of his ears, smelling like mashed garlic gone bad.

Next to him is his best friend and best man—my adoptive brother, Aaron Oberman. People often remark that Aaron and Jude look like siblings, with Aaron being the uglier, shorter and less accomplished one. But his taste in clothes and life in general is as expensive as Jude's.

He's poorer than Jude, but has a relentless drive to spend as lavishly as his best friend. Which is why his tuxedo nearly outshines the groom's.

But nothing can outshine Aaron's smile. He's beaming like *he*'s the happy bride. I might beam too if I were a heartless asshole who didn't care that he was selling his adoptive sister off to a sociopath for two million dollars. Not sure if Aaron knows the depths of Jude's depravity. But it wouldn't matter, because money matters more.

Aaron's mom Sherry is seated in the front row, in an eye-catching burnt-orange damask dress. Most people don't realize that we aren't actually related by blood. Her chignon is the same shade of auburn as my carefully curled hair. Our eyes are similar as well—moss green ringed with gold, although hers are often vacant and focused somewhere "beyond" as she silently recites some Buddhist scripture. Even now, in the midst of the wedding festivities, she moves her thumb over the beads on her japamala. It's made with a hundred and eight small blue lace agate beads and one larger one, all strung together with off-white silk threads. I've never seen her without it, even in her sleep.

Her eyes meet mine briefly, then drop to her lap. If she knew what I was doing—and why—would she try to stop me? Or would it not matter because I'm not her real daughter and Aaron is her actual flesh and blood? I wish I knew, but Sherry would never tell me, and I'm too cowardly to ask. I want to believe she loves me—that she treats me as well as she treats her real daughter, Finley. Otherwise...

I don't know what I'd do otherwise. Fear has muddied my mind since I found out *I* need to pay off the two million dollars my brother owes some loan sharks...or face the unimaginable consequences.

Despite my slow progress, I'm already close to the altar. Jude's smile widens, his unblinking eyes on me. The large stained-glass panel behind him is backlit by the sun, casting various colors into the chapel.

My mouth dries. My pulse beats wildly, like a sacrificial lamb's.

I glance out the open windows to the bright sky. So beautiful. Not a wisp of cloud anywhere on the endless azure expanse.

Dear Buddha, please strike this ceremony with lightning. I'll give up meat for the rest of my life.

There is no explosion of heavenly electricity. A few birds chirp as

"Here Comes the Bride" swells to a climax. But then, Buddha isn't really known for lightning strikes.

My grip on the bouquet tightens as cold sweat slickens my palms. Tremors wrack me. Jude's eyes gleam with the satisfaction of a hyena about to rip into its prey. He wants to make me suffer for daring to leave him eight years ago.

Dear God. Please! Just one *lightning strike. You can bypass the chapel and hit me directly. I don't care.*

The doors behind me open with a thunderous crash. *Yes! Thank you, God.*

Joyous relief nearly turns my knees into jelly. I spin around, hoping for a spectacularly messed-up entrance, one with lots of rubble and clouds of dust. Jude's grandmother is superstitious. She'll never let the ceremony continue. Ideally, she won't let me marry into the family at all.

What about the money?

The question hammers in my head, but my sense of self-preservation says I should flee. God is against this marriage. Surely, he'll strike down the loan sharks as well.

The buoyant sensation in my heart instantly fizzles as I take in the sight of the man at the entrance. A dark tuxedo molds to him perfectly from broad shoulders to narrow waist. The unknotted tie hangs around his neck, and the top two buttons are undone, showing a hint of a strong, lean chest.

Whispers rise in the chapel as I take him in. Slanted, dark brows over a pair of sharp gray eyes that mocked me only a month ago. A perfectly straight nose and the firm, confident line of his surprisingly full lips. Expensively cropped black hair looks like a crown, and the set of his strong jaw says he doesn't give a fuck.

I blink to clear the vision. But no. It's still him. Bryce Huxley, in the flesh, looking like he's just stepped out of a fashion shoot for dissolute bad boys.

What's he doing here?

He was the first—actually the *only*—person I could think of when my family was about to face bankruptcy and needed two million dollars. He hates my guts now, but he owes me one. When I rescued his golden retriever from a hit-and-run accident ten years ago and took care of her, Bryce promised he would do me a favor—anything within his means. No time limit.

I've never called that marker in. I did it for the dog, not for Bryce to owe me something.

Still, I didn't expect the son of a bitch to not only ignore my plea, but act like he had amnesia about the promise. Hopefully he doesn't think crashing the wedding is what I wanted, because I wasn't thinking about marrying Jude at that time. The deal to sell me off to Jude came after Bryce turned me down and humiliated me at his office.

"Bryce Huxley! What a surprise," Jude calls out, then takes a step forward. Rivals since high school, they never got along. "You weren't invited, but you're welcome to sit in the back and toast to us later. After all"—he spreads his arms magnanimously—"we have a history." His tone is triumphant, almost gloating—*I won. Again.*

He comes down the steps of the altar, grabs my hand and yanks me up toward him, causing me to drop the bouquet. He doesn't seem to care; his arm wraps around my waist, pressing our bodies together. Cold shivers spider over my spine and neck, making my scalp prickle. Nausea roils in my belly.

"I'm not here to toast to you." Bryce glances at Jude's hold on me, then looks me in the eye. "What you said in my office—does it still hold?"

Confusion clouds my mind as I desperately try to remember exactly what I said. Didn't he trample all over me and basically tell me to go fuck myself? "Well—"

"Yes or no?"

My mouth dries. I didn't say anything that wasn't true. "Yes. But—"

"Fine." He raises his hand, palm up. "Let's finish our talk."

"Our talk...?"

"The favor."

Shock snuffs all the thoughts in my head. I stare at his hand blankly for a moment, trying to decide if I'm hallucinating. He was so resolute and final when he had me dragged out of Huxley & Webber.

Bryce's eyes remain as calm as a lake, but he cocks an eyebrow. The small shift in his expression jolts me out of stupefaction. *He won't wait forever.*

I don't know what he'll demand. Two million is a lot of money, and we never got around to discussing how I'd pay it back before he kicked me out. But...

My heart pounds so hard I feel half dazed, my body trembling. Bryce couldn't possibly be any worse than Jude, could he? The memory of the two years of abuse and humiliation Jude heaped upon me is a weight that may never leave. And he hasn't gotten any better since. Being with him will mean—

Dread clamps around my neck. I can't be with him again, especially when I might have another option. Bryce might not be much better, but at least he isn't an out-and-out sociopath. He might hate me, but at least he'll try to be respectful in public. Jude loved to humiliate me in public. It stroked his ego, made him feel powerful and manly.

I lunge forward before Jude can react, flying down the aisle in my heels toward Bryce. Brilliant exultation flares in the depths of his eyes.

"You whore!" Jude spits. I can hear him running behind me, trying to catch up.

And then it all becomes too much. My knees buckle in mid-stride and I start to fall. Surprise flashes in Bryce's eyes as he lunges forward, catching me and throwing me over a shoulder in one smooth motion.

Aaron takes a few steps forward. Some of the guests jump to their feet as well, seemingly ready to take action. But Aaron hesitates, obviously unwilling to put himself between Bryce and Jude. The guests look at each other, unsure what to do. Only Sherry breaks the tableau, counting her beads and chanting her mantra, her gaze fixed somewhere beyond the white cross on the wall.

"What the *fuck* are you doing?" Aaron shouts finally, his chest heaving.

"Sealing a deal and saving the family," I say, but it's anybody's guess as to whether or not he hears me.

Bryce turns and starts walking out, but something tugs at my train.

"Stop!" Jude says. "She's my woman!"

I lift my head and look at his distorted face, his eyes burning with unholy fury. I flip him the bird—something I've wanted to do for a long, long time. I'm not anybody's woman, and *especially* not his.

Bryce spins around. I grab his jacket and twist to see what's about to happen between the two men.

"Put her down!" Jude snarls. "She's mine—"

The rest ends in a high-pitched whimper as Bryce's foot connects with his knee with a shudder-inducing crunch. I gasp with shock—and schadenfreude.

Jude's face goes bright red, his eyes bulging. His mouth gapes open in a silent scream then closes as he clenches his jaw. Veins stand out on his temples as he clutches his knee with one hand, the other still grasping my train.

Bryce gathers some of the material in his own hand and yanks the train out of Jude's grasp. He turns and starts to walk out with me still on his shoulder. "Might want to do something about your grip strength," he says in a voice loud enough to carry through the entire chapel, "if you plan to use that hand for more than just jerking off."

2

FIONA

—TWO MONTHS earlier

THE SoCAL SKY is an immaculate blue as the dark mahogany coffin with copper details is lowered into the ground. Only the best for my adoptive father, Zachary Oberman, even in death.

People in black circle around, wearing somber faces and expensive perfumes. A few women let out muffled sobs and sniffles. My eyes remain dry as I stare at the fresh red roses falling on the top of the coffin. I'm not sure what I'm feeling right now, but it isn't mere grief.

We weren't close. He only adopted me because his wife couldn't cope with losing their seven-year-old daughter Finley in a drowning accident, even after a year had passed, and other options weren't effective. Zachary considered therapy bullshit—a waste of time.

He assessed my frame, coloring and features to make sure they matched Finley's as closely as possible. He had me sing to make sure I could carry a tune, then instructed an assistant to facilitate the adoption.

He also gave me a long list of things I could and couldn't do, the most important one being that I must answer to Finley or Finn, whichever his wife preferred, even though he allowed me to keep my given name on paper.

In addition, I was to behave like an angel, just like Finley. I had to act sweet and cute around Sherry, control my attitude and words, study hard so I didn't bring home bad grades, and never let her worry about me.

Not only that, everything Finley did, I had to do as well, including the violin. She was almost a prodigy, and Sherry had been proud. If I couldn't play, that wouldn't do for Zachary. But without Finley's talent, I had to make up for it with persistence and effort. Zachary said he'd provide the best of instruction to mold me—and then delivered exactly that.

I strove to meet every demand, terrified of coming up short and understanding that if I didn't pass muster, I'd be sent back. I'd overheard too many adults' careless whispers and realized that, at the age of seven, I was too old to be desirable for adoption. People want cute babies, not skinny, awkward girls.

I didn't want to be sent back again, like some mistaken online purchase, and was terrified at the prospect of being passed around among foster homes. The one that took me in after my first adoption failed was awful, with a man who often drank too much and lost his temper. He never hit me or the other kids, but he would curse, call us "stupid dogs" and frequently forgot to feed us.

I never complained because the next home might have been worse.

I could never forget what my first adoptive mom whispered when she thought I was asleep.

"I feel so bad about sending her back," she'd said to her husband. "What if she ends up with someone like that man...? You know, the one in Lancaster County who beat his foster kids?"

"Yeah, but we can't keep her. We only have so much energy and money, and the baby in your belly is the priority," he'd said.

Now that I'm older, I realize most foster parents are good, well-meaning people. But I was too young and too scared.

I drop a rose into the grave. *Goodbye, Zachary.* Although he only saw me as a tool, I'm grateful in a way. After all, he was never stingy with me, always the nicest clothes, best private schools and extracurriculars. I even had a pony. He did all that to soothe his wife, but I benefited greatly.

Sherry grips my forearm, her eyes wet with tears, and looks up at me. I'm still not sure if she sees me or the shadow of Finley. The moment I entered the Obermans' household, Zachary hugged me, calling me Finn. Sherry followed suit, then held me at arm's length and laughed like she couldn't have been happier. There were tears in her eyes. "My Finn, welcome home!"

The way Sherry looks at me dismays me from time to time. I can't decide if what I've done has helped or hurt. It might've been better for her to face the reality that her daughter died a long time ago. From what I understand, Sherry became a Buddhist after Finley's death because she needed to believe that good karma would reincarnate Finley into a better life.

Shifting my weight awkwardly, I look away. Zachary would probably call me ungrateful if he knew my inner conflict. But it's exhausting to be a stand-in or a tool. Sometimes I just want to be me—Fiona, not Finn.

Where's Aaron? He was standing next to Sherry only moments ago, but now he's nowhere to be seen. But then, he's been distracted and even a little anxious since the funeral started. He's also been giving me a death glare every time he notices me. Not sure why his hostility has grown even more intense. The entire estate will go to him. Zachary told me upon my graduation from Harvard that he wasn't leaving me a penny. Apparently, the family legacy belongs to a *real* Oberman.

Once the burial is over, Sherry leans on me, visibly wilting. I take her to the long, winding path in the park next to the cemetery. It's beautifully maintained, with lush greenery and trellises covered with white jasmines, designed for people to take an emotional break. The view should soothe her frazzled nerves and grief over losing her husband, who, despite his flaws, adored her.

"Do you have to go back to Wisconsin, Finn?" Sherry asks, after a while. "You've been away for so long."

I squeeze her hand, hoping I'm giving her the comfort she needs. Losing Zachary has to be devastating. He treated her like a hothouse flower and protected her from the ugliness of the world. I can never repay the debt of gratitude for everything Sherry's done for me. Although Zachary treated me like a tool, she's cared for me like her own flesh and blood. She gave me a home when I had none, and provided me with the attention I needed as a young, insecure girl, from attending every school event to teaching me how to do makeup and bake a peach cobbler. I doubt a kid abandoned by her birth mother would be able to speak three languages fluently or have a Harvard degree without Sherry.

"You have Aaron," I say. He's always loathed me for taking his sister's place. "You're just a fucking fake, taking Finley's place!" he screamed within an hour of meeting me. "A horrible, disgusting stand-in!" Zachary glared and had the butler "remove" him. Although Zachary spoke to Aaron, the attitude hasn't improved. His hatred has only gotten worse over time. Zachary protected me, but it wasn't because he cared about me. He needed to preserve Sherry's fragile mental health.

"Sons are different," she says with a sigh. "Do you have to work for that cheese company? That family can more than afford to take care of you. If you want to continue your career in marketing, there are so many companies in Los Angeles. I hear you're good at your job."

"I am, but the company needs me." The owners treat me well, and I don't want to leave them hanging. "I'll be back for the holidays."

"And for your birthday," she says, her fingers tightening on my arm.

"I'll see what I can do." But I know I won't be coming home for that. The Obermans celebrate Finley's birthday, which is also the day Zachary brought me into the Oberman household. My real birthday is forgotten, and it's a little awkward—even emotionally draining—to blow out candles on a cake with another girl's name on it. Besides, Aaron can't stand celebrating anything about me.

"It's been so lonely without you. Should I move to be with you, then?" Sherry looks contemplative. "I don't want you to give up anything for me."

Horror and guilt wind through my heart. I went to Monroe, Wisconsin specifically to see if I could heal from the trauma of the last two years of college because I knew I would never recover if I stayed in SoCal, where Bryce and Jude live. In addition, I wanted to find a purpose and sense of belonging away from the Obermans. Who knows how long the family's going to need me to play the fake daughter? Sherry shouldn't abandon her real son and everyone she knows in SoCal to be with me in another state.

"Please. Mom." I put a hand over hers. "I don't want *you* to give up your friends and family in L.A. for me."

"Your father's gone now. What do I have left?" she says, looking down.

A huge lake appears to our right, and she switches places with me so she's on that side of the path. After Finley drowned, Zachary filled in the pool at the family mansion and turned it into a field of wisteria, the child's favorite. After I moved in with the Obermans, I discovered that I'm highly allergic to wisteria. But Zachary gave me medication and instructed me not to mention it to Sherry, since it'd only distress her.

"This looks dangerous," Sherry says. "Do you want to turn back?"

I don't tell her I can swim, since Finn isn't supposed to be able to swim. "No. It's okay." Turning back would mean possibly running into Aaron, and I don't want to deal with his hostility. "Let's walk a little more. I won't trip and fall. I promise." I give her a reassuring smile.

She looks at me for a moment, then finally nods. "True. You're older now."

We walk along the lake, the cool breeze toying with our hair. I don't say much, just listen to Sherry's gossip about the people in her social circle. It's amazingly wide, and includes the Huxleys. "Your father hired Bryce Huxley to take care of the estate. Can you believe it? He used to be so little. He'd come by to play when you two were young and toddling around." She laughs, apparently oblivious to the tension gripping me.

Bryce. My heart clenches with pain, but I force a smile. He never came by after I was adopted, so the playtime must have been with Finley. Sherry gets confused sometimes, especially when she's going through an emotional upheaval.

When I met Bryce at Harvard ten years ago, during our sophomore year, he was amazing—made me feel seen—but then overnight he began to hate me, and with good reason.

If you clarify—

What? That I was being blackmailed? Then I have to tell him what I was being blackmailed with. And deal with all the consequent ugliness.

There's no evidence, and he would never believe me. He judged me back then, but when I finally offered to explain before leaving for Wisconsin, he texted that I was dead to him. He wouldn't be any different now.

My breathing starts to hitch. I close my eyes and inhale deeply. *Don't think about that chapter of your life. It's over.*

"Huh. Look at the two of you. Strolling along like you got nothing to worry about."

I open my eyes and look at a couple of men in front of us. They're in black suits with white dress shirts, sans ties. The top two buttons are undone, and an exaggerated swagger lends them a disreputable air. The one on the left has a small scar at the corner of his thin mouth. Younger than the one on the right, he takes a step forward.

"How fucked up is it that you two are living such a carefree life while refusing to make good on the loan?"

The loan? I rake my eyes over them. They don't look anything like bankers or financial advisors. The Obermans are old money, and they don't deal with people like this.

Before I can speak, he continues, "We hadda *inconvenience* ourselves to come here to collect." A huge gold ring glints on his index finger as he pokes my forehead with unexpected force.

I stagger back, frowning. "You must be mistaken. The family has a bank it deals with."

"I must be mistaken," he mocks in a falsetto, looking at his friend. "You sayin' you don't owe us? Lemme tell you somethin', honey. When one of you owes us, *alla* you owe us."

I glance at Sherry, but she looks just as confused as I am, and slightly anxious. Zachary was too straitlaced to deal with people like this. Which leaves—

"We are a good, respectable family," Sherry says. Her diction is more pronounced, her spine straighter, a sign that she's becoming upset. "This behavior is simply unacceptable."

The men look at each other, chortling. "Our *behavior*." Scar Mouth moves toward Sherry. "Pay up, bitch."

I slip between them, standing before her like a shield. His meaty paw smacks my shoulder with enough force to bruise. I wince, grateful he didn't touch Sherry, who's in her sixties and too delicate for this kind of physical confrontation. Anger flares in his beady eyes.

"You gettin' in my way?" He shoves me to my right, hard.

I gasp as I lose my balance and fall into the lake. Along with the splash comes an agitated shout from one of the men. Despite L.A.'s warm weather, the water is frigid, chilling me instantly. I sink, gravity sucking me into the murky depths. Little bubbles brush past me, and my survival instinct jolts through me, adrenaline pumping through my veins. Zachary made sure I could swim, and it's coming in handy as I kick myself up toward the surface.

A large object splashes into the water. Auburn hair waves like kelp...

Sherry!

Panic roars in my head, drowning out the pounding of my heart. She never learned to swim. She avoided the water entirely ever since Finley died. *Did the assholes push her in, too?* Damn it, that's practically murder!

I propel myself toward her. She flails, bubbles rising. My hands brush against her arms, but she shoves at me, jerking her hands and shaking her head faster. She opens her mouth as though trying to speak, although nothing comes out under the water.

What is she trying to do? Doesn't she know she's making things harder for me?

I give her a stern look—well, as stern as I can manage given the situation. *I'm not leaving without you.*

I grab her and frog-kick us up, even though she thrashes against me. My task is a thousand times more difficult with her flailing. *Is being in the water triggering her?*

When she's overstimulated, she has episodes. I don't want to imagine what she'll do once we're out of the water.

Finally, we break the surface. My arms and legs feel like jelly by the time I drag us to shore. I gasp, desperately sucking air into my starved lungs. Sherry supports herself on both hands, coughing and sputtering water. I look around quickly. The men aren't around anymore. *Did they freak out and run after Sherry fell into the water?* She might've jumped into the lake before they could react. I'm not sure how she'd react when faced with the possibility that her daughter might drown—again.

"Mom." My voice is hoarse. "Mom" feels so strange and unnatural on my tongue. I've avoided calling her that as much as possible because it enrages Aaron. "Mom! Are you okay?"

She coughs some more, then shakes her head slowly. Her clothes stick to her body, and stringy hair plasters her skull. She turns her head toward me, her face bloodless, her lips trembling. She studies me, as though to make sure I'm breathing. Then she shoves herself off the ground and launches herself at me.

"You stupid, stupid child!" she screams, hitting me. Her fists are so soft, they feel like soaked cotton balls. Her muddy japamala beads smack my chest. "What's wrong with you? You never, never try to protect me! You protect yourself! How am I going to go on if anything happens to you?"

Tears stand in her eyes, which are unsteady with heartrending fear, relief and fury. She continues to scream and hit me. My falling into the water must've been horrifying, recreating the nightmare she wants to forget at all costs. Seeing Sherry suffer because of me makes my heart heavy with an uncomfortable cocktail of emotions I can't pinpoint.

"Mom, it's okay," I say, pulling her into my arms. She resists, like she knows I'm just playing along. "Shh… I'm fine. We're fine. Please, settle down. Please."

"Why did you risk yourself like that?" she sobs, pressing her fist over her heart. "*Why?*"

"It's for good karma," I say, knowing this will comfort her. I don't understand Buddhism, not the way Sherry does, but talking about good karma can soothe her.

"Finley," she whispers, her gaze vacant. "Finley." Her thumb brushes over the japamala beads, and her eyes light up with a fervent zeal. "Namo Amituofo, Namo Amituofo, Namo Amituofo…" she chants with the fanaticism of a mother who wishes her dead child well in the afterlife. She looks around, reciting under her breath.

"Mom, what are you looking for?" I ask.

Instead of answering me, she continues to repeat, "Namo Amituofo." Her eyes skitter right past me.

Suddenly, she crawls toward the water. "Mom!" I say, putting my arms around her.

She shoves at me with almost superhuman strength, still reciting the two words. She stares at the now-calm water, then stretches her hand out, the japamala hanging from her thin wrist. Although her mouth says, "Namo Amituofo," her eyes scream for Finley.

The water laps at her muddy knees. I cling to her, desperate to keep her on the shore.

"Finley," she sobs. "Finley." She passes out.

3

FIONA

THE MACHINES BEEP. I look at Sherry lying on the hospital bed. The doctor says she's fine, thank God, just in shock. She's become more fragile over the past few weeks, but losing Zachary and having the thugs manhandle us was probably too much to bear. She's lived her life in wealth and luxury, cocooned and protected.

I shiver as chills run through my body, and realize my clothes are still wet. Now, out of the sun, they've gone cold and clammy. I need to change before I catch a cold—or worse, get hospitalized for hypothermia or something.

The door to the private room bursts open. Aaron in his funeral-black suit barges in. He glances at Sherry on the bed, then turns his burning eyes toward me, his chest heaving. "What the *fuck* have you done to Mom?"

"Me?"

"Yes, you!" He points a finger at me.

Fury and adrenaline pump through my body. "Do you owe money to some loan sharks?" I ask in a low voice.

His eyes narrow. "What are you talking about?"

"Two sketchy-looking men came, demanding repayment of some 'loan.' Said something about the entire family being responsible for the debt. One of them pushed me into that lake by the cemetery. Then Sherry fell in, too. I'm not sure if they shoved her, or if she jumped after me."

The explanation seems to dampen his rage. His gaze flicks away as he opens his mouth then almost immediately clicks it shut.

Apprehension bites my gut. "How much?"

Irritation and defiance stiffen his back. "Not that much. Half a mil."

My eyebrows pinch as surprise cuts through the earlier unease. It would be a staggering sum for most people, but not for a family like the Obermans. They're blue-blooded upper crust with a vast wealth that has passed down over four generations. Money is like water to them—something that just exists for the family's use without their having to think about it.

"Well, pay it off before they come back to harass Sherry."

His mouth flattens. His transparent expression shows pride warring with bitter reluctance.

"I'm flying back to Monroe tomorrow morning," I remind him, so he understands that, *if* there's a next time, Sherry might be on her own.

He spits out a word in a voice so small, I can't make it out. Probably something like *bitch*. Aaron's vocabulary for cursing me out isn't very creative.

"I need to head back and change." I start toward the door.

"Can't," he says, louder.

Can't...? I stop and face him. "What do you mean?"

"I can't pay it," he grinds out.

"Why not? You just dropped over two hundred grand on a car." Aaron drove a brand-new Maserati GranCabrio to Zachary's burial.

"That's different."

"I'm sure, but half a mil isn't a big deal, not for you."

"That's the principal."

That's the principal? "What the hell are you talking—"

"The half-mil is just the principal of what I owe those guys."

Uh-oh. "How much do you owe, in total, with the interest?"

"Two million." His voice is as small as mosquito buzzing.

What the hell? "How did you let the amount grow to four times the principal?"

"Hey, shit happens!" He scowls and sticks his chest out. The bravado doesn't mask the defensiveness underneath. He knows he fucked up.

"Well, whatever. Just pay it off." Two mil is a lot, but still, something the family should be able to handle.

"I *can't*. There are no liquid funds."

"Sell your car, then."

"Won't be enough to cover the loan."

"Maybe you shouldn't have bought it in the first place."

"It's a fucking amazing car!"

My jaw slackens with shock. "More amazing than not having creeps come after you and your family?"

"Someone like you will never know or appreciate it." He exhales harshly, then admits in a tiny voice, "There's no money."

I let out a hollow laugh. "Stop joking around. It's not funny. Look, I don't want whatever Zachary left behind. It's all yours. I'll put it in writing if you want."

"I'm not joking. There's really *no money*. The company isn't doing well, and the house is already mortgaged to the hilt."

My eyebrows hit my hairline. "Are you telling me the family has no money? At all?"

"Do you fucking understand English? *There's no money!*"

I blink slowly as my mind processes. "Is the family about to go bankrupt?"

"Probably. That'd be the easiest way to shed the debt."

I close my eyes briefly. How could the family go belly up like this? How is it even *possible* that the company isn't doing well? Oberman Events is one of the most exclusive event-planning firms in the world. They only cater to corporate or wealthy clientele whose minimum budget is at least half a mil. "Except for the two mil you owe those men. They don't look like the type to abide by a bankruptcy court ruling."

Aaron says nothing. But the lack of denial is telling.

Damn it. "Does Sherry know how bad things are with family finances?"

He shakes his head. "Dad and I don't—didn't—want to worry Mom with stuff like that."

Good. She wouldn't be able to bear it. "How did you end up with loan sharks?"

"I was trying to make things better."

"That doesn't explain how five hundred K turned into a two-million-dollar debt."

"Yeah, well... I went to Vegas to fix things."

"Vegas?" A horrible realization dawns on me. "You went gambling?"

"It's the easiest way to make a quick score!"

Blood skyrockets to my skull. "The house always wins!"

"Over time! Not with every single customer. And I know how to count cards."

Oh my God. "But you still lost half a million dollars."

"I was tired and made a mistake or two."

I look deeply into Aaron's defiant gaze. He always believes he's far better than anybody else, smarter than the world. "Did Zachary know?"

He shrugs.

So Zachary knew, but couldn't stop him. "All right. I'll take Sherry with me tomorrow, so they won't harass her. You deal with them on your own."

"It won't work." He shakes his head and looks out the window. "There's no place you can hide to get away from them."

"What do you mean?"

"They're everywhere. Do you think they're going to let you leave?" Aaron scratches the tip of his nose and sniffles, not meeting my gaze. "If you're lucky, they'll slash your tires. If not, things could get a bit more personal."

"Are you telling me I can't return to my life unless you make good on that 'loan'?"

His mouth twists. "Don't sound ungrateful! Remember what my parents did for you!"

"Yeah, I know. *Zachary and Sherry* did a lot for me. Not you."

"You owe it to them!"

I stare at him, my heart racing furiously. "I don't have two million dollars! I've never had that kind of money!"

"Borrow it," he says, like I can just go out and pick up that money on the streets.

"Aaron." I pinch the bridge of my nose. "What bank will lend me that much without any collateral?"

"Didn't Dad buy you a condo?" he says, with more force than necessary.

Is he still upset about that? "No. He offered, but I declined." Specifically because I knew it would trigger Aaron. "I've been renting an apartment."

"An *apartment*? What kind of stupid are you?"

"Oh, I don't know. But definitely not get-myself-in-debt-for-two-million stupid!"

He opens his mouth, but a soft moan comes from the bed.

Sherry! Has she been listening? I rush to her side, but her eyes remain closed. Hopefully she just had a dream.

I shoot Aaron a glare hard enough to break his skull. "You keep her comfortable. Say whatever you need to say so she *doesn't know what you've done.*"

I spin around and leave the room. Aaron claimed I wouldn't be able to leave, but that's what he thinks. *Seriously, who's going to track me and Sherry all the way to Monroe?* It's a small city—really more like a town, compared to Los Angeles. It doesn't even have its own airport, so I have to fly to Madison then drive forty more miles. Way too much work, when they can squeeze the money out of Aaron here in L.A.

Besides, my sympathy for him hit rock bottom after that crap he said about his Maserati. I'm not going to be part of his mess when he doesn't even take the disaster he's created for himself seriously.

Checking for an available flight for Sherry, I go to the lobby and slice through the crowd. As I exit, the same two men who confronted me and Sherry stare at me, then jerk their chins up, smirking.

My skin crawls.

"Where you going, pretty lady?" Scar Mouth calls out.

Ignoring them, I hurry toward the parking lot.

"Hey, I'm talking to you."

Keep walking. Keep walking.

He doesn't lay a hand on me like he did before. Too many people around. "Don't even think about skipping town without making good on the IOU."

A chill skitters over me like scorpions. "Aaron's in there." I jerk a thumb at the hospital.

"Did you already forget? When one of you owes us, *all* of you owe us. You ain't going anywhere. Neither is your mama."

I spot a black Escalade with its hazard lights on. The driver's face is difficult to see through the windshield and huge sunglasses. He gives me a mocking salute.

Horror coils around my gut. My knees tremble, and I stiffen my legs to not betray myself.

Just what the hell kind of people did Aaron get tangled up with?

4

BRYCE

"HURRY!" Ares yells. We make a break for it.

My heart pounds as my brother Ares, my identical twin Josh and I run as fast as our legs can carry us. Mom lets out a soft cry as she follows. The cookies she gave us churn in my belly. My vision gets fuzzy, everything going out of focus. Even though it's dusk, the sunlight is somehow blinding, making me squint.

I don't understand why Mom tries to grab us like this. She and Dad argued loudly when they didn't realize we were listening, and he threatened that she'd never see us again. But kidnapping us like this... Isn't it too extreme?

You're such a good boy. My good boy.

Mom's words ring in my head. She always called me a good boy. I was always sweet-tempered and obedient. Even Aunt Jeremiah told Dad I might be too nice to survive at the family's law firm.

You're a good boy, Bryce.

Mom always looked me in the eyes when she said it.

I can always count on you.

The tenderness in her blue eyes. The gentle smile on her lips. Her light fingers stroking my chin and neck.

I love you the most.

Maybe she was scared she might not see us again. Dad always says he doesn't make threats, only promises. It's the way of the family, and Grandma and Dad always told us that Huxleys don't use empty words.

But would Dad keep Mom away from us forever? She *loves* us.

Right?

A soft sob comes from behind us. *Mom.* My heart feels funny, like a splinter's gliding into it. I slow down a little to look back at her. I don't want her to cry. I need to let her know I'll always love her because she's our mom. I'll never abandon her.

She grabs my shoulder. I wince, but swallow a pained cry. She probably doesn't mean to hurt me.

"Got you!" The smile on her face isn't normal. It's a little scary, her eyes too bright and wide.

"M-Mom...?"

"No!" Ares yells. He runs toward us, headbutting Mom hard. She loses her balance, but she doesn't let go. Ares bites Mom's hand. That loosens her grip, and he shoves me toward Josh.

"Get outta here! Now!" Ares screams, then bites Mom's hand again.

Blood and saliva seep from the wound. Mom screams, then knees Ares in the belly. He doubles over, but he doesn't loosen his jaw. If it's possible, the muscles clench tighter.

I freeze, sick to my stomach. It's my fault Ares is hurt. *I have to go help him.* But Mom... How can she be like this?

Josh grabs my arm. "We have to go." His eyes are wide with shock and fear.

Mom was always so gentle. And beautiful. The person who held and comforted me when I scraped a knee. Read me stories. Told me legends from her home country of Nesovia. Slipped me an extra cookie when I begged, saying, "Please! Please, Mommy. You know I love you the most!"

But the woman in front of me, restraining and attacking Ares, is nothing like the one I've known. Confusion and horror turn my mind blank, unable to process what I'm seeing.

Holding my hand tightly, Josh starts running. I follow, my body moving on autopilot. I can't look back and have Josh get taken, too.

Ares, I'm sorry. It should be me she's hitting, not him. A hot fist clenches around my neck. I struggle to suck in air, and the sound of my breathing grows louder and more ragged.

"Bryce, no! Don't leave me!" she screams, then lunges for me, her arm stretched out. Somehow she catches the hem of my shirt. I fall face-first, my hand slipping out of Josh's grip.

The impact makes me see stars. She flips me over and lowers her head until her nose is touching mine. "My baby. You know I love you the most. We should stay together. Remain a happy family of five. Don't you want that?"

Then her hands wrap around my neck and start to choke me. I struggle, my arms and legs flailing. My vision dims. *Am I going to go like this?* Fuck. No matter how I struggle to inhale, nothing can get past the tight hands around my throat.

A dog barks somewhere. A girl screams in a voice so familiar it sends a chill down my spine. "Let him go!"

Her shout penetrates the terrifying fog. Mom's hands lose their strength, then fall away. The weight on me vanishes.

The girl holds my prone body, her presence wrapping around me like a shield. Her warm hand cups my cheek, the gold-ringed green eyes looking down at me with concern and care. The tension inside me eases. I can finally breathe.

"Fiona," I whisper, clutching her. "Fiona." I repeat her name as though I can find salvation through it.

"Bryce." She looks down at me, the sweetness in her gaze leaching away, replaced by cold mockery. "I always found you disgusting," she says, her voice choppy and harsh. She shoves me away.

"No!" I roll and fall into a pit, falling and falling and—

I jackknife up in bed, sucking in the cold, dry air. My heart races with the vestiges of panic. Clammy sweat covers me from head to toe.

Fuck. Another nightmare. I press the heels of my palms against my eyes, willing the spasming nerves behind them to settle. I can't go into the office like this. The Fogeys—the elders of the family—will worry, even if they don't say anything too overt. Ares and Josh will notice and wonder if I'm okay.

We all know what Mom's kidnapping did to us, even though we don't delve too deeply into it. We're lawyers, not psychotherapists. And

The Fogeys hired the best therapists money could buy for us. They probably did a decent job. I quit waking up crying and having nightmares every night. Now I don't cry. And the nightmares are only occasional.

Not ideal. But manageable. Ares, Josh and I are all still a little bit broken, but most of the time, we're okay. When we aren't, we pretend we are. And when we can't pretend, we offer each other what support we can.

After all, we're Huxleys. *Pietas et unitas.* Without loyalty and unity, we're nothing.

When my pulse is back to normal and I'm no longer gasping like a fish tossed up on land, I put on workout shorts and head to the home gym to run. Since Gardy passed away, the only way for me to quickly shed the aftereffects of a nightmare is a hard run, lasting at least half an hour.

I step onto the treadmill. *I should get a new dog.* Maybe another golden retriever...

Except I keep finding reasons not to. Much as I adored Gardy, the last few years of her life were hard. Watching her grow weaker and sicker was painful. Not only that, every time I saw her, it reminded me of Fiona Oberman—a girl as beautiful and treacherous as my mother.

Unlike my mother, though, Fiona lacks self-respect, I think gloomily as the treadmill accelerates. My arms and legs pump, my heart beating faster. My head begins to clear.

Why did my nightmare have to end with Fiona holding me, then tossing me aside? It never involved her until today.

I shake myself mentally. Fiona isn't likely to reappear in my life ever again. She knows how much I despise her. She's a traitorous bitch, but she's not an idiot. But Mom? Mom has no shame, and now that Josh and I are thirty, she'll be back. She didn't finagle Dad into giving her the right to visit us again as adults just to stay away for the rest of her life.

The family should've put her in prison. Or, failing that, hired a discreet hit man. Grandma actually might have, if Mom weren't the only daughter of Nesovian mob boss Vincent Dunkel. He might not love his daughter, but he could never afford to look weak by failing to protect his own flesh and blood. Also, The Fogeys wanted to end any entanglement with the mob as quickly as possible. Dad got the divorce he wanted. Ironic, since Mom tried to kidnap us to avoid getting divorced. But the family has always been firm on never getting involved with organized crime. And Dad had already discovered what an unhinged lunatic Mom was by then.

Mom can come back and make a big fucking stink all she wants. But she'll never be able to deceive and manipulate me. I'm no longer her innocent little boy.

You know I love you the most.

Bullshit. There's no love or purity of heart—except for the blood members of my family. *Pietas et unitas.* Loyalty and unity. The motto is engraved into our psyches the moment we're born. We might squabble with each other, but if anybody else tries to fuck with us?

Oh, hell no.

You're a good boy.

Yeah, not anymore. Aunt Jeremiah no longer worries about my not having the right temperament to swim with the sharks of Huxley & Webber. I'm no longer the naïve kid who believed "I love you" actually means anything. It's just a tool for manipulation.

After the thirty minutes are up, I warm down, stretch and shower. Select a dark charcoal three-piece suit. A gift from my stepmom Akiko, it was hand-stitched in Tokyo by the same tailor who dresses all of the men of her zaibatsu family in Japan. She worked so hard to chip away at my distrust and sullenness after Mom tried to kidnap us...

The images come again: Mom managing to nab Ares, but losing Josh and me because Ares resisted and bought us time to escape.

Self-reproach drips like poison: *it's my fault Ares got taken by Mom.* I close my eyes, exhale, and imagine water leaking from a faucet—then turn it off. Nobody needs that guilt, especially not me or Ares, the one who suffered the most. He fought so that Josh and I would be safe and happy, not so we would dwell on the past and what could've been.

I take extra care styling my hair, ensuring it's slicked back perfectly. Loop a muted burgundy tie into a trinity knot. A Cartier Tank on my wrist, onyx wolf-head cuff links and I'm ready to face the world without letting anything touch me.

The family law firm Huxley & Webber takes up most of a sleek skyscraper. Every Huxley born is expected to work—and thrive—at the firm, and most of us do exactly that. My brothers and I did exceptionally well—Harvard undergraduate and Harvard Law. I'm content with my career and the work I do. Dealing with The Fogeys can get a bit annoying. After all, my dad and aunt are name partners and can be meddlesome from time to time.

I'm half an hour early. Aunt Jeremiah joins me in the elevator, holding a travel mug full of coffee. Her blood-red hair is pulled back into a knot, and the same shade gleams on her lips. Her skirt suit and stilettos are jet black.

It's one of her court appearance looks. Somebody's going to die, and it's not going to be her.

"Good morning. You look a little pale."

Her observation makes my eyebrow twitch a little. Does it show that I had a nightmare? Even though I had the run?

"Should sleep more," she says.

"How did you know?" I often sleep poorly, but have never mentioned it to anybody in the family. Nobody knows I have bad dreams, not even my doctor.

"You didn't leave until two last night."

"Neither did you," I say, trying not to sound defensive.

"Yes, but I'm a vampire. Haven't you heard?" A corner of her mouth curves upward. "You aren't."

"You should still sleep, if only during the day," I say, running with it. "As for me, I have to put in the time. Divorce cases are delicate."

"There's nothing delicate about a Hollywood divorce, sweetie. They're going to sling mud at each other, saying shit that will undermine your position and make you wish you could feed your client into a wood chipper."

"Jesus." I suppress a shudder at the imagery. I wouldn't put it past her to do exactly that if a client pissed her off. She believes in winning, not doing damage control for idiots who can't keep their mouths shut, no matter how wealthy they are. That's why, despite her dictatorial attitude, people still beg her to take their cases. They know she doesn't lose.

The elevator dings, and we step out of the car together onto the half-full floor. Nobody can afford to slack off when one of the partners is known to arrive early. I stop by the break room to grab a coffee, then head to my office, shutting the door with my heel. My assistant won't be here for at least an hour. She has to drop off her kid at daycare because her husband is out of town.

What would it be like to be able to trust your spouse with something as important as your own children? Amélie, usually sharp and sarcastic, glows when she talks about her family, especially her husband. Apparently, it was love at first sight.

Yeah, right. More like a psyop by the guy. There's no such thing as love, much less at first sight. He's just waiting for the perfect opportunity to backstab her.

I haven't told her, but if she ever needs to divorce his ass, I'll do it pro bono. I'll ensure she gets everything, including the kid, the house, the car—even his underwear.

I turn my attention to the huge stack of documents on my desk. The first one's about the Oberman family trust. I frown slightly while sipping my coffee. Why Zachary bothered wasting his money discussing the situation with me is beyond my understanding. The trust has been hollowed out completely by the trustee, who basically let Aaron do whatever he wanted. Zachary sought advice on undoing it, but unfortunately, that wasn't how the trust was set up. If there had been more time and Zachary could have afforded the fee, I might've pored over everything and found a loophole to exploit. But the man had a sudden heart attack, leaving everyone stunned, including me. Now there's nothing left of the estate except debt. I doubt it could pay the latest fifty-thousand-dollar invoice from Huxley & Webber.

The firm will try to collect, but we'll probably have to eat it. Grandma will lecture me to be more careful about avoiding deadbeat clients. But who would've thought a family with a history like the Obermans would be teetering on the verge of bankruptcy?

Even if I'd known the family was insolvent, I would've still taken Zachary on, on the off chance that he'd mention Fiona. See if that would stir anything. She made me think she was some kind of angel, only to stab me in the heart.

And he did speak to me about her with a faint smile, but I felt nothing. Who cares if she moved to Wisconsin, or that she works in marketing at some cheese company, or that she's still single? She's probably still pining over Jude Morven… Although if she wanted him, she should've stayed in L.A., where he's living off his family's money, like the pathetic, invertebrate parasite he is.

Yeah. She's so stupid she didn't even stay in L.A. to chase after that loser "soul mate" of hers. Why should I have any feelings for her? I'm too rational for that.

Since I'm not going to get paid, I push aside Zachary Oberman's files and start reviewing the Hollywood divorce. I swear—if Bebe Brooks makes one more social media post about her imploding marriage with Xavier, I'm going to break her fingers.

"WHAT DO you mean I can't talk about that piece of shit? I'm *American*! I have *rights*!" Bebe's impressive tits heave under the low-cut dress. Those breasts are real—and made her an overnight sensation on some pseudo-porn site, where she got her start. Now she does more respectable acting, but the melons are still the stars.

My day was going fine until she showed up for her appointment because she had to talk about "something important." I maintain my bland smile despite her shrill screams and the beginning of a headache. She seems to believe that, of the two of us, she knows more about constitutional law.

"Yes," I say in my most professional tone. "You do. But you aren't free of the consequences from exercising those rights."

Bebe has a coquettish physical quality that serves her well on screen. She pouts, obviously upset that I'm not siding with her. Tears spring to her eyes, then start falling in rivulets. "He's an *asshole*!"

"Do you want him to keep FruFru?" I should get a prize for keeping my expression blandly polite. *FruFru*. The couple's French poodle allegedly attacked four gardeners. Not that anybody can blame the dog. If some asshole named me FruFru, I'd bite some gardeners, too.

"No!" More tears fall, jacking up my impatience.

"Then please do as I say. I can't help you if you keep scoring own goals."

"But you're Bryce Huxley! You can—"

The door to my office bursts open. Amélie stumbles in, but is immediately pushed aside.

"Bryce, I can't wait anymore! You have to hear me out!"

Fiona. The voice hits me like a bucket of ice water. I stare, then blink slowly. Maybe Bebe's tears have given me a brain tumor and I'm seeing things.

But an illusion couldn't push my assistant aside. Fiona is even more beautiful than I remember, her auburn hair pulled back into a low ponytail to show off her exceptional cheekbones and delicate features, those large cat eyes and the lush mouth that tasted like honey and nectar. I could never get enough of kissing her, stroking her taut, smooth skin. The impact of seeing her is—

Uncomfortable, I decide. The weird tightening in my gut is nothing more than indigestion, the shaky boom of my heart just an aftereffect of too much coffee this morning.

Fiona doesn't seem to be having a great time, given the pallor and dark circles under her eyes that her makeup can't hide. Her black pantsuit makes her appear even thinner than she is—she's shed weight she didn't need to lose since graduation, giving her an air of fragility that wasn't there before. Her black shirt is buttoned all the way to the top, like she can't bear to show any skin. Or maybe she just doesn't want me to see any.

I still don't know why she changed so quickly back in college. It was like somebody flipped a switch in her heart. We'd been dating for a semester after she saved my dog. I fell for her so hard, so fast, that even Josh was a little worried. But I brushed his concern off, believing she and I were happy—on the same page. Disbelief and fury hammered me when I walked in on her rolling around in *my* bed with Jude Morven. My vision went red, blood boiling as rage burned.

"How could you?" I demanded in a shaky voice.

She gave me an unreadable look as she wrapped her arms around Jude. "Just decided to trade up. Besides, I never enjoyed sleeping with you. You make my skin crawl."

Time should've dulled the cruel response's edge, but recalling it still hurts. At least my heart doesn't bleed like it did back then.

I torched the fucking mattress, along with all my love for her. I wanted to kick my own ass for ever thinking that she was genuine or beautiful—my angel.

"Who is this tramp?" Bebe screeches, jumping to her feet. Her tears vanish.

Normally I'd find the term amusing, especially coming from my trashy client. But Fiona fucked Jude, used to wear very little for him and clung to him even when he had other girls on his arm, so I guess "tramp" fits, although I'd add "pathetic" as well.

"Nobody. An old acquaintance," I say coolly. That's the nicest way to describe my relationship with Fiona.

Pain flashes in her golden-green eyes. Instead of sheer derision, a small ache of my own unfurls in my heart. I harden my jaw. *What the hell's wrong with me? She turned her back on me first. She* messed up, not me. She deserves nothing, especially not sympathy.

"Why the fuck is this acquaintance interrupting my appointment? Does she know who I am?" Bebe raises her inch-long lacquered talons.

I quickly move around the desk. I can't let my client commit assault and battery with witnesses in the room.

"I'm so sorry. I told her you have appointments, but *she wouldn't listen*," Amélie says, looking at Fiona like she'd love nothing more than to murder her.

Fiona bites her lip, not meeting Amélie's gaze. "You made me wait more than three hours. I thought you were messing with me."

Apparently appalled at being called an unprofessional liar, Amélie glares at Fiona. "Well, are you satisfied now?"

"I'm sorry," Fiona says.

Given Amélie's temperament, she probably didn't take kindly to Fiona's appearing out of nowhere and demanding to see me. So she undoubtedly put Fiona in an area without a direct view of my office.

My eyes linger on Fiona's soft lips. Then I recall how she said she finds me disgusting.

"Call security and drag her out," I instruct Amélie.

She nods. "Oh, I will be *happy* to—"

"Wait!" Fiona says. "You said you'd do me a favor for saving Gardy!"

I pause as the memory of how we met floods my mind. Some asshole had hit my beloved golden retriever, and it was Fiona who found her, took her to the vet and cared for her until she could reach me. Gardy wasn't just a pet, she was a source of comfort and sanity after Mom's attempted kidnapping, critical to my recovery. When I offered to pay, Fiona declined. "No need. It's what any decent person would do. I'm just glad Gardy is fine."

The smile she gave me soothed the jagged edges that had stayed inflamed for over a decade. I couldn't help but smile in return. "Okay. But any decent person would repay you for your kindness. If you ever need anything, you let me know, and I'll take care of it. No limit, no expiration date."

I meant every word. I wanted to help her somehow, save her day, no matter what it cost. Except she never called in the favor, while we were dating or afterward—probably because she and Jude were having too much fun cutting me up.

Guess Fiona finally remembered the impulsive promise I made and decided to cash it in. Fine. I don't want to owe her anything anymore.

"Bebe, can you give me five minutes?" I say.

"You want *me* to wait?" Bebe's eyes widen incredulously like I told her she has to recite the Book of Psalms before she can divorce Xavier.

"Don't you want to win?"

"Ohh! Fine. FruFru is *mine*!"

"He will be." I glance at Amélie. "*Five* minutes. Not a second more."

She nods, narrowing her eyes at Fiona, then escorts Bebe out and closes the door. I prop myself against the desk, resting my hands on the smooth edge, my legs spread and stretched—a picture of indolent arrogance—and wait for Fiona.

Her chest heaves as she takes a shaky breath. My eyes drop for a second. *Her tits aren't that remarkable after Bebe*'s. It's an uncharacteristically petty thought. But somehow I can't seem to look away from her.

She starts to take the seat Bebe vacated.

"I didn't tell you to sit."

Her eyes flicker with surprise and a hint of humiliation and desperation. The last doesn't shock me. She wouldn't be here, with someone she said sickens her, if she had any other option.

And I wouldn't be listening to a treacherous ex if I hadn't made a promise. But regardless of how revolting she is, I'm going to be the bigger person and keep my word.

I glance at my watch. "Four minutes and forty-two seconds."

Her cheeks turn bright red. She stiffens her spine as she stands before me, standing a foot away from the tips of my well-polished loafers. "I need two million dollars," she blurts out.

I tilt my head and regard her thoughtfully. I didn't see anything in Zachary's estate that would require a large cash infusion. It's bankrupt, but nothing a decent bankruptcy proceeding won't take care of. The Obermans don't need a law firm of the caliber of Huxley & Webber for that. "Two million."

She nods. "A loan. I'll pay it back."

I? What about Aaron, or Sherry? "And if you can't?"

Her breathing shifts, growing less steady. She closes her eyes briefly, as if to gather courage, but the fluttering lashes betray her. "I have a stable job. I'll pay it back."

"People with stable, well-paying jobs don't generally dig themselves into two-million-dollar holes."

"Bryce."

My name is a plea on her lips, and it sounds almost too sweet to be real.

It isn't *real. She's trying to use you, to backstab you again.*

Still, the impact of her voice makes my gut clench. Her eyes look up into mine like I'm the only thing that can save her world, and my heart beats wrong, like it's torn between the desire to believe the illusion she's weaving and the desire to strangle her for trying to play another game with me. I loathe myself for reacting like this, and I hate her for making me feel this way, as though all the ugly words and deeds between us never happened.

Some things can never be unsaid. Some things can never be undone.

Her phone pings. She ignores it, but I want to break eye contact, to get a moment of reprieve to regroup before I deliver my blow. I need it to hurt so bad she'll never come crawling back.

"Check it," I order her.

She hesitates, her eyes lingering on my face.

"*Now.*"

She looks down. I breathe a little easier as the prickling sensation lessens. Her fingers flick over the screen. She tightens her grip around her phone. Her lips part to let out a shaky breath, and her eyes fleet everywhere, unable to settle, as though she's searching for a solution to an impossible problem.

Finally, she looks at me.

I'm not the answer, sweetheart.

Suddenly she drops to her knees. The abrupt gesture of self-humiliation is stunning, freezing the gears in my head. *What the hell is she up to?*

She bites her bloodless lip. Her hand reaches out and rests on my knee. The touch sends a shocking heat through my veins. Her fingertips flex, digging into the muscles. Sparks of something far too dangerous and uncontrollable start to erupt.

A jolt rushes up my spine. A knot of desire, loathing, disbelief and fury twists inside. I grip the edge of my desk tighter. My breathing roughens. It takes all my discipline to remain still and wrestle back some self-control.

I clench my teeth at her attempt at manipulation. If she thinks she can play me with moves like this, she's wrong. The visual—her on her knees, a hand on my leg, looking up at me—only reminds me of seeing her like this with Jude, and how she cried her heart out on her knees when she thought he might never wake up from his coma.

She could blow me right now, and I wouldn't be stirred to do what she wants.

Fuck her and her methods.

"It's a matter of life and death," she whispers. "Please."

The way she says *please* is just like the way she used to when we were in bed. *But she probably did the same with Jude.*

Still, my dick hardens, and I hate myself for responding.

I loathe her for still having the power over me.

"That's your problem." My voice is arctic.

She merely stares at me, light in her eyes dimming. Why is she trying to make me feel like the villain?

It takes two heartbeats before she places her palms on the floor and slowly pushes herself up. The tight tension in my gut eases, but only a little.

Her breathing is erratic. If it were anybody else, I might be worried that she'd pass out. She starts to undo the top button of her shirt, but her fingers shake too much.

I let out a cold laugh. "Sweetheart, don't flatter yourself. A woman who's been around the block as much as you isn't my type. On top of that, you can't even be faithful." I rake her body insolently with my eyes. "You have nothing I want. Not anymore."

Dropping her hands, she turns red, then white, then back to red. Her eyes lose focus and wander aimlessly, tracing nonexistent patterns on the carpet.

Two knocks at the door. I push myself off the desk. "Your time's up."

The words seem to jolt her out of the trance. "Bryce, you said you'd do me a favor!" she says. "Anything I asked!"

"Yes. Which is why I took five minutes out of my busy schedule, with a paying client, to listen to you, just like you asked. Now I owe you nothing."

She turns so pale so fast, I ready myself to step forward and catch her. I don't care if she gets injured, I tell myself. But I can't have her injured on the premises, because that would be a lawsuit.

The door opens, revealing Amélie and two security guards.

"Take her away."

"No!" Fiona reaches for my wrist, and I pull away. I'm not letting her touch me, skin to skin.

The guards take her, linking their arms with hers and tugging at her. She twists and flails. "No! You liar!"

I smile and wave. I suppose she's somewhat right. Telling me what she wants as a favor shouldn't count *as* the favor. But if this isn't the outcome she wanted, she should've tried to make an appointment, not that that would've done much good.

All the people near my office crane their necks to see the show. Let them. Why would I care that Fiona's embarrassing herself?

"Where's Bebe?" I ask.

"Miss Slinky Writhemore said she needed to touch up her roots and left. Apparently, she forgot a hair appointment." Amélie doesn't roll her eyes, but it's in her tone. "This," she says. "This is why aliens kidnap us and stick things up our butts." She shuts the door as she leaves.

I let out a soft breath at the restored peace. Where did Fiona ever get the nerve to demand anything from me?

I start toward my desk, then catch a glimpse of a black shoe. It's a stiletto with a pointy heel. I pick it up. Not a designer item. Probably something picked up at a department store clearance or something.

Huh. The Fiona I knew always splurged on pricey shoes. She always had better footwear than clothes in her closet.

Still, it's a sexy item. Guess her taste hasn't deteriorated, even if she quit spending a small fortune on shoes. I start to toss it into the trash, then stop. *If she comes back for it...* I could ask her how I was supposed to know where she lost her shoe, but Fiona can be annoyingly persistent. She might even try to use it as a way to worm her way into my schedule again.

Two million dollars. What the fuck?

I open the bottom drawer of my desk, toss the stiletto inside and lock it. If she comes back for it, she can have it. Otherwise...

...it can rot there.

5

FIONA

THE GUARDS AREN'T rough as they drag me out of Bryce's office, but they aren't exactly gentle either. They take me to the staircase, make me walk down twenty-six floors—they're so damn fit that they do it without breathing hard—pull me through the lobby and finally deposit me on the street outside the Huxley & Webber building like a piece of trash. They probably don't normally drag unwanted guests out with such enthusiasm and thoroughness. Likely Bryce instructed them to do it, and if I go back to get my shoe, it'll be a repeat of the humiliating scene.

Bryce has changed so much since graduating from Harvard. Sharper-edged, more aloof—meaner. But all that is hidden underneath an even more beautiful package—the stunning dark gray eyes that I can't look away from, and the broader and more powerful frame under the expensive outfit and accessories worn like armor. But even if he wore rags, you'd think twice before approaching him. There's a force of will and presence that say *back off*...or pay the price.

Well, I paid the price.

Despite the Los Angeles sun, I'm chilled to the bone and can't quit shaking. None of the banks wanted to lend me a penny. Nothing could be used as collateral. The family is broke.

When I realized I was out of options, Bryce was the only one I could think of to turn to. Not that he'd help me out of kindness, but he made that promise. Although I have lied to him and treated him badly, I always knew he was honorable, the type to keep a promise no matter what.

Guess I was wrong.

I raise my shaking hands and claw at the top button of my blouse, needing more air. *The collar's so restricting...* Bryce thought I was offering him my body—*as if!*—but I couldn't breathe in his office. Panic clenched around my throat, and his presence loomed over me, his hatred suffocating.

I squint at the sun, and fill my lungs—but it doesn't do much to make me feel better. My knees are still weak, and they ache from having hit the floor in Bryce's office as my legs gave out.

How humiliating.

What stunned and pained me was that he thought I was offering sex. *I'd never.* I know he doesn't want me—not after how badly our relationship imploded—and the idea never occurred to me. He must think the worst of me now. The sheer disgust in his eyes and voice told me more eloquently than the venomous words he used.

Guess the memory of the old betrayal hasn't gone hazy with time. When I let him catch me in bed with Jude, he looked at me with so much disbelief, pain and anger. I said things I can never take back. He called me the names I deserved, then punched the hell out of Jude.

Even as I shoved him away from Jude, acid burned in my gut. Bryce clenched and unclenched his hands, and I wished he'd hit me, too, so the guilt wouldn't cut so deeply. But he merely backed away.

"You just betrayed the one person who would've never turned his back on you." He tilted his chin at Jude, who was watching the scene with a bloody smirk. "I hope he's worth it."

He wasn't. He never was. But Bryce would never know the full truth. And even if he did, what would that change? Some things can't be unseen. Wounds might heal, but they always leave scars.

I should've known better than to think he would help, no matter how desperate I was. I didn't mean to collapse like that in his office, but my legs turned to noodles as fear cleaved through me. The photos that arrived on my phone flash through my mind. Aaron's "loan collectors" took pictures of Sherry doing her Buddhist meditation and napping. Although I doubt they were actually in the room with her, they had to get past security at the mansion gates to get the shots they sent.

Your mom's pretty for a woman her age. Think she can pay it off on her back?

Another wave of nausea sweeps through me. *What kind of sick people say things like that?* What's most terrifying is that I'm sure they'll follow through if I can't find a way to get the money. It won't just be Sherry in trouble, but me and Aaron, too.

If Bryce won't help, who can I turn to? Aaron said he'd ask around, but who's going to lend money to a gambling addict? You might as well set your money on fire. Not only does he not have a job, the family business is going under. He says it won't be liquidated and he'll remain an executive, but I don't trust anything he says.

Actually, I can't take anything *anybody* says at face value anymore. Bryce not only refused me, he outright mocked me. Of all the people I know, I thought he would be the last one to lie.

If I told him who hit his dog at Harvard, would he have helped? He wanted to know to get justice for Gardy. But would he have believed me? I only found out much later, but there's no proof I can give Bryce that Jude is the one who ran over the poor golden retriever. Without bothering to check the thousands of videos and photos individually to make sure they were the ones I wanted gone, I wiped Jude's phone, laptop and cloud clean, making sure he wouldn't be able to retrieve anything, not even his contact list.

That was the only way I could think of to escape from the man who'd become my nightmare.

–Aaron: I got something.

Sudden exhaustion weighs on me. Dread, really. When Aaron says he's got something, it means he's found an easy way out, not a smart way out.

Please. Don't let Aaron have gotten involved with another loan shark. It'll only make things worse.

–Aaron: All you have to do is say yes.

–Me: Me? What am I saying yes to?

–Aaron: Come home, and I'll tell you.

Given how much he hates to acknowledge me as his sister, my gut warns me to ignore him. I so want to, but life often involves doing things we'd rather not do.

I suck in more air, then slowly make my way to the rental, take some antihistamine pills and start driving. He won't leave me alone until I hear what he has to say. My day's already a complete mess, so who cares if Aaron dumps more shit on it? Can't be worse than what I went through in Bryce's office.

Although the family fortune has declined, the mansion is the same, at least outwardly. Dark ivy covers the stone walls. There aren't any pools or ponds on the grounds to avoid triggering Sherry.

Wisteria blooms all over. Sherry plants more of it every year because it was Finley's favorite, and I don't dare mention that I'm allergic. Zachary was the only one who noticed, but he told me to take antihistamine and suck it up.

In front of the door are Aaron's new Maserati—the sight of it makes my molars grind—and a black Maybach I've never seen before. The latter better not be another of Aaron's new splurges or I might just stab him and plead temporary insanity.

The massive, solid oak doors are polished until they shine like gold. The huge vase in the nook between the foyer and living room holds a bouquet of fresh lilies from the garden. Not a speck of dust lies anywhere. The air holds a faint scent of cleaning solutions, and hidden speakers play Bach softly.

Only some furtive glances from the staff betray the undercurrent of nerves. They're wondering how long they'll still have a job. I wish I could reassure them, but I have nothing to share.

"Hey."

I turn around at Aaron's voice, eyebrows pinching at the exuberance in his tone. *What's he so happy about?* He's the one who got the entire family into trouble by messing with the wrong kind of people. Sherry and I don't deserve this.

"Where you been?" he demands impatiently. "If you'd stayed home like I told you to, things could've been wrapped up faster."

"I went to Huxley & Webber." My words are flat. His brash optimism doesn't inspire me much.

He scoffs. "Lawyers can't fix this problem."

"I wasn't planning to sue." The kind of people Aaron got entangled with aren't the type who can be controlled by the law. It's always faster to break bones, and sex trafficking is profitable. From the gestures and comments the men made, they're probably familiar with both. Hope Aaron doesn't think he's safe because he's got a penis. Not all sex-trafficking victims are female.

"Good. Because I've got the solution." He rubs his hands and looks like he expects me to jump around with excitement.

"What is it?" I try to hide my weariness and impatience. I just want to go upstairs and soak in hot water until my knees quit hurting. My pride will take longer to recover, but there's nothing I can do about that. Looking at Aaron's face only intensifies my resentment and anger. If he hadn't messed up so badly, I wouldn't have had to go to Bryce, the one man I never wanted to see again.

"Me." A familiar man steps out from the kitchen with a smirk tugging at his lips, setting them into a cruel line. He's in a blue V-neck shirt and slacks, looking as preppy as he did in college.

My mouth dries. Adrenaline spikes, but my feet stay rooted to the spot. Jude Morven isn't the kind of man you can simply run from.

"You." I manage to croak that one word.

"Hello, Finn," he purrs, smiling. It's so genuine, it's terrifying. Whatever he's happy about can't be good for me. "Long time no see."

He reaches for my hand. I pull my arm back like I'm evading a snake. A shriek wells in my throat, but I somehow push it down. If Sherry hears me scream, she'll panic—and the family can't afford another hospital visit.

His reptilian eyes narrow. "You've changed. You used to love holding hands with me."

"No," I rasp. "This is just how I am."

Scowling, Aaron jabs his finger at me. "What the fuck kind of attitude is that? He's here to help."

"How?" My eyes slide to Jude.

But it's Aaron who answers. "He's going to make those guys go away. After all, two million's nothing to my man Jude." He clasps Jude's shoulder with an *aren't we best buddies?* smile.

Every time he smiled like that in front of Jude, I got pushed into a deeper level of hell. Jude is the main reason I left SoCal, but Aaron is a close second.

"Do you still sing well?"

Jude's soft question sends nausea roiling through me. The world sways, but I blink to maintain my vision. I can't drop like I did earlier. Any sign of weakness is a surrender, and I'll suffer more for it.

"I don't sing." I manage to push the reply out despite the tremor racking my body. I clench my hands, but I can't hide my shakiness. "I never liked it."

"You're just out of practice." He smiles again. "Once you start, you'll remember how much you love it."

6

BRYCE

I LEAVE the office early to get my place ready for poker night with my brothers. It's a tradition we've kept since the kidnapping—one of our therapists said we needed a way to bond and get over what happened.

And for me in particular, I think he wanted me to overcome the guilt. After all, it's my fault Mom was able to grab Ares. Being alone with her totally fucked him up, made him not only emotionally closed off with the opposite sex, but obsessed with some girl he calls "Queen." He's had, like...what? Five or six girlfriends in his life, and he's thirty-two. Actually, it's amazing that he had even one girlfriend, because he doesn't like being touched. Hard to be in a relationship without physical contact.

He's only married because he wants a promotion to junior partner. Otherwise, he'd be dating Rosy Palm.

Josh, of course, went in the complete opposite direction. A total playboy. If there's a willing woman, he'll poke his joystick into her.

But he doesn't commit.

Thick wrought-iron gates open when my Ferrari arrives, and I drive through the succulent garden. The stone walls surrounding the property are thick enough to stop anything short of a tank. The mansion's windows are bulletproof, and the turrets have cameras—and guns, although I haven't had the occasion to fire any since Mom has stayed away.

Which is a little sad—it would've been nice if she'd violated the terms Vincent and The Fogeys negotiated. Whatever might've happened to her as a result of her coming for me would've been self-defense. But Vincent is apparently too scary to fuck with, even for somebody as psychotic as her.

Now that we're officially thirty, though, she might come slinking around again. Hopefully she'll show up at my place first, so I can finally off her and spare my brothers the trouble.

Who's the good boy now, Mother?

I step inside the house. The place has been immaculately cleaned by the daily staff. The caterer lays out platters of cheese, roast beef and pork and crackers on a lazy Susan on the round dining table. I place down Padrón Cigars 1926 Serie Maduro, two bottles of Pétrus 2020 and a Hanyu 2000. Good cigars and drinks are a must-have for poker night.

Josh arrives first. He glows—probably got laid or destroyed some opposing counsel. To him, court victories are like orgasms. In my opinion, victories are better than sex or women. Victories, at least, will never betray you.

"No Hanyu Ichiro Malt card series?" Josh says as his eyes sweep over the table.

I cock an eyebrow. "Are you worth it?" Before the distillery in Japan shut down, it produced a few sets of premium whiskey with labels featuring cards. I won a complete set for over a million bucks at an auction.

Josh puts a hand over his heart dramatically. "Who was he, Bryce? This...this man who hurt you so?"

I snort. He's probably just still sore about losing the bid for the set.

Ares walks in, looking like he hasn't slept in days. If he were still single, I'd guess that a case wasn't going well, but now that he's married...my money's on some matrimonial issue. Although he acted solicitously toward his new wife at the last family dinner, he probably still has hangups about touching and intimacy.

"I'm gonna win some big money!" Josh rubs his palms together. "Feeling lucky today."

"Yeah? Well, don't cry after I take all your money."

"Ha! Bet that card series and we'll talk."

"You wish."

"Start," Ares says. He's trying to sound calm, but there's an uncharacteristic gloom underneath. He's usually better at pretending everything's fine in his world.

I shoot him a look, but he remains quiet. I pick up a cigar, cut and light it, then start shuffling the cards. Ares and Josh grab their cigars and pour themselves whiskeys.

"Can I spend the night here?" Josh says.

"Why? I'm not a hotel."

"There's this chick who won't leave me alone."

This chick. Bet Josh doesn't even know her name.

"How many times did you sleep with her?" Ares asks.

"Once, of course." Josh's tone says, *I'm not crazy.*

I shake my head. Josh never sleeps with the same woman twice, and many of them get upset when they realize they aren't special enough for a second round. If that was all there was to it, it wouldn't be so annoying. Just his problem. But they confuse me with Josh and stalk me from time to time. "You need to stop saying shit like 'I'm looking for my soul mate. I just know she's out there.'"

"But I do," Josh protests, his eyes wide with faux innocence.

"Right. And you have to stick your dick into them to see if they're the one." I slide cards to all of us.

Josh spreads his hands. "How else can I tell?"

"From the way your heart feels?" Ares suggests. "When you don't care about somebody, nothing stirs inside. But if you do, even a little, you get that reaction, even if you can't pinpoint exactly what it is."

What he's saying reminds me of my reaction to Fiona earlier. But then, anybody would react if they'd run into an ex who betrayed them.

"Did you feel it with your wife?" Josh asks.

Ares merely looks at his cards.

I look at my hand, then take a puff of my cigar. Josh glares at his, but I don't buy the act. He does it all the time to confuse us and extract any advantage he can.

I've got two aces. Nice.

"By the way, what were you so smug about this afternoon?" Josh asks me suddenly.

"Me? Smug?"

"You looked like a cat after a successful hunt," he says.

Huh?

"There was some kind of commotion," Ares clarifies.

"Oh, that? An uninvited guest interrupted my day, and my assistant did her best to keep her out, but..." I shrug, then deal the three community cards.

The four of clubs. The seven of hearts. The two of clubs. *Ugh.* Ares tosses a hundred-dollar chip into the pile. I call. So does Josh.

"Who on earth managed to get past Amélie?" Ares says, his eyes on his hand.

The taut frown betrays him—he never frowns during a game. He's thinking about something else, which is interesting. He's just as competitive as any of us. Money isn't the object—a hundred bucks a chip is nothing when we're all worth over two billion each. But winning? Now, that's everything.

I stare at my hand. Not the best, but too early to fold. "Fiona Oberman," I say, trying for casual.

Ares cocks an eyebrow. "Fiona? Doesn't she know you hate her?"

"Yeah, but when I was young and dumb, I made a promise to do her one favor. She finally came to collect."

"Wow. But still... She couldn't find anybody else to turn to for help?" Josh says.

"What did she want? Not representation, right?" Ares asks. "She would never trust you that much."

I snort. *Whose fault is that?* Trust and Fiona do not go together.

But I meant it when I told her she'd turned her back on the only person who would've always stood by her. When she rescued Gardy, she earned my loyalty. Then later she earned my affection by acting sweet and lovely, hiding her rotten core with what must have been practiced ease. If she had kept on acting—or even broken up with me before hopping into bed with Jude Morven—I would've stood by her.

But sticking a knife in my back? That was the end of us.

I tap my chin, trying to calculate the probability of winning. Josh's curious gaze bores into my face. He doesn't have to speak for me to know what he's wondering.

"She wanted to borrow money," I say.

"Did you tell her that if she can't pay you back, you'll want a pound of her flesh?" Josh asks. He knows me too well to believe the meeting was amicable. Not only that, he witnessed my anger and disbelief firsthand back when she cheated on me.

"Of course," I say, not wanting to get into specifics, "especially when she begged so prettily." *When she fell on her knees. When she tried to unbutton her shirt.* I mocked her, but the more I think about it, the more irritated I become. Just what the hell happened to the girl who charmed me with her gentle soul and steely determination? How could I have misjudged somebody so badly? I learned my lesson after Mom's kidnapping. I quit trusting empty words and gestures. I only believe what I can see with my own eyes.

But it doesn't matter anymore. It's been years. I'm wiser and more experienced, and no amount of pity-acting by Fiona Oberman is going to fool me again.

Another card dealt. The king of hearts.

Shit.

Ares raises. What does he have? Josh and I call, not giving up yet.

"Did she take your offer?" Josh asks.

She offered to suck me off. I keep that to myself. It'd be too humiliating for her for me to air, even to my brothers. *Consider it an old-fashioned courtesy from me to an ex,* I think, imagining I'm saying it to Fiona. "Too much fucking pride. Funny, considering her family's on the verge of bankruptcy."

Ares shoots me a look full of skepticism.

"She'll come around, though." I feign nonchalance, even though the prospect of seeing her again sends a zing through me. She has no other option. Banks aren't stupid—they know the family's gone belly-up. But after the way I had her dragged out, she might just stay away to preserve what's left of her pride, assuming there's still any left.

She looked really desperate, a small, gloating voice in my head says.

"What other choice does she have?" I ask rhetorically.

"A sugar daddy?" Josh says. "SoCal is full of 'em. She doesn't even have to limit herself to single men. Mistressing is a lucrative business."

I scoff, even as the possibility of her all over a man old enough to be her grandpa fills my mouth with bitterness. "Don't be ridiculous. She's too old for that."

"She's barely thirty." Ares looks at me like I'm stupid.

Josh says, "*And* she keeps in shape. She looks like she's twenty-two. A lot of guys would tap it."

Has he seen her lately? She looks younger than her age, but not twenty-two. Besides, she doesn't keep in shape. She's too thin. Not sure why. Maybe she got a boyfriend who wanted her to lose weight after college. How stupid. When a man tells you to lose weight, you ought to crush his balls and find a man who'll love you the way you—

Stop. Why am I thinking about this? Who cares about Fiona's post-college love life? Still, the idea of her with another man feels...

I shake my head. The odd burning sensation in my gut isn't from thinking about her with some other men. It's from too much whiskey. "That's disgusting," I sneer to hide the weird heat in my belly. Another card—the queen of diamonds. *Damn it.*

Josh shrugs. "Not my fault she's a babe."

Ares throws in more chips.

"You seem confident," Josh says to him.

"I'm always confident."

"You taking your wife to the art auction exhibition?" I ask Ares, not wanting to discuss Fiona's prospects as a trophy wife or mistress anymore.

Who would marry her anyway? Even the position of mistress seems too good for her. Maybe just a plaything at the most. Something you use once and discard.

That evening, I don't win a single hand.

7

BRYCE

MUSIC loud enough to split skulls booms in the dimly lit VIP room at Z. Top-shelf bottles of liquor litter the bar, and women gyrate around in outfits that could get them arrested for indecent exposure. Strippers, strippers and more strippers.

This isn't my kind of scene, but I need an outlet. I've been too restless since seeing Fiona a few weeks ago. Nightmares with Mom trying to kidnap us keep reoccurring, and they always end with Fiona calling my name. Recently, though, the finale to the dream has morphed into her not only calling my name but kissing me senseless.

Waking up with tingling lips and morning wood isn't a good way to start the day, especially when they're caused by a devious, duplicitous ex. I still can't forget the way she looked in my bed with Jude, long hair disheveled and lips swollen. Or the cruel, taunting words she said, each one a bag of acid that exploded on impact.

The weird texts about her—and photos—that started in the last two weeks haven't helped either. They constantly disrupt the calm I'm trying to achieve. I keep blocking them, but whoever's behind the harassment continues to get new numbers.

If I find out who's behind it, I might just feed them into a wood chipper.

–Unknown: Don't you owe her one? So do the right thing.

Why should I? The taunting question begs to be texted, but I hold back. I'm not taking the bait. The longer I glare at the text, the more it seems like the culprit is Fiona. She has to re-engage if she hopes to get my money. *Well, dream on, baby*. I'm not playing the game.

After all, it's a tired cliché. She texted me before leaving for Wisconsin, too, claiming she wanted to explain "what really happened" with Jude. I refused. There's only one kind of bullshit excuse, the same kind Mom used when she got caught after almost killing Ares.

I did it for you. I did it out of love. You're a good boy—I thought you'd understand how much I wanted us to be together.

Words mean nothing. Only actions matter. My experience over the years has taught me that love can be used to justify anything, no matter how vile.

"Hey, man!" Barry, an associate at the firm who planned this gathering and provided the strippers, wraps his beefy arm around my neck and shoulder.

I roll my eyes with a small, friendly smile, but don't bother to pull away, since there's no escaping him. A former football player for the University of Georgia, he's one of the most physically imposing lawyers at Huxley & Webber, thick muscle all over his broad, solid frame. He tries to tone it down with bleached yellow hair, too much tan and a Georgian drawl that he lays on thick, "lahk frostin' on a cake." He even sports a vaguely stupid grin. Most clients are disappointed to learn he's their lawyer, until they discover he's one of Jeremiah's favorites.

He's one of the meanest, smartest and hardest-working associates. And he never misses an opportunity to party. Ares's wedding ceremony tomorrow has provided him a perfect excuse.

"Where's Ares?" he says, letting me go now that he's sufficiently happy he's done a proper man-greeting. I'd bet the year's bonus he has no idea if he's talking to me or Josh.

"Home," I say.

Barry's eyes widen. "What? Why? I told him about this bachelor party last week!"

I snort. I know my older brother too well. "He didn't say he'd attend, did he?"

"I reminded him yesterday. And this morning!"

I shrug. "He's glued to his wife." Probably tasting whatever she wants to eat because she has a justifiable hangup about food. "You know that he isn't technically a bachelor, right?" Ares wants to have a big ceremony to make up for the hasty Vegas wedding. He treats her like a queen and has apparently gotten over his revulsion at being touched. True love does indeed conquer all—for some people.

"Ah," Barry says, raising a sausage-sized finger. "But he doesn't remember the wedding! So he's sort of like a bachelor."

"Mm. Well, you two will just have to agree to disagree. He said to tell you to spend more time with your wife."

"Hey, she never complains. I'm a great husband."

My eyes slide to the strippers around us. "If you say so."

"I only look. Never touch." Barry raises his hands, palms out, all innocent.

"Eye-fucking is eye-cheating."

His jaw drops. "What century are you from?"

"The twenty-first." I clasp his shoulder, then scan the area for Josh. He generally enjoys Barry's parties and would definitely come to make up for missing Barry's own bachelor party in Vegas. He was pretty sad about it, but work comes before play.

I discover my twin in a corner, busy necking with some chick. Not a stripper. Her dress is tight, but not too revealing. He never lacks female companions, but then, he has a decent mug.

Since he's about to get lucky, I head to the bar. My phone pings. Another unknown number, another photo.

The shot shows Fiona at some store, trying on a wedding dress. My hand clenches around the phone. *What's the point of this?*

I should look away, but I can't. The dress is classy, with a long train and intricate lace. *Can she afford it?* She's two million in the hole.

Or is this some kind of taunt—she's marrying money, so she doesn't need me? But if she could've gotten a sugar daddy this easily, why didn't she? Surely, it would've been less bruising to her ego, unless her groom-to-be is so foul that not even two million bucks can make up for it.

I tap my phone thoughtfully. Something about her behavior doesn't add up.

She's lost even more weight since she barged into my office. Her fragility is more pronounced in the tight bodice, and the way it shows her bare shoulders and arms. The fact that I notice anything about her is irritating. But the angle of her pose and the way her eyes are slightly lowered—her mouth set in a vulnerable line—remind me of her on a rainy night nine years ago when we were still in school.

She'd left a frat party without Jude, who was sprawled on a couch with three girls. Her various attempts to catch his eye had failed, and she probably didn't want to stick around anymore. I shouldn't care, but it was after one a.m. and raining hard. My hatred and contempt for her kept reaching new heights since the night I'd caught her in bed with him. She'd continued to debase herself for Jude's attention—a total doormat for a guy who wasn't worth it.

Just what the hell did she see in him? He was popular enough, his family was wealthy enough, but he was a snake and everyone knew it. But she still simpered and hung on to him. If she'd left me for a guy who was legitimately better, I'd at least have understood. But she'd picked a complete bastard who treated her like dirt and openly cheated on her.

Karma. Still, bitter satisfaction wasn't what burned in my gut. I didn't want to think too much about it, since it would only piss me off.

I watched her unsteady steps from a window. Probably drunk. I looked away, reached for another beer, then stopped.

If anything happened to her... *Shit.* I'd always wonder if I could've prevented it. Even if the victim was somebody I loathed.

So I followed her out. She didn't get into a car—Jude must have driven—and didn't have an umbrella. She just ambled along the dark sidewalk, in and out of the few streetlights, letting the chilly early-spring rain soak her.

I glanced at my umbrella, then at her. *Nah.* That was more interaction than I wanted. Ever since her betrayal, I'd looked straight through her. Let her words glide off me without showing anything to her.

She was dead to me the moment she backstabbed me.

I maintained a few yards between us. She didn't seem to notice anybody was following. *Jesus.* Shouldn't a girl be more aware of her surroundings at night? She could get into trouble.

Stop sounding like you care.

Suddenly, the rain intensified, wind picking up. A blinding bolt of lightning split the sky. She stopped and looked up at the streetlight to her right. Her lashes fluttered in the rain, and her mouth pressed tight, the corners turned downward. Her shoulders heaved slowly. If she was crying, the drizzling water hid the tears.

An instinctive impulse to reach out surged, and I squelched it—*hard.* She didn't deserve to be comforted, especially not by me. If she regretted choosing Jude over me… Well, too late for buyer's remorse.

Still, that image of her in the rain has been etched to my subconscious. And the photo that just arrived reminds me of that night for some reason.

Did she know I was following her? Is she sending me these things because she thinks there might be some kernel of care for her still inside me? Something other than sheer loathing?

If she thinks she can leverage me against myself, she's mistaken. I'm not going to bail her out of the trouble she's in. What Josh said about her becoming a trophy wife or mistress pops into my head.

Let her marry some old geezer. I don't care. I really don't.

My belly burns like there's a hole in my gut. I grab a glass of whiskey, then block the number and let out a sigh of frustration. I'm not finding an outlet for my restlessness here tonight. Maybe call one of the girls? But no one looks good as I thumb through my contact list.

My cousin Huxley Lasker would know some hot model. On the other hand, he's still in the honeymoon phase of his marriage and wouldn't welcome an interruption late at night. I'm not sure how long it's supposed to last. For God's sake, they have a baby, but they're still lovey-dovey. Sometimes they don't even act married, more like teenagers being stupid in love.

"Hey, Josh!" A pair of arms wrap around my neck, and a stunning brunette presses her huge, firm tits against my chest. "I missed you," she coos, long fake lashes fluttering as she looks up at me adoringly. A thin film of sweat covers her otherwise lanky body. The dark mirror behind her reflects her backside. Her ass is rather lacking. Huh. Not Josh's type.

I tilt my head and gaze at her thoughtfully. Has my twin ever slept with her? "How did you get invited?"

"Barry said I could come. And you did too when I texted you, silly! You said you'd be in a white shirt and black jacket." Her hand roams over both.

My eyes flick to Josh—no jacket. *That asshole.*

"Why did you run out like that?" the brunette says, pushing her breasts harder against my chest. "We never got to talk about the next step."

I lean back and swallow the whiskey. "There's a next step?"

"Well, *duh*. Every relationship has a logical next step." She looks up at me expectantly, like I should know. Except I don't. The one I thought would go somewhere ended in betrayal. The subsequent ones... Well, they fizzled, like soda left under the SoCal sun for too long.

"Like...?"

"Marriage!"

I cough up my whiskey. *Holy shit.* How the hell do you go from a casual fuck to marriage in "one logical step"?

"I want to marry well. To a young, handsome, rich guy. I mean, if I have to marry, I might as well marry one who's got everything, right? Besides, you were amazing in bed. And I think you liked it when I sucked you off. You didn't complain when—"

"Okay, okay, okay!" *Too much information,* but then, she seems like the type to overshare. And be very honest about her mercenary needs.

"Don't make this hard." She pouts. "I mean, I have a backup, but he's not as young or handsome. I'd really prefer to marry you."

I should tell her I'm not Josh, so she can stop before she embarrasses herself further...but now I don't want to. Not after she so casually told me she has a backup, like she's proud of keeping some poor guy dangling in reserve. I feel sorry for the man. Most backup guys don't know they're backups until it's too late. Like me in college.

Besides, I don't want to make things easier for my twin. He and I sometimes mess with each other, but this is going a bit too far. Not only that, he probably got tired of dealing with her, so he's trying to foist her off on me. That asshole. "You know what? That sounds about perfect."

She claps her hands. "You agree, right?"

"Of course! Why don't you pick out a ring, sweetheart? And send the bill to me?"

Her face falls a little. "Well...but shouldn't *you* pick it? To show you care?"

Oh jeez. She wants money *and* love. "Of course I care, but I have a really big case right now." I smile ruefully. "I have to win it to make partner. Don't you want to be Mrs. Joshua Huxley, the wife of a partner and a rising star at Huxley & Webber?" I sweep my hand from left to right, showing her the beautiful vista of the future she could have if she'll just buy an engagement ring and send the bill to my brother.

"Oh my God." Her eyes twinkle as she clenches her hands and hops in excitement. "That sounds amazing."

"I know. You're the only woman who got this far. Most women... They just couldn't hang."

"Really?"

"Really." I nod, putting on the solemnity I'd reserve for a murder trial—if I ever decide to practice criminal law. "You're the best of them all. The most beautiful, the most intelligent, the most charming... Imagine the kids we could have together."

"Oh my *God*! You want *kids*?" she squeals.

"Of course. We have to leave our legacy to someone."

She hugs me. "I love you, Josh."

I pat her back. "I love you too."

"Let's go celebrate." She tugs at my arm. "This way."

I follow her out, although I don't plan to celebrate. Now that I've exacerbated the woman problem for Josh, I plan to go home, puff a good cigar and go to bed. Our stepmom Akiko will be upset if I stay up too late and look tired in the pictures tomorrow. She's a firm believer in taking as many great photos as possible.

"Who's this brainless bimbo? Your plus-one to the wedding?" comes a familiar, sneering voice, one that's always reminded me of a mixture of chicken grease and mayonnaise.

I cock an eyebrow and turn to confront Jude Morven. I haven't seen him since I graduated from Harvard undergraduate. I went off to Harvard Law, and didn't care where he ended up.

The bastard still looks like a snake, albeit older. The recessed lights hit his slightly wavy golden hair, neatly styled and held stiffly in place with wax. The eyebrows are probably shaped and plucked—they weren't this tidy in college. The eyes are the same cold and soulless blue. If he ever wanted to go into acting, he'd be amazing at playing serial killers; all he'd have to do was be himself.

His skin is slightly tanned, which must've taken a lot of effort. The fucker burns, and he was paler than pizza dough from fall to spring in Massachusetts. He's wearing a black button-down shirt with three buttons undone and black slacks. He tries too hard to look imposing and cool, especially since his frame is on the slender side.

Our enmity started in high school, with him initiating it. I never understood why until Josh told me that Jude hated me for beating him in everything. Apparently, until he met me, he was number one—in golf, tennis, academics and girls.

"He can't beat *you*, either," I pointed out in confusion.

Josh shrugged. "But *you* beat him first, not me. So he's fixated on *you*. And he's so hung up, *he can even tell us apart now*."

Hardly anyone outside the family can tell us apart. "What a freak." It wasn't my fault Jude couldn't measure up, and I dismissed a rivalry that only he cared about. He wouldn't let it go, though, and it pissed him off that a girl he liked asked me to prom.

So his much-delayed revenge was sleeping with Fiona—in my bed. The difference was that the girl in high school wasn't dating him. Fiona was in a committed relationship with me—or so I thought. The commitment obviously didn't run very deep if she could throw it away to sleep with a guy who hated my guts. Of course, I didn't let him go unpunished. I turned his face into hamburger meat.

"I'm going to be his *bride*," the brunette crows, tightening her hold on me, which gets a smirk from Jude.

Whatever confrontation is to come isn't going to be pretty. I don't want her witnessing it. "Sweetheart, go pick out your ring, okay? And call me."

"I will. Love you." She wags her fingers goodbye and leaves, her step springy.

Jude watches her go. "Pathetic. You always knew how to pick the worst women. Typical loser. Make sure to buy the most expensive item on the registry."

Not worth an answer. "So you're getting married? To what? A water moccasin?"

A corner of his mouth quirks. "Finn Oberman."

I study him, my eyes level and steady. There's the same smarmy smile. The same inferiority complex. I don't believe for a second he's marrying her. He treated her like trash back in college, somebody you deign to allow to warm your bed, but would never marry. Even a piece of shit like Jude would need to have a modicum of respect to make somebody his wife. He has too much pride to marry someone "beneath" him. Fiona was just a tool he found to claim superiority over me, nothing more.

Besides, she left him as soon as we graduated. Went to some dinky little town in Wisconsin and cut all ties. Didn't bother with reunions or alumni associations, either. It's like having the diploma in her hands suddenly wised her up, although it doesn't explain why she cried like her world was ending when Jude went into a coma from a nasty car crash he had a month before graduation.

"You remember her, don't you? I had her send you an invite," he says, his eyes on mine, gauging my reaction.

"Never got it." She hasn't contacted me since I had security drag her out of the office. Didn't even try to convince me that the favor I owed her couldn't be fulfilled by listening to what she wanted from me. Maybe she doesn't need the two million so badly after all. Or perhaps her pride couldn't handle any more abuse. Regardless, I can't decide if I'm disappointed, relieved, irritated or happy that she's staying away.

"Disobedient little bitch." He glares at me, as though somehow it's my fault I didn't get the invite. "Have you ever heard her sing?"

I deliberately keep my expression relaxed. She hummed for me when I was suffering from nightmares involving Mom. When Fiona cradled me like she'd protect me from the old memories of Mom's treachery and softly crooned nameless tunes with her lips so close to my temple I could feel the heat from her mouth, I could breathe easy and sink into her warm comfort. Guess that was also something Fiona and Jude laughed about. "She sings like shit."

"No. She sings like an angel. You just have to coax her a little. Or, you know, she has to care about you." The nasty smile on his lips reaches his eyes as he scrutinizes my reaction. "I guess it was neither in your case."

I give him a cool stare that betrays nothing, even though my insides seethe.

A triumphant glint flashes in Jude's eyes. He knows he's hit a sore spot. "Jealous, aren't you? She's picking me, just like she did before," he says, then laughs as though he's thrilled he's scoring a point against me after all these years. "What's it like to know she's mine—that she was mine even when you thought she was yours?"

I shoot him a condescending look. "Only a fool believes a woman's heart is worth anything, Jude. It's fickle, vicious and useless. Still, I'm happy for you. Guess she didn't tell you that you were her *second* choice."

The smugness fades. "You're lying."

"Oh, no. She came to me first. *Begged* me. On her knees. You should've seen how pretty she looked."

His face turns red; his hands clench. He'd throw a punch if he thought he could get away with it.

My smile grows genuine as I slap his shoulder, like we're best buddies. "She only went to you because I turned her down, Jude. But taking in garbage I don't want suits you, man. It's like you were born for the role."

He stares at me, disbelief and outrage rolling over his face. His reaction is laughable. Did he think I'd have nothing to say? Or that I'd let him walk all over me?

I straighten his shirt, smoothing the collar down a bit, then step back. "Have a happy wedding."

8

BRYCE

A SOFT TOUCH on my shoulder from behind. I start, then spin on my feet.

"You can't run from me forever."

The words are said in an even softer voice, but my mouth dries anyway. Mom stands before me, looking as beautiful as ever, her blue eyes on me. Her small smile is full of a satisfaction so deep it spikes my veins with anxiety.

I'm not a helpless child anymore, I tell myself. I'm an adult now, bigger and stronger than her. She can't drag me away. Not now, not ever. She has no hold over me—

"You used to be so adorable and cute—a good boy. But look at you now. All big and grown. So respectable and wonderful." She takes a step forward, then another. "Still a perfect, good boy."

I'm rooted to the spot, my legs feeling like lead. I raise my palm. "Stop."

"Why? I've waited so long for our reunion."

"I never want to see you again."

An incredulous laugh erupts from her chest. She grips my hand. "But you're seeing me now, aren't you?"

My skin crawls at her touch. Her skin is buttery soft and smooth, but it only makes me want to recoil. I try to pull away, but she holds firm and I can't free myself. *What the fuck?*

"You're mine."

Panic swells. *No.*

Suddenly, someone else grips my free hand. "Bryce."

I turn and gaze into Fiona's green-gold eyes, which slide to Mom for a second before she turns her focus on me. *What's she doing here?* Her warm grip chases away the chill Mom's touch brought. The dread in my belly eases, and the anxiety recedes.

"Come with me," Fiona says. "Everything's going to be fine."

She tugs at me, and like magic, I can move my legs. She lets me go, then runs ahead. I follow her along a long, dimly lit corridor.

Abruptly she turns, cradles my face in her hands and crashes her mouth against mine. Her lips are soft, giving under mine like a ripe peach. The taste of her—all woman and sugar—drives me wild, and she smells like rosewater and warm female flesh, an intoxicating combination.

I push my tongue into her mouth, needing more. She moans and sucks on my tongue, tunneling her fingers into my hair. The heat underneath my taut skin is unbearable. She drives me crazy. She always did. All the blood in my body pools in my dick. She rubs herself against me.

The more she strokes me with her tongue, the more the layers of chill and ugliness Mom brought fall away. I cling to Fiona like salvation, fuse my mouth to hers like I could meld our bodies if I just kiss her deeply enough. I don't know how I stayed away from her for so long—

She pulls me down until I'm on top of her, her back on the floor. She's in a stunning white gown—very much like the wedding dress I saw in the pictures. *When did she change?* But I never get to ask the question; she hikes her skirt up to her waist, raises her knees and spreads her thighs, beckoning. My mouth waters.

"Like what you see?" she teases softly.

"You know I do." My voice is guttural. I run my palm along her soft inner thigh, heading for the gorgeously flushed flesh, but she wags a finger.

"Uh-uh. You can't touch me there."

"You spread your legs for me. You're mine."

"I can spread my legs for anybody." She dips a finger into her opening, keeping her eyes on me. Pleasure clouds her gaze. "Including myself."

Lust clutches me. I've never seen her touch herself, and the sight makes my dick ache, my fingers itch. Her breathing hitches.

"Let me stick my fingers into your pussy. Find the spot you can't resist while I suck your clit."

She shakes her head, her eyes narrowed. She thrusts two fingers inside herself. When she withdraws them, they're slick. She bites her lip. *Jesus.* The visual is too much. The need to hammer into her thrums in my skull. I want to fuck her through the floor and into the dirt below. I want to defile her, hate her and love her at the same time until I get this maddening obsession out of my system.

"Not a good idea," she says breathlessly. "I'm waiting..."

"To come?" I say when she doesn't say more. My dick hurts so much, but most importantly, the need to touch her rides me like a monster I can't resist.

"No. She's waiting for *me*." Jude appears in a tux and starts to fall on her. I grab him before he can touch her. My fist connects with his face until blood spurts from his nose. Satisfaction sears through me.

I've *always* wanted to do this. It's almost as good as sex with Fiona.

Fiona's scream echoes, the impact of the shriek hitting me like a concrete block—

I blink. My eyes struggle to find something tangible in the utter darkness. I rub them, smell the soft lavender scent—potpourri from Akiko. She sends it to me every so often because she suspects I don't sleep well, but also knows if she worries too overtly, I'll withdraw.

I run a hand over my face. The lavender smells nice, but it doesn't do a thing to keep nightmares at bay. Nothing worked until I met Fiona.

For some reason, holding her helped me sleep. The nightmares stayed away when she hummed for me, her fingers threaded in my hair. But I'll be damned if I admit she had anything to do with my improved sleep back then. She's no human Ambien. It was just a coincidence.

It sounds annoyingly unconvincing even to me.

I turn, burying my face in the pillow, chills and heat chasing each other through my body. *The damn nightmare*. What the hell was that—Mom, Fiona and...Jude at the end? Tonight isn't the first time I've had a messed-up dream involving those three. If I were still seeing a therapist, he'd have a field day with it...especially since I'm still hard.

I don't blame my dick too much. After all, I'm healthy, in my prime, so when a hot chick masturbates in my dream, yeah, I'm going to get an erection.

But I'm awake now. The dream's over.

My penis continues to throb. If it could talk, it'd say, "Grab me, fucker. For God's sake, gimme a break!"

The problem is that the only thing I can think about right now is Fiona—her legs spread, her eyes dark with pleasure, her cheeks and mouth flushed with heat. I'm *not* jerking off to that. No. No way.

My mood hits rock bottom when I finally drag myself out of bed three hours later. I haven't slept a wink and my head feels like it's full of wet cotton balls. Thank God I'm not working today. I need to get some pills to help me sleep through the night. I quit using them after my last birthday—didn't like the dependency—but screw it.

My dick still refuses to get the memo. It's semi-hard. I ignore it and shower. "This is going to be a great day," I tell myself as I get ready to attend Ares's wedding. My brother is disgustingly happy with his wife, and he deserves that more than anybody else.

The ceremony is held on a wide green field. It's just the Huxleys and some friends. Nobody from Lareina's side of the family comes, but then, "attending a wedding" is not a valid excuse to leave prison. But she's probably happier without them anyway. And it avoids a potential murder, because Ares might just kill them if he ran into them.

"Here Comes the Bride" soars in the air. Lareina appears in a stunning white gown. Although the ceremony was hastily arranged, you'd never be able to tell. There are beautiful orchids, lilies, jasmines, tulips and other flowers I can't begin to name, along with a live band and fantastic catering.

Lareina's backless dress is something straight out of a fairytale. Hundreds of diamantes sparkle, and the bodice is sewn with countless little pearls. Ares spared no expense to ensure his wife would get a dream wedding, the kind befitting a queen.

Josh and I stand as Ares's groomsmen. My phone continues to buzz. Probably more photos from Jude, who's trying desperately to get my attention—and reaction. How pathetic can he be?

But how pathetic are you*, thinking about something that only happened in your dream? You're wondering if she spread her legs and plunged her fingers into her pussy in front of Jude...*

A ball of acid burns in my gut. My heart says it's jealousy, but I refuse to accept that. Why should I get jealous? I don't feel anything for her.

Too late. You got hard.

God, I hate arguing with myself.

After the vows are exchanged and Ares and Lareina march out to Mendelssohn while rose petals rain down on the couple, Josh pulls out his phone, then stiffens and glares at it. "*What?*" He turns to me. "Marriage? Are you *crazy*?"

I do my best to look confused. "What?"

"Stina!"

I make a big deal out of frowning and scratching my head. "Doesn't ring a bell."

He stares at me in disbelief. "The girl from yesterday! You told her to buy a ring because I wanted to propose!"

"Oh, *her*. Yeah. You sent her to me, so I just returned the favor." I give him a what-did-you-expect shrug.

"You were supposed to act like you'd never met her before—"

I snort. "Didn't have to act. I never *had* met her. But I thought you might want to get something going with her, since you didn't outright reject her."

"I did, but she burst into tears."

My jaw drops. "So you sent her to *me*?"

"I was trying to help you. I was about to tell you that before you cut me off."

"Help me?" I fold my arms and wait. "This ought to be good."

"Yes! You've been uptight and irritable for weeks now. Ever since Fiona visited your office."

It takes considerable willpower not to clench my teeth. However, any reaction would be admitting he's right, and I'll be damned if—

"So you could've just released your built-up pressure with Stina, and voilà, back to normal."

I sigh. "I'm not uptight and irritable, and I certainly don't have any 'built-up pressure.'"

"You made an intern cry." He says it with the triumphant finality of a lawyer unveiling his best exhibit, the kind that will destroy the opposing counsel's entire case.

"He fucked up!"

"But making him cry?"

"Hey, if he can't handle constructive feedback, it's on him. Huxley & Webber isn't some kindergarten."

Josh puts a hand on my shoulder. "Bryce, you need to get laid. That's my 'constructive feedback' for *you*."

"I don't want sex."

"Why not? Sex solves all sorts of issues. It's better than therapy. Cheaper, too. Think about it." He slaps my shoulder, then goes off to say something to Aunt Jeremiah.

I shove his ridiculous advice out of my head and turn away. The spot on my thigh that Fiona touched tingles, almost as though she still has her palm on it. She looked so...pitiful and beautiful, so treacherous and hot at the same time. If she hadn't retreated... If she'd actually unbuckled my pants and pulled my dick into her mouth...

Security wouldn't have been called in. No. I would've clenched her hair and fucked her mouth, thrusting deep into her throat. I never did that back in college because I didn't want her to choke, but now?

I'd order her to hollow her cheeks and maintain good suction, because it'd be about me—and my pleasure. Then, when I'd had enough, I'd come in her mouth, making sure she swallowed it all. If she spilled even a drop, I'd make her do it all over again.

Then—once I'd had my fill—*then* I'd call security.

Maybe you should've done that. Then you wouldn't be having all those fucked-up dreams about her. Or an erection at your brother's wedding.

Damn it.

I breathe in and out a few times. *Be a good brother. Make a toast and dance and do everything that you're supposed to do at a wedding.*

As Ares and Lareina start their first dance, my phone pings. I look down at the screen. A photo from another unknown number. Fiona in a wedding gown. Her gaze unfocused and her mouth unsmiling, she's sitting on a stool in a white room full of ivory lilies. Doesn't look like a happy bride. Isn't she marrying Jude, the love of her life? She should smile, glow radiantly.

Or perhaps Jude decided he doesn't want her after all. And it's very possible that he simply lied last night to piss me off. What started out as an unrequited rivalry on his part has morphed into hatred on both our parts. He'd love nothing more than to seize an opportunity to mock me, using Fiona like he did before.

But if not Jude, then who's the groom? Maybe some old geezer with money?

I narrow my eyes at the photo. *Is she trying to beg me to come save her from a marriage she doesn't want?*

How shameless. She deserves whatever fate throws at her.

But...

I think about some stooped, balding asshole touching her. His mottled hands. His thin, dry lips pressing against hers, his quivery fingers undoing the laces on her dress and stroking her taut flesh—

Revulsion and rage swell. In my mind, I'm already grabbing the collar of the old man's shirt and hurling him away. I haven't felt such raw possessiveness in...forever. But it isn't caring, either; I want to grab Fiona and shake her for being a cheap idiot then pound into her until she's begging for mercy.

Jesus. What's wrong with me?

Then another ping—from a different number. The new photo isn't of Fiona, but Jude in a tuxedo in a white room much like the one in Fiona's photo. Several vases of lilies of the valley sit in the background. His hair is slicked back, his eyes bright. The smirk twisting his mouth is full of smugness.

–Unknown: Perfect groom for the perfect bride.

So he really *is* marrying Fiona? This piece of shit, who treated her worse than the dirt on the soles of his shoes?

Despite what I told Jude last night, I might not have been her first choice. She might've gone to him first, then come to me after he didn't give her the answer she needed fast enough. Or...maybe she's just that crazy about him. The years apart might've shown her she couldn't be without him. Who the hell knows what's going on in her head?

My mouth tight, I block the number. She wants to brag that she's marrying the man of her dreams? Well, let the traitorous bitch marry that snake. It's a perfect pairing.

I shake my head. She's never changed. Yet my gut churns with acid. I simply can't understand—

Ignore it. She wants that asshole.

I forcibly wrench my attention back to Ares. But the wedding-night scenario reappears. Except this time, instead of the wrinkled hands, Jude's hands glide over her body, his mouth on her lips, his cock entering her—

The last image nearly blows the top of my skull off. The pressure has built so tight, my sternum feels like it's about to crack.

Over my dead body they're going to have a fairytale wedding and live happily ever after.

Pulling at my tie and loosening it, I get up and start to leave. I have a wedding to go fuck up.

9

BRYCE

IT BARELY TAKES an hour to reach the place where Fiona and Jude are getting married. Speeding helps. Thankfully, their wedding made the local gossip columns, which in turn made it easy to find them.

The venue Fiona and Jude picked out is done in an ostentatious and overwhelming amount of white, and actually sports onion domes. Where are we? Moscow?

But then, Jude does have an ego. Maybe he equates himself with a czar.

Giant banners with photos of Fiona and Jude hang everywhere. The fucker didn't bother to use her real name, putting *Finn Oberman* on the banners. Ridiculous how she's so into a man who won't even call her by her real name.

When we first met, she said everyone called her Finn, but it doesn't suit her. She's more like a little rose that you didn't know was there, but once you notice, you can't look away. So I've always called her Fiona.

She's smiling in every picture, her eyes wide and bright. Jude, on the other hand, grins like a man who's rediscovered a toy he lost and had forgotten about. No affection glows in his gaze, just a need to possess.

How can she not see that? Or perhaps she does see it and doesn't care. After all, it's Jude. She's always made an exception for him.

For a moment, I hesitate. *What am I doing here?* Crashing the wedding like a prince on a white horse? Am I trying to save her?

I'm no prince. I'm nobody's prize, really, if you get to know me. But suddenly her photo from earlier flashes in my head. The heavy sense of oppression, helplessness and grief in her eyes. I think back to that rainy night at Harvard.

Frustration, irritation and the need to break something tighten around my neck. I rip at my shirt buttons, undoing the top two, and drag in more air.

Finally, clarity settles in my head. I'm no prince...and she's no princess. This isn't a fairytale where I rescue her and we live happily ever after. It's a story where I ruin her wedding to an asshole, and then get to torment and use her until I get this constant restlessness and craving for her body out of my system. Once I get to fuck her a few times, I'll be satisfied—able to permanently evict her from my life and never think of her again.

The faint melody of "Here Comes the Bride" floats in the air.

I follow the sound. On the double doors are portraits of Fiona and Jude. Good *God* they're desperate to let everyone know they're getting married!

I kick the doors. They crash open with a deafening bang. Fiona stands in the aisle, near the altar. Jude and Aaron are with her—the latter of course being best man, since he's almost as big an asshole as Jude.

The music fades. Whispers rise from the guests. Fiona stares at me, her mouth parted. She blinks as though unable to believe I just crashed the wedding. Shock, confusion, disappointment, hope and uncertainty all pass over her gorgeous face. My heart inexplicably tight, I wait to see which will remain.

Finally, she frowns.

Don't like what you see? Too bad, sweetheart. You shouldn't have sent me those photos—actually, you shouldn't have barged into my office and shown yourself in the first place.

Jude reacts first. "Bryce Huxley! What a surprise." He smirks, malice glinting in his eyes, then starts to step forward, hiding Fiona behind him like a dog guarding his bone. "You aren't invited—"

Aren't invited? Oh, is that how you want this to go? Trying to make me look like a socially maladroit fool? Derision tugs at my mouth.

"—but you're welcome to sit in the back and toast to us later."

Hope he isn't expecting me to thank him for his "hospitality," after that bullshit about the invitation last night.

"After all, we have a history." If he could, he might just crow like a rooster.

But underneath the gloating is a hint of nervousness and wariness. He snatches Fiona's hand and yanks her toward him. She drops the bouquet, but he doesn't seem to care or notice as he wraps his arm around her waist and pulls her tight against him.

"I'm not here to toast to you," I say. I slide my eyes in Fiona's direction. She's pale, sweat filming along her hairline. "What you said in my office—is it still valid?" The question is her last chance to make her stance clear—me or Jude. Not that I'm going to change my plan to fuck up this wedding. But her answer will determine *how* I'm going to fuck it up.

Her eyebrows pinch together. "Well—"

"Yes or no?" My voice is cold. A small part of me—the one that's never gotten much wiser over the years—wants to say, *Choose me, Fiona. You've always abandoned me—always chosen him over me. So pick me this time.*

She licks her lips. "Yes. But—"

"Fine." I raise my hand, palm up. "Let's finish our talk."

"Our talk...?"

"The favor."

She reels back a little, as though dazed. She stares at my hand, her eyes unfocused.

I cock an eyebrow, hiding an unfamiliar feeling of uncertainty. Is she going to pick him? I'm not exactly sure what I'll do if she does, but it won't be pretty. She doesn't get to blast into my life, then invade my dreams. She doesn't get to send photos and dare me to do something about her situation, then act innocent.

A slight tremor racks her body. Indecision fleets across her beautiful face, calculation flashing in her eyes. Even now she's trying to weigh me and Jude, to see who's going to benefit her more.

Just what the hell did Jude promise her? Respect as his wife? His wealth?

Suddenly she lunges forward toward me. My heart crows with jubilation.

Finally.

"You whore!" Jude grinds out, then runs after her.

Her cumbersome dress must've tangled with her feet—she starts to fall.

Shit. I lunge forward and catch her, then in one smooth motion push her over a shoulder. Her weight feels good. Too good.

Aaron steps forward, his face red. Numerous guests rise, without any idea what they want to do.

Sherry Oberman only counts some beads and murmurs things under her breath, seemingly oblivious.

"What the fuck are you doing?" Aaron shouts like a clown.

"Sealing a deal and saving the family," Fiona mutters.

I start walking out.

"Stop! She's my woman!"

I feel something tugging me and Fiona back. I spin around. Jude is gripping the end of the train, his knuckles white. Ah. That explains the little backward jerk.

Jude's face is twisted with impotent fury and embarrassment. I almost laugh at the scene. Seeing him like this is surprisingly entertaining.

"Put her down!" He reaches for Fiona. "She's mine—"

With great relish, I kick his knee hard enough to make it crunch. He yelps in shock and pain. His eyes bulge, and a vein stands out in his forehead as he wraps his hands around the knee.

What a beautiful sight. Hope the moment is forever etched into his brain.

I yank the train out of Jude's hand, then turn around and start to leave, with Fiona on my shoulder. Unable to resist, I raise my voice loud enough to carry. "Might want to do something about your grip strength if you plan to use that hand for more than just jerking off."

10

FIONA

My heart hammers as Bryce carries me out of the venue. Oh my God. Now what?

Jude screams. Aaron is shouting. Guests murmur, and Jude's parents seem about to faint. Sherry acts like she hasn't witnessed anything out of the ordinary as she recites her mantra, probably praying that this is more good karma for Finley.

"Can you stop by the dressing room and grab my purse?" I say quickly as Bryce strides past the bride's room. "To your left."

His body heaves as he sighs, then kicks the door open and snatches the black purse I left on the vanity. He unceremoniously dumps me into his Rolls-Royce, then climbs behind the wheel. As my body sinks into the buttery leather seat, reality starts to reassert itself.

The wedding didn't happen. I didn't marry Jude. And Bryce is here...next to me.

I turn my head slowly to stare at his handsome profile, from the straight nose to the high forehead and the taut line of his mouth. Why did he do this? He couldn't have known about the ceremony...or did he? Jude wanted me to invite him, but I didn't bother because I knew he wouldn't care.

But maybe he does care.

My head is too jumbled to make sense of what's going on. Everything that happened since he walked into the ceremony feels like it occurred in a drunken haze, although I haven't touched a drop of alcohol.

Bryce glances at the rearview mirror. "Jude is limping toward us."

My eyes dart to the mirror to my right. Sure enough, Jude is coming—fist raised and looking like he's going to use it. No need to worry about appearances when the wedding's already been ruined.

God, I hate him. I feel a sudden need to put on a show the jerk won't forget and show him I've always despised him. So I put a hand on Bryce's cheek and press my lips on his, knowing Jude can see us. They're very familiar but also different—warm, but harder and more recalcitrant. Like I used to, I run my tongue over Bryce's lips, then pull the lower one in and suck gently.

He doesn't open his mouth. None of the tender passion from when we were dating shows on his face. Instead, his eyes slide toward me, studying me without blinking, as though he wants to see how far I'll go.

My skin cools. This isn't the Bryce from before—sweet, strong and protective. The Bryce sitting next to me is harsher and sharper, full of thorns and jagged edges. If I get too close, I'm going to get shredded.

Suddenly, all my confidence disappears. *Why did I think he would hold any kind of feelings toward me?* He's only come for me because he wants to humiliate Jude. Didn't I see enough of their rivalry while the three of us were at Harvard?

I feel like a fool, standing on a stage, playing a role I can't possibly pull off. I sit back and straighten up, my eyes focused ahead. He runs the pad of his thumb over his mouth, then lets out a scornful laugh. "Was that a joke?"

"What?" I say shakily.

"You used to kiss better. Don't tell me your skills have gotten rusty over the years." He looks in the rearview mirror, smirking. "Time to let him fume in our exhaust." He glances over. "Get it...?"

He floors the Rolls-Royce, leaving Jude behind. I can see him shaking his fist.

Bryce doesn't say anything as the car weaves through the L.A. traffic. I stare at my hands and run the pads of my index fingers along the edges of my thumbnails over and over again. Anxiety—different from what I felt when I was about to say "I do" in front of everyone—thrums in my heart. I'd like to believe Bryce came with good intentions, but I know better. He might've decided he doesn't want to be the asshole who broke his word, but it's taken him too long for me to trust him completely.

But he said we'd finish our talk from the office, so that means he's open to lending me the two million. I can't ask for more than that right now. I'll figure out the rest as it comes along. After all, it's become clear that no matter how carefully I plan my future, one unexpected event can derail everything.

First things first—I need to come up with a way to convince Bryce I can make regular payments on the two million. Jude forced me to resign from my job in Wisconsin and refused to let me apply for another position in L.A., saying his wife doesn't need to worry about money. But I can probably find a job fairly quickly. I have lots of experience in marketing. Many of my campaigns have added significantly to the bottom line. Actually, my old company might rehire me if they haven't found a replacement yet. The hours are reasonable, and I rarely, if ever, had to work overtime. I can probably get a side gig to pay the loan off faster.

So for the moment, anyway, my course seems clear. Hash out the terms with Bryce. Get in touch with my boss in Wisconsin. Find a position as soon as possible and make payments. I should consider taking Sherry with me. Now that the family's gone bankrupt and Aaron's turned into a gambling addict, her staying in SoCal doesn't seem so desirable. Wisconsin's far enough away that she'll be at least somewhat insulated from his idiocy.

Suddenly, I realize the car isn't going toward Huxley & Webber. Instead, it's headed to—

A huge mansion appears in front of us. Unlike the ornate Oberman estate, this one is more contemporary, with rectangular wrought-iron gates. But the walls seem overly tall, like the chief concern is privacy, and excessively thick, like the other main concern is safety. Which is weird. Bryce isn't some celebrity hounded by paparazzi, and doesn't live in some hotbed of crime.

He drives along a winding road. Succulents in various shades of green, purple and red cover a vast garden with walking paths made with flat white rocks. Up ahead is a sprawling two-story building with turrets that look almost medieval. I spot at least ten security cameras, but I suspect there are more.

He stops the car in front of the mansion.

"We're talking here?" I ask.

"Yes." He gets out.

I follow him. The front door of the mansion is massive, made of thick wood that could likely withstand a battering ram. The inside is done in cool gray and ivory, with some marble and crystal. A postmodern oil painting in blue and red hangs in the foyer. The splash of color stands out, making the place feel less sterile.

A nook at the corner between the foyer and the rest of the house holds a gorgeous crystal case with the name *Bryce Emmanuel Huxley* engraved on the latch. Inside is a long cane with PIETAS ET UNITAS etched in elaborate silver filigree. The knob is a silver wolf's head. It looks expensive and dignified.

A gigantic kitchen boasts state-of-the-art appliances. Copper pots hang from hooks above, and a huge wooden butcher's board occupies the black granite counter mottled with white and gray. Given how spotless everything is, either he never cooks or his cleaning staff is amazing. My money's on the former—none of his pots have a single ding.

He takes me to the living room with two plush leather armchairs and three leather couches, all of them pale gray. The center table is a glass top supported by the sawed-off trunk of some massive tree, maybe an oak.

Remembering what happened in his office, I wait for an invitation to sit. Bryce heads to the wet bar and pours some whiskey into a glass. "Want some?"

The offer is tempting, but I need a clear head. I didn't sleep at all last night, and the adrenaline from earlier is wearing off. "No, thank you."

He takes a sip while studying me over the rim of the glass. His gaze is so intense, I feel like my skin is burning. "How much do you owe Jude? Two mil?"

"No. He hasn't given me any money yet. He thought I might run if he gave it to me too fast." That was what he claimed, but I know better. He wanted something to dangle in front of me, so he could watch me squirm and struggle. He enjoys that—gives him a sense of superiority and fulfillment that nothing else can.

Bryce nods. "Good. I don't want you having an excuse to meet him again."

"Believe me, the feeling is mutual." I'd gladly give up a kidney not to see Jude ever again.

Bryce's eyes bore into my face, like he wants to gauge if I'm being truthful. I look him in the eye.

"I can tell," he says finally. But his voice is so flat, it doesn't seem sincere.

"Can you?" I say softly, pained. Although I'm grateful he interrupted when he did, part of me wishes he hadn't let me go through the hell of preparing for a wedding with Jude. But then, he might've done it to show me that he's the one in charge. It's impossible to forget the frustration and helpless fury in Bryce's gaze when Jude used me to taunt him back when we were in Harvard. The memory still makes me want to squirm and look away in shame. At that time, I felt like I had no choice—I was too young, panicked and afraid of being abandoned unless I was perfect, like Finley would've been if she hadn't died. But I should've opted for honesty, even if it meant public shame and being kicked out of the Oberman family. "I didn't think you'd do anything, especially not after what happened in your office."

"Barging into my office was rude."

"So is going back on your word."

"I'm neither polite nor forgiving."

"Maybe not now. But you used to be nice."

Something dark flashes in his eyes as his mouth twists into a cynical line. "You mean I used to be a sucker." He sits down and stretches his legs. Still no invitation to sit.

Guess he's still unhappy with me. But if that's the case, why did he rescue me from the wedding? He didn't bring up the money just now or want to continue our talk just to kick me out again.

Bryce swirls his drink and studies the movement in the glass.

Although he looks like a lazy lion, my skin crackles with the tightly suppressed energy coming from him. He's barely controlling some kind of urge I can't fathom.

"You said something about wanting to borrow money and pay it off," he says.

I nod. "A fair proposal."

"Fair?" He cocks a skeptical eyebrow.

My hackles rise. Even though I don't have many cards to play, he doesn't get to question my sincerity. "Yes. You give me something, I pay you back."

"How very transactional." His eyes chill.

Frustration suffocates me. What does he dislike about what I said? I didn't say anything out of the ordinary. If we were having this discussion ten, even eight years ago, I might've thought there were simmering feelings underneath, but it's been too long. We haven't stayed in the same place, emotionally—we've moved on. "Because that's all there is to it. You should've given it the consideration it deserved. Instead, you mocked my proposal, then insulted me."

"You're the one who got on your knees," he says.

I gasp at his outrageous framing of what happened. "My knees gave out!"

"What—too shocked I didn't offer to just give you the money? The idea of actually having to pay back the two million was too much?"

I bite my lip. He's acting like I'm a witness he needs to break. Inexplicable tears sting my eyes, but I blink them away. He wasn't like this before. Yes, he hated me, but he never treated me like he wanted to destroy me. Back in college, he sneered at Jude and generally pretended I didn't exist. I thought that hurt, but this is much more painful. I thought I'd moved on, but maybe I haven't made as much progress as I believed.

"When did you become such a jerk?" I whisper.

"I was always a jerk."

"No. You weren't like this before. You were *nice*."

His eyes flash dangerously. "Are you calling me a good boy?" The muscles in his jaw bunch. "Do you think you know me because we used to fuck? If you understood anything about me, you wouldn't have done what you did. And you certainly wouldn't have thought you could come beg for a favor afterward."

The rough displeasure in his tone says that talking about our past won't be productive. We're just talking in circles. If I tell him what really happened, will his attitude change?

He brings his glass to his mouth and knocks back the rest of the whiskey. His legs are spread, the free arm draped over the back of the couch. The muscles on his strong frame are both thicker and leaner, the words sharper and colder. He gazes at the world like everything's at his feet, and nothing can touch him.

Bryce exudes a confidence and authority he didn't have when we were in college, but they aren't his only new trait. An impenetrable shield is up around him, keeping everyone at arm's length, including me.

Especially me.

I realize with gut-wrenching pain that the truth about the past won't penetrate that shield. He might listen, but he wouldn't believe. I can't even present him with evidence. What could I show him? The pictures and videos are gone. And Jude would never admit to anything because he'd rather cut off an arm than say anything that could restore my relationship with Bryce.

Don't look back. Move on. Focus on what's important now.

"Let's discuss the loan and repayment. I don't have a job at the moment. I had to leave mine in Wisconsin, but I'm sure I can get a similar position. I might even be able to go back to my old company. I was very good at marketing."

"Why go to the trouble?" His eyes rake me with arrogant thoroughness, as though he wants to make sure I'm at least as good as he remembers. "You can just do what you do best. Work it off on your back."

Of all the...! "You said I wasn't your type," I shoot back, furious.

"Sometimes a man wants a fast-food burger."

Humiliation heats my face. "I take back what I said about you being a jerk. You've become a complete asshole!"

He gives me a smile so arrogant I want to slap it off his face. "And proud of it."

"You really want to have sex with me?" I can't believe he's saying this after giving me crap in his office.

"You didn't think I destroyed your wedding out of love, did you?"

"No. But it's two million dollars." My mind reels, unable to process what Bryce is saying. The situation feels like something out of an over-the-top movie. Except *Indecent Proposal* had a happy ending. This isn't going to have a Hollywood ending. I'm too old and jaded to believe in such nonsense. Things like that happen to other people. I'm just hanging on to my veneer of respectability and happiness with white knuckles, hoping nobody finds out I'm an unworthy fraud.

"Yeah. I'm probably going to want more than one burger."

"Why?"

"You're in no position to demand an explanation, Fiona. If you don't want to pay with your body, forget it. You have nothing else to offer."

Despite his hard voice saying the topic is finished, I can't stop. Maybe I'm a masochist, but I need to know just how low he plans to push me. "How many times?" I ask shakily.

His eyebrows pinch briefly, and coldness flashes in his eyes. "Until I get tired of you."

"Aren't you tired of me already?"

"Guess not. I was tempted when you put your hand on my thigh. If it hadn't been my office and people weren't waiting..."

My whole body burns with shame at the reminder. He rejected my explanation about my knees giving out, and he's not going to believe the gesture was devoid of any sexual overtones on my part. Abruptly I realize he'll never take anything I say at face value. The loss of trust cuts my heart like a shard of glass. I knew I lost something valuable when I was forced to let Jude use me to hurt him, but seeing what I truly lost leaves me flayed to the deepest part of my soul.

I take a moment to suck in air and recenter myself. "Not good enough. I need a number."

He shrugs carelessly. "Three hundred."

"Are you *crazy*? Ten!"

He lets out a laugh. "Are *you* crazy? You think sex with you is worth two hundred thousand bucks a pop?"

I falter. *Put that way... Still—*

"Even at three hundred, I'm overpaying. Your body isn't worth over sixty-five hundred bucks. Not even top-end escorts get paid that much."

My mind goes blank, unable to come up with a counterargument. Still, I hate him for making me like a commodity. "You're such a bastard."

He gives me a look. "You're the one who wanted a number, Fiona. Don't blame me for the consequences of what you've done. You're a big girl. Ask a question, suffer the answer." A faint smile curves his lips, but it doesn't reach his eyes. Instead, in their depths is a simmering combination of grim satisfaction and challenge. He doesn't think I'll go through with it.

After all, he doesn't really need me for sex. Certainly not enough to pay me. He's young, handsome and rich. He can get any woman he wants with a snap of his fingers.

I flick my narrowed eyes to his crotch. His pants are tighter, although maybe he isn't fully erect yet.

He wants my body...

Fine—his lust will be my weapon.

11

FIONA

My eyes holding Bryce's, I move my hand to the side and lower the zipper hidden under the rows of tiny pearls. The bodice hangs forward, gaping open. I tug at the ribbon at the small of my back, and the tight clutch of the fabric loosens.

I slowly lower the dress, inch by inch. His eyes follow, the intensity searing my skin. Triumph thrums in my veins.

Just as the neckline is about to dip below my nipples, I stop. "Does this count as one? After all, I need to work on reducing the three hundred."

His Adam's apple bobs. "That depends on how far you take it." His voice remains hard, with a hint of guttural roughness that wasn't there before.

"We're going as far as we need to," I purr, then let the dress glide down my skin, the chiffon whispering in the silent room. The silk caresses my nipples, then strokes my belly like a lover's touch.

His eyes flare as he realizes I'm not wearing anything under the bodice. My nipples bead in the cool air. I rock my hips slightly, helping the dress slip past.

The white fabric pools at my feet, the copious material covering up to my shin. I stand in front of Bryce in nothing but a garter belt and white silk stockings, no other underwear. I waxed two days ago, so there's not a strand of hair on me.

Heat erupts in Bryce's eyes, but he doesn't move. The tent at his crotch rises higher. I drop my eyes, then lift them to meet his.

I step out of the dress I despise and sit on the glass-top coffee table. It's so low my knees go higher than my hips. Putting a hand behind me for balance, I slowly spread my legs. His gaze drops to my most private flesh, the impact sending sizzles up my spine.

"Like it?" I say. "Never seen me waxed before, have you?" I take my index and middle fingers and run them gently over the soft folds on either side of my pussy, not showing him the prize. Not yet.

"Spread them," he orders me, unblinking. He reaches for his glass, then stops, as though belatedly realizing he knocked back his whiskey already.

Licking my lips, I slip my index finger between the folds without spreading them. I stroke my clit leisurely, eliciting a soft sigh of satisfaction. I might be exaggerating my reaction a little, but it isn't difficult to be turned on. Bryce has always had an irresistible ability to make my blood boil.

I move the finger lower, gliding it along the slickening flesh until it reaches my pussy. I tease the opening, biting my lip. Heat curls in my belly.

He unbuttons his shirt—although he had two undone already. His cheeks flush—a sign he's seriously turned on. I widen my knees, moving my finger more vigorously over myself. Every stroke bumps against my clit, and the wetness spreads.

"Fuck yourself with your fingers."

I only push in one finger, my eyes defiant. I know I'm being naughty and challenging, but I don't care. I want to show him he doesn't hold all the cards just because he tries to make me feel cheap.

His jaw stiffens. He tightens his hand around his whiskey glass. I push another finger in, then pump them the way I like the most. Fast, but not so fast that I'm chasing a quick climax. I move my pelvis to the rhythm.

The pleasure builds much more quickly than I expected. I haven't had a decent orgasm in ages, the kind that leaves you shaking to the core. By all rights I shouldn't have one now either, but Bryce's gaze upon me intensifies every sensation.

"Fuck yourself to an orgasm if you want this to count."

At his velvety command, my breathing shallows. Although the wickedness of having him watch me masturbate is a huge turn-on, I can't seem to go over. I thrust harder. My muscles grip my fingers, but something is missing.

I need a vibrator, I realize. I'm not going to come like this.

Dismay ripples, then is quickly replaced by another thought—*Just fake it. Nobody's going to know.*

I faked it all the time with Jude, and he never noticed. Men only see what they want to see.

I pump my fingers faster and arch my back, moving my hips. Then I squeeze my eyes shut and let out a soft scream, quiver a little and then pant as I slowly "relax."

After a few minutes, I pretend like I've recovered. But when I open my eyes, Bryce is looming over me, his hands on each side of my head, his crotch close to my pussy. He's still in his clothes, but I can see the strong chest through the gap in his shirt.

I gasp, and he lowers his face closer to mine. His eyes roam over my every feature, as though he's seeing me for the first time. "When did you learn to play such a transparent trick?"

"Wh-what do you mean?" I stammer.

"Come on. Faking, sweetheart?"

I bite my lip, then quickly put on an air of bravado. "Don't be ridiculous."

"I've seen you come countless times. I know what you look like when you're lost in an orgasm."

"Maybe I've changed."

"Maybe *you* have, but your body hasn't." He shifts, one hand going to the back of my neck and holding me. The other travels down and pushes three thick fingers inside me. The invasion stretches me, shock waves rippling out. I gasp, staring up at him in surprise. "See? Your cunt can never be satisfied by two of your slim, anemic fingers. It wants to be filled tight. Like this."

He pulls back a little, then thrusts them in, deeper and harder this time. I moan helplessly as pleasure washes over me.

"And your angle's wrong. Your hips need to be like this, so my thumb can rub against your clit. Your body has always been greedy for me." The pad of his thumb circles over my clit as he pumps his fingers. Electric jolts shake through me, tingling my nerve endings until I'm writhing against him.

"And your tits want to be sucked and nipped." His mouth closes over my nipple.

My back arches, this time like a bow pulled tightly. He knows exactly how much suction I need, how to flick his tongue to produce the maximum reaction.

The sensual assault overwhelms me. I was wet before; now I'm soaking.

I brace my heels at the edge of the table as I arch, rock, buck...and come. But he doesn't stop touching me. He thrusts harder, his thumb circling over my swollen clit, and his mouth sucks the other breast like he's a man on a mission.

I whimper, aroused and alarmed that he's turned the tables on me, even as my pelvis moves shamelessly against his hand. Another brutal orgasm breaks over me. I grip him hard, digging my fingers into his hair, holding his head to my breast.

He turns a little, letting my nipple out of his mouth. His breath fans over the overstimulated tip, making me shiver with prickling pleasure. "You like that? But this greedy little body is still unsatisfied." He pushes in deeper. "It's still begging for more, getting wetter. It wants to be really filled." He unbuckles his pants, pushing his clothes down.

His cock springs out, and I tremble at the size. The shaft is thicker than I remember, dark veins pulsing along the long length. The plum-shaped head is rounder and bigger. Precum drips down.

He wraps his large hand around the shaft, but can't hold it all. He gives it a good pump, his breathing roughening. My mouth dries.

Still, a sliver of sanity wins out. "No sex without a rubber."

"Don't worry." He pulls out a foil packet from his pants pocket and tears it with his teeth.

The second he sheathes himself, he drives into me, balls deep. I cry out at the ruthless invasion. The feel of him can't compare to his fingers—so thick and long and hot and pulsing. It hits the spot deep inside me just right, making my vision haze with a pleasure so intense I can't breathe.

The rhythm he sets is brutally hard and fast, his balls slapping against my ass with each thrust, the bobbing making my breasts jiggle. I twist as ecstasy swells, crackling through my veins. He returns to my nipple, sucking it in and trapping it between the roof of his mouth and tongue. The pleasure building inside me is so intense, it's almost painful. I pant helplessly, moans vibrating through my arched throat.

"Please... Bryce... It's too much..."

He shows no mercy, driving into me with ruthless focus.

Lust burns white hot. I wrap my legs around him to control his thrusts and get him to slow down, but soon I realize I'm actually using him as an anchor so I can move my pelvis to match his cock.

A tidal wave of an orgasm crashes through me. I scream, clutching him hard, afraid I'll be lost if I let go. My pussy spasms, clenching his cock. It's almost like my body needs a moment to gather itself. But he doesn't stop. He is a man on a mission to show me who's in charge.

Without giving me a chance to catch my breath, he slams into me.

"Give me a second—"

"Why? You're taking my cock like your pussy is made for me," he says between pants. His cock feels even thicker and longer. *How is that possible?* "You're gripping me like you can't bear to let go." He rams into me so hard that I feel it all the way to my tingling scalp.

Another intense climax washes through me. I can't even scream as I shake under him. He drives into me a couple more times, then finally lets out a guttural groan as his entire body tenses and he empties himself.

I lie on the table, limp as a rag doll, struggling to drag in air. My heart hammers so fast and loud, I can't seem to hear anything over the sound of my pulse.

Bryce wasn't like this before. He was insatiable in bed, but not so ruthless and driven. Even though he's given me multiple orgasms, not one was about us. It was more about something else—dominance... control...who belongs to whom.

He's made his point. I'd forgotten how my body reacts to him—it's like he's made of some unholy aphrodisiac. Or maybe I thought I wouldn't respond to him like that anymore because of our breakup.

I tense at another thought: *Is he seeing somebody?* He's from the Huxley family, and their motto—*pietas et unitas*—is famous. Loyalty and unity. The family lives by it. Some of them don't commit at all, but if they do marry, they're faithful to their spouses. But I'm not a Huxley, so Bryce doesn't owe me anything. He might have a girlfriend he cherishes, but wants me on the side as a fucktoy for when he feels horny but doesn't want to jerk off.

"What's going through that head of yours?" Bryce says, studying my expression. His edge has dulled a little, but is still sharp enough to hurt if I try to get too close.

"Just wondering if you have a girlfriend." I aim for nonchalance, but my voice breaks a little at the end, which, thankfully, he doesn't seem to notice.

His eyebrows snap into a dark scowl. "If I did, I wouldn't have fucked you. Unlike some people, *I* don't cheat." He sounds insulted.

I look away briefly as the familiar ache burns in my heart. "And if you meet somebody you like while we're doing this...?"

"Then I guess we'll have to put this on hold, then resume after I break up."

I gasp. The sheer *presumption*. "I can't be your eternal fucktoy. I might not want to live in L.A. for that long."

"Perhaps you should focus on satisfying me three hundred times, then."

"Two hundred and ninety-nine!" I glare at him.

He laughs mockingly. "You better keep an accurate account. If you mess up, who knows what'll happen."

"You—"

He dips his face to kiss me and shut me up.

I quickly turn my head. His lips brush my cheek. I shiver. *So close.* "No kissing on the mouth." My tone is flat and firm, brooks no debate, but of course a highly trained lawyer like Bryce wants to argue.

"Ridiculous. You still have my cock inside you and you can't bear to kiss?"

Right on cue, his penis twitches. I flush at the sensation, which is much more delicious than I'd like.

"What kind of game are you playing now?" he demands.

"Not a game. It's one thing for you to stick your dick in me, another for you to kiss me on the mouth. It's far too intimate and affectionate." He'll never kiss me like he used to—with all his affection and care, like I'm the world's greatest treasure. My heart might just break, and I don't want to show any more vulnerability. I'm scared he'll use it against me. "Plus, you don't deserve it."

Rage flares in his eyes. "*I'll* decide what I deserve." He grips my hair and tries to kiss me again.

"I'm not consenting to the kiss. Are you going to force me?"

He stops, then scrutinizes my face—one heartbeat...two... "Are you telling me if I kiss you, it'll be rape?" He's so close, his breath tickles my cheek.

I nod jerkily.

He stares at me like I just told him clouds are made of ice cream. Finally, he pulls back and laughs. The sound is unpleasant—nasty, even. "How ludicrous. Fucking you any way I want isn't rape, but kissing you on the mouth is?"

I stay stubbornly silent.

"Fine. We'll have it your way."

12

BRYCE

Hot water sluices down my suds-covered body, washing away every hint of Fiona on me. Her scent disappears, replaced by the mint and sandalwood of the soap. Foam swirls down the drain—like what happened to our college relationship, when I was more innocent and naïve.

When I believed she might be the one.

I thought if I sated my sexual frustration and erased every trace of her from my skin, I'd feel liberated. No more thinking of her. No more getting erect at inopportune times. Instead, all I can do is remember how amazing it felt to be back inside her.

Damn it. I shove my wet hair out of my face in frustration and cut off the shower. Sex with Fiona hasn't done a thing to quell the annoying restlessness that's been plaguing me. No, that's not quite right. The satisfaction was there when she came around my cock twice, and I lost my mind with pleasure. I hate to admit it, but I've never felt as good with any other woman.

But then she had to ruin it by acting like kissing on the mouth was equivalent to rape, then looking at me like I'd smashed her heart.

Brazen. Shameless...!

She's the one who betrayed me and trampled all over my dignity, pride and feelings. Did she honestly believe I ruined her wedding with Jude just to be able to return to playing her lap dog?

My biggest mistake back then was letting her soften me into being the kind of boyfriend the world considers "good." Well, the time of my being that kind of idiot is over. Forever.

The problem is my dick. It's incredible how a penis can have its own logic and stubbornness that have nothing to do with my brain's decree.

I shake my head. I honestly thought I was beyond such nonsense.

Still. It was bitterly satisfying to watch her struggle to maintain her superior attitude. She tried to pin me to a number, then spread her legs and touched herself to provoke me.

Did she expect tenderness or something else more meaningful out of sex? Before, we had sweetness, laughter, joy and trust—at least, I did. Now, I won't spare her any. She said I didn't deserve to kiss her. It's she who doesn't deserve anything.

I put on a shirt and shorts then walk out of the bedroom and head downstairs. I pause when I see Fiona standing in front of the coffee table. She's covered herself with the wedding dress. Guess she wasn't brazen enough to stay in just the garter belt and stockings. Or maybe she's realized they won't get her what she wants.

When she took off the dress and showed what was underneath, my blood shot to the boiling point instantly. A toxic combination of bitterness and victory sizzled in my veins as I took her in. Her softly rounded breasts rose and fell, their tips rosy and pointed, begging to be sucked. Her waist was still nicely taut, her hips flared just enough to fill my palms if I wanted to grip them as I screwed her brains out. The sight of her hairless pussy was more erotic than any porn. I'd never seen her waxed there before, and I loved it that nothing was hidden from my view. The silken stockings encased her long, shapely legs, their snowy color giving her an air of innocence despite her state of wanton undress.

She wore those for Jude—for their wedding night. But it was me who got to enjoy the view, not him. The realization is still gratifying. Bet he's still fuming—maybe in his wedding bed, *alone*.

She's staring at the floor as though studying the pattern in the marble. But I was in the bathroom for half an hour or so. There's no way she just stood there all this time, doing nothing.

"You can go," I say, my tone more curt than I intend. But it's best I don't give her any sort of opening.

She starts. "I don't have a ride."

"I'll call you an Uber—"

"Actually, I don't *have* anywhere to go."

I fold my arms and squint at her. "What happened to your place?"

She licks her lips, shifting a bit. "I didn't get a rental. I've been staying at the family estate, but it's...not a good idea for me to go there right now."

"Like I care?" If the mansion's about to be foreclosed, that's her problem, not mine.

"Jude and Aaron are likely to be there."

That shuts me up. Those two don't deserve to give her a hard time. If anybody's going to make her suffer, it's gonna be me.

And although she didn't mention it, her mother is probably going to be at the Obermans' mansion. After all, where can a widow without any job skills go? She might blame Fiona for not marrying Jude and jeopardizing the two million dollars.

But I don't want Fiona in my house. It's my sanctuary. As a matter of fact, I regret bringing her here. I never bring women here, preferring to go to their place or to a hotel nearby. I should've done the same with her, but I wasn't thinking clearly as I drove away from the wedding. I was riding too high on triumph and elation.

"How about a friend?" I say.

She looks away with an awkward shrug. "Don't have any."

I raise an eyebrow. "Are you telling me you never made any friends all these years?"

"Not anyone close enough for me to crash with in L.A."

Again, hard to believe. *Don't girls have sleepovers with friends all the time?* Even I had one or two with some boys, although my dad and stepmom were paranoid about my and my brothers' safety. As far as I know, Fiona doesn't have a sociopathic mom trying to kidnap her and leave her to die in a fire. "Are you proposing that you stay here? You're that eager to pay off your debt to me?"

She flushes. "I don't break my word."

I snort. "That remains to be seen." Cheaters cheat because they fundamentally *don't* value their word or the trust people place in them. That sort of attitude doesn't change just because they're dealing with somebody who isn't a significant other.

I pour myself whiskey. This time I don't offer her any. In my peripheral vision, I sense her shift again.

"What's wrong? Need to use the bathroom?"

She shakes her head. "No. I… My legs are stiff."

"Then sit. There aren't any land mines in the cushions."

"I didn't think there were, but back in your office you were upset when I tried to sit without an invitation." She sinks into the smallest of the couches and arranges herself. The poufed skirt makes her look like an innocent fairy in my living room, her hair tumbling over a slender shoulder and her cheeks slightly rosy. Her mouth is soft, her lips full and vulnerable, the kind that beg for a kiss that starts out gently but morphs into something hard and intense.

Heat starts in my belly and spreads through me, all the way to my fingertips and toes. I hate it that I notice how pretty and kissable she is.

Back at the office, huh? If she's fishing for an apology, forget it. I pull out my phone with a nonchalance I don't feel, my body propped against the bar. "I gave your information to my banker. He'll reach out tomorrow and arrange for a wire for two million."

"Um. I don't know if they're the kind of people you can just wire money to."

I tilt my head. "What does that mean?"

"They're loan sharks. I don't know if they bank like normal people." She clears her throat.

What in the world…? "Are you crazy?" My hand tightens around my phone. It's that or shake her until she develops some common sense. "You borrowed money from loan sharks?"

"Not me. Aaron," she says defensively.

My jaw drops. "What the hell? *You're paying off Aaron's debt?*"

She nods.

I stare, trying to understand. The entire conversation has taken on a surreal tone. "Why? He's a big boy. Let him handle it." Somewhere in my head, a voice says, *If she doesn't have to take care of the two million, you won't have any leverage over her.* But I don't care. It's stupid of her to take on that kind of debt when she doesn't need to. Didn't anybody advise her?

"I wanted to, but they came after me and Sherry. I couldn't let them hurt us."

"But loan sharks?" I shake my head.

Fiona lets out a hollow laugh. "I had the same reaction. But what can I do? They can have Aaron and do whatever they want to him, but I owe Sherry everything. I can't let her suffer."

I've seen Zachary's wife a few times at social functions. Pretty, but a bit fragile. Pleasant enough, and well mannered. But I can't picture her doing anything that'd inspire such devotion from Fiona. Sherry's always lost in some Buddhist scripture or mantra. Won't touch meat or alcohol, saying taking a life is bad. Apparently, plants don't qualify as "lives."

Fiona continues, "I don't know exactly how to make the payment, but I'm sure they'll be in touch soon. They text every day. And I'd prefer to not involve Aaron, since he might try to take the money and run. He has a gambling problem. Did you know that?"

"No, but I'm not surprised." Aaron was at Harvard as well, two years ahead of us. He was a piece of shit back then, and the rumor was that, in addition to the usual drinking, he indulged in drugs, hookers and every other vice known to man. Nobody made a big deal about it, especially not the administration. The Obermans donated a large sum of money each year, and the amount jumped while Aaron and Fiona were attending. "Anyway, I can arrange for the money to be paid however you want, although I don't encourage cash. Too dangerous."

"I know. I'm not going to be that reckless."

"Really? Because you've been reckless ever since you reentered my life." Fiona was reckless when she barged into my office...when she decided to marry Jude...when she sent me those photos. And now she's trying to pay off money her brother owes to some loan sharks. Concern clouds my better judgment, and I sit next to her—then immediately realize it was a mistake.

This close, I can smell the scent of us on her. It's like she belongs to me in every way, and if I push her back and spread her, she'll welcome me into her wet, tight pussy with a soft moan, then beg me to use her for my pleasure.

A prickling sensation spreads. My dick hardens like it didn't just explode inside her less than an hour ago. My fingertips twitch, and I curl my hands, refusing to touch her. I don't want her to think she's in charge. She will never be in charge. I'm never giving her that much control and power again.

"I was desperate," she says. "But now I'm not. I have the money, and once I pay them, they'll leave me and Sherry alone."

I sigh. "You realize the loan sharks are probably just going to jack up the interest, right?"

She blinks in bewilderment. "Why would they?"

"Because they can. Because they're assholes. If Aaron went into debt while gambling, they probably have mob connections."

"Well..." She shakes her head. "I'll deal with that when it happens."

"How? Are you planning to borrow more from me?"

Her cheeks redden. "I'll think of something."

I detect a slight tremor underneath her firm tone. "Are you paying off the extra with your body too?"

"I don't like to think about hypotheticals." Suddenly she clears her throat and stands up. "Actually, I need to go."

Flustered? "Where to?"

"To..." She hesitates. "To get my things."

"I said *where*, not why."

Not meeting my eyes, she shrugs. "Jude's place."

"Why? Now that you got fucked by me, you want to hop back into his bed?" The nasty question is out before I realize what I'm saying. The words are full of old wounds and pain, and I want to smack myself for inadvertently revealing a glimpse of the hurt I've been harboring.

"Don't be crude," she says sharply.

I inwardly sigh with relief that she didn't notice anything. I put up an even higher and more unbreakable wall.

She continues, "He had all my things moved there last night. All my shoes and clothes and stuff."

"So? You aren't crawling back to him, regardless of the excuse."

"It's not an excuse—"

"If you go anywhere near him, the deal's off. You won't need to wear clothes for what you're here to do."

Her expression starts to crumble before she blinks away all signs of vulnerability. "You are *such* an asshole now."

"No. I was always an asshole. It's just that I wasn't an asshole with you."

Something halfway between anguish and disbelief flashes across her face. Her hands clench into fists. "You know what? I'm not wasting my breath talking to you."

"Good. You aren't paying off the loan by talking. Now go take a shower, unless you want to smell like you just got fucked," I say, selecting words for maximal pain.

Her complexion turns red, white, then back to red before she spins around and walks upstairs.

"Third door to your right," I call out. That's the only guestroom with an en suite bathroom that's fully stocked.

The slamming of the door is the only answer. I cock an eyebrow. *Temper, temper.*

Now… Will she come out in the same dress with nothing underneath once she's showered? I can strip her of the damned outfit, have her grip the back of the couch and take her from behind, this time shooting my cum all over her bare back, reapplying my scent to her.

If I take her until her pussy is raw, perhaps this endless hunger can be satisfied. But part of me says that's the worst kind of strategy. She's expecting that—and likely has counterplans for it.

I don't want to see her in the wedding dress she picked out to marry Jude Morven ever again.

I head to my closet and pick out the oldest T-shirt I own. The pale gray cotton is faded, but clean. It even has a couple of small rips around the neck, thanks to Josh. The least attractive. Perfect. Then a pair of brand-new boxers, still in the plastic packaging.

I leave them on the bed for Fiona and grab some documents I need to review before tomorrow, then settle into an armchair with a glass of Yamazaki 18. But my focus isn't wholly on the paper. Part of me is hyperaware of Fiona upstairs—in the shower, naked and wet and covered with slippery suds. When she washes her private parts, does she glide her fingers through her folds, then rub, making herself feel good at the same time? Her clit and pussy are probably still sensitive. I remember how long they remain like that after she comes. Is she rubbing herself for another quick orgasm in the shower? Or is she trying to ignore the awareness between her thighs?

I sip the whiskey, letting the liquid fire burn down my throat all the way to my stomach. But the heat in my gut has nothing to do with the fine liquor. It's all about the woman upstairs.

If she had her phone, she might stay hidden upstairs, but her purse is still in my Rolls-Royce. Well, when I see her in my old T-shirt, I'm not going to feel this uncomfortable or worked up. I picked it specifically because it's going to look ridiculous on her.

But she doesn't come out of the room for the rest of the day. Even though her purse and phone are still in the Rolls.

I have to read the documents three times, constantly distracted by images of her in the damn shower.

13

FIONA

MY EYES automatically open at six—just a habit I've had since college. I blink as the gears in my head start engaging. The soft sheets smell a bit like Bryce—the same detergent, most likely. Even though it's just soap scent, nothing more, every time my bare legs brush against the soft material, it feels erotic, like it's Bryce's warm hands gliding over my hypersensitive skin. The sensation doesn't dissipate but pools between my legs. It's ridiculous, but I'm wet and slightly swollen. If Bryce came into the room right now and slid a finger down my folds, he'd crow smugly with victory.

Damn him.

I thought he might slip into the room and demand an encore, but he didn't try anything. It's almost like he's trying to be a gentleman.

Instead of providing relief, it's just unnerving. It's obvious he has the upper hand, and that he wants to humiliate and use me, just like Jude did. I wish my body would wise up, like my head has, but it craves the pleasure only Bryce can give.

So unfair. Billions of men out there, and he's the only one who can make me lose my mind with sex.

He probably sold his soul to the devil.

My belly growls urgently. I didn't have anything to eat yesterday—

too nervous before the ceremony. Afterward, I couldn't eat because I didn't want to face Bryce in nothing but a T-shirt and boxers. My nipples were still sensitive and pointed, and the feel of the cotton rubbing against them was just too much.

I've never felt like a horny nympho until now. Sex before and after Bryce was okay. Jude could never manage to give an orgasm. I just faked it because having him on top of me was nauseating. Most of the time I told him I was on my period, including that time he made me stage that sex scene in Bryce's bed. Jude acted like I was diseased, thank the Lord. I had a couple of boyfriends after heading to Wisconsin, but I could never really relax around them enough to enjoy myself.

I gasp as a horrifying possibility surges into my mind. Surely I didn't let my emotional guard down enough to climax like that with Bryce, right? He hates me. If I show him even a hint of vulnerability, he'll use it to shred me.

No, no. I slap my cheeks a couple of times. *My reaction to him is one hundred percent physical.* Like having an orgasm with a battery-operated boyfriend. Not all sex toys are equal. Some work better than others. Bryce just happens to fall in at the head of the line.

Food, coffee, then an action plan. In that order. I can't let myself be maneuvered into doing what Bryce wants. I still don't know why he wants to have sex with me when he had to have had plenty with other women after we broke up. I'm a realist—there's no way he didn't sleep around. Even when we were together, girls eyed him like they wanted to devour him. And there's no way he still harbors any kind of nostalgia for what we had before.

For men, sex is just fun. Maybe a method of stress relief and relaxation. But nothing serious.

I sigh. I wish I'd protested more vigorously when Jude moved my things to his place. Or at least found a way to grab them before Bryce got so nasty about my going for them yesterday. I could've snuck inside before Jude came home—he probably had to deal with the guests, venue and caterers and go to the hospital for his injured knee. But it's too late now.

I check the clock on the nightstand. Six thirty. Bryce is probably gone by now. The morning traffic is horrible in L.A., and he was always punctual.

I tiptoe out of my room. Nothing but heavy silence. I quietly pad to the kitchen. On a stool in front of the counter is my purse. Good. I look to see if there's anything for breakfast. Two cups of coffee in the coffee pot. Guess the machine made it automatically. A used mug in the sink. I let out a soft breath. Yup, Bryce is gone. I can take the leftover coffee without any problem.

I pour myself a mug and sip the surprisingly aromatic brew. Guess he indulges on pricey coffee beans. Not surprising, though. He loves the finer things in life, and doesn't care how much they cost. Must be nice to be rich—*with his own money*. Even before the Obermans went bankrupt, I never felt like I could touch a penny of their money. I had to wait until Zachary or Sherry noticed a lack and provided for me.

I open the fridge. Nothing but a carton of milk, some juices and two tubs of whipped cream cheese. The pantry has egg bagels and a box of cornflakes, my favorite breakfast. I pick up the cereal. Still sealed. Does he have another box that's already open? The only things on the shelves are peanut butter, various jams and some pasta.

Guess not.

I stare at the cereal. If I open it, he's going to know I rummaged through his kitchen and ate his food. I hate to take more than the money we agreed on. How about the bagels? I don't care for them, but I'm too hungry to be picky. But...a brand-new bag. Ugh.

I have my purse, so I can just head out and get something. *Draw a line. Keep our relationship clear, just between creditor and debtor.*

"That cereal won't jump into the bowl on its own."

I jump and scream at the same time. The box of cornflakes hits the floor. "Oh my *God*! You scared me!" I press a hand over my racing heart as I turn around to face Bryce.

He's in a black three-piece suit with a blue-gray tie, knotted perfectly. His near-black hair is slicked back, showing his high forehead. His dark eyebrows pinch tighter, and his mouth settles into a flat, vaguely displeased line.

Is he that unhappy about my dropping his precious cereal? Good

God, I'll buy him a new box if it's that upsetting. I start to bend down to pick it up.

He grips my forearm and stops me. "Take off that shirt."

What? Gasping, I yank away from him and cross my arms in front of my chest. "No."

The muscles in his jaw flex. He steps forward, invading my personal space. He smells like the detergent on my sheets and the shirt...and something else—minty soap and male flesh.

My mouth dries as I recall how the bedsheets felt against my bare skin. Alarm flares inside me at the wetness pooling between my legs. Just what kind of spell has he cast on me that I'm turned on by his scent?

From the way his dark gaze bores into mine, I wonder if he knows what he's doing to me. *Oh God...*

"Fiona—"

"Don't you have to go to work?" I say hurriedly.

An impatient sound growls deep in his throat. Closing his eyes for a moment, he exhales heavily. "What were you doing in the pantry?"

"Looking for an open box of cereal."

"You know I don't eat cereal."

I blink as the most unlikely implication sinks into me. "Did you buy it for me?"

His eyelashes flicker, then he nods curtly. "Yes." The tips of his ears turn pink.

Just that simple answer chips away at my guard. But then I remember how he asked me to take off my shirt just now, probably wanting a morning quickie before work. I keep my voice neutral. "How much do I owe you?"

"Thank me with a kiss."

The tinge of tenderness I felt just a second ago vanishes faster than a drop of water on a hot pan. I step back, and he steps forward. He drops his eyes to my lips, and they tingle like he's caressed them.

He's just peeved at my trying to set boundaries. He wants to torment me, and he can't do that without crossing all my lines.

My eyes flick to his mouth. Memories of our kisses play in my head. Sometimes he kissed me teasingly, his lips moving as softly as butterfly wings, coaxing and cajoling, sweetly inviting me to kiss him back and stroke my tongue over the seam of his mouth. Then there were times he turned me around and kissed me like he missed me so much. But the best was when he cradled my face in his hot hands and fused his mouth to mine, thrusting his tongue in with ruthless drive, like he was intent on stealing my breath, my heart and my soul.

Every single one of them was too intimate, made my blood heat and belly flop. They knocked at my heart, breaking whatever shield I had around it with ease. They might not have the same impact now, but I'm not risking anything. Especially after learning that he's even better at sex than before.

My pulse throbs as he continues to advance slowly. I take another step back, blindly fumbling for my purse and pulling out one of the tens I keep in the side pocket for emergencies.

He grips the counter behind me, trapping me against the granite. The heat radiating from him makes my mouth dry. A small tremor runs through me.

He starts to dip his head. Quickly, I slap the ten-dollar bill over his mouth. "Here! For the cereal. Keep the change."

Something hot and dangerous flares in his eyes, but I don't back down. Instead I raise my chin in defiance. He pulls back, scowling darkly.

"After I eat, I'll go and get some clothes and stuff, so I can give you back your precious shirt."

He glares at me. "You're going out in nothing but my T-shirt and boxers? To let everyone get an eyeful of what should only belong to me?"

I scoff at the ridiculous display of possessiveness. Just because I owe him two hundred and ninety-nine more times doesn't mean I need to act like his exclusive property. "My body isn't for your eyes only."

"It is until you fulfil your end of the deal." He looks at me like he's just found a strand of hair in his dessert. "I already ordered some clothes." He wrinkles his nose, speaking like he's doing something so unpleasant that he'd rather eat broken glass. "My personal shopper should drop them off later this morning."

"You know my size?"

He raises his hands and makes squeezing motions, dropping his eyes meaningfully at my breasts and hips. "You haven't changed much, Fiona, and I have an excellent memory."

I pause. *He still remembers my size from shopping in college?* From the slight tightening of his jaw, I realize he's also referring to the pain I caused. Bittersweetness knots my gut, and I blink to stop the tears from welling. "Thanks. That was...um...nice of you."

His eyes narrow. "Necessary to make sure I get my money's worth. Three hundred is really overpaying." His gaze drops to my bare legs meaningfully.

That insufferable, rude, socially unacceptable jerk! "Two hundred and ninety-nine, now."

He opens his mouth, but his phone pings. He glances at the screen, then starts to leave. "Whatever. Keep track. And wear something sexy tonight."

My jaw slack, I stare at his retreating back. *Hot, cold, hot, cold...* What I wouldn't give to be able to strangle him until he picks one or the other.

Inhaling deeply to control my temper, I pour a bowl of cereal and dump milk on it, which is also new and unopened. Obviously, he got them yesterday, probably for me, since he hasn't touched anything except the coffee as far as I can tell. When we were in college, he only had coffee and maybe a bagel or a croissant for breakfast. I was the one who had cornflakes, and he always made sure to stock his place with some for me.

Tears of sadness sting my nose. Logically I understand there's no point in playing *what-if*. But my heart wants to think about it, to go through the full catalog of regrets.

I let out a long breath, trying to steady myself. "Don't look back," I tell myself. "Just forward. Always move forward."

After all, reliving my past hasn't been good for me emotionally. Thinking about how my own parents discarded me when I was just a newborn hurts until I can't stop tearing up. My first set of adoptive parents throwing me away like trash because they got pregnant is salt over an old wound that refuses to heal. If they didn't want me enough to keep me no matter what, they shouldn't have adopted me in the first place. Their actions taught me that only some kids are loved. And that fear of not being lovable stayed with me with the Obermans when I learned they didn't love me for me, but for resembling their beloved, perfect Finley.

I'm always terrified of not being perfect, but also exhausted and resentful of the need to be flawless, lest I be cast aside again. I bask in the affection people give me because I'm perfect, but also despair I won't be loved if people found out how flawed I really am.

I don't know what I'm supposed to be anymore because I don't think I can maintain my façade for much longer. Choosing Bryce at the wedding probably already destroyed whatever illusions Sherry and the family's acquaintances had about me. If I had even a hundredth of the confidence and self-assurance Bryce has—

Stop thinking about what you love the most about him.

I shake myself mentally and take my phone out. Notifications have exploded in the last few hours. More than a hundred texts from Jude calling me names. "Bitch cunt whore" is one of the nicer ones. But then, he always had the worst names for me. He used them with relish, loved the way I bit my tongue and faux-fawned over him, while people around us looked at us like we were circus freaks. He thought they admired him for being able to do whatever he wanted and still keep a nice girl by his side. He never saw the pity, disgust and disdain in their eyes.

Aaron has also sent me a bazillion texts. His names are slightly more literate, like "ungrateful little bitch," along with ranting about how I plan to pay the money. The loan sharks need their money, and I'm being selfish and thoughtless by leaving Jude. How is he supposed to deal with my irresponsible behavior?

He's obviously forgotten who was irresponsible enough to borrow money from loan sharks to begin with!

But yelling at him won't solve anything.

Nothing from Sherry. That's a little surprising—and deflating. I didn't expect her to applaud my decision yesterday, but I thought she'd at least ask if I was okay. If I were her real daughter, she'd definitely show more concern.

I press a hand over the ache in my heart. I should be used to this. Sherry's only worry is to get good karma for Finley's reincarnation. She told me Finley died too young, before she could accumulate enough good karma, so she has to do it. I shoot her a quick text:

–Me: In case you're wondering, I'm okay. I hope you're okay, too. Please let me know if you need anything.

I stare at the screen for a while. Nothing. Not even three dots.

Okay. I put the phone down and do the dishes—including Bryce's mug—and look out the window facing the backyard. There isn't a single succulent to be seen. Instead, the massive garden is full of shrub roses blooming in stunning carmine—a little surprising, because they don't seem like something Bryce would pick. I thought he'd prefer something more masculine and less high-maintenance. A field of agaves or black dahlias, maybe.

I stare at the gorgeous red flowers and think about my immediate plans. Zachary's death and Aaron's mess have derailed my life. It's time to put it back on track.

First, a job. Then a place of my own—a small studio apartment. Then a decent used car, since I had to sell mine in Wisconsin when I was forced to marry Jude.

My fucktoy phase will end within two years. Bryce was insatiable before, and he's even more sexual now. He'll burn through the three hundred—no, two hundred and ninety-nine—pretty fast.

Also—as soon as the clothes arrive, I need to get on birth control. Condoms will still be mandatory. But I need reassurance that soon this will be all a distant memory without any permanent baggage.

14

BRYCE

Booming music throbs, the rapid beats pounding through me. A sea of people below jump and sway to the vibrant tune, lost in the music, alcohol and drugs.

The VIP lounge on the upper level isn't as crowded. Z serves the best liquor and has the hottest chicks. I need a little break and distance after what happened this morning.

Josh's already got a couple of girls with him. Probably going to take one to a hotel nearby if he "feels the necessary chemistry." I, on the other hand, feel nothing as I survey the women gyrating around the club.

Damn it. I run a hand over my face roughly. I told Fiona to wear something sexy tonight. What will it be? Something so hot it makes my blood boil? Something so plain and boring that I might just laugh at her defiance? Or maybe nothing at all just because I ordered her to wear something.

Even as my body tightens with anticipation, I stay put. I'm not confident I won't lose control. And control is everything when you're dealing with somebody as treacherous and beautiful as Fiona Oberman.

A redhead next to me places a hand on my thigh, pressing her tits against my arm. The low cut of her tight black dress leaves almost nothing to the imagination. Not at all like the practically nun-like outfit Fiona wore when she came to beg for money.

Then there were the garter belt and stockings from yesterday...

And my old shirt this morning. Damn it, it was supposed to look like a worn-out sack of potatoes over her with holes. Instead, it was so thin I could see the outlines of her nipples.

I could almost hear her panting and moaning my name. *"Bryce, please. Please, I need more."*

I wanted her out of the shirt instantly, but when I unthinkingly told her to take it off, she crossed her arms like I was some kind of pervert.

If she hadn't crossed her arms, I might've yanked the shirt over her head myself. Then knotted it, trapping her arms above her head, and sucked her nipples...

Or I might've just pushed her to her knees and filled her insolent mouth with my cock. I was so tempted when she pressed that ten-dollar bill against my lips.

But there was a hint of naked vulnerability underneath the daring attitude, so I backed down.

I shouldn't have. All I've been thinking about at work is her. Her voice. The way she smells—all sweet and female with my soap over her. Her softness. Those small but sensitive breasts and that amazing pussy I can never get enough of.

Even as I focus on her body, regret seeps through. All that's supposed to be left between us is my unresolved need for her body. I shouldn't have bought the cereal and milk last night when I realized she was staying. Shouldn't have tried to kiss her after that immensely satisfying orgasm or asked for one in the morning, like some lovesick idiot. None of our intimacy from before remains now. Hell, it wasn't even real back then. The only one who cared was me. I was the fool who believed it was love, when she was just playing a game.

The idea is infuriating and humiliating. I hate myself for not being able to move past it, as though I'm walking away from an unfinished story. Whatever was between me and Fiona ended with her betrayal—why hasn't my heart gotten the memo?

Love isn't real. Deceptions are a dime a dozen. The time when we held each other and whispered sweet nothings and laughed and kissed and lost ourselves in each other is over. I mourn it because it was beautiful. But I should know better. Lovely moments don't last. They always end before you're ready, and they leave deep scars.

But scars do eventually heal. The ones Mom left are scabbed over. The ones from Fiona will mend, too. I'll make sure of it.

When I glance down at the slim, well-manicured hand, the redhead glides it upward leisurely, but with a clearly seductive intention. She knows the score, and she's just looking for a good time, nothing more.

Part of me wants it, needing something—anything—to push Fiona out of my head. Another part recoils at another woman's touch.

Right now, the latter is winning—my dick lies inert. Bastard.

"You're so tense," the redhead says into my ear. Her moist breath feels sticky and unpleasant, but I let her continue. Her eyes drop to the untouched whiskey in front of me. "Why don't you have a drink? Take the edge off?"

"I'm a tequila fan." A lie, but I don't want to touch anything when I'm not sure about the chain of custody. Anybody could've slipped something into the drink. Mom's side of the family—the criminal side—loves to drug people. Her brother Harvey once put something in Ares's whiskey to try to get him to work for the mob as their legal counsel.

Perhaps I'm being overly paranoid, but I'd rather be careful than regret it later. Mom, Harvey… I wouldn't put anything past those two—or anybody from the Dunkels. My maternal grandfather, the Nesovian crime lord Vincent, is sick, and Mom and Harvey are fighting to take control of "the family business." Supposedly, Vincent said he'd hand over control to whomever could bring his grandsons to see him before he croaked.

I hope he dies alone and miserable, and before he can put anybody in charge of his pathetic criminal enterprise. In a just world it will fall apart from internal strife—maybe even a civil war. If he'd agreed to put Mom in prison for what she did to us, I might've gone on my own to see him. But Vincent cared more about the optics of being a strong crime boss who protects his daughter than making her pay for her crimes.

He doesn't get to act like a loving grandfather now, after all these years, without an apology. But I already know what he'd say: *I love you, my boy. I did it for you.*

Whatever. Too little, too late.

The redhead makes a soft humming noise. "I bet I can make you learn to *love* whiskey. You just have to have it right." She takes a sip of the amber liquid, then cups my cheek and presses her mouth against mine. She pushes the fiery whiskey past my lips. I swallow reflexively, then shove her away. Her tongue is too invasive, and feels nasty in my mouth, like an overgrown slug. It leaves my blood cold.

She laughs. "Oh my God, don't tell me you're a prude. I don't believe you came here to just sit and watch."

I say nothing as the warmth from the liquor spreads. The sensation is a bit disturbing. It was only a mouthful, and my tolerance is high.

"I like you." She smiles at me like I'm the last piece of chocolate left in the display case. "Why don't we go somewhere? Let me make you feel good?"

She pulls me up, and amazingly enough I find myself standing. The girl's smile widens. I glance back at Josh, but he's occupied, probably testing for a soul-mate bond with a woman whose name he won't remember tomorrow.

The redhead and I step out of the VIP lounge, where the deafening music pounds us with near-physical force. The pulsing of the beat makes my head spin. *What the hell?*

"I've got you," she says when I sway a little. "Just lean on me. I'm *much* stronger than I look."

Prickling sensations spread through my body. Heat starts in my belly and expands. My skin feels too tight. The air seems to thin, and I yank at my tie, undoing the knot and pulling it down. But that isn't enough. My collar is suffocating. I unbutton the top button, then drag in more air. *Still not enough.* My vision blurs for a second.

"Are you okay? Let's go outside," she says.

Great idea. Outside means more air.

We burst out of the club. The cool, slightly smoggy air hits my face, but somehow my lungs can't haul in enough oxygen. The heat from my belly spreads everywhere, even to my face. My cheeks burn, and my fingers feel shaky.

The streetlights are hazy halos against the dark of the sky. I turn to the redhead. "It's foggy."

"What is?" she says as she continues to lead me away.

My head feels like it's been shoved under water and time seems to slow. But my body burns, and my cock is so swollen, it hurts. Electric sparks sizzle in my veins. I feel like I'm going to die if I can't ram my dick into a warm pussy—any pussy.

A small alarm bell goes off in my head. *This...isn't like me at all.* Unlike Josh, I don't screw indiscriminately.

I'm drugged.

The whiskey. I didn't think it would be drugged, since she drank from the same glass, but she might have taken an antidote beforehand.

Only two people in my life would do something like this—Mom or her brother Harvey. My eyes cut to the redhead. Who does she work for? What's her next move?

Where is she taking me?

Red drags me into a dimly lit space. I stare at her. "Where the hell are we?"

"The presidential suite at the Aylster. I want to splurge." She says it in a nasal, whiny voice she undoubtedly thinks sounds sexy.

I squint, trying to focus, but her face is a little too blurry. The gears in my head turn sluggishly, like they did when Mom fed me and my brothers drug-laced cookies before attempting to kidnap all of us. The similarity is eerie.

"We're going to make each other feel good." Red runs her tongue over her lips. The gesture looks like something out of a third-rate porn movie shot by a first-time production company.

Not like what Mom gave me. It's much worse. My cock twitches. The heat in my blood is unbearable. I feel like I'm burning from the inside out.

Every nerve screams for relief. Am I going to spontaneously combust? But giving in would be surrendering to the manipulation. *Nobody gets to play me.* "What did you feed me?"

"What, the whiskey?" She smiles. "You tasted it."

Her mock-innocent answer is suddenly infuriating. The long-buried frustration, guilt and recrimination over my childhood helplessness pound through my veins, and I explode, shoving her roughly. "Don't lie to me!"

Before the back of her skull can hit the carpet, I'm already on her, straddling her, closing my hand around her neck, tight enough to threaten, not injure. The fire in my veins feels wrong. My brain says what I'm doing is fucked up, but my body wants to rip her dress off and violate her.

What the hell is the point of this drug? To manipulate me? To blackmail me? My cock throbs. I wouldn't put anything past Mom or Harvey.

"Who sent you?" I demand between clenched teeth.

"Nobody. I just...want you. Heard you were a good boy." She smiles coyly, her eyes flicking between my eyes and mouth. "I've always dreamed of corrupting one."

A good boy. My skin crawls. *Mom.* Her poisoned words ring in my head in a loop. *You're such a good boy. My good boy. I can always count on you. I love you the most. My good boy, I love you, good boy, good boy—*

Fuck, fuck, fuck! I scream in my head to break the cycle before the nightmarish memories overtake me. I'm nobody's good boy. I don't need any fucking love.

Just control.

I lean down, my face half an inch from Red's. "Listen very carefully. You tell Zoe Dunkel I'm not playing her game. I don't give a shit about her or what she wants. She isn't my family. Next time she pulls something like this, I'm going to end her."

Red swallows, the seductive bravado suddenly gone. "Aren't you just a lawyer?"

"*Just* a lawyer?" I let out a nasty laugh. "You know whose blood flows in my veins?"

She flinches. She knows who I am—a grandson of the biggest and nastiest mob boss in Nesovia. The desire to take my fury out on her is as strong as the need to fuck her right now before my cock explodes.

I could push her skirt up, rip off her panties and shove my dick into her now, and she wouldn't say a word. A few good thrusts, and the pressure that's been building will be gone.

Wouldn't that feel amazing? Do it. Just take her.

No way. The drug keeps breaking down my inhibitions and defenses, steering me toward the basest path. I grit my teeth. It's not going to beat me. *I. Am. In. Control!*

I pull away from her, then stand up. "Get out."

She rolls to her hands and knees and pushes herself up. Stumbling on her heels, she scrambles out as quickly as she can.

The second the door slams, I impatiently unbuckle my pants and shove them and my boxers down below my ass. My cock springs out, swollen and thick, angrily red and veins throbbing. I grip it tightly. The heated slickness coats my dry palm. My nervous system screams for relief. The touch is both relief and agony.

I groan deep in my throat as I pump my hand and jerk my pelvis desperately. If I can just blow my load once, the pressure won't be so unbearable. As I fuck my own fist, my mind conjures up images of Fiona.

How much I want to bend her over and ram into her. How much I want to keep my cock inside her until she forgets what it's like to have her pussy empty. I want to hear the sounds she'll make when she can't take it anymore. When she's too raw and every thrust is equal parts pleasure and pain.

I curse as my spine stiffens, and streams of white shoot from the tip of my cock. It splashes on the carpet, and a deep regret unfurls that it isn't somewhere on Fiona instead.

I breathe hard, wait for my cock to settle down, but it only hardens further in my hand. I let go and step back. Whatever Mom fed me won't let me rest.

Damn it.

The priceless silk of my suit feels like sandpaper scraping me raw. I rip out of my clothes, discarding them like trash on the floor. But it isn't enough to give me peace. Now the air feels unbearable on my bare skin.

I don't know how long the effect will last, but I can't return home like this. I don't know what I'll do if I see Fiona.

My dick aches fiercely at the thought of her. I bite my lip and throw myself on the bed. The cool sheet provides some brief relief to my hot body. I let out a soft breath, relaxing a little, even though my dick's harder than ever.

But the respite is short. The fire in my gut burns brighter, greedier. I want to bury myself balls deep in Fiona and explode inside her.

Not just to get over this intolerable erection, but to regain the sense of peace she gave me when she held me in her arms back in college. My body would go lax, her fingertips gliding lovingly from the base of my skull all the way to the bottom of my spine, as though to push the nightmares away.

My teeth clench. That phase of my life is over. It's never coming back. There's only sex between us now.

I grip a pillow until my knuckles turn white and squeeze my eyes shut. A big mistake. My mind is instantly full of her—the soft sound of her voice. The view of her finger dipping into the opening of her pussy, her swollen clit ignored. How much I wanted to suck it into my mouth yesterday and push her to a brutal climax.

If she hadn't had the wedding dress around her, I might've lost myself in her like we had traveled back in time.

I move against the mattress, pushing against its softness like it's Fiona. But of course it can't compare. Every time I sink into her, I feel like I'm rediscovering heaven.

Even after the betrayal, she can still make me feel like she's my safe place.

Fuck, fuck, fuck. How stupid am I? How pathetic—

I come again, the sticky fluid coating my belly. But the lust doesn't dissipate. My dick doesn't even soften halfway before it's hard again.

I flip over, throw an arm over my eyes. My breathing grows more labored. What the hell... *How long is this going to last?*

My phone rings, the sound jarring. I ignore it, but it keeps ringing. I concentrate on slowing my racing heartbeat, but the lust only increases, until it's burning like an inferno.

Not letting my body control me. I grit my teeth and focus on evening out my breathing. *Come on. One, two, three...*

Suddenly I freeze as I realize my hips are moving. A sense of shame and helplessness lances my heart. A scream wells in my chest. I need something to distract myself—dissociate myself—from this. But I can't think of anything except how delicious Fiana looked this morning and how much I regret not taking advantage.

The phone rings again. Relief washes over me. *Maybe it's Josh.* He probably decided the girl of the night wasn't his soul mate.

I hit the green button without looking at who's calling. Through the speaker comes a familiar voice.

"Bryce? When are you going to be home?"

Fiona. A blaze sweeps through me, and my heart pounds. "Shit."

"What? *You* told me to put on something sexy and wait for you."

My mind grasps "something sexy," and my dick throbs. I clench my hand around the phone.

She says, "It's already eleven."

She sounds irritated, but her voice is somehow nonetheless soothing. I grit my teeth. I can't have her see me like this, when I'm out of my mind. I might say something I'll regret, reveal something I shouldn't.

Need a distraction. "How did you get my number?" Part of me wants to beg her to come and put me out of my misery. *No. Hell no.*

"How did I—?" A huff. "You never changed it! Look, if you aren't going to be home soon, I'm going to bed and docking it off the number. It's you who's bailing on this 'date,' not me."

Go to bed. But the words catch in my throat as I struggle for control. Finally, I grit out: "The Aylster. Presidential suite. *Now.*"

The second the words are out, I bite my lip hard, the bitter taste of blood filling my mouth.

15

FIONA

How curt. And weird. Bryce didn't sound like himself, like he was both angry and relieved. If he was upset that I called, he should've answered my texts. It isn't easy to stay up this late when I usually get up by six. But I couldn't just fall asleep, knowing he wanted to take his second time tonight.

Maybe he wants to role-play and got annoyed I didn't call sooner?

I shake my head. We used to be so in tune. A single glance, and I knew what he needed, whether it was a kiss or a hug or comforting humming or sex. Now, I never have any idea. He threw me out of my office, then changed his mind. He mocked me for "offering my body," then demanded I pay with my body.

The man is fickler than a weathervane in a hurricane.

Or this might be his way of screwing with me. After all, he made it clear he'd never forgive me for what happened...which is probably deserved. He's doing everything in his power to punish me for that past humiliation—also understandable from his perspective.

Part of me wishes I hadn't bothered with the text, asking to meet and speak to him—just gone over to him and explained what really happened between me and Jude before leaving for my job in Wisconsin. However, when Bryce said I was dead to him, my courage died. Or maybe I was just relieved that I didn't have to relive the trauma and shame. I felt like I owed him an explanation, but even if I'd given him one, he might've still accused me of making excuses. He might've been more disappointed and annoyed that I wasn't the perfect angel he'd initially assumed when I saved his golden retriever.

Stop thinking about what might've happened.

An Uber drops me off in front of the Aylster. The concierge comes to me with a polite smile. "Ms. Oberman? The presidential suite is this way."

Guess Bryce told the hotel.

I nod and follow her, carrying a box of condoms in a paper bag. Can't be prepared enough. It's possible Bryce arranged for some, but birth control matters more to me than him. After all, my consequences would be far more immediate—and dire.

The concierge takes me to a waiting elevator, swipes a card over the reader, then hands it to me. The car moves upward silently.

I exhale, trying not to fidget. The mirrored doors show a woman with her hair shiny and unbound, cascading around her shoulders in auburn waves. A respectable black trench coat with the waist cinched tight with a fabric belt. The heels I picked out are strappy and scream sex.

Bryce wants something sexy. I plan to give it to him—and show him that just because I go along with his demands, it doesn't mean he's in control. If I can't establish that, our time together is going to be disastrous.

He already wants to establish his control and possession over my body. I need to make it clear that sex doesn't mean he gets to own me until he gets his fill—because I know perfectly well he isn't going to count all the way up to three hundred. He's just being a jerk because of how we parted ways. Once he gets bored, he'll stop, but my life needs to go on.

Hopefully that will happen sooner rather than later. And hopefully we won't harbor any residual feelings for each other. A clean slate, everything totally even. Hell, if I ever get married and need a divorce lawyer in the future, it'd be nice to be able to consult Bryce without any hard feelings.

The elevator stops with a ping. The doors open. A sign in the hall says the suite is to my left. I walk along the thickly carpeted corridor, taking a deep breath to calm my nerves. I can play whatever game Bryce wants to play.

There is a pair of massive double doors at the end—and a platinum plaque to the right that reads PRESIDENTIAL SUITE. I swipe the card. The lock clicks open.

I run a palm over my hair and stride inside, my heels silent on the lush carpet. A giant vase full of fresh white calla lilies sits on a stand to my left. The floor-to-ceiling windows show a spectacular view of L.A., countless lights glittering like gemstones in the dark.

Next to an ivory baby grand piano is a trail of clothes: a white shirt, black vest and jacket, pants and underwear, all thrown haphazardly. Cushions litter the floor, some flung far from the big sectional. Socks and shoes lie under the glass-top coffee table. A tie at the foot of the bed. The tips of my shoes almost kick the cuff links glinting on the floor.

What the hell happened here? It isn't like him to leave a mess all over. He's surprisingly tidy. Even when stripping for sex, he's always left his things in a neat pile near the bed.

Except... The only time he was a wreck was that time he had a horrible nightmare earlier in our relationship. I walked in on him after a late-night group study session as he swiped his hands over his desk, sending everything crashing on the floor, including his laptop and phone. He threw the Babs Bunny mug I left on the nightstand that morning. The ceramic exploded like a bomb against the wall. I jumped, my heart pounding with shock and concern. He yanked at his hair. I dropped my bag and rushed forward. He swiveled his head toward me, but his eyes were glazed and unfocused, lost and haunted.

"Fiona...?" he croaked.

"Yeah, it's me."

Something tight and agonizing on his face crumbled. I pressed a tender kiss on his cool, unresponsive lips, then held him, stroking his back. The skin was icy, but slick with sweat. His chest rose and fell erratically. He wrapped his arms around me and buried his face in my neck, sucking in air desperately. Shudder after shudder racked through his big body. He struggled to even his breathing, but it didn't seem to help. I pulled him down on the bed, since I didn't want anything on the floor to cut his bare feet, and held him and crooned softly, hoping the steady gentle rhythm of the melody would help him regain control.

The shudders eased. His breathing grew regular. I stroked his hair, and his back. "What happened?" I asked.

"Just a bad dream." His voice was rough.

"Wanna talk about it?"

He shook his head, his hair tickling my skin, and clung to me. "It's enough that you're here."

We fell asleep, holding each other. And I never saw him react that badly to a nightmare again.

Uneasy, I step over a pillow and move closer to the bed. The sheets are twisted. If I didn't know better, I might worry that he had another nightmare episode. But he was obviously awake when we spoke on the phone. So what could've caused such a mess?

I pull the condoms out of the paper bag and toss them on the night table. The air smells faintly of mint, sandalwood and sex. My eyes scan the area—no sign of female clothes. Apprehension tightens my chest. Something's definitely not right.

A hand grips my wrist. "Fiona."

Bryce. He spins me around, taking both my wrists in his hands. I gasp as he pins me against the wall by the nightstand, my hands trapped above my head. He leans forward until his naked body is pressed against mine. His erection throbs against my belly. My pulse gallops at how hot he feels.

"You really came." His voice is low with surprise.

"Well...you asked me to. Didn't you?"

His cheeks are slightly flushed, his mouth even redder. The air in my throat catches at the darkly possessive gleam in his eyes. His pupils are so wide that the irises look nearly black. It reminds me of the time his eyes glazed from the nightmare, but there isn't any of the vulnerability from the past.

He pushes a thigh between my legs, spreading my knees, making me feel exposed even though I'm the one who's still wearing clothes. His cock is trapped between our bodies. *Is it even bigger and harder than last night?* My breathing shallows as I remember how amazing it felt when he invaded me, filled me and stretched me. Is tonight going to be even better?

He lowers his head to my mouth, and I turn my chin so that his lips graze along my jawline. He inhales sharply with displeasure. The hands around my wrists flex in a silent warning.

"I said no kissing on the mouth." I look up at him, meeting his eyes.

Savage possessiveness and a need to conquer burn in their black depths. My mouth dries, and I run my tongue over my lips without thinking. His eyes follow the movement, and his grip tightens as he tries to chase my lips.

"No!" It comes out more sharply than I want, but recalling the past has weakened my emotional shield. A kiss might feel too much like it was before—when it wasn't just a prelude to sex, but a way for us to show each other we cared. I can't afford to wallow in the past and become vulnerable, not if I want to leave this arrangement unscathed.

Something that looks like pain passes over his gorgeous face, but I'm just imagining things. A rejection from me doesn't have the power to sting him.

He puts his mouth on the side of my neck, right over my pulse point. A frustrated groan rumbles in his thickly muscled chest. He nips the delicate skin until I feel a small tingle, then he licks. Hot shivers vibrate through my body. He uses his free hand to undo my belt and unbutton my thin coat. All the while, he ravages my neck, sucking and biting and licking, as though he's punishing me for denying him my mouth. His hot breath fans over me. The prickling sensation spreads, pulsing all over until it ends between my legs, making my clit throb with the need to be touched.

I admit in the back of my mind that—maybe—I was looking forward to another night with him when he told me to dress sexy. After all, he's amazing in bed and we have great chemistry. Transaction or no, he would never deny me pleasure.

He spreads the lapels of my coat and trails his hot mouth down over my collarbones. I clench my thighs as more liquid heat pools in my already-slick flesh. My thong's going to be a mess.

Still pinning my wrists to the wall, he pushes away my coat. His eyes drop, and he takes his fill.

The black strappy underwear provides very little cover—and what is there is made of sheer lace. The satin bands crisscross my body like rope bindings, and tiny scraps of lace cover my nipples and make a tiny triangle over my crotch. A thin string made of the same material wraps low and snug around my neck like a collar with a platinum heart in the center. A garter belt and fishnet stockings complete the look.

While he looks, I look. My eyes roam all over his physique. The incredibly wide shoulders and the slabs of muscle over his chest. The ridiculously defined six-pack, and the narrow hips and thick thighs that say *power.*

His cock is so erect the head touches his belly, leaving a streak of precum on his abs. How long has he been like this?

"Did you get hard thinking of me?" I ask, my voice raspy.

"I already came twice thinking of you."

I gasp at his raw response. My eyes fly to his face. *His cock is this stiff after* two *orgasms?* Even when we were in the throes of young love, he wasn't this insatiable.

"No way," I whisper, trying to pull away and failing when his grip remains firm.

Heat blazes in his eyes, burning away whatever sanity and control he's been hanging on to. He pulls the coat down my body, then picks me up and tosses me on the bed. I gasp as I bounce on the soft mattress. The sheets underneath are wrinkled, and my hand touches something sticky.

I glare up at him. "I'm not going to sleep with you in a bed where you had sex with another woman."

He leans over me, his hands on either side of me, trapping me between his legs and arms. A smug smile tugs at his mouth. "You look pretty when you're jealous."

I want to deny I'm jealous, but it'd only make me look foolish. "I don't want you getting an STD and giving it to me."

He laughs. "Don't worry, there was no other woman." He looks into my eyes. "I told you: I came twice thinking of *you.*"

Oh my God...

He grips my hair and dips his head, then stops when we're only hairsbreadths away from kissing. "Oh, I forgot. No kissing the princess, right?"

Before I can process the resentment and wistful longing in his voice, he pulls my nipple into his mouth while pushing away the thin strap between my legs. He groans when his fingers dip into my slick depths.

"How long have you been wet?" Without giving me a chance to respond, he moves his fingers inside me so hard that I shake. "Were you thinking of me?"

I shake my head, not wanting to answer and stroke his ego.

His eyes flare. "Were you thinking of someone else?"

I grit my teeth as the pleasure builds. I'm going to get my orgasm, and he's getting whatever he wants out of the arrangement. I don't owe him any explanations. I can't afford to offer any. I need to remember what this is about and keep my heart insulated.

He lets out a mocking laugh at my defiance, then flicks his tongue over my left nipple. I moan at the teasing stroke, how good it feels. He sucks the tip of my breast with single-minded focus, and I grip his hair. He pumps his fingers, and my pussy grips them. He barely grazes the bump inside me, the one that makes me go wild. He keeps a steady pace, enough to build the fire, but not enough to make me explode.

"You bastard," I grit out. "I can't believe I ever thought you were nice."

He laughs with the nipple in his mouth, the vibration sending streaks of sharp pleasure to my core. I press my feet on the bed for better mobility, to rock against his hand, but he just rides the motion, maintaining a constant, unfulfilling pressure.

"Do you get horny thinking of me?" he asks against my breast. "Does it ever get unbearable? Do you ever finger-fuck yourself, remembering all the things we did together?"

No, no, no, I shake my head. Even as he goads me, his eyes are glazed and unfocused with raw vulnerability. I've glimpsed that before, when I walked in on him after he'd just had a nightmare. Part of me wants to cradle his face and press a kiss on his mouth as tenderly as before, but I pull back.

I don't want to give in and let my guard down. I don't want to remember the nights when I thought of him, wished I could hold on to him, kiss him until we were out of breath and have him glide into me over and over again until I forgot all the ugliness in my life.

I don't want him seducing me into hoping this can be anything but a deal. He and I… We've been through too much to believe in fairytales and happy endings.

"Do you—"

Blinking away the bittersweet tears before they fall, I put a hand over his mouth. "Shut up and fuck me."

16

BRYCE

SHUT UP AND FUCK ME.

I cock an eyebrow and stare into her luminous eyes. If she'd demanded that even half an hour ago, I might've just gone ahead and done it. I probably wouldn't have been able to control myself enough to tease her. But two orgasms and a bit of time have shaved off some of the drug's maddening urgency. The need for her boils in my veins, but not to the point that I'll do everything she wants, thank God.

And making demands when she won't even let me kiss her properly? I hate it that she's denying me that comfort, something that goes beyond just sex. For an instant, I thought that she might press her lips over mine in sweet solace as worry pinched her expressive face when she looked around the messy room. And my heart skipped a beat.

But I should've known—she never loved me. Even when our relationship was at its peak, it was one-sided. For whatever reason, the people I love and trust the most always hurt me while claiming to love me. If I'd learned that lesson when I was eight, I wouldn't have let myself be so helpless again.

I lick Fiona's palm, feeling and tracing the lines with the tip of my tongue. Her eyes widen, and she lets out a shocked sigh. Amazing that she forgot her hands could be so sensitive. I found out the second time we slept together.

I move my fingers inside her, winding her up just enough that it's torturous, but not so much that she can climax. She wants to use me like a human dildo to give her a few orgasms, but I'm not her boy toy. She'll never play me again, physically or emotionally.

Her breathing grows more erratic. She rocks against my hand, and I slow the pace a bit, denying her the peak she's chasing.

"Tell me who you think of when you touch yourself."

She shakes her head again.

"I'm getting awfully tired of your defiance, Fiona. You won't let me kiss you, and you won't be honest with me. What the hell am I getting in this bargain?"

"My body. You're getting my body," she says, her jaw clenched.

"Seems like a bad deal." I brush the tip of my middle finger over her G-spot. She arches her back, but the knot of tension inside her doesn't break. I know her body. As responsive as she is, she struggles to go over the edge without some hard and relentless pushing. The first orgasm is always elusive for her, although the subsequent ones are easier.

"Bryce," she moans softly, then bites her lip to contain the rest of her plea.

"My questions weren't that difficult." I rip the scrap of lace that passes for underwear and inhale and exhale softly over her folds. She smells like soap and woman and lust, making my mouth water.

She writhes, fisting the sheets. I take her hand and wrap it around my cock. As I thrust into the soft sheath, I feel like the top of my skull is about to blow off.

This is what I should focus on—the raw, physical lust. Once I sate myself, I can forget her and walk away. Shed her and our past like a snakeskin.

Her pussy clenches and unclenches around my fingers. Nice, but it'll be better around my dick. My eyes land on a box of condoms on the nightstand, and my control starts to go.

I grab one, then sheathe myself. She licks her lips, her eyes full of expectation. Gripping her wrists, I use my knees and spread her thighs as wide as possible. Her throat works as she looks up at me. The green-gold of her eyes is so dark, I feel like I could dive into their depths and never come back up.

I dip my cock into her opening. A groan wells in my throat. Holy shit, she's so slick and hot. My blood boils. I half expect to see steam coming out of my pores.

I keep my thrusts shallow and steady, building a rhythm and slowly stretching her. She moans with bliss. She used to love being stuffed, but this isn't going to be enough.

Suddenly, I ram into her hard. The pleasure burns under my skin, tightens my balls as my flesh slaps against hers. Her pussy clamps down on me, but I change my angle to avoid hitting all the good spots inside her.

"Noooo," she sobs. "Don't... Please."

"Sweetheart, you know what I want. Put that mouth to good use. Kiss me or answer my questions." Although Fiona can be surprisingly bold, she can also be shy, especially when I ask her to verbalize her needs. It was always one of her most endearing contradictions, and I'm going to use it now.

Before the night's over, she's going to kiss me like she used to. I know it'll be fake—only done for an orgasm, not because she has any feelings for me—but for some inexplicable reason it seems significant. Maybe I just need to feel like I'm more than a nice, hard cock.

I push into her again and again, deep and hard, continuing to edge her. God, she feels amazing. I could do this all night. Whatever drug was in the whiskey makes it impossible for me to lose my erection for more than a moment. And with Fiona sweet and soft in my arms, I don't think I'll ever go limp.

The selfish part of me says I should come, while denying her, since I'll be erect again soon. But I don't want to. We should both be in sexual purgatory, teetering on the brink.

"Bryce... You asshole," she says between gritted teeth.

"Not the right word, sweetheart." I rest my head in the crook of her neck and bite the skin there. "You know what you need to do." I pull her earlobe into my mouth and nip. "Kiss me and you can come."

"No."

"I can do this all night, probably into tomorrow, too."

She lets out a panicked breath. "What did you do?"

"Got fed some kind of drug. But it's pretty good, eh?" I chuckle dryly at the ridiculous non-joke. It's so ironic how two women I loved the most backstabbed me the hardest, when I least expected.

"Not funny. Damn it, Bryce..." She rolls her hips.

I let her. She's positioned herself so I'm grazing against her clit, but it won't be enough. It'll only make her more desperate.

She squeezes her eyes shut, panting. I flick my thumb over her nipple with each thrust. She arches her back, moving wantonly against me for more. She's gorgeous when she's chasing her pleasure.

Her eyebrows pinch as her mouth firms. She's made a decision. My mouth curves into a victorious smile, and I wait for her to lift her head and kiss me like she means it—like she still cares, even if only a little.

"I can get wet when I think of your naked body and how you look when you're hard. It's dangerous but exciting," she says, her voice low and husky.

I freeze for a moment. A bitter mixture of disappointment and self-mockery pulses in my heart. Should've known. She wouldn't say anything so overt before. But now, the words fall from her lips like broken expectations.

She grows quiet. Only when I resume thrusting, she continues, breathless.

"I think about the things you did in order to make me come. Sometimes it's your mouth on my clit, sometimes it's your fingers stroking and pumping me, but most often I think of you inside me."

I curse. I haven't tasted her in so long.

"You're so big, it's almost uncomfortable, but you feel amazing, too. I don't know why, but when you set your mind to it and start to ram into me, it drives me insane. Sometimes I feel like I could get an orgasm out of each thrust." Her face flames.

Our eyes meet. Tears glint in the corners of her eyes, but then she blinks and they're gone. Why is she sad when I'm the one who's been screwed?

I feel like a fool for trying to... *What? Make her act like she cares?*

My control evaporates. I sit up, bringing her along with me. My ass on my heels, I impale her. She loops her arms around my neck, her body vibrating with unfulfilled need. I drive into her hard. Her breasts bob, nipples scraping against my chest. She groans, then clenches her teeth to contain the sound.

"Let me hear you, Fiona."

She shakes her head.

"I'll stop."

She clutches me. "Don't."

I push into her over and over. Gravity helps deepen the invasion. She throws her head back, gasps and moans pouring out of her slightly parted mouth.

Her plump, rosy lips beckon, but I ignore the temptation. She told me she didn't consent to kissing, and I'll be damned if she'll ever be able to claim that I forced myself on her.

I push her back on the bed, grip her hips and continue the relentless drive. Her moans grow louder and sharper. The tension in her muscles reaches its peak, and I increase my tempo.

She screams, twisting and arching. "Oh my God! *Bryce!*" Her arms wrap around me. She's honest in her climax, clinging like I'm the only one keeping her safe as her senses spin out of control.

Her limbs start to relax, but I'm far from finished. I want to punish her for denying me, and I want to punish myself for begging for it like an idiot.

I drive into her, harder and faster. Now that she's come once, it's easy for her to climax again and again. She comes, spasming around me, digging her nails into my back.

I don't stop. She looks at me, eyes wide. "Bryce," she manages between sharp, uneven breaths. "You... You aren't—"

"My stamina's gotten better over the years," I say, my forehead on hers. "You've been missing out."

A few more hard thrusts and she comes again. She shakes. "Oh my *God*!"

I cradle her flushed face. Her eyes are glazed with an overload of pleasure, and every inch of her gorgeous body trembles with another impending climax.

The pressure inside me expands until my vision almost dims. I pull out, rip off the condom and jerk off, giving my dick two good pumps with a guttural groan. The white stream jets all over her belly and breasts. The sight of her covered with my cum is even better than I imagined.

Mine. All mine.

I rub the fluid over her, glide my slick palm over her pointed nipples. Tight pinches earn me blissful gasps.

"Fuck, this is hot," I say, unable to tear my eyes from the view.

She nods, then breathes out shakily, relaxing. Probably thinking, *Thank God it's over.*

Except if she'd bother to look down, she'd see that my cock is still erect.

I grab another condom. The foil rips and her eyes fly open. "What—?"

"As you can see, I'm not finished."

She glances down and her jaw drops.

I laugh softly. "Told you my stamina's gotten better."

"You can't be serious."

I flip her over on the soft mattress. My cock nestles between her taut ass cheeks, and her breathing hitches with excitement. "Serious?" I lay a kiss on her nape, pulling a soft gasp from her. "Baby, I'm just getting started."

17

BRYCE

NINE FORTY-FIVE A.M.

By now, I should be showered, dressed in an I'm-gonna-fuck-you-up suit and meeting a client who's more anxious than an abandoned chihuahua on the Serengeti. Instead, I'm still in the suite, my body parked in the armchair near the bed, nursing my third iced Americano. The chilly drink doesn't do a thing to ease the suffocating knot in my chest.

My hair has long dried, slicked back and firm with the gel the concierge sent up earlier. A black Armani suit and a muted burgundy tie wrap around me like armor—not my favorite, but it's a spare Amélie sent from the office. Of course, she included a note:

> *Your freshly pressed power suit has arrived. Along with it comes my hopes that you remembered your toothbrush (and your standards).*
>
> *I took the liberty of having the inseam shortened by 2 inches. Figured it would help draw attention from your bleary eyes and undoubtedly rumpled hair from last night's exploits.*

Ever your servant's servant, etc.

-Amélie

The suit, of course, fits perfectly.

Fiona hasn't stirred. She's on her stomach, face half buried in one of the fluffy pillows. Hickeys dot her neck and shoulders. There are more on her chest and stomach. I wiped her down last night when she finally passed out...I think. It's difficult to be sure—I remember very little of what happened after I called her.

Now that overheated blood has quit pooling in my dick and a fresh dose of caffeine has burned the rest of the drug out of my head, remorse kicks in. Even though my memory of last night is fuzzy, there are fragments of feelings floating around in a kaleidoscopic way: I'd die without her; I wish she'd look at me the way she did before; a stupid craving that we could go back to the way things were, even though it can never be. She's changed—or rather, shown me her true colors.

People don't change. They just eventually reveal what's underneath.

We both know the score, and what we have right now isn't about being nice to each other.

I'm just being responsible, making sure she's okay after last night, I tell myself for the tenth time since six thirty, when I should've left the hotel to head to the office. Part of me wants to prove I'm impervious—it isn't too late to walk out—but I swat it aside. Whatever ridiculous things I wanted last night weren't me. It was the damn drug.

I can't believe I ever thought you were nice. I have no clue what made Fiona say that. I probably did something to earn it.

I swallow more of the dark coffee to wash away the bitter taste in my mouth. No more Mr. Nice Guy. That's what I've been striving for—and apparently achieved. Should be happy, but I'm restless.

My phone vibrates.

–Dad: Are you okay? Amélie says you're sick today.

I inhale. He knows something's up. I've never called in sick, never complained about the impact Mom's kidnapping attempt left. I've become a master of faking wellness, both physical and mental, in front of my family. So when Amélie told him I'd called in sick, he undoubtedly had to check in.

–Me: I'm fine.

–Dad: Akiko wants to stop by.

–Me: I'm not home right now.

I love my stepmom. Although we have our differences, some of them cultural, she's one of the sweetest and most patient people I know. She's from a Japanese zaibatsu family, ultra-wealthy, that owns a massive multinational conglomerate, and could've married anybody, not a divorced man with three highly traumatized boys in therapy.

She expresses her love with bento boxes so beautiful, it's almost a crime to eat them. She tiptoes around our childhood trauma, always worried that she might say something to make things worse.

–Dad: What's going on?

–Me: A long story. I'll talk to you later.

There is a pause. Then:

–Dad: We WILL talk. Your grandma's worried.

Hmm... Guess it won't be one on one with Dad, but with all The Fogeys. If Grandma is worried, Aunt Jeremiah's going to show up too. Not to provide emotional support—that isn't Aunt Jeremiah's forte—but to advise and strategize.

"Mmm..."

I glance over at the bed and put the phone away. Fiona finally stirs, slowly turning. Her hand stretches out, touches the empty spot next to her. Three grooves form between her eyebrows, then she slowly blinks her eyes open, looking at the ceiling.

"Hey, Siri," she says, then stops, her scowl deepening. Her voice is hoarse and rough. She curses under her breath. "What time is it?"

"It's ten seventeen a.m."

She lets out a soft sigh. "Thank you."

A corner of my mouth quirks up. But then, she's always courteous... to others. Just not me. She wouldn't have cheated on me if she'd thought I deserved any consideration.

"You're welcome," says the chirpy artificial voice.

Fiona lies motionless for a bit, then shifts in my direction. Her sleep-glazed eyes meet mine. Her eyelids flutter.

"Good morning," I say quietly.

"Ack!" She jackknifes up, then bends over, her elbows digging into the soft duvet. "Ow, ow, ohh..."

Placing the coffee on the table next to me, I almost start to get up to check on her, then catch myself. But the question slips out anyway. "You okay?"

She gives me a hard stare. "What do you think? You aren't allowed near me for the next three months."

I feign innocence, relieved she isn't going to talk about the inane desires I displayed because of the drug. Hopefully she assumed I was acting emotionally off due to being drunk or something. "What's the problem?"

"*What's the problem?*" she repeats incredulously. "Are you kidding? I'm sore all over."

"Well, multiple orgasms can have that effect..."

"It's not the multiple orgasms. It's *you*! My God, who does it all night—*for real*—without any break? Did you steal your dad's Viagra or something?"

Murder flashes in her eyes, but when her cheeks are flushed from sleep and her neck and chest are mottled with the marks I left, she looks ridiculously cute. I laugh softly. "You can ask him."

"Seriously?"

"No." I laugh again at her expression. It reminds me a little of Gardy when she was a puppy and had a biscuit taken away by Grandma, who worried that she was getting too obese. That poor puppy couldn't decide how she should react.

"I didn't steal his Viagra, if he even has any. But I'll ask for you. Tell him you're curious."

"Don't you dare! It was just a rhetorical question." Her eyes drop to my iced Americano. She lets out a longing sigh.

I pour her some hot coffee from a thermos room service sent up and dump some sugar in. "Here."

She bites her lip.

"Oh for—! Stop acting like taking a cup of coffee is some kind of surrender. I don't want to engage with a woman who hasn't had her morning caffeine."

"Fine." She takes the mug and takes a long sip. "Thank you." Her eyes close. The tension drains from her face and shoulders. The blissful, unguarded expression reminds me of the peaceful mornings we had at Harvard.

As soon as the memory pops up, I push it back down. The two million wasn't to relive the past; it was to get her out of my system. Reminiscing is for the weak and foolish. Life is about internalizing hard-learned lessons and moving on.

After a couple more sips, she turns to me. "So. You now have two hundred and ninety left."

I snort. "Don't even think about ripping me off. It's two hundred and ninety-eight."

"What we did last night counts as *at least* nine, not one."

"Most definitely *one*. I was just getting my money's worth."

She gives me a long, hard stare. If she could turn the coffee mug into a knife and stab me with it, she would.

I don't really intend to do the full three hundred, of course, just enough to give some closure to our past. There's no way our relationship was so deep that I really need three hundred nights' worth of sex to get over her.

I stand and straighten my jacket. "The suite's yours for the day. Relax, use the hot tub and order room service. A limo will pick you up at six."

Her expression sharpens with suspicion. "Where are we going?"

"Not we. *You*'re going home." As soon as I finish saying it, I realize that I've referred to my home as hers, too.

Her eyes sharpen—she noticed, too. A multitude of feelings fleet over her face: wistfulness, confusion, curiosity, nervousness. Her tongue flicks out, wetting her lips.

She's going to bring up something I'm not ready to discuss. I pull back, withdrawing physically and emotionally. "I need to go."

Before she can react, I walk out and step into the elevator. *That was close*. How could I let my guard down so easily? It was easy to be vulnerable around her before, but I should know better now.

My watch says it's only eleven. I should probably head to the office and get some work done. That's a better use of time than obsessing over my reaction to Fiona.

I text the concierge to send some Epsom salts for her as I stride across the lobby. It's surprisingly busy, with guests arriving and bellhops carting suitcases back and forth. A huge banner says, *Welcome to the Sunny SoCal Super-Signing!* A convention crowd.

Across the lobby, a brown-haired woman sits in a cushy ivory armchair next to a small end table, flipping through some glossy fashion rag and sipping a cup of coffee. My heart hammers with shock as I zero in on her. I thought I'd never see her again.

An expertly tailored azure wrap dress fits her like it's painted on her slim, toned body. Her skin is milky and ageless, without a single line on her beautifully sculpted face. The high cheekbones are the envy of all—I know, because she gave them to me.

She looks up and our eyes lock. Dense lashes frame the soulless blue. A wide smile stretches her crimson lips but fails to warm her expression.

My skin crawls.

Run! And if you can't run, kill her!

Cold sweat slickens my back as I stay rooted to the spot. My fingers twitch, my pulse throbbing in my head. It feels like I'm eight again, small and vulnerable. My mind replays her twisted face as she held Ares and tried to reach for me and Josh.

"Come back here!" she shouted. "You're mine! My sons!"

Helplessness slams into me. My breathing shallows. I've wondered so many times what I'd do if I ran into her again. I told one of the therapists that I'd grab her and shake her until she apologized for what she did, but the reality...

I loathe myself for my powerlessness, for being overwhelmed by the old panic.

She winks, raising her cup in a mocking salute.

The gesture jolts me out of my trance. *I am* not *letting her fuck with me.* Hands clenched, I start toward her. She rises from her seat. A churning gaggle of convention women and bellhops pass between us. When they're gone, Mom has disappeared, too.

I stop and shove a hand through my hair. *Did I imagine her? Is this a lingering side effect of the drug?*

I reach the armchair and look around the lobby carefully. No sign of Mom anywhere—and she would stand out. Zoe Dunkel isn't the kind of woman you can overlook.

My heart rate starts to settle. Exhaling slowly, I shake my head. *Might be the stress.* One of my therapists said that mild hallucinations are actually common when under excessive strain. Being drugged to turn me into some sort of mindless fucking machine should definitely count.

I drop my eyes—

On the table before me is an elegant white cup with a bright red lipstick mark on the rim.

18

BRYCE

So I *didn't* imagine Mom?

Anxiety and dread throb at the base of my skull. I scan the lobby again, to no avail.

Where did she go?

Okay, time to think. Red was sent to seduce me last night. Mom has to want to check on her handiwork.

I start toward the elevator bank. The area is heaving with convention attendees. No Mom.

I turn back and walk out onto the street. Cars, pedestrians, arriving guests dragging their suitcases from the trunks. Loud honking and voices buzzing. I make a slow three-hundred-and-sixty-degree turn. No brunette in blue.

I drag in some air and force myself to take a mental step back. I could be overreacting. It isn't like Mom's the only woman in the world with red lipstick. My eyes drop to a random blonde's mouth, which is painted bright scarlet.

A man approaches from the left and places a meaty hand on my shoulder.

Adrenaline jets through my veins. I twist around, fist raised.

He lifts his free hand, palm out. "Easy, big guy. Harvey wants to talk." He gestures toward Nieve, a bistro inside the Aylster.

I freeze for a moment, cursing my luck. "Got nothing to say to him."

I start to turn, but the man puts pressure on my shoulder. "Let's keep things dignified. Nobody wants a scene."

My first urge is to break his pug face, but Harvey probably brought more than one minion to do his bidding.

When I turn toward the bistro, Harvey waves with a broad smile from a table just inside the window, showing off straight white teeth. A black suit makes him stand out against the ivory interior. He's built like a tank, wide and thick, with more power than he lets on. A relatively trim waist says he's vain enough to worry about having abs. His mahogany hair is slicked back, revealing a forehead with lines that make him look like a deep thinker rather than a potential mob heir. His pale amber eyes and heavy lids are nothing like Mom's. He took after Vincent, got the narrow nose and thin lips. Not attractive, but charismatic.

I head inside and sit, my body sinking into the leather seat. A waiter fills my glass with water. "Talk."

Harvey laughs. "Hello, dear nephew. I missed you. It's been, what? Twenty-two years?"

Two beats.

My silence doesn't faze him. He grins. "Have a drink."

I drop my gaze to the water and give him a do-I-look-stupid look.

"Did you get my birthday present? I had it hand-delivered for your thirtieth. A Glock and an AK-47. For self-defense. When Zoe shows up again"—he points a finger gun in my face and pulls the trigger—"*pop* goes the weasel."

He waits for me to react. I merely stare at him.

A deep frown. "It's unfair of you to show no gratitude. Actually, your entire family is a bunch of ingrates." He takes a sip of whatever he's drinking and sits back. "You know Zoe sent you a bunch of presents? Mostly age-appropriate toys, I heard, but it's your mom."

Haven't heard anything about that, but it wouldn't surprise me if The Fogeys sent them back without informing me.

"Probably not anything as useful as a gun. After all, she cares about herself the most. Your family returned them, along with mine. That's the only reason I let the *insolence* slide. The Huxleys are rude to everyone. They even turned away Father's gifts for you." Harvey's expression turns reptilian—cold and soulless. "He's lonely, Bryce. Misses you and your brothers very much."

I yawn mightily, feigning boredom. I didn't miss his emphasis on "insolence." He seethes with resentment against my family, wants to humiliate us and force us to our knees.

Over my dead body.

"But look, I get it. You think he chose your mother over you guys. But what else could he have done? She's his own child. And prison isn't a pretty place, especially for the daughter of Vincent Dunkel. She'd have suffered over a little indiscretion."

Did this motherfucker just call the kidnapping a "little indiscretion"?

"Besides, he didn't want to lose another child."

Another child? I frown, but ignore it for the moment. "It was prison, not death." The law doesn't believe kidnapping your own children merits the death penalty, even if you do leave one of them to die in a fire.

"Yeah, well, maybe it would have been death—for her. Besides, he was in a vulnerable emotional state back then." Harvey shrugs. "Swayed by her tears, you know how it is. Lucky for you, I'm not like my father. If I'd been in charge, I'd have made her pay."

"Isn't she your *beloved* sister?" I heard Vincent was furious with Mom, but eventually decided to protect her. Made some low-level sucker take the fall instead. That's the Dunkels—blood is thicker than water.

"She was impolite to you and Josh. And almost killed Ares. Made your entire family unreasonable toward us."

"Look, Harvey. You want to use us as pawns in your internal struggle, I get it. But frankly, I don't give a shit who wins. None of us do."

Harvey's smile doesn't falter, which is creepier than if he started yelling. "You think you'll be better off if Zoe takes the reins? Twenty-two years, Bryce. She's waited and prepared for twenty-two years to retake what she thinks is hers. You, Ares, Josh. Prescott." He adds Dad to the list. "And, of course, the *family business*."

"In Nesovia?" I snort a laugh. The country is so medieval in its attitude toward women, they can't even control their own money before the age of thirty without being married. Most Nesovian men would fornicate with a dog before taking orders from a woman.

Harvey waves the point away and purses his mouth. "Father's ill. Doesn't have much time left. The only thing he wants is to see you and your brothers and shower you with all the love he couldn't before."

"I'm thirty now. It's too late."

"Is it? When a man faces his mortality, he doesn't believe anything's too late. He told me and Zoe whoever could give him the 'complete family' he wants will inherit the business." His eyes burn with anger and resentment at being denied what he's believed would be his all his life. "I want to bring you and your brother into the family fold, and have Ares join the business in an advisory role."

"Is that what you call drugging him and trying to force him to sign a contract?"

He waves the hand again. "Just a little drink to help him relax and think better. No harm in it. Besides, why are you upset with me? Zoe does the same thing."

I narrow my eyes. Is he trying to direct my wrath toward Mom? Hoping I'll side with him in an "the enemy of my enemy is my friend" kind of thing?

He continues, "She's the one who only sees you as a means to an end. She wants to use you to move Father to tears and have him give her the business."

Can't imagine Vincent in tears, even though my memory of him is vague. I saw him a few times when I was little. He was always a bit too stern and controlled, handing out lollipops with a dark frown on his face when he ran out of things to say to us.

"Being near death makes one sentimental. Father has gotten emotional lately. Won't even let us battle it out—winner take all. Tragic. It would've been quicker and cleaner."

Indeed. It would've been great if Mom and Harvey hacked each other to death.

"Even more tragic," Harvey says, studying his coffee, "is that your family won't hire an expert to permanently take care of Zoe."

Does he seriously think we'd hire a hit man? "We aren't like you."

"Sure, I get that. And Father respects it. He admires your loyalty to your family. Wants us to learn from it. You wouldn't believe how fast his attitude changed when he found out Lareina married Ares. Before, he considered her a potential tool to extract money from the Hayworth fortune. Now… He'd murder us if we touched his precious granddaughter-in-law. Guess things changed when she became family." Harvey shrugs, then focuses on me again. "Help me out here, Bryce. Come to Nesovia with me, meet Father, tell him how much you miss him, and how I convinced you to give the relationship a chance."

"Why should I?"

"Because your hatred for Zoe is personal. You wouldn't hate me if I wasn't related to your mother."

"If we weren't related, I wouldn't even know you existed."

"Don't be rude. I'm giving you a chance to protect yourself and the people around you. You think just because Zoe and I can't kill each other, we're going to play nice? That's not how it works. And Father never said anything about collateral damage." He pulls a finger across his neck.

Is he threatening to kill other members of the family? Or is he warning me that Mom will?

He continues in the same even tone. "Since I'm a civilized man, I showed my familial affection by whacking the groom's other knee after you kicked him and took his bride. A stand-up move, by the way. A real man always takes what he wants. Father was proud. You're a true Dunkel."

"I didn't do it for Vincent."

"Doesn't matter why you did it. Father admires you for it, which *does* matter." Harvey shrugs. "Unfortunately, your mother doesn't believe in being civilized. You probably already know she drugged you last night. She wants to breed one of her young, nubile sycophants with you. After all, infants are much more malleable than a trio of adult offspring with minds of their own, and no old man can stay stonehearted when he's presented with a girl who's pregnant with his first great-grandchild."

For fuck's sake. The entire plot is sociopathic, but also very much Mom.

"She's working under a deadline, you know."

"She is?"

Harvey nods. "Father's reinvestigating what really happened to our youngest brother."

Vincent had a third kid? I really don't need another uncle as insane as Mom and Harvey.

"You never met him. He died young, before Zoe married your father. Was the baby of the family, the *apple* of our father's eye. The golden child who could do no wrong." No hint of grief passes over Harvey's face. He's probably happy that a potential rival was eliminated so early, without his having to dirty his hands. "Could be she had something to do with the helicopter crash that killed him. Father doesn't want to jump to conclusions—'cuz, you know, I could've set her up, a lot of things could've happened—so he's going to do his due diligence. But Zoe..." A shrug. "She isn't known for her patience or finesse."

No. She prefers blunt force. Seducing Dad and getting immediately pregnant. Kidnapping us. Trying to get in the way of Ares's marriage. And Red last night. If what Harvey said is true, Mom isn't going to play nice. She needs a quick result—something to save her ass when Vincent finds out that she caused the crash and killed her own brother.

Harvey shifts, a hint of triumph glinting in his eyes. "Right now, she's here to see if the girl she picked is full of your cum, except"—his eyes flick upward—"that girl you left up in the suite isn't the one she sent you."

19

FIONA

SOON AFTER BRYCE WALKS OUT, the doorbell rings. I shrug—*ow!*—into a bathrobe, all my muscles protesting, and then stand up.

My legs almost give out. *Thank God Bryce isn't here to witness this.* His head would never be able to squeeze through any door. The bathroom mirror shows hickeys all over my neck and chest. I pull my hair forward, then yank the lapels tighter to hide the red marks.

The second I open the door, a uniformed server pushes in a beautiful cart laden with spotless, shiny silver domes. The elderly man opens each with a flourish, only to reveal a bowl of cornflakes and a jug of milk in a gorgeous crystal jug. There is also a small bowl of fresh berries and whipped cream on the side and a fresh pitcher of coffee.

"I didn't order this," I say, crossing my arms. I still sound hoarse, and I wince inwardly. Given how much I screamed last night, it would've taken a miracle for me not to damage my voice.

"Mr. Huxley did." The man hands me a lavender silk and satin satchel. "And some Epsom salts for you." He shows me a slip, and I scrawl my name on the paper.

I keep my arms folded and stare at the food and Epsom salts with apprehension. What's this about? Act nice and confuse the opponent?

If it is, he's succeeded. I am completely confused. He talks like a complete asshole, then does little unexpected things like this. Like the cereal in his house. Like having clothes and shoes for me delivered to his place.

And last night, he clung to me desperately, like he couldn't bear to let go. Then he cajoled, wheedled and coaxed me all night long, trying to get me to kiss him, growing more determined each time I turned away. It's almost as though he needed some sort of confirmation that I still care about him. If I'd sensed even a hint of vindictiveness in his dark gaze, I might've scoffed and pushed him away. But he seemed sincere without the usual shield he put up around him—or the asshole-worthy snarks. When he looked wounded at yet another rejection, I almost forgot myself and kissed his eyes.

Don't, I tell myself. It wasn't Bryce—it was the drugs talking. Whatever he had last night must've taken down his inhibitions. Part of me wants to believe his behavior under the influence last night was the real deal, but I'm not gambling with my emotional wellbeing. It took a lot of therapy and healing to feel normal after leaving Cambridge. And although I'd like to believe I'm stronger after the ordeal, it isn't entirely true. Whatever is keeping the fragments of my heart together now isn't strong enough to withstand another onslaught.

Exhaling, I sit down and start on the cereal, remembering when we first met. It's so silly how I thought maybe my life could be different just because Bryce said, "You don't seem like Finn. The name doesn't fit you somehow." Such a small thing, but in that moment I felt seen—like I wasn't just Finley's shadow, just a tool to soothe Sherry's pain. I didn't realize until then how uncomfortable and stifled I'd been, living in that identity.

And on our first date, I automatically ordered grilled halibut, but Bryce noticed I'd eyed a steak and baked potato on the next table and asked if I didn't really want that instead. That was when I realized I didn't even let myself *like* things unless Finley had loved them too. And it was also the first time anyone had told me to take what *I* wanted. My heart melted. I think that's when I started to really fall for him, because he didn't measure me against Finley. I was just Fiona.

Tears prickle my eyes. It was the most wonderful time of my life, when I felt loved...except it shattered at the end.

You never deserved that kind of love.

I wipe the tears away and laugh at myself. Yeah. Who am I to think I could do better? If Finley hadn't drowned, nobody would've looked at me twice. I would've been passed from one foster home after another and probably fallen through the cracks like so many unwanted kids. Or gotten abused by some asshole like that man my first adoptive parents whispered about.

I finally managed to get out of the toxic situation and went to Wisconsin. But now I've been dragged back, where things are so much worse than before. Zachary told me the harder I worked, the better my life would be. But in my experience, it's the opposite. The harder I work, the worse my situation becomes.

I sip coffee to wash away the bitter taste in my mouth and check my phone. Nothing from the loan sharks. *How strange.* Aren't they eager to get their money back? Why so silent now?

Maybe they got arrested by the police. Or better yet, run over by a truck...

Three knocks at the door. I sigh. What did Bryce send now? I put down my phone and open the door. "You should tell Mr. Huxley—"

"Finally!"

Aaron!

My heart in my throat, I try to slam the door in his face, but he's faster. He pushes the door open, shoving me hard as he invades the suite.

"You stupid— Argh! What the fuck were you thinking running away from the wedding? Do you know what kind of trouble you've caused? *You fucked me over!*" Aaron screams, spittle flying everywhere.

He doesn't seem to be exaggerating his predicament. He sports circles so dark, they look like black eyes. His cheeks are sunken. There are lines on his forehead that weren't there before, and no razor has touched his face in days.

His wrinkled suit is the same as the one from the wedding, just dingier—he probably hasn't changed, either.

I stare in shock, registering only half his screaming. It isn't like him to overlook grooming. Aaron cares way too much about his appearance.

"How did you find me?" I ask.

He opens his mouth, then shuts it. Probably did something shady and won't admit to it. "You can't hide from me. I'm much smarter and more resourceful."

Of course. "I told your loan shark I'd pay." I say the words slowly, trying to hide my impatience and irritation and get through to him.

He spins toward me, his fists tight and shaking. "Don't lie to me!" he screams. "They came for me at the house just this morning, while Mom was at a temple to pray." His red-rimmed eyes glare at me. "I was left alone to fend for myself! It was so *unfair*."

I blink. His nostrils flare. He breathes hard. Not a hint of relief that Sherry was spared the scene. Just fury because he undoubtedly had to grovel to avoid getting his knees broken or something.

What's happened to him since college? I don't recognize my adoptive brother anymore. Although Aaron was never nice to me, he was always a good son. He strove to meet his father's lofty expectations and humor his mother to keep her depression and emotional outbursts at bay.

The Aaron I knew would never have been this self-centered. What little respect I had for him dies.

"It's your debt," I remind him impassively. "Sherry has nothing to do with it."

"So? She's my mom. She has some money set aside that she could use to help me out." He sounds betrayed. "I just found out."

My shoulders sag with relief. She'll be able to maintain a decent lifestyle. The woman's powerless and wouldn't know what to do if she had to earn her own money. "Well, good. But it's her money, not yours."

"I'm her son! I deserve that money!"

"She deserves to live out the rest of her life in dignity, Aaron!"

His face reddens with guilt and embarrassment, but his eyes glint with resentment. He hates it when I act like a daughter to his mother because I'm "trying to replace Finley in Sherry's heart." He conveniently forgets that it was his father who brought me in to do just that.

"Why are you so upset, anyway?" I keep my tone calm to avoid escalation. "I was the one marrying a monster, remember?"

He glares at me. "Jude's no monster."

"If you like him so much, *you* marry him."

"Shut up, dumbass!" Aaron points a finger in my face. "You're going to go to him, get on your knees and beg for his forgiveness. He was nice and sentimental enough to agree to marry you because of shared memories. But now, he'll probably just keep you as a mistress or something." He shakes his head, muttering something about pearls and swine.

"I'll do no such thing."

"Yes, you will." He grips my arm and starts pulling me toward the door.

I dig my heels in. "Stop it! What's wrong with you?"

"You asking me what's wrong? You fucked up the wedding and you now want me dead! Jesus, my life is worth more than two million! Jude's being gracious by offering to pay that much for your body. It isn't like you're a virgin."

"Oh my God! Medieval much?"

"Shut up. You owe it to my dad for giving you a home!" He tightens his hold and yanks me to the door.

"No!" I try to pull away, but he's much too strong. I scratch his hand hard enough to leave red marks, but he's beyond caring.

"We can do it the easy way or the hard way," he grinds out. "Your choice."

"What the hell kind of choice is that?" I shoot back, fury and helplessness overpowering my senses.

He twists my arm up behind my back. A burning sensation shoots along my upper arm and scapula. I cry out.

"Wow," a woman's voice says. "Is that the easy way? What would be the hard way? I might be able to learn a thing or two."

Aaron and I freeze, his hand still holding my arm in a painful lock. He loosens it slightly, not letting go, but the pain eases, thank God. I glance sideway at the person who interrupted, not all that hopeful.

The door is somehow open, and a fortyish brunette in a fashionably tight blue dress is standing in the doorway. She doesn't seem willing to help me. She actually seems to be entertained.

She leans closer. Her blue eyes glow with unholy interest, and the smile is a bit too wide. A dangerous vibe emanates from her.

Aaron doesn't seem to share my evaluation. He shoves me aside and turns to her. "Lady, this is family business, nothing to do with you. Now get out of here before I fuck you up."

She straightens and puts a fancily manicured hand over her chest. "Fuck me up?" She points at Aaron. "You?"

"Yeah, me." His chest puffs out like he's a rooster gearing up for a fight.

She snickers. Genuine amusement glitters in her eyes. Every hair on my body stands.

Suddenly she lashes out, a backhand that connects with Aaron's face hard enough to make a cracking sound. His head snaps to the side and he bends slightly, covering his mouth with one hand. She steps closer and kicks his balls with a stiletto.

He screams and falls, curling onto one side.

"Say it again." Her voice is calm, almost dulcet. "Say you're going to fuck me up." Another kick, this time to his stomach.

He groans, wrapping his arms around his belly.

"Come on. Say it and I'll stop." She smiles, not even breathing hard.

She's lying. The steely glint in her ice-cold eyes says she won't stop until she's convinced Aaron's learned his lesson.

Red spreads on his hands. I squint. *What the...?* I let out a gasp when it hits me—*blood!* Her shoes aren't just any old footwear.

"Stop it!" I say. "You're going to kill him!" Aaron's a horrible human being, but he doesn't deserve to die.

She frowns in confusion. "So?"

So?

"What's wrong with that?"

My throat dries. "Because..." I cast about helplessly. "Murder is bad...?"

"Oh, sweetie." She laughs. "Murder isn't bad. Getting caught is."

"You'll *get* caught! The body alone... There are security cameras inside the hotel—the cops are going to know!"

"Cameras, a body..." She shrugs, her palms turned upward. "Do you think he'd be the first body I've had to bury?"

My knees tremble. *Oh my God.*

"You look like you're about to lose your room service, so I'll let him live. But you'll need a stronger stomach if you want to bear a great-grandchild for my father."

What? I just stare, unable to process.

She kicks Aaron one last time. He remains limp, doesn't even moan anymore.

"How did you get in?" I ask shakily.

"The door was open. You should keep it closed for security."

"Right." I'm never opening one again without checking first.

"You should be grateful. You're lucky I dropped by when I did. Imagine what could've happened." She saunters to the room service table, looks at the empty cup of coffee and tsks. "And you shouldn't drink coffee when you're trying to get pregnant. It's not good for the fetus."

"I'm not trying to get pregnant."

"Not trying?" She turns her head, the motion like that of a possessed doll. "Why do you think I sent you? Not so you could just enjoy his body, you stupid whore. You better not have lied to me. You'd better be ovulating, and you *better* have ensured he came without condoms. He should've emptied every one of his swimmers into you last night. Wouldn't have been able to find any respite without being balls deep."

The more she says, the more lost I become. I've never even met this woman before. But there are enough clues for me to figure one thing out. "Are you talking about Bryce?"

"Obviously. I already have someone else working on Josh." She tilts her head, her arctic eyes studying me up and down. "Although...you're sort of disappointing. I thought I was going to get somebody with bigger tits, a tighter waist and longer legs. A bit more flair and sex appeal. You're sort of...drab. Small tits. Slightly paunchy."

My jaw drops at the way she catalogues what she perceives to be my flaws in that flat tone.

"You like dairy, don't you?" she says, waving a hand vaguely in my direction as she heads to the minibar. "The extra fat around your hips." She sighs, then pulls out a bottle of Merlot and studies the label while twirling a corkscrew between her long fingers. "I want the best for my son."

Son?

"He deserves better. You're..." She twirls the corkscrew in the air.

"You're *Bryce's mom?*"

"Of course. *The* Zoe Dunkel, in the flesh. Couldn't you tell? We look alike." Her smile dares me to disagree.

I can still see Aaron's prone body on the floor in my peripheral vision. I keep my mouth shut.

"Did he even fuck you last night? How many times did he come inside you?"

Nausea roils through my stomach. "That's disgusting. He's your son."

Her eyes narrow. "Take off your robe. Let me see."

"What?" I cross my arms. "No!"

She strikes before I can take my next breath. Her hand grasps the robe lapel, her forearm putting enough pressure on my neck to cut off some of the air. I stumble backward, with her pushing forward, until my back slams into the wall. I start to twist away, then scream when she raises the corkscrew toward my face. I squeeze my eyes shut and jerk my head to the side, praying she slashes my cheek rather than something more important.

"Stop being ridiculous and open your eyes before I gouge them out." Her licorice breath fans over my cheek, sending chills down my spine.

Adrenaline burns in my veins. I shake from the need to run or flee, neither of which is possible. She's much stronger than she looks.

Panting, I obey, then inhale sharply. My heart pounds a thousand beats a minute at the sight of the corkscrew a hairsbreadth away from my left eye.

"Open. Your. Robe," she commands. "No argument unless you want to go blind. You don't need eyes to bear children."

I undo the belt with trembling hands. Humiliation and fear clutch my throat. I spread the robe, thinking of her violent attack earlier. She's still gripping the lapel, so I can only open it so much. Or so I plan to tell her if she gets upset.

Her eyes glide from my chest to belly to crotch. She sniffs, then wrinkles her nose. "Good. I guess you did all right after you gave him the meds. At least you aren't totally useless." Her tone says that useless people don't get to live. She eases the pressure off my neck and takes half a step back, although the corkscrew remains perilously close to my eye.

My eyelashes flutter, the sensation of brushing against the cold metal sickening. A sob catches in my throat. My eyes burn from keeping them open, but I don't dare blink.

"Here." The woman drops a small Ziploc bag full of powder into my bathrobe pocket. "Use this next time. It's more potent than the compound from last night. And remember: there are other girls after him. Whoever gets pregnant with his baby first wins."

My mind freezes with shock and disbelief. She's psychopathic. Absolutely mad.

"Since you did well last night, I'm going to do you a favor. I'll clean up that trash, still breathing, because you seem fond of him. But you should warn him—the next time he manhandles you, he's dead. I'm not risking anything happening to my key to the kingdom." Her gaze drops to my belly briefly, then she tosses the corkscrew on the floor and struts away, dragging Aaron by his collar on her way out.

When the door shuts behind her, I wrap the robe tightly around myself and drop to the floor. I stick my head between my knees and focus on breathing as my heart races faster. The adrenaline still sizzles in my veins. *Just what the hell was that?*

Wait a minute... She said I gave Bryce "meds." Given the way she spoke, I doubt she wanted to feed him Tylenol.

He was insatiable last night, refusing to go limp, drowning me in orgasms once he realized edging me wasn't going to earn him a kiss.

She *drugged* him—her own son. So that he'd impregnate some random girl.

I cover my mouth as another wave of nausea roils. What kind of people *do* things like that? Has she done it before? Does he know it was his mother who drugged him?

That might explain why he waited until I was up and ordered room service and Epsom salts. He probably felt guilty about the entire incident.

Why didn't he warn me, so I'd be prepared? Now I'm on his mother's radar. She's seen me—and worse, has taken Aaron, who'd sell me out in a heartbeat just to see me suffer—and thinks I'm going to give her a grandchild.

No. A great-grandchild for her father.

Oh God. Uncontrollable tremors rack through me. What do I do now? Can I even run? Will that psycho woman let me?

As my predicament becomes clearer, resentment and anger start to rear their heads. Bryce has to know his mother isn't normal, but he dragged me into it anyway. If another girl drugged him last night, he could've just spent the night with her and left me out of it. We don't have the kind of relationship that requires fidelity. And getting entangled with his Looney Tunes mom wasn't part of the deal, damn it.

I jump to my feet and put on my clothes—or try to. The underwear is ruined, and the only things still intact are my trench coat and shoes. I slip into them, cinching the belt tightly. I open the Uber app, my fingers clumsy with nerves.

The question on the screen: *Where to?*

The burst of energy that got me moving drains away. I lean against the wall, then slowly slide down until my butt hits the floor. My teeth dig into my lip until it bleeds. I look out across the room and out the window to the vast panorama of Los Angeles spread out below.

I have nowhere to go.

20

BRYCE

"Fiona!" I scream, bursting into the suite. Fear pounds in my skull as I look around.

Mom is a sociopath. If she finds out that Fiona isn't the girl she sent...

I don't dare imagine the consequences. The woman didn't think there was anything wrong with kidnapping her own children and leaving one to die in a wildfire, all the while claiming she just wanted to have a happy, intact family.

"Fiona!" The yell is half choked with shaky terror.

My eyes roam the suite. The breakfast is mostly eaten. No sound from the bathroom. A bottle of unopened Merlot on the room service cart—

I didn't order that.

The tip of my shoe hits a corkscrew on the floor. My heart stops. A potential weapon. Who used it?

My hands tremble. I squat to study the tool, then let out a sigh of relief when I don't see any blood on it. Not that that means Fiona is safe. It could've been what she picked out to protect herself with. But no blood at least means Mom didn't use it on her.

I collected and read every tabloid account of her "glamorous" life as a wealthy woman in Nesovia. I wanted to understand what moved her to go to that extreme to avoid divorce. Mom claimed she merely wanted to keep our family of five together, but The Fogeys didn't buy it. According to them, she dazzled Dad in a whirlwind romance, pretending she had no idea who he was, to pull Huxley & Webber into her father's empire. Vincent wanted to expand into America and needed good lawyers who could assist.

When Dad discovered who she really was and what kind of insanity she planned to bring to the family, he initiated divorce proceedings against her. She insisted she loved him and the sons they'd had together, and it culminated in the kidnapping.

Vincent agreed to the divorce and gave Dad what he wanted, except for two points: Mom going to prison and staying away from us forever. She didn't go, and she apparently cried and pleaded until Vincent negotiated with The Fogeys to keep her away from us for twenty-two years.

The articles I've read didn't portray her in the best light. She lived like a socialite with many lovers. Whispers of abuse spread—beating lovers for displeasing her. Many of the men complained she was freakishly strong and fast.

I recall how she struggled to nab me, Ares and Josh. She wasn't that physically capable back then.

She's prepared for twenty-two years to retake what she thinks is hers.

I shudder at the memory of Harvey's warning. She could've gotten stronger, physically and otherwise. Twenty-two years is a long time to nurture a grudge.

This time she won't give up so easily, especially if Vincent's sick. And even more so if she thinks she could get into trouble for killing a baby brother I didn't even know existed.

I stand up and scan the room. A discarded robe, no shoes or trench coat. No sign of a struggle, either. A thick blackout curtain to my right shifts. I swivel, fist raised just in case. But the fight leaves me when I spot a figure huddled under the window.

Fiona has made herself as small as possible, legs folded and face lowered and hidden in her knees.

Crouching before her, I look for signs of abuse or injury. No blood that I can see. She isn't making any sound of pain. Did she hide—and Mom somehow missed her?

Apparently she did. I inhale slowly, settling my nerves. Showing anxiety won't help. "Hey," I say gently. "Fiona."

She curls up more, making herself even smaller.

"You're safe. It's just me."

"Go away." Her voice is muffled against her knees.

The sight of her huddled like a scared child makes me want to strangle Mom. I push down the anger and keep my voice soft. "Sorry, can't do that. Let me see you."

"See me? So you can gloat about how much you've messed up my life?"

An immediate denial dies on my tongue as she jerks her head up, eyes flashing. The sight of unshed tears reddens my vision. Blood seeps from a cut on her lip. She isn't sporting bruises, but that doesn't mean Mom was gentle. She knows plenty of ways to hurt without leaving a mark.

"Who did this to you?" I start to cradle Fiona's face, but she turns away. My hand trembles, and I drop and clench it. "Tell me who scared you."

"Why do you care? What are you going to do if you know?"

Her furious distrust pains me, but I have no one to blame but myself. Remorse pools like acid in my stomach. I should've anticipated Mom's behavior after the encounter with Red. This is on me. "Was it my mother?"

Fiona lets out a hollow laugh. "Not entirely. Aaron found me first."

Rage beats at my chest. *That fucking weasel.* "I'm going to murder that fucker."

"Then your mother arrived," Fiona adds woodenly. "She hurt Aaron, then threatened me with a corkscrew. Did you know she had a woman drug you last night?"

I nod.

"What happened to her?" she asks, her face taut.

"I kicked her out. I don't want to be anybody's pawn."

"So you called *me* here?" Fiona's breathing grows shallow and unsteady. "Knowing what could happen? That *I* could become a pawn instead?"

"I was too out of my mind with the drug to think that far. I was—"

She jumps to her feet, her chest rising and falling rapidly. "Your mother didn't just say hello, Bryce! She came here to tell me that if I don't get pregnant with your baby, *she'll kill me*. She thought I was the girl you were supposed to sleep with! She made me show her my body to make sure we'd had sex! If I didn't, she was going to stab my eyeballs because I don't need them to get pregnant!" Her voice is shrill with helpless fury and shame.

I slowly unfold my legs and modulate my tone. "She won't touch you, Fiona. She won't—"

"*Yes, she will.* You know why? Because the problem isn't killing someone, it's getting caught! And who'll care enough to search for me if I disappear? No one. Not a *single person will care*." Her last statement comes out a shaky yell. She clamps her mouth, but her chin trembles.

More unshed tears glitter in her green-gold eyes. She isn't just saying this out of anger. She believes it deep in her heart, and Mom's actions stirred her fear. Remorse slices my heart. "That isn't true. I'd look for you."

"Riiiiiight." Sarcasm drips from Fiona's tone. "Oh wait, you would. Because you still need to collect your two hundred and ninety-eight."

"That's not—"

Shaking her head, she hugs herself. "This isn't what I bargained for. It was supposed to just be sex. Why couldn't you have just slept with that other girl last night? I wouldn't have cared."

Pent-up fury erupts at her casual suggestion that I have sex with another woman and that it wouldn't have bothered her at all. It overwhelms the burgeoning guilt. I grip her arms. "Do you think I wanted this to happen? Do you think I want to have a mom who's this crazy?"

Fiona gives me a look that says I'm just as awful as my mom. I'd give up a kidney to wipe that expression off her face.

"You told me your mother was nice and sweet," she says between gritted teeth. "Remember? When we were at Harvard?"

"My *step*mother. Akiko. I always wished she could be my mom—*my only mom*—and at that time it felt like she was, because my real mom stayed away."

"Well, she isn't staying away now. And she won't stay away, either. She says she's sending more women for you to impregnate, and that I'd better hurry up. She even gave me this to help." Fiona slaps a bag full of white powder on my chest. "This is supposedly more potent than what you had last night."

I curse, trying to figure all of the angles. Mom's out of control. She let Lareina's cousin out of prison to fuck Lareina up because she wouldn't play ball. Although there was no concrete evidence to convict Mom in court, Ares, Josh and I knew. She will only escalate—every criminal does, for a bigger payoff, more thrills and a greater reputation. In Mom's case, she has to establish a rep brutal enough to make up for her lack of penis.

What Harvey said fleets through my head. Vincent's become more sentimental now that he's older. He doesn't want anything to happen to Lareina because she's now family. After getting the cousin out of prison, Mom hasn't gone after Lareina probably because she was worried about how things would look to Vincent.

I look at Fiona's pale face. If we got married, it'd keep both of us safe. Mom wouldn't be able to send more women because Vincent wouldn't approve of her trying to sow discord between a newly wedded grandson and his wife. And she wouldn't be able to harass Fiona anymore because she'd be family.

"Let's get married," I say.

"What? *Marry* you?" Fiona stares at me for several heartbeats. "*Are you fucking crazy?*"

"It isn't that terrible." I try not to sound insulted. Objectively speaking, I'm a great catch. Young, smart with a trust fund worth over two billion. Healthy, in shape and not bad looking. Once Fiona has a moment to think it over, she'll see that, too. "The thing is, we'll *have* to get married if we want her off our backs."

"Oh my God. It's bad enough I'm stuck with you until I pay off the two million, but *this*?"

My impatience rises at her horrified expression. Perhaps she needs a starker reminder of what she's facing. "You only have two options: me or my mother."

Fiona slowly blinks. Twice. Then she covers her mouth, runs to the bathroom and promptly loses her breakfast.

21

BRYCE

My head throbs, but I refuse to skip poker night with my brothers just for a headache. Especially since Josh would give me shit until I wanted to punch him in the face—he wants a chance to avenge himself. He isn't thrilled he lost a thousand bucks on our latest wager because my legal theory was the one the SCOTUS adopted in the latest ruling. Apparently, he believes winning a thousand bucks in a poker game will make us even, although I'll still be the smarter and better-looking twin.

But more important is the need to warn my brothers of what Mom and Harvey are up to. She's as psychotic as ever, but Harvey? He was a bit *too* helpful and forthcoming. Didn't even try to drug me. It's like a viper trying to cuddle with you—can't possibly turn out well.

I have four Tylenols, which are slow to kick in. Or perhaps the cause isn't physical, but mental. My mind keeps replaying what happened since that chick drugged me. There are a lot of what-ifs, but no matter how I slice and dice it, I made the best decisions I could, given the circumstances.

Josh is hosting tonight's game, and has catered a massive deli spread centered around roast beef, as well as put out a box of Cohiba Behikes to puff for the evening. Hibiki Blossom Harmony whiskey is also here for us to indulge in. Delicate and fleeting, it's one of my favorites.

Josh doesn't give anybody a chance to talk, too eager to start. He deals before I can pour my first whiskey.

I take a sip of Hibiki and glare at my hand. A king of spades and a ten of clubs. Not bad, not bad at all.

Josh tosses a chip into the pile with a sly grin, which nobody should trust, since he lies well. He can beat a lie detector with ease, and a couple of lawyers at the firm have used him to prove the unreliability of lie detectors in court.

"You've sighed four times in the past two minutes. That bad of a hand, or something else?" Josh asks, peering at me over his cards.

I knock back my drink.

"Amélie said you were sick this morning." Ares frowns. "You still feeling bad? We could've changed the date."

"I'm not sick. It was Mom."

The atmosphere around the table changes instantly. Gone is the light mood, replaced by a suffocating oppressiveness.

"She came to you?" Ares bristles. Out of the three of us, he harbors the greatest hatred for her. Well deserved, since she nearly killed him.

"What did she want?" Josh demands.

I rub the aching spot between my eyebrows. "I should clarify. I spoke with Harvey, and didn't get to talk to her. She went after Fiona."

"Harvey, too?" Ares clenches his hand around his cards, probably fantasizing that they're Harvey's neck. He still hasn't forgiven our uncle for drugging him in Las Vegas.

"He was civilized, considering. Gave me info about what's going on with the Dunkels and lots of warnings about Mom—like I would ever trust her again." I roll my eyes, then share what Harvey told me.

"We had another uncle?" Ares shudders. "I can't decide if I should be grateful or sad that he's out of the picture."

"Are we supposed to shed some tears for poor Vincent's loss?" Josh sneers. "Given how Mom and Harvey turned out, I'm sure he would've been just as cold-blooded and ruthless."

"Are you okay, though? What did Mom want from Fiona? Did she try to bribe her into betraying you?"

I frown at the direction Ares's mind has gone. "Why do you say that?"

"She betrayed you before with Jude. Why wouldn't she sell you out?"

I shoot a quick glance in Josh's direction. He must've shared every detail he knew with Ares, who didn't really know much about what happened between me and Fiona. Back then he was busy applying to law schools, among other things.

"Second time's easier," Josh says.

"She dumped Jude at the wedding." The incident hasn't remained a secret. After all, Jude is a minor celebrity of sorts. It's just that The Fogeys haven't had time to get nosy yet. Dad's leading a high-profile class-action lawsuit against some pharmaceutical company that lied about the side effects of an entire class of their drugs. Jeremiah's busy with two high-maintenance clients who refuse to understand that calling and texting her every hour isn't conducive to winning.

"So? Maybe Jude made her sign a shitty prenup," Ares says uncharitably. "After all, people like her only care about herself."

"You'll never get us to feel anything sympathetic toward her, not after she hurt you the way she did. Had you on a bender for a week. Bitch."

I pull my lips in. My brothers' hostile expressions say that it's my turn to tear her down, but for some inexplicable reason, I don't want to.

Have the fiery depths of my rage against her lessened in the last few days? I frown, but I can't shake off my heartache at the hollowness in her eyes when she said nobody would notice or care if she went missing. She wasn't faking that.

"I really fucked things up with her." I knock back another Hibiki and explain what happened with the redhead and then Fiona. "It put her on Mom's radar."

Ares sighs heavily. "Ah, geez."

"Yeah."

"At least Fiona hasn't been blinded." Josh sounds like he's torn between relief, horror, sympathy and old grudges. "So what's the plan?"

"Well, I'm proposing to marry Fiona—"

Josh erupts instantly. "Are you out of your fucking mind?"

"—because that way, both of us are protected from Mom's machinations."

"She must've jumped at that," Ares mutters.

"Yeah, she did. Jumped to the toilet and threw up." I scowl.

Ares and Josh high-five each other and laugh.

"Who's she trying to fool?" Ares says. "Everyone knows you're her best option. Her family's gone bankrupt and Jude obviously isn't going to marry her."

Josh puffs on his cigar. "Is she playing hard to get?"

"No, she—"

Ares snaps his fingers. "Maybe she couldn't keep her breakfast down because she suddenly got pregnant from your proposal."

"No." I exhale with exasperation. "She heaved until nothing came out, then ran out, asking me not to follow because she needed to gather her thoughts before we could talk."

"Did she text you *yes* after a couple of minutes?" Josh says.

I shake my head. "She hasn't texted or called." I hate it that I'm worried about her. I don't want any part of the tender feelings that were there for her before. I'll be damned if I let myself be vulnerable to her again.

"You aren't serious about marrying *her*, though, right? If you just want Mom to quit sending you drug girls, you could marry anybody." Ares leans forward eagerly. "Actually, my wife's friend has an assistant who might work out. A nice Korean woman. Speaks great English and is highly capable. Graduated from a top women's university in Seoul. You'd probably hit it off."

I rub my forehead. "It isn't that simple." The bone-deep skepticism in Fiona's eyes when I told her I'd look for her won't leave me alone.

She betrayed me first. She approached me for money first. And she sent me those photos, silently begging me to get her out of marrying Jude. I saved her in spite of an ugly past that left me heartbroken and humiliated. Intellectually, I know I've done more than what was necessary for her, but emotionally, I feel like I owe her a little, even though it makes no sense.

"How come?" Josh asks.

I consider for a moment, then finally zero in on the most obvious answer. "If anything happens to her, I'd feel responsible. I don't want to carry that guilt for the rest of my life. You know Mom wouldn't just yell at Fiona. She might use a corkscrew on her for real."

Ares and Josh look at each other, silently acknowledging the point.

I turn to my twin. "You need to be careful, too. Mom is apparently working on you as well."

"Nobody's drugged me yet," Josh says, although his eyebrows pinch, creating deep grooves between them. "And I've had a vasectomy, so Mom won't be getting a baby out of me."

"Vasectomies fail," I remind him. "Our cousin Huxley's dad fathered seven boys in four months because his came undone."

"Let's just say my surgeon's better than his."

We finish most of the whiskey, but don't play any more cards.

22

FIONA

I STAND outside Bryce's gates and stare at the security pad. I don't have the code or anything. Didn't need one to leave his place last night, and I didn't think to get one when I walked out of the hotel room in panic and fury.

I bought a shirt and skirt, along with some underwear, and walked around the city until it started to get dark, then called for an Uber. The easiest solution would be to contact Bryce and ask him for the gate code, but I don't want to be in touch with him until I've decided what my next step should be.

Is there a good next step?

The gates open and a modest car comes out. I trot over and wave at the driver. A man with a straw hat lowers the window and squints at me suspiciously, a thick-knuckled hand resting on the steering wheel. "Yes?"

"Hi. I'm Fiona. I'm Bryce's"—my voice falters as I search for a suitable word: *plaything, sex partner, debtor, friend?*—"ex-girlfriend."

The man's eyes sweep over me, taking in my disheveled hair and the trench coat. "He didn't say anything about anyone coming over." He could've easily said, "You look like a freak and I'm calling 911," in the same voice.

"I'm actually staying here for a bit. Can't really go home."

He nods slowly. "Is that a fact?"

"I'm not a weirdo, I swear. And I really am staying here. The backyard has really pretty shrub roses. Red. I saw them earlier. And if you let me into the house, I can show you my clothes in one of the upstairs bedrooms."

"Oh." He blinks in surprise, then gives me another once-over. "Bryce doesn't bring women over. Been with him five years and never seen one."

What? Given Bryce's sexual appetite, it's hard to believe. Maybe he likes to take them to hotels. "Well, he brought *me* over. I couldn't have known what he has in the backyard otherwise." A tall, thick wall surrounds the entire mansion.

The man chews his lip for a moment. "All right, I guess. But you can't go into the house. Housekeeper set the alarm before leaving."

"That's fine. I'll just wait in the yard."

The man nods and lets me walk past the gates. I sigh with relief and weariness, then head to the backyard. My calf muscles ache from so much walking. Stilettos aren't very practical for long hikes. I toe off my shoes and lie on the freshly mown grass, staring up at the darkening sky. The evening breeze carries the scent of the surrounding roses.

Suddenly I realize I'm smiling, and I smack my forehead. What's *wrong* with me? I'm entirely too pleased that Bryce hasn't brought any woman over in the last five years. I've already decided I have no territorial feelings about him. I'm not entitled to them.

Besides, there's a bigger problem: his mom's threats and what to do about them. Bryce suggested we marry, but that's got to be the worst solution. He must've regretted it as soon as he blurted it out.

I'm still pissed that he didn't tell me about the possibility of running into his psychotic mom, but now, anger isn't the only thing I'm feeling. It must've been incredibly hard to have a mother like that. Just like I couldn't choose how I was born, he couldn't choose whom he was born to. Apparently she stayed away for a while, but she must've raised him when he was little. The first time I saw the nice, off-campus house that he and his twin brother shared, with its sizable yard, I thought he must've been raised in luxury and thoroughly spoiled by his wealthy and powerful family. After all, who at Harvard hasn't heard of the Huxleys? But now, after actually meeting his psychopathic mother... His childhood might not have been much better than mine.

Still...marriage? Just the idea is wild. We don't even like each other. Well, he certainly doesn't like me, and I doubt anything will change that. The things that I did to him... If he'd done them to me, I'm not certain I could forgive him.

Jude wanted to make sure I couldn't go back to Bryce, even if I managed to break free from his own clutches. *Asshole.* I almost wish it were Jude who'd come to the hotel to confront me. He deserves a beating more than Aaron.

I hope Bryce's kick at the wedding crippled Jude for life—or at least causes him lifelong pain.

My phone pings, and I tense. *Bryce?* I'm not ready to talk to him yet.

–Sherry: Are you really all right? Where are you, Finn? I thought you'd be back by now. I've been offering incense and prayers.

I sag a little. Not Bryce, but not somebody I want to talk to right now, either. I'm actually a little surprised Sherry finally remembered my existence and texted. She didn't even glance in my direction when I took Bryce's hand at the wedding.

Many girls I grew up with said they turned to their moms, sisters or best friends when they needed to discuss something. I didn't have any of those. Sherry's always been too obsessed with getting good karma for Finley's reincarnation. I'm never certain what she sees when she looks at me—a girl she's adopted or Finley. To be honest, Zachary probably never knew either.

Girls my age didn't like to open up to someone who was awkward and standoffish. Besides, many of them knew I was adopted, and some probably heard the reason from their parents' gossip. L.A. is a big city, but its wealthy elite social circle is small. Girls whispered and speculated, but they didn't befriend someone like me.

–Me: I'm fine. I'm sorry about the way the ceremony ended.

–Sherry: So you're really okay? You haven't come home.

–Me: I've been staying with a college friend. Are you okay? Nobody's tried to hurt you?

The loan sharks *still* haven't gotten back to me. I make a mental note to text them again.

–Sherry: Not that I know of. I've been away to offer incense.

Of course. She needs to pray to make Finley's next life better. Apparently, the fragrance from the burning incense is supposed to honor Buddha and incinerate "negativities." Anything beyond that is also beyond me—I'm not well versed in the religion the way Sherry is.

The memory of the harsh way Zoe attacked Aaron flashes in my head. I squeeze my eyes shut, hoping Sherry won't have to pray for Aaron's reincarnation as well. As horrible as he is, no mother deserves to bury another child. And no amount of incense will ever provide Aaron with a better life, given what a horrible human being he is. He'll be lucky if he doesn't get reborn as a cockroach's lower intestine.

–Me: Did Aaron come home?

–Sherry: No. I haven't heard from him since last night. Why?

–Me: Did he text you or anything?

–Sherry: No. What's wrong, Finn? Did he do something?

Oh, did he ever.

–Me: No, just wondering. Can you text me when he gets in touch with you or comes home?

–Sherry: OK. But wouldn't it be easier if you just text him?

–Me: I'll try.

I won't try, but I don't want to have a debate with Sherry. She's convinced her son is an angel. I just want to make sure Zoe hasn't killed him.

I put the phone down and drape an arm over my eyes. How did my life go from making videos for social media to promote cheese to my being chased by loan sharks and my ex's lunatic mother?

And Bryce's proposal is ridiculous. *Us? Married?*

No. I shake my head. It isn't happening.

My phone pings again. I lift it fast, hoping it's Sherry telling me Aaron's finally home.

–Unknown: You fucking lied to me.

What?

–Unknown: You aren't the merchandise I picked for my son. How dare you trick me!

Tension wrings my gut.

–Me: Is the guy you took still alive?

–Unknown: How am I supposed to know?

My palms dampen with cold sweat. I should've expected this sort of response based on her actions at the Aylster.

–Me: I can tell the cops what you did to him. And your threats.

–Unknown: And I can carve your tongue out of your mouth and hang it up on my rearview mirror. Don't write a check you can't cash, little girl.

The air thins in my lungs.

–Unknown: Did my son even fuck you properly? Aaron says Bryce hates you and will never have you as the mother of his child.

–Unknown: Answer me!

–Unknown: You think you can ignore me? Think you're so special?

My breathing roughens.

–Unknown: You screwed around on him. Infidelity is unforgivable. I've been faithful to Prescott since our divorce, even though he remarried that mealy-faced hypocrite.

–Unknown: I should've killed you at the hotel.

–Unknown: Stay away from my son if you value your life.

–Unknown: Actually, I'll kill you anyway for hurting my son in college. You don't get to abuse my precious baby. My prince, my good boy.

Three dots appear, signaling more insults and threats are heading my way. I block the number and drop my shaking hand. I was hoping she'd never find out who I was, but of course Aaron sold me out.

Bile rises in my throat. I curl up on my side and gag a little, even though nothing comes up. I doubt she knows where I live, but it's only a matter of time before she finds out. Will she really kill me? Will she hurt someone else to get to me? She wouldn't touch Bryce, but what about Sherry?

Although she's never been an attentive parent, she doesn't deserve to be tortured by someone like Zoe. Now I wonder what she'll do to the girl who was supposed to have slept with Bryce last night. It's clear she doesn't regard any of us as human beings, just tools.

I start to stand, to pull myself together.

Another pinging from my phone—and my mouth dries.

–Unknown: Did you just block me, you disrespectful wretch?

–Unknown: You're so fucking dead.

–Unknown: You're next.

A photo pops up. A bloody finger on a gray concrete floor, with poor fluorescent lighting. I scream. The phone slips from my grip. I press a hand over my racing heart. Horror pumps through my veins. *Oh my God. What the hell was* that?

I reach out with a trembling hand and pick up my phone, then study the picture carefully, clenching my teeth to avoid hurling.

The finger is long and slim with a long, lacquered pink nail. Not Aaron's. Is this from the girl who was supposed to have slept with Bryce last night? My pulse accelerates.

I feel sick. Clammy sweat mists over my spine. A feeling of overpowering helplessness wells up, and I clench my hands, hating it. When I left Harvard, I vowed I'd never let myself be swept away by other people's actions and decisions. I moved to Wisconsin to reclaim my life. But ever since Zachary died, I've let circumstances and other people dictate my life to the point that I'm stuck with a guy who hates me, dealing with a psycho who sends me a picture of a bloody, severed finger and being told I have to head into marriage that's doomed to fail to ostensibly keep me safe.

Lights come on inside the house. Bryce is home.

The pent-up frustration, fear, bitterness and impotence erupts like a volcano. I march up to the window and knock. "Bryce! We need to talk!"

23

BRYCE

I DROP my keys in a small Bizen-yaki bowl in the foyer and stride into the living room. The lights come on automatically as the system detects my movements.

No sign of Fiona. She hasn't called, either. It's already after ten. Where is she? When is she going to contact me? Or is she doing this on purpose to be passive-aggressive? Should I make the first move and reach out to her?

A rattling sound comes from one of the windows facing the backyard.

Bang, bang, bang.

Not rattling this time, *knocks. Who the hell managed to get past security?*

I reach for a Glock just in case, but a figure presses itself on the glass from the other side of the window. I blink to make sure I'm not imagining things. Limp hair covers most of the face, but I could recognize Fiona even if she hid her face in a paper bag.

She wasn't in the best mood when she walked out. I hoped she'd had time to calm down and think things through, but her wild look makes me lose that hope.

Well, tears, screams, it doesn't matter. *I can do this.* I open the French door to the backyard and step outside. "What are you doing out here? Why didn't you come inside?"

She pushes the hair out of her face and squints at me. "Seriously?" She snorts. "Apparently, I'm not supposed to be inside your house. That's what the guy who let me pass through the gates said. So I told him I'd wait out in the backyard until you got back from work or wherever."

"You should've come inside anyway."

"And get arrested? Your housekeeper apparently set the security system."

"I would've bailed you out."

She shoots me a skeptical look. Guess I deserve that, based on our interactions since I crashed the wedding. If this had been when she first barged into my office, I would've relished seeing her squirming behind bars. But now, such pettiness seems low—

Whoa. The abrupt thought leaves me dazed for a moment. When did the sharp edge of my anger start to dull? I always told myself I'd never let it go. It wasn't just a matter of being vindictive, but self-preservation. Only idiots repeat the same mistake.

I refortify my emotional and mental shield, stiffen my spine and gesture at her to come in. "Come on. Let's get you inside."

Stilettos dangling from her hooked index finger, she walks past me. The scent of freshly cut grass wafts from her. I resist an absurd urge to hug her and take a moment to be glad that she's okay—and she's back. Part of me says she'd *better* be back to pay off the two million. But another part is just relieved she doesn't seem harmed.

Fiona sniffs. "You smell like cigars and alcohol. Did you go out after work?"

Her eyebrows pinch in irritation, and the tight vise that's been around my skull all afternoon and evening eases. I almost laugh with relief. It's good that her spirit hasn't been broken after her encountering Mom's psychotic behavior. I can deal with an angry Fiona. I just can't with a Fiona who is sad and lost.

"Yeah." I close the French door and gesture toward a couch, which she promptly takes. I sit next to her, facing her with one knee bent and on the couch. "What about it?" I keep my tone nonchalant and casual.

"Wow. You weren't even worried about what happened this morning. But of course it wasn't you Zoe threatened, just me and possibly some other women."

The reminder makes me scowl. "Trust me. I'm definitely on her radar. Both of us are." I take a moment to gather the thoughts and the arguments I made in the morning to convince her that a quick marriage is the best way to get Mom off our backs. Given the state of panic Fiona was in, I'm not sure how much of it stuck. For all I know, she might've dumped all my words along with her stomach contents.

She scrutinizes me skeptically. "Did she send *you* a picture of a severed finger, too? Because I don't think she did. If she had, you wouldn't be so calm."

"What?" The vise around my head retightens. "Show me."

She unlocks her phone and pushes it in my face, her hand slightly shaky.

I study the picture, my heart thudding heavily. It looks like a photo to hang on a wall for a low-budget Halloween party. The lighting's third rate, and the background is just a concrete floor. The finger is feminine, with a long nail. I stare at it for a while. No way to tell if it's from last night's redhead. I didn't pay attention to her hands. But Harvey's warning is genuine. Mom's had twenty-two years to strategize and prepare.

I recall her determined expression when she tried to kidnap me and my brothers. The proud conviction that she was doing the right thing, no matter what anyone else said. She no longer just wants the family back. No, she wants the power her father wields—since it's the only thing that kept her under control. The condition that forbids her from approaching us is over. Vincent is old and sick. Nothing can stop her now.

"I can't tell if it's real," Fiona adds in a small, subdued voice.

For a nanosecond, I debate lying, but opt for the truth. Fiona deserves that much. "Mom wouldn't send a fake photo. It'd make her look weak if we found out."

Fiona pales so fast that I ready myself to catch her. She sways a little, but rallies without my help. "What am I going to do?" she mutters, pressing the heels of her trembling hands against her temples.

"I've already given you the solution. We can get married."

"That's *not* a solution. That's the worst thing out of your mouth. We don't even like each other. How is a *marriage* supposed to work?"

Fiona isn't saying anything I haven't thought of—but when she says it, it sounds so much worse. Like she's declaring how much *she* hates *me* because I was falling in love with her until I discovered her in bed with Jude. I already know she doesn't respect or care for me—you don't cheat on someone you respect and care about. But hearing it still hurts, salt on an old wound that hasn't quite healed.

With the pain comes a spark of anger. She shouldn't get to scratch at the old wound, even if my own damn mother is pushing us into an impossible situation. I'm trying to be the good guy here and save both our asses. She should demonstrate some appreciation, not scoff.

"And your mom hates me now." Fiona gets to her feet and starts pacing. "She's pissed that I'm not the one she sent you."

My mouth dries. "How does she know?" Did Red spill the beans? Given how terrified she seemed of my mother, I thought she'd keep her mouth shut and pretend everything went according to plan.

"Aaron talked. There's nobody he wouldn't throw under the bus to save his own butt."

Motherfucker. I never liked him. What little respect I had for him dropped to nothing when Fiona revealed that he expected her to fix his financial mess. Now I outright despise him.

Fiona continues: "She wants a baby. There's no way I'm getting pregnant with your child, and I'm pretty sure you don't want to have a baby with me either. So how is a piece of paper going to fix our problem?"

"We don't have to have a baby to fix the problem," I state flatly as my mind lays out all the facts in a logical sequence.

"Oh, really? Because Mommy dearest sure seemed set on one when she was holding that corkscrew to my eye!"

I raise a placating hand. "If you're family, she can't touch you."

"Not convinced." Fiona stops pacing and glares at me. "I'm not even thirty, Bryce. I can't risk dying in the next few months because I happened to displease your mother." She rips at her hair. "Why is my life like a bad soap opera?"

I let out a hollow laugh. "Because you got tangled up with people with a bad soap opera life?"

She gives me a look. "Oh, please. You?"

I nod. "Mom probably didn't tell you this, but she tried to kidnap me and my brothers when we were little. Josh and I were eight, and Ares was ten. She fed us cookies with something that made us lethargic and malleable, and she caught Ares. Josh and I escaped."

My voice gets rough as I relive the moment. The terror and helplessness that should have faded still feel fresh and vivid in my mind. The old guilt lingers.

Fiona's face betrays confusion and disbelief. Guess it wasn't something that could happen even in her wildest "bad soap opera" scenario.

"She did it out of 'love.' To avoid divorce. She thought if she could keep us, she'd keep the perfect family. It didn't matter what she had to do or who she had to hurt as long, as she could keep the family whole. I don't know how she felt after she lost me and grabbed Ares instead. I was her 'good boy'—the one she loved the most." My mouth twists with bitterness. "To her, I was probably the one who should've understood the best, gone along with her plan. To this date she calls me her good boy." Red called me the same thing, and remembering causes a wave of revulsion to wash through me. I clench my hands to hide the reaction. Need to lay out the relevant facts...

Horror ripples over Fiona's expression. A hand covers her mouth as she stares at me.

"Ares escaped. He always was strong. Still is. Mom eventually got caught, but didn't suffer any real consequences. No jail time. No condemnation. Not because my family forgave her. My grandmother would've flayed her alive, but Vincent—my mom's father—was simply too powerful a crime lord for the family to cross."

Fiona's eyes widen. Probably never guessed a family as respected as the Huxleys would be tied to the mob through marriage.

"The compromise was that Dad got full custody of us and the divorce he wanted. I was relieved, since I didn't want anything to do with my mother. But the family elders conveniently forgot to mention that she could try to worm her way back into our lives once all of us kids had turned thirty. Guess they either didn't want to worry us...or maybe they hoped she'd find somebody else during those years and start another family to be obsessed with." I shrug.

"But she didn't, did she?" Fiona says hoarsely.

"No. She apparently spent all that time obsessing about us."

"And your stepmom," Fiona adds. "Zoe mentioned her."

"I'm sure, but she won't touch my stepmom." She can't afford to, no matter how much she despises Dad's second wife. Akiko is a master at playing politics within the family. She understands and respects the complicated family dynamics and history and has never expressed any desire to rock the boat, so to speak. She'd never keep us away from Zoe if we wanted to see her, but if my mother crosses Akiko, she'll strike back using everything at her disposal. And as a member of a powerful zaibatsu, she's a lot more influential than she lets on. Mom already has too many enemies. She doesn't want to add another power player to the list.

Fiona continues to look at me, her eyes unblinking as she processes what I'm telling her.

I consider my words, to impart the seriousness of the situation without overly alarming her. "Vincent—my mother's father—is older and has grown much more sentimental about family. He seems to regret the decision he made to save Mom and discard us the way he did. Based on his behavior, I'm guessing he thought my brothers and I would understand his untenable situation and let it go. Except we didn't. As far as we're concerned, that side of the family doesn't exist. So he's overcompensating, insisting that Mom and her brother bring about a tearful, heartfelt reunion between us and him."

"What happens if they fail?"

I run a finger across my neck. "Or maybe something worse, if their mob brains can think of nastier options." I shrug. "Outwardly, it's about the family reunion, but in reality, it's about control over the mob. Mom knows she has a better chance of swimming to Mars, so she's trying to create a great-grandchild to soften his heart."

Understanding dawns on Fiona's face. I give her a few minutes to think it through and figure out the implications.

Finally, she exhales and shakes her head. "That still doesn't mean we should get married. I have plans for my future that include a man who loves me and a family I can really belong to. I'm not going to throw that away just to keep your mother away."

Fiona's dream isn't unreasonable, but the idea of marrying a man who'll love her makes my jaw clench. The nasty, acidic feeling in my belly is jealousy. I'm not dumb enough to deny that. Unfortunately, the awareness doesn't lessen the frustration of knowing that I'm never going to be that man. I can't be, when I'll wake up every morning wondering if today's the day she'll betray me.

I could try giving her another chance, but in my experience, people never change, not where it counts. Just look at my own mother. A moment of hesitation was all it took for her to take advantage. The fact that she got to hurt Ares kills me. I should've been the one who was grabbed and left to die in that fire.

"Okay, let's say we don't get married." I recline and stretch out my legs. "What's your plan to get my mom off our backs?"

Surprise fleets over her face, and her expression softens for a second before it firms. "Our backs? I'm going to worry about mine, thank you very much."

"Fine. Your back."

She glares at me. "I don't know, since it hasn't been twenty-four hours since I got this big news thrown in my face. But don't worry. I'll figure something out."

"If you think going to Wisconsin will save you, you're wrong. She has tentacles everywhere in the country. If she doesn't want to send her own men out there, it doesn't take that much money to hire someone."

Fiona's jaw drops. "Are you trying to scare me into marrying you?"

I shrug. "Just giving you the full picture. Mom doesn't care what she has to do or who she has to hurt to get what she wants. The ends always justify the means. And she holds a grudge."

"That's..." Fiona shakes her head, like she can't think of a word. But then, Mom has that kind of effect on people. "So she's literally going to kill me for having gotten in her way last night and continue to drug you to get women pregnant?" Horror and shock twist her face. "Oh my God, she's basically attempting to have you raped to suck up to her father."

"I guess."

"It doesn't bother you?" Fiona asks in a hoarse whisper.

I shrug again. "It's just...what it is. Mom has never cared about anyone else's agency or consent. She just does what she wants."

Fiona gives me the strangest look. If I didn't know better, I might think it was pity or sympathy. She doesn't seem to notice the tears filling her eyes, probably because they aren't falling. The unexpected intensity of her reaction is stunning. I start to open my mouth to tell her I'm used to it and it isn't a big deal, but—

"I don't know how you can sound so blasé. The Bryce I knew in college would never have been okay with somebody messing with his life like that. You were always headstrong and proud, and I admired that about you because those were two traits I wished I had." Her voice cracks.

Her broken tone clenches my heart, and the horror and sympathy in her words take me back to the past, when she fooled me into thinking she reciprocated my feelings.

She exhales softly. "One year with the two million dollars between us cleared and settled. I want to give us an opportunity to live our lives freely without anybody meddling in them. I'm hoping that by then, your mother will give up or her brother will find a way to deal with her."

The depth of my desire to want to take her at face value is terrifying. But I can't allow people I love to get hurt because I stupidly believe someone I shouldn't. The guilt would destroy me. So I force a light laugh. "A year? Are you kidding? Do you think you're worth two million dollars a year?"

Fiona shoots me a death glare.

I continue, "I say you owe me two years—actually, more like four. No, really more like forty."

"How did you get to *forty*?"

"Fifty thousand a year?"

If this were a video game, her rage gauge would explode. Her chest heaves as she puts her hands on her hips. "Bryce, I know it's difficult for you to understand, but I'm not as cheap as you think."

I should quit pressing her buttons, but I can't stop. "It *would* be difficult—"

"Arrrgh!"

She comes at me, her face crimson with rage and a finger pointed in my chest. But she steps on one of the discarded stilettos, losing her balance and pitching forward. She grips my shoulders to catch herself. At the same time, I catch her waist, cushioning her fall with my body.

She immediately pushes herself up, sitting in my lap. From the fury burning in her eyes, it's obvious she's pissed at my provocation and her own clumsiness. I don't think she realizes that she's sitting directly on my crotch.

My blood, meanwhile, flows south, my body completely oblivious to her anger. I had her for hours last night, but I want her again. Badly.

"You make it *so* hard for me to be nice to you," she says between gritted teeth.

I smile up at her, lifting my hips so she can feel my hardening cock. "I don't know. I think you're being pretty nice."

The flush on her face spreads to her neck and chest. "You bastard."

My grin widens. "From time to time." I hold her hips and rock against her, making sure to give her the stimulation that never fails to excite her.

Her breathing shallows. "Let me *go*, you jerk."

"Me, a jerk?" I widen my eyes innocently. "You're the one who threw yourself at me."

"You *provoked* me."

"Just correcting your math."

She wraps her hands around my neck, tightening her grip.

I palm the sweet curve of her pelvis and ass. "You gonna choke me, baby?"

Her eyes narrow. "You'd love that, wouldn't you?"

"If I get to be inside you at the same time." I rock my hard dick against her.

Heat flares in her eyes, but there's also a tinge of self-directed cringe and fury. "You're impossible!"

"So kiss me. Make me shut up," I dare her, looking at her soft, sweet mouth.

Pursing her lips, she shakes her head. "Don't even think about it."

"What's the difference? Is your mouth more precious than your pussy?"

"Too intimate. It would almost be like I *liked* you."

The flat statement cuts. It hurt when I realized she never reciprocated my feelings ten years ago, but being told right to my face raises the pain to a whole new level. I hate it that she makes me feel this way.

Well, who cares if she doesn't like me? She still craves my body.

I want to feel her clench around me, climaxing from my touch. I unbuckle my belt, then push down my pants and underwear. I shove at her skirt and slip a finger past the thin fabric of her thong, almost groaning at how slick she is.

"Your mouth might hate me, but your pussy loves me." I dip a finger into the opening, getting her juices on my finger. Her own fingers flex, but she doesn't move away. I glide the pad of my thumb over her clit. Her eyes start to flutter closed.

I tap her clit twice, eliciting a sharp gasp. "Look who's making you feel good."

Her eyes blink open, glazed with rising pleasure.

"Tell me you want me," I command, watching her flush with need.

Her teeth dig into her lip.

"Oh, I forgot, your mouth *doesn't* want me."

I push three fingers into her. Her back bows, her chest shuddering. Using my free hand, I undo the belt and buttons of her trench coat and shove it off her shoulders. The arch of her spine pushes her pretty tits against the fabric of her shirt. I cup her breast and run my thumb back and forth across the nipple. Her pelvis moves to the rhythm of my plunging fingers, bliss unfurling over her beautiful face.

I watch her expression break, her lips part, as she struggles to breathe. A glimmer of triumph shimmers in my veins. She can claim that she dislikes me, how I'm all wrong for her, but her body knows better.

My dick grows impossibly hard. Her cream drenches my shaft. The urge to shove into her tight depths is strong, but I resist the base desire.

I remove my hand from between our bodies. She moans in protest. I lay my cock along her folds and rock against the slick channel. The tip of my penis bumps against her throbbing clit with each glide. Her fingers dig deeper into my shoulders as she grinds her hips against me, writhing shamelessly.

I move faster and harder, holding her close, our bodies pressed tightly against each other. Somehow the act of doing it on a couch with just enough body parts exposed for sex feels lewder and more illicit than being naked. The ceiling lights shine on her face as her tension builds.

She throws her head back as she catapults into climax. Her flesh spasms along my shaft, and I can't hold back. I come, the thick white fluid spurting against her. My cum mixing with her slick juice is a sight to behold.

We lie together for a moment, recovering. Then I pick her up and carry her to the bedroom. That was just a small taste. Time for the main course...and to prove to her how much her body wants mine.

24

FIONA

I SHIFT A LITTLE IN BED, not opening my eyes. Don't know what time it is and don't care. I'm too exhausted from last night, not to mention hungry. I haven't eaten anything since breakfast yesterday. Meeting Zoe killed my appetite for the rest of the day.

I don't know what Zoe fed Bryce, but it must've been something potent. It's been over twenty-four hours since she had him drugged, but he was insatiable again last night. I came way too many times. Toward the end, it was all I could do to cling to him and scream until my throat turned raw. It's a real mystery—how can a man drive me so wild with lust, yet make me want to murder him with my bare hands at the same time?

Afterward, he clung to me, burying his face in the crook of my neck, his big, strong body shuddering like a wounded animal. I ran my fingers through his hair, just the way he loved when we were together in college, then hummed a wordless tune softly until the tension in his muscles melted away.

Bryce once asked me what song it was, but it doesn't have a title. I just came up with it when I noticed he was too tense to fall asleep. "Maybe I'll call it 'My Special Song for Bryce,'" I told him with a shrug, my cheeks slightly warm. Although one of the reasons Zachary chose me was that I was musically adept and could carry a decent tune, my ability could never measure up to Finley's—a fact that the Obermans brought up many times.

He cradled my face and smiled at me like I was the life-giving sun. Except *he* was the sun that warmed *my* soul. I was never certain if I could be worthy of happiness, but he made me feel like everything was possible if I'd just reach for it.

And I dreamed of myself, with him, creating a family I could belong to. My life didn't work out the way I wanted, but I could still comfort him in his sleep. I ran my fingers through Bryce's hair and hummed for him. He stirred my shocked sympathy when it dawned on me that he had no idea that what his mother was doing was basically rape. I couldn't even speak. He's a *lawyer*! He should've realized it before anybody else.

But Zoe's abuse when he was small might have been so bad that he copes by pretending what she's doing isn't as horrific as it actually is. Or maybe his lawyer brain just doesn't work right when it comes to his family. Nothing is more complicated than families.

It's also possible that I'm just more sensitive about consent than most people. After all, Jude took me against my wishes for two godawful years. If he hadn't nearly died and I hadn't had the opportunity to hack into his phone, laptop, and cloud storage, he might've continued until I couldn't bear it anymore and done something unthinkable—and irreversible.

"Good morning, Fiona," comes Bryce's cheerful voice. The mattress dips as he sits near me.

I pull the sheets over my head and bury my face in the pillow, closing my eyes more tightly. "Go away." I wince at how hoarse I sound. "You're not allowed to come near me for the next seven days. Minimum."

"Seriously?" There's laughter in his voice. "Even when I come bearing a gift?"

That makes my eyebrows twitch a little. "What gift?" I ask suspiciously. If he says, "My hard, eager dick," I'm going to murder—

"An Americano."

I open one eye, lift the sheets a fraction and sniff, inhaling the beautiful, heavenly aroma of fresh coffee. I push myself up. "Gimme."

Before I can extend my hand, he wraps my fingers around the handle of the mug with a small smile. "Thanks." I take a sip. The warm liquid soothes my raw throat. "Not bad," I say primly. "Still, stay away from me for a week."

He cocks an eyebrow. "Are you going to hold a grudge?"

"Maybe." I focus on the coffee. "I think I'm entitled, don't you?"

"But you got to attack me, get on top of me, and strangle me. Don't you think that's worth a little forgiveness?"

"Let me think about it for the next seven days. *Alone*."

He laughs. Of course he's in a great mood. He got laid. He strokes my left cheek gently. "Looks better now."

"What?"

"Your face. Not so haunted."

I trace the tingling trail his fingers have left on my cheek, torn between the desire to erase the sensation and hold on to it. "I'm a resilient person."

"Or maybe my dick's just that good."

"Trust me, it's not you, it's me." I pat him on the chest, wanting to continue the light mood. When we're like this, I feel like we're back in time, filled with affection and laughter. I wasn't afraid to kiss him or show him how much I adored him. I probably fell for him way too fast and deep. The sensation of being seen was just too heady and addictive.

I'd had boyfriends before, in high school, and they liked the shadow of Finley I portrayed. But Bryce... He liked *me*. Called me by my real name. Watched movies that *I* was interested in. Gave me flowers that *I* wanted. Dined in restaurants that had food *I* enjoyed. There was no room for any part of Finley between us, and I clung to him desperately, never wanting to show even a glimpse of imperfection, lest I not measure up.

My heart aches for all that's been lost between us—things I let slip through my fingers because I was too young and scared when Jude blackmailed me. Hell, I'm still scared of not being good enough, not deserving to belong. I'm almost thirty, but every time I'm around Bryce, I feel like I'm still twenty, desperate to be perfect so I can be worthy of love and acceptance. The skin around my eyes grows hot with sudden tears, and I blink rapidly to clear them.

"Don't you have to go to work?" I ask, wanting some peace and quiet to reconcile the many facets of Bryce. I thought I knew him at Harvard, but I realize I only saw a very few sides.

"No. I told them I'd be in late."

"Two days in a row?"

He shrugs. "I rarely take vacation days. The firm will get over it."

"You mean your family. Everyone knows they own the firm."

He grins.

"Nepo baby," I mutter, although I can't fully disguise the half-teasing tone.

"Did you just call me a nepo baby?" he demands with mock outrage.

I nod with a small smile.

"Hey, I'm an amazing attorney. You'd be honored to have me on your side. Anyway, I drafted a short agreement for our unholy matrimony."

I stiffen. I guess it makes sense to put everything in writing when something as important as marriage is at stake. "Fair enough. Guess you need to ensure I don't get a penny of your money..." I shrug.

He snorts. "You already got *two hundred million* pennies of my money."

My cheeks warm at the pointed reminder.

"But we won't put that in the agreement, unless you want me to," he says.

"It's fine. Do I need to hire a lawyer?"

"Up to you. But if it helps, it's in plain English."

"Wow, I'm shocked. I was expecting it to be in legalese so dense nobody except the name partners at your firm could understand it."

Bryce chuckles. "Now *that* would be an asshole move."

"Yeah, it would be." It's weird to admit to myself that despite our history, he hasn't been a total bastard. He can be contrary and irritating, but he hasn't gone above and beyond to be a vindictive dick. I don't know what to make of that. He hasn't forgiven me for my betrayal, so why not cut me down? Humiliate me worse than Jude did?

But he hasn't. He flipped out with worry when he found out about his mom's "visit" with me. Part of me wants to believe it might mean we have a future together, the kind that I lost when I acted so stupidly ten years ago. But realistically, I know I'm being blindly optimistic. He's never going to love me or want to create a family with me. I'm not sure if I could if the situation were reversed. *If I caught him in bed with another woman while we were dating, especially if the woman happened to be my rival...?*

Bryce hands me the piece of paper to review. As promised, the document is in plain English. There are three main points: one, we have to be faithful to each other; two, we have to share the same bed each night; three, absolutely no babies. The duration is set to two years.

I narrow my eyes. "I guess you're not going to change the length of our fake marriage?"

"No. Two years, unless you want to go for forty."

"Don't be ridiculous. You don't want to be stuck with me that long."

An odd expression crosses his face, then his eyes widen slightly.

"What, did you forget an appointment? If so, we can discuss this later."

"No." He shakes his head slowly. "It's something else. Not important."

Bullshit. I trust his initial, undisguised reaction more than his Harvard Law-trained words. "So, I guess this means we don't have to do that sex countdown."

"I didn't say that." He leans forward. "After all, can we really go two years without sex?"

"Well, *you* probably can't." I shoot a meaningful look at his crotch.

"*Me?* You're the one who created this huge wet spot." He points to the bed. "I had to put a towel over it because I'm a gentleman and I don't let my partner sleep on the wet spot."

My face heats, and I shake my head, self-conscious and annoyed at the same time. Bryce and I have always had amazing chemistry. He makes me so wet that it's embarrassing sometimes. It's never happened with anybody else, but I'm not stupid enough to admit that. Bryce would crow until I wanted to throw the Americano in his face. And I really need this coffee.

"So how are you going to do the sex part?" *Time to move on from the wet spot.* "I don't want to do the countdown if I also have to be married to you for two years."

"We'll play it by ear."

Why does that sound like, "We'll do it every day"?

"But I am at your service anytime you want to jump me, just like last night." He spreads his arms with a smug smile.

My fingers tighten around the mug. "How absurdly generous. I'll keep that in mind."

"Oh, and I want to add that I'm always in the mood."

And that sounds like, "I'll help you get in the mood, baby." Given our chemistry, it's very possible that he could seduce me if he put his mind to it.

And part of me wants to see what he'd do.

I shake myself inwardly and read the rest of the document. It says that we don't have any claim over each other's premarital assets, but I'm to live with him at his home. *Fine.* We're to keep our assets separate while married, and under no circumstances commingle anything. *Also fine.* It should make our break cleaner.

"Birth control?" I ask.

"I can supply condoms, and if you want, you can go on birth control."

I sigh. There's nothing objectionable about the terms. "Okay. Give me a pen."

He hands me a sleek Mont Blanc. I scrawl my name at the end of the document and date it. He takes the pen and signs. As I watch him jot down today's date, my stomach flutters with nerves and something else I can't quite put my finger on. Anxiety floods me. It's nothing like what I felt when I agreed to his payment plan for the two million dollars.

Oh my God, I'm really marrying Bryce. I breathe slowly in and out, trying to focus on the air moving through my body.

It's going to be okay. Two years will pass in the blink of an eye. It'll be like living with a roommate.

Besides, he's too smart to not figure out a way to end our

relationship as quickly as possible. I can't imagine his wanting to spend any more time than he has to with me. Once the Zoe problem is resolved, we'll go our separate ways even if it hasn't been the full two years.

"So, when are we getting married?" I ask, praying it'll take at least a month before the ceremony.

"Today."

25

BRYCE

Fiona stares out the car window, her expression pensive. She agreed to the marriage and didn't object to any of the terms, but something doesn't sit right with me. Maybe it's the dejection on her face, as though she's given up.

It bugs me that she hasn't even glanced at me ever since she signed the paper, even though I really shouldn't care what she does as long as I get what I want.

She might be sulking because she didn't get the kind of proposal she's always dreamed of. Tough shit—I didn't think I would marry the woman who smashed my heart to pieces either, so we're even. Still, part of me squirms. Last night when she held me and hummed for me, my heart beat unsteadily. It was disorienting, like I'd been catapulted back in time. The mental and emotional strain that had been with me for so long eased, allowing me my first true rest in...forever.

I thought maybe there'd been a change of heart on her part. But much to my disappointment, she acted like the soothing, intimate moment last night didn't happen. I thought she'd say something about the past to excuse her betrayal, even if it was just to give me the tired "It just wasn't working for me" line.

I couldn't bring it up, either. There wasn't a way to raise the topic without sounding needy and vulnerable. And I can't afford that with Fiona.

Today, she's in a pretty ivory sundress and strappy sandals, like she cares at least a little about the ceremony. Her pink toenails look cute. I put on a black three-piece suit with a tie because anything else would be wrong for the occasion.

I park the Lamborghini at a county clerk's office near a courthouse. She starts to reach for the door.

"Wait."

She turns toward me with a small frown. "Is there anything else to discuss before we get married?"

"Not discuss, exactly, but..." I pull out a velvet box from my jacket pocket and pop the lid open.

Her jaw slackens, her eyes zeroing in the ring in the center. "Oh my God."

I pluck the glinting ring out and slide it onto her finger. The princess-cut diamond is set on a classic platinum band, and is perfect on her slim hand, just the way I imagined it at the store yesterday. Classy and elegant while discreetly hinting at wealth and prestige.

"You like it?" My tone's super casual.

She lifts her gaze to meet mine. "It's *huge*!"

"Only ten carats."

"You're the only guy I know who would say 'only' ten carats."

"Because it's not that big." Why isn't she answering my question? *Does she not like it?*

Her eyes take in the discreet logo inside the box. "It's Sebastian Jewelry."

"I couldn't get something cheap." My tone's definitely grumpy now.

"Because you always get the best."

A shrug. "It wasn't that expensive. The piece isn't custom made." Still, I didn't think that was going to be an issue. The band is unique, with a rose etched on either side of the diamond. The flowers reminded me of the Fiona roses in my garden, and it seemed to fit her. Perhaps I misjudged, and she doesn't want to settle for a premade item.

She sighs. "Thank you. It's really beautiful."

Relieved, I start to smile, but she adds, "I guess...I didn't think about props."

She's lost what little romanticism she had since the graduation. I study her, from her slightly arched eyebrows, long, thick lashes and thoughtful green-gold eyes to her soft, lush lips pursed in a mild self-directed recrimination.

Everyone becomes jaded, maybe even a little fatalistic, with some scars to show, as they navigate adulthood. But she was always a bit too jaded, like she'd lost something precious despite having struggled mightily for it, and she was convinced she'd never have it. She didn't even tell me it was her birthday until the day after. If she'd been like other girls, I might've thought she was testing me, but she had very few expectations. I had to plan an emergency celebration, and her shocked, pleased smile was the greatest reward I could've hoped for. The hug—and the sex afterward—was fantastic, too.

I realize with a pang that we were truly happy back then...and I miss it more than I want to admit. I've been furious ever since she threw it away for a guy who wasn't worth it.

"How are we playing this when people ask about us?" Fiona looks at me. "We're going to need a story to go with the ring."

I clear my throat to shake off the pain, sorrow and anger, then put on a careless façade. "We stick as close to the truth as possible."

"So, how romantic was the proposal?"

"Very."

"Flowers?"

"Yes, red roses," I say, thinking of the shrub roses I planted.

"Like the ones in the backyard."

"Precisely."

She stares at the ring for a moment. She refused to say that she liked it, but I hope she does, not because I care what she thinks—*I don't*—but because she has to wear it for the next two years. It'll be difficult if she hates it. I'm not buying her another ring, I decide stubbornly.

She strokes the cool band, her eyes lowered. "Do you want it back when all this is over?"

Suddenly, my throat feels tight. I didn't think about what would happen once our deal ended. Strange, since we signed a contract for it.

It's almost like we're any other couple about to get married, only focusing on the present. "No, it's a gift." My voice is stiffer than I intended. "Besides, what am I going to do with it? It's not like I can reuse it with the next woman."

Fiona drops her hand in her lap. Her expression turns inexplicably self-deprecating. "You're right. What was I thinking?"

I get out of the car, then walk around to open her door. A hand at the small of her back, I lead her inside.

Paola smiles at me. In her late twenties, she's one of my favorite clerks because there's no gossip she can't not share, and she tells me everything about everyone.

She pushes back her long braids and waves. The rhinestones on her electric-blue nails glint as she does so. "Hey, Josh, what's shaking?"

I laugh. "I'm the better-looking twin."

"How am I supposed to know which is which unless you start talking to me? Both of you *claim* to be the better-looking twin." She chuckles. "So what brings you here today?"

"I'm here to get married. This is my fiancée, Fiona."

Fiona smiles and presents the ring.

Paola gasps, planting a hand over her impressive bosom. "Oh my Lord, that's *gorgeous*. And so big!"

Fiona's smile widens, although her eyes fail to match the wattage. "Yes, he really spoils me."

"Girl, how come I never heard about you?" Paola looks Fiona up and down, cataloguing every detail as quickly as possible. The gleeful glow on her face says she's dying to tell everyone about my *fiancée*. "Bryce really kept you under wraps."

"I wasn't *hiding* her," I say with a light laugh.

Fiona steps up. "We met when we were studying at Harvard. But after we graduated, I went to Wisconsin for work, so..." She shrugs. "But recently I came back, we ran into each other, and the rest is history."

"That sounds like a movie! How was the proposal? Did he go down on one knee?"

"Of course. With lots of red roses."

Paola's eyes close and presses her hand deeper into her bosom. "Oh my God, that is *so romantic!* I'd die if it happened to me."

If only that was how Fiona reacted. She threw up, like marrying me was the most disgusting thing imaginable. If Mom hadn't sent the photo with a severed finger, Fiona probably would've stayed stubbornly uncooperative. I shove aside the sudden bitterness and feign a happy groom-to-be.

"Thankfully, she didn't die. There was some leaping about with joy, though. Almost twisted an ankle in her heels—"

"Let's not get carried away, dear." Fiona covers my mouth with her hand, a wary caution in her eyes. I push it away, kissing the fingertips.

"Baby, you know the way if you want to shut me up." I let my eyes fall to her mouth.

She flushes and gives me a meaningful look. "Not in front of an audience."

"Oh, don't mind me," Paola says, fluttering her lashes. She would love that. Might even pull out her phone to record it.

Fiona turns to her with a sweet smile. "Can I give you my information first?"

"Yes, of course," Paola says, her hands dropping to the keyboard. Then she gives me a small wink. "She's a keeper."

26

FIONA

SHE'S A KEEPER.

If only Paola knew. I can't believe she bought our lies. I guess sticking to the truth as much as possible helped. After all, we did meet at Harvard, and there are a lot of red roses—in his backyard. And he was on one knee for about half a second last night between dropping me on the bed and climbing on top of me.

So yeah. Truckloads of truth.

The clacking of Paola's keyboard is like the sound of someone hitting a button that releases more and more anxiety into my system. I wipe my clammy hands on my thighs. I feel like a mouse trapped in a maze it can never escape. *Two years,* I tell myself. *Two years, and I'll be fine.*

I glance at Bryce as he checks the information on the marriage license to make sure everything is proper. How does he really feel about all this?

He has to hate me, but there are times he does or says things that make me think that perhaps he doesn't *truly* hate me. And that's what makes him so dangerous. With other people, their regard for me is crystal clear. I don't have to second-guess myself, and they also don't make me think that there could be *more*. But if I start to believe that with Bryce, he'll break my heart, and I can't let him. If I have my heart shattered again, I'll never recover.

It took me so long to piece my life together, to heal my emotional wounds. I even went to a place where nobody knew me so that I could really start fresh. Despite the loneliness, it worked. I never let anybody become too important, so no one would have too much power over my emotional wellbeing. Nobody is allowed to do what Jude did to me.

"Judge Mansfield is available if you don't have anyone else in mind and want to get everything done today and hold the ceremony later," Paola says. "I'm sure he'll be thrilled to marry you."

My smile hurts my cheeks. "That's wonderful. You're such a gem."

"Not at all. I'm so happy for you guys. This is one of the most exciting things that's happened since I started working here."

"Really?" You'd think a clerk's office would have more interesting gossip than a couple getting married.

"Yeah, there's a betting pool for which Huxley twin is getting married first, and *I* won." She twists a little in a restrained dance.

"Am I going to get a share of that?" Bryce asks, leaning against the counter.

"No, but I'll buy you a drink." She taps the back of his hand, then winks. My chest suddenly feels uncomfortable, like I'm having heartburn.

Not even glancing at me, Bryce laughs, which intensifies the acidic feeling. "Deal. I'll take you up on that one of these days."

"Hey, you know my number."

I start walking away—I've seen enough. Bryce says bye and catches up to me with wide-legged strides.

"Are you jealous?" he asks, a smirk in his voice.

I look straight ahead, maintaining the same pace. "No." It'd be absurd to admit it. Just because we're getting married doesn't mean we have any claim over each other. Our relationship is worse than just dating. At least with dating, you don't have a set end date. This marriage is doomed to end in two years from now.

"As fun as it is to see you worked up, don't worry. She doesn't like me that way."

I give him a look.

"It's true. She's dating a hockey player. But even if she weren't, I wouldn't cheat on my partner. It'd be disrespectful." He holds my eyes. "And hurtful."

It's as though he's daring me to explain why I did what I did to him back then. Although intellectually I understand that I was a victim too, deep in my heart, there's shame. Shame that I didn't know better, that I wasn't more careful, that if I had been smarter, I would've been able to stop Jude.

I opt for something I should've said before leaving for Wisconsin. "Bryce, I'm sorry. I shouldn't have done that to you."

He takes half a step back and stares. And it hits me—I've never apologized to him for what happened, ever. We never got a chance, especially after Bryce said I was dead to him. But I should've made more of an effort. If I had, we might've been able to get some sort of closure, let go and move on—a much healthier outcome than what actually happened. "I should've said it before I left for Wisconsin. It was thoughtless of me. I know it sounds like I'm making excuses, but at the time, I just had to leave as quickly as I could without really talking to anybody."

He gives me a long look. "Why? What happened?"

His expression is soft and gentle, like that of a man who's willing to listen and forgive. I'm tempted to break down and unload everything. However, the years-old shame claws the churning words back down from my lips. I choose my response with care. "I...needed a new beginning. Wisconsin felt like the perfect place, far away from L.A. and... from the people I knew. Contrary to what you might've thought, my relationship with Jude was awful. Just terrible. And my biggest regret was hurting you. You were so good to me. You deserved the very best of everything." I manage a smile, but from his taut face, I know it's not a very good one.

Several beats pass, the entire courthouse seemingly frozen. *It's too late. Too little, too late.*

Finally, I say, "Why don't we just go see the judge?" It comes out as a croak.

Bryce gazes at me for a moment, then gives a curt nod. "Okay."

~

Judge Mansfield is an older gentleman, hair gray with lots of wrinkles stretching over his face. Maybe in his early sixties, he's in a white button-down shirt and slacks with a brown knit vest. A plate of half-eaten sugar cookies is next to him, crumbs covering the desk.

When he notices us, he smiles, eyes twinkling, and gets up to greet us. "How good to see you." He shakes hands with Bryce, clasping his shoulder with the other hand. "How's your grandmother?"

"Doing well, thank you." Then Bryce mouths, *I'm Bryce.*

The gesture surprises me. Although Bryce and Josh are twins, they look totally different if you spend more than a minute studying them. There's an air about them, a kind of electrical charge that makes them unique to each other.

The judge laughs. "Thanks for taking pity on an old man." He turns to me. "And who is this beautiful young lady?"

"This is Fiona, my fiancée."

"How lovely." He extends a hand. "Nice to meet you."

I pump his hand. "The pleasure's mine."

"So, what's the occasion?"

Bryce hands him the marriage license. "We're getting married."

"Well! Congratulations!" Judge Mansfield looks back and forth between us. "What a lovely surprise."

"I'd like you to marry us, if you have the time," Bryce says.

"No fancy ceremony?" The judge's curious eyes flick to me, gauging my reaction, but I merely paste on my perfect good-girl smile.

"That'll come later," Bryce responds, wrapping his arm around my shoulders and pulling me closer.

I respond by looping my arms around his waist, letting his body heat seep into me. "We want to make it official as soon as possible."

"In that case, it'll be my pleasure." The judge smiles and clasps Bryce's shoulder in a fatherly gesture. "I can't believe it. It feels like it was only yesterday when you were a tiny little baby I bounced on my knee. Look at you now. Taller than me and wanting to start a family of your own."

"There's no baby yet," I add quickly.

"Maybe not now, but there will be one soon. You know Catalina is looking forward to one. Marrying into the Huxley family is like gaining the biggest ally you can have, the kind that will always watch your back and keep you safe. You're a lucky woman," the judge says to me.

"Thank you." I try to sound joyful, but can't hide the wistfulness. He's describing the kind of family I'd love to have, but won't. That will be for some future woman Bryce falls in love with and marries. When his family finds out what happened between me and Bryce, they'll never forgive me. Actually, they might already know. Josh and Ares have to be aware of our ugly college breakup, and might have told them already.

Still, I manage to maintain a smile as the judge asks his assistant and clerk to come in to be our witnesses, then starts the civil ceremony.

"Do you, Bryce Huxley, take Fiona Oberman as your lawfully wedded wife, and offer her your love, strength, support, loyalty and faith as long as you shall live?"

Bryce raises his chin. "I do."

Anxiety knots my gut. Bryce doesn't believe in the vow, but he says "I do" with such conviction that it makes my heart ache with longing.

Judge Mansfield nods and turns to me. "Do you, Fiona Oberman, take Bryce Huxley as your lawfully wedded husband, and offer him your love, strength, support, loyalty and faith as long as you shall live?"

Inhaling shakily, I look at the judge, then at Bryce. The question feels like an indictment about how I've treated Bryce before. I haven't given him any of those. But at the same time, I'm getting a two-year-long chance to close the old chapter and start a new one, one where I redeem myself for my past.

"I do," I whisper.

Bryce's shoulders relax a bit. *Was he nervous that I'd reject him?* I reach out and squeeze his hand to let him know turning away from him was the last thing on my mind. Smiling a little, he pulls out another velvet box bearing the Sebastian Jewelry logo. Inside are matching wedding bands. He slides the smaller one on my finger.

I stare at the simple, elegant platinum band. Something beneath my feet seems to shift, telling me my life is about to change in a big way.

Giving Bryce a tremulous smile, I gently push the bigger band along his finger. In my head, I hear something closing—like a door shutting off a line of retreat, forcing me to walk forward.

"I now pronounce you husband and wife." The judge beams. "You may kiss the bride."

I freeze at the declaration. I was so focused on the change in my marital status that I totally forgot about the kiss at the end of the ceremony. Bryce turns to me. His eyes are expectant, but he doesn't make the move to kiss me.

Guess he remembers my rather heated words from before that kissing me without my consent would be rape. I don't want to embarrass him by refusing to seal the ceremony with something as traditional as a kiss. But I don't want to set the wrong precedent, or an expectation that I have feelings for him.

Putting my hands on his shoulders, I stretch up on my toes and place my lips on the corner of his. "Husband."

Something like disappointment and regret flashes in his eyes. But then he smiles. "Wife."

Unlike my whisper, his word is firm and possessive.

I flush. I don't know what the future will bring, but I promise myself that I'll be the best wife I can, as long as the marriage lasts.

27

FIONA

As we walk out of the judge's chamber, Bryce's phone pings. He checks the screen with a small frown, then shakes his head. "I have to go."

"I thought you took the entire morning off." I was hoping to have lunch together and maybe figure out some of the details for going forward.

"I did. But apparently..." He rolls his eyes.

"Okay. You go ahead. I'll just get an Uber."

"Don't be silly. Take the car—I'll Uber." After placing the fob in my hand, Bryce walks off.

I stare at his back for a moment, puzzled. He's giving me his Lamborghini to drive? I'm a good driver, but surely he doesn't trust me that much... *Does he?*

I checked my phone's notifications. Nothing from Sherry. Hollowness pierces my heart. It's been three years since she quit sending me birthday wishes. Technically, today is Finley's birthday—don't know my real one, since my biological parents weren't thoughtful enough to share that info when they abandoned me—but it became mine when the Obermans adopted me. Zachary spent a lot of time, money and energy to update it on the official government papers to make sure I could be the perfect Finley substitute.

Except it seems like I haven't measured up in the last few years. Sherry would never ignore the birthday otherwise.

Isn't this what I wanted? To be Fiona, not Finley? But somehow Sherry's silence feels like a rejection. Before, I chalked it up to the fact that Zachary's health wasn't good, but now there's no excuse. Sherry doesn't want me either, even though I've done everything she expected of me. Resentment simmers, but confusion and surprise soon follow. I realize I wanted her to continue in my mother's role as long as possible, so I could lie to myself that I wasn't truly alone. Now I can't even pretend. Did I really want Sherry to act maternal even if she only saw me as Finley? Was I *that* desperate deep inside?

I shake myself mentally. I've always been alone, from the very beginning. I was discarded by my birth mother, and my previous adoptive parents didn't want me either. I shouldn't have wanted the Obermans to be any different. They made their preference clear all the times they looked the other way when Aaron bullied me for "stealing" his sister's place. To be fair, back then he was too young to understand that I was there to be Finley's substitute for his mother. Somebody—an adult, most likely—clarified my role for him.

I put my phone away and start to leave the courthouse.

"Such a gentleman, letting you take the Lambo."

My steps slow as I glance at a tall man in an expensive-looking suit. His hands in his pockets, he wears a harmless smile. However, there's a subtle edge that screams danger. His broad, powerful shoulders fill his jacket, and there's the barest hint of menace in his relaxed posture. His dark hair is slicked back, showing a high forehead. His amber eyes crinkle slightly with a smile, but there's a cold calculation in his gaze. He might think he's slick. Most people would be fooled, but not me. I've been dealing with snakes all my life—people who tell me how much they like me only to discard me as soon as they don't need me anymore.

"Do I know you?"

His smile grows more brilliant. "Of course you do. Or you will. I'm your new uncle."

I tilt my head. "Uncle?"

"Yes. Harvey." He watches me closely with an expectant smile. If he thought I'd go, "Oh, of course! I've heard so much about you from Bryce," he's in for a major disappointment.

"And your Cupid," he continues.

I frown with confusion. "Cupid?"

"I brought you and Bryce together." He places a hand on my shoulder. From somebody else, the gesture might seem friendly. From him it's mildly threatening, like a viper slithering along your skin.

"I have no idea what you mean, and I don't know any uncles," I say, stepping away from his touch.

He looks at the hand I rejected, then shrugs. "We should have a proper conversation. How about a late brunch?"

"No, thanks. I need to get going."

"Fine. I suppose we can talk out here. I don't mind." But his cold eyes say he most definitely minds and pressure me to agree to the brunch.

I stubbornly keep my mouth shut. Bryce didn't say anything about anyone coming over to the courthouse. And after meeting his lovely mom, I'm not risking—

"I saw you met my sister. Zoe always makes an impression, eh? I guess she did on you, too."

My mouth dries. *This is the mob uncle Bryce mentioned.* I doubt this man's going to be any better than Zoe, especially since he's fighting with her for control over the criminal enterprise. "She did. But look, I don't want anything to do with you or your sister."

"Sure you do. Your brother owes me two million, which you plan to pay back."

"How do you know—? Wait, are *you* the loan shark?"

"Bingo. Although I prefer the term 'preferential lender.' Whatever you call it, it's one of my more minor interests."

I pull out my phone. No way am I letting that sum of money hang over my head, especially if the person's Zoe's archnemesis and brother. I don't want to give anybody the impression I'm picking a side. "Great. Why don't you send me your bank information so I can wire the money today?"

He puts a finger on the edge of my phone and lowers it. "Don't be so cold. There's no need. We're family now. Consider it a wedding gift."

Oh, hell no. "No thank you. Two million is not on the registry," I say with a forced smile.

He gives me a look. "Honey, you think I got where I am by coloring inside the lines?"

"I have no idea. But it's my policy not to accept anything from anyone that might come back to haunt me."

He lets out a soft chuckle. "You're interesting. But it's a gift, not a trap."

I let the statement hang, not responding, but he keeps staring at me like he needs me to say something before he can continue. "Okay," I finally say. It's the only neutral thing I can think of.

"Seriously, the two mil is yours. Consider it...compensation for you keeping my nephew as happy as possible, for as long as possible."

I scowl at Harvey. He's talking to me like I'm just a tool. Probably a shared sibling trait, albeit he's more civilized than Zoe.

He leans so close that I can smell the cool aftershave on his skin. A chill runs through me, but I don't back down.

A genuine smile tugs at the corner of his mouth. "Besides, a couple million is nothing between family, right?" He leans forward. "You can just give me something suitably reciprocal later, if it bothers you that much," he says into my ear, making me shiver. He pulls back and straightens his jacket. "Like maybe nine months from now."

28

BRYCE

BARRY POUNCES the second I step out of the elevator. "I can't believe you got married without telling me!"

It feels like an old *Twilight Zone* episode. "How the hell—?" I ask, striding down the long hall to reach my office.

He follows. "Paola just called."

"That was quick, even for her."

"She's just happy she won the money," he says sourly.

"Oh, that betting pool?"

"Yeah. I lost." He scowls. "The least you could have done was warn me."

I snort. "Imagine me playing the world's tiniest violin."

"You're so damn cruel. Hey, how about a post-bachelor party?"

"And have my wife stab me the moment I get home from it? No thanks."

"She doesn't have to know."

"Women *always* know." I gesture to the office and the building at large. "This firm *runs* on women who know. Speaking of which, why is the floor so quiet?" I frown as I look around to locate the reason I had to come in. "Where's Bebe? I should've heard her scream from miles away."

"Jeremiah kicked her out. Threatened to sue her if she wouldn't shut up. Then told her to make an appointment."

"She did? Huh… She's rarely that nasty."

"She's in a mood." He lowers his voice. "Apparently one of her clients misrepresented some pertinent facts, and it really fucked things up for the case."

I shudder. My aunt hates losing, and if the misrepresentation costs her the case, she'll murder the client. My phone pings, and I check the message.

–Dad: My office. NOW.

"Gotta go. Partner calls." I wave at Barry and head to Dad's office on the next floor.

As a senior partner at Huxley & Webber, my dad has one of the nicest corner offices, with a fantastic view of the city. In a few years I'll get one, too, but I'll keep my old furniture because it's comfortable and functional.

Dad's seated at his massive mahogany desk with a sleek laptop and some papers on top. Expensively cropped dark hair frames his confident face. A bespoke black three-piece suit—a gift from Akiko last Christmas—and a muted blue tie completes his legal shark look.

His dark eyebrows are pulled together. Under them, his wide-set, pale gray eyes gleam with calculation as he gazes at me over steepled fingers.

"Have a seat." He tilts his head at one of the cushy armchairs. His voice is, as usual, modulated. He has a booming voice that would make any stage actor envious, but he rarely uses it at full volume, because he thinks that raising your voice equals admitting defeat.

I take the seat and prop an ankle over the opposite knee, then wait for him to start.

"You aren't where Ares was. There won't be a promotion to partnership," he says flatly.

"I know." I shrug.

His frown grows darker. "So why did you suddenly elope? You didn't tell me. You didn't tell anybody. I had to hear it from Eric."

So Judge Mansfield made a call. I expected Paola to gossip with lawyers at the firm, but not him.

It doesn't matter. My goal was to get people here talking about my revised marital status. Mom undoubtedly has spies at the firm. Although Huxley & Webber thoroughly screens everyone's background, including janitorial staff, nothing's foolproof.

"Do you know how it made me feel to realize you'd gotten married without telling anybody?" Dad continues. "Not to mention Akiko! She's hurt."

"Mom was going to hurt my wife, Fiona," I say somberly. "I had no choice."

At the mention of Mom, Dad stiffens. "That bitch."

"Mom's after me. Vincent is apparently much sicker than we thought—at least sick enough to put family first."

"Really? Too bad he isn't dead yet," Dad says.

"Agreed." I fill him in briefly on what Harvey told me. Dad's face turns red, green, then back to red. "Anyway, marrying Fiona gives us some protection against Mom's machinations."

Dad heaves a sigh, his shoulders slouching. "I'm sorry, son. If I hadn't been so blinded by love back then..." He rubs his forehead. "I feel like an idiot."

"Don't, Dad. If you hadn't met her, you wouldn't have created us. Do you regret that too?"

He snaps his head up. "No. Never. You and your brothers are the greatest accomplishments of my life."

I smile with affection and understanding. "Look, you've always done the best you could. None of us blame you for what happened. That's all on Mom."

"Thanks." He tries to smile, but lets out another heavy sigh instead.

I clench and unclench my hands. How I loathe Mom for dragging the family down after twenty-two years.

"Your grandmother wants to meet your wife," Dad says.

"I'll check my calendar."

"Ah, no, Akiko is hosting dinner tonight. Bring her."

I bite back a groan. "Tonight? But it's Fiona's birthday."

I was going to give her a surprise lunch until Amélie said Bebe was acting up in the office and nothing short of my presence would calm her. If we have dinner with Akiko, we'll end up starving. Besides, I don't know how Fiona's going to feel about meeting my family so quickly when our marriage is temporary. Although I told her it was for two years, I don't plan to stick to the timeline. It's going to end when Mom's out of the picture...and I no longer feel that weird pinch in my heart every time I think of Fiona and I quit getting erections around her. That shouldn't take two years, so introducing her to the family seems like a type of fraud. On the other hand, keeping her away from the family would look sketchy as hell to Mom.

"Fine. I'll tell her to make a cake," Dad says gruffly.

"It'd be better if you just told her to make bigger portions."

Dad gives me an expression full of mournful regret. An honest reaction, since he would never show that he's unhappy with Akiko's food. "She seems to believe if I have more than three bites, I'm going to get diabetes, hypertension, heart attack and a stroke all at the same time."

I snort. "At the rate things are going, you'll outlive us all. Just tell her not to labor so much in the kitchen. Since we're pressed for time, it'll be best if she orders a few pizzas instead."

Longing fleets over his face, but almost as quickly as it appears, he shakes it off, glaring at me. "Stop whining. You'll eat what she makes."

~

I STEP inside my office and do a double take. I step back out and glance at Amélie, who gives me an I-did-my-best shrug. Shaking my head, I stride inside and shut the door, then face my brothers.

Ares is propped against the edge of my desk, giving me a dark look that's all disapproving eyes and an even more disapproving, flat mouth. Josh, on the other hand, paces like a caged panther, clenching and unclenching his hands, face red and looking ready to explode.

I'm not fooled. Ares is the one about to have a volcanic eruption of a temper tantrum, while Josh is managing his fury by pacing.

"How could you?" Ares says as he pushes himself off the desk to stand straight.

I knew it.

"What were you thinking?" he says. "Did she infect you with some kind of brain parasite?"

Josh keeps pacing, nodding in agreement with everything coming out of Ares's mouth.

I shrug. "I already told you I didn't want the guilt—"

"The hell with guilt! *She didn't feel guilty when she fucked Jude Morven in your bed!*" Tendons stand out in Ares's neck. He's barely restraining himself from screaming.

I'd applaud his control, but he's salting a wound that hasn't healed yet. I inhale deeply to control the raw pain. "Ares, I know you mean well, but Fiona's my wife now."

His face scrunches with disgust.

Josh stops and turns to me. His mouth opens. I know what he's about to ask before he says the first word. "Can you—"

"An annulment is out of the question. It's either this or dealing with Mom's women and drugs."

"You could marry somebody else," Ares says.

"I'm not marrying a stranger." The very idea of a stranger living in my home makes my skin crawl.

"This won't stop Mom, not really. She's going to escalate," Josh says.

"Tag-teaming me, are you?"

"It's not tag-teaming. It's just stating the truth," my twin adds.

I narrow my eyes. "Okay. Do you *want* Mom to force me to make a baby so she can ingratiate herself with Vincent?"

"Of course not, but—"

"You realize it's rape, right?"

Ares and Josh stop, both shocked. "What?"

"That's what I said too. But Fiona pointed it out to me. If Mom tries to force me to have sex with women I don't want, and especially if she uses drugs, it's rape. Like date rape. I'm not consenting, right?" I rub my face, weary. "We're so fucked up that we don't even recognize some of what she does as abuse. We're just so worried about her doing something worse. In some messed-up way, I guess being drugged and forced to be an insemination machine is better than being kidnapped or left to die in a fire."

Ares's expression shifts, softening a little, but then he quickly juts his chin. "All right, fair point. Still, I'm not on board with you marrying Fiona."

"Neither am I." Josh's voice lacks its earlier heat, but his brow is still knitted. "What if she betrays you again?"

"I doubt she'll side with Mom. She didn't make the best impression."

Josh scoffs. "It isn't like Jude was known as Mr. Charming back then either."

"The hardest thing in dealing with people is that you can never know what they're really thinking," Ares says. "I just don't want you to get hurt." He gives me a pointed look. "Again."

I nod. "I know. I appreciate it, but give her a chance, okay?"

"She never even apologized," Josh grumbles.

"She did."

Surprise crosses his face.

"So let's be civil at dinner tonight."

Ares bites back a curse. "Fine. I'll try, but if she does anything to hurt you again, I'm going to kill her."

"Unless I kill her first," Josh says.

My brothers look at me like they're expecting some reassurance that she won't, but all I can manage is a blank smile. It dawns on me that even though she apologized, I'm never going to be certain of her unless I know what made her betray me in the first place.

29

FIONA

As the gates to Bryce's house magically swing open, I understand why he wanted me to take the Lamborghini. He didn't want me stuck out here again like last night. The garage doors open on their own to let the car in as well.

But once I get to the entrance to the house, the security pad blinks red. I run the fob over it a couple of times, but it remains red. I grab my phone and text Bryce.

–Me: In the garage. How do I get into the house?

A moment later, he sends me a six-digit code. I stare at the number with surprise, uncertainty and confusion—Finley's birthday. Is it a coincidence? Seems unlikely, but...I don't want to give it more meaning than I should.

–Bryce: Did you get in okay?

His message pulls me out of my daze. I quickly enter the number on the smooth screen, which has a scrambled number pad. The system turns green and the door unlocks with a metallic click. I push it open and step into the nook between the living room and the kitchen.

–Me: Yes. Thank you.

–Bryce: Do you still like pepperoni pizza?

–Me: Yes. Why?

–Bryce: Because I'm going to pick one up to share.

As I look at our text exchange, it's almost like we're back in college. We used to split pepperoni pizzas and sip Diet Dr. Pepper when I stayed over at his place.

–Me: How about some Diet Dr. Pepper?

I send the message before I realize what I'm doing. I bite my lip, wondering if he's going to think I'm being overly sentimental...or maybe presumptuous.

–Bryce: I can grab that, too. I'm leaving the office in half an hour.

–Me: That early?

–Bryce: Shitty traffic, and we have to go out for dinner.

Dinner? Then why the pizza...?

Is this some weird way of trying to celebrate our fake two-year marriage? In any case, isn't necessary to cut his workday short for it.

–Bryce: With my family. Paola told everyone, and of course, The Fogeys want to meet you.

I inhale sharply. He called the elders of his family The Fogeys in college, and I'm guessing that hasn't changed. Something like an electric charge runs through my nerves, leaving me shaky. I drop onto a couch and try some deep breathing. But it doesn't settle my anxiety.

–Me: Do we have to? I'm only your wife for a little while.

–Bryce: Sorry, it's mandatory. My stepmom is cooking, and there's no avoiding it. Unless you want them descending on our house, which I'd prefer to avoid.

I prop my elbow on my knee and rest my forehead in my palm. A small throbbing starts at the base of my neck—the beginning of a tension headache.

–Me: If we're having dinner with your family, why are you getting pizza?

–Bryce: Because that's also mandatory.

What?

–Bryce: Trust me. You'll thank me later. Gotta go.

I blink, dazed and dumbfounded like I just got sucked into a tornado. Realistically speaking, I suppose it only makes sense that his family wants to meet me, although...don't they know about the ugly history between me and Bryce? Ares and Josh know for sure. They were at Harvard when it happened. I ran into them a few times later, and they both looked at me with loathing and contempt. The only reason they didn't punch me in the face was my gender.

Is this going to be some kind of dinner of disapproval? The family wants to warn me to be good to Bryce or else...? The judge said I was lucky to marry into the Huxleys because they're loyal, but he doesn't know the history. They'll never accept me as one of their own.

I run my clammy hands on my skirt, then stop. *Oh* shit*! I can't go like this.* I picked this dress because it was the most bridal-looking one, but they probably don't want to be reminded of my new status as Mrs. Bryce Huxley. I rush to the closet to find something else, but...

Jeans won't do. A blue wrap dress with a floral print in darker blue? I put it on and look at the mirror. Much better. And a pair of nude pumps. I redo my hair, twisting it into an updo. Reapply mascara and blush. Then I undo my hair and brush it vigorously. Still... Something's off.

By the time I'm done, my hair's in a French twist, and my apprehension is through the roof. There's no scenario under which his family's going to like me. Forget *like*. I'll settle for indifference. At least it won't be hate.

"Fiona...? I come bearing pizza and Diet Dr. Pepper!" comes Bryce's voice from below.

"Coming!" I say, checking the time. Five thirty. A little too early to eat, but then I realize I haven't eaten anything since breakfast. Suddenly I'm famished.

I hurry downstairs. The heavenly aroma of pizza laces the air. Bryce stands by the counter, in a black suit he wears like armor. My pulse accelerates at the slight slant of his eyebrows, the piercing, intelligent eyes and gorgeous lips—the only thing soft on him. The sight of the wedding band glinting on his finger has a combination of fluttery anticipation, guilt, wistfulness, remorse and something else warm and sweet I don't dare name pooling in my heart.

I want his family to not hate me with a keen, aching desperation. My fingers tremble, and I clench my hands to hide it. I promised myself to be the best wife possible, and refusing to meet his family would be breaking that vow.

He lets out a soft sigh, his eyes darkening with the desire I've come to recognize so well. “Damn. You look good enough to eat. Maybe we can skip the dinner.”

“No. Your family will be disappointed.”

“They can wait.”

“No.” *I don’t want them to hate me any more than they already do.* “Let’s have the pizza. I didn’t have any lunch.”

“You should’ve raided the fridge,” he scolds as he takes out two plates and glasses from the cabinets.

“Didn’t think about it. Next time.” I place a slice on a plate and hand it to Bryce, then serve myself as he pours the soda into two glasses full of ice.

We take the stools at the counter, the moment surprisingly companionable and homey. Over the pizza I can smell Bryce’s mint and woodsy scent. This hasn’t changed either in all the years since our time in college. Every cell in my body seems to relax. Sex was great back then, but I also missed peaceful time like this, when we could just be easy with each other and enjoy something as mundane as pizza and soda.

I take a small bite, then stop as something not so pleasant pops into my head. I hesitate for a second, but decide honesty is the best policy. “I forgot to tell you earlier, but Harvey approached me after you left.”

“What?” Bryce stiffens, his eyes roaming over me for signs of injury. “Are you okay?”

I nod, my heart warming at his protectiveness. “He didn’t hit me or anything like that. Much more civilized than your mother, actually. He said he’s the one who lent the money to Aaron, and I don’t need to pay it back because it’s a ‘wedding gift.’”

Bryce turns livid, the muscles in his jaw working. “*Son of a bitch.* Then what happened? What did you tell him?” he asks urgently.

“I told him no. He’s going to try to get something out of me. He even said I could give him something reciprocal. There’s no way I’m owing him anything worth two million, no matter what.”

“Good girl.” Bryce relaxes a little, then frowns. “I’ll take care of this. And the next time you see him—if there’s a next time—call 911 and report him for harassment. That’s the least he deserves.”

30

FIONA

THE SINGLE SLICE of pizza I nibbled on sits like a congealed lump of cheese and dough in my belly. Bryce, on the other hand, seems completely relaxed despite having eaten half the pizza.

"Is your stomach feeling okay?" I step out of the black Maybach he chose to take us to the dinner and lay my hand in his.

"Yeah. Why?" He peers at me. "Is everything okay?"

"I guess." It's probably just my anxiety. Bryce told me about the people I'm going to meet during the drive, but instead of soothing my apprehension, it only made my stomach churn worse.

How much do they know about our past, or the situation with Zoe? Everything? Nothing? I should ask, but every time I open my mouth, the words get caught in my throat. They probably won't like me or approve of our marriage...assuming they don't hate my guts already.

Bryce's parents' home is large and has an opulence that says *money* without appearing vulgar or overly materialistic. Next to the circular driveway in front of the main entrance is a small parking section for staff and visitors. A silver Maserati and a black Cullinan occupy two spaces. Although there are two more empty spots next to the cars, a red Lamborghini is parked sideways, blocking both.

"Yes!" Bryce says with a small fist pump.

I look at him. "What?"

"Aunt Jeremiah's already here. Which means we're free to leave whenever." He points to the Lamborghini. "That's her car, and she always parks like an asshole. Although if you tell her I said that, I'll deny it to my last dying breath."

I make a zipping motion across my mouth.

He grins, puts a hand at my back and escorts me inside through towering double doors. A massive tapestry hangs from the ceiling in the spacious foyer. Against the dark navy background, silver wolves snarl around a shield. Underneath are block letters.

"Pietas et unitas," I murmur.

"Loyalty and unity. The family motto," Bryce explains. "We live by it, we die by it. Family is everything."

"It was also on the cane in your house."

He nods. "It's custom made. Every Huxley gets one when they're born. A kind of welcome-to-the-family gift."

I take a moment to look at the coat of arms. If I were truly a Huxley by marriage, seeing PIETAS ET UNITAS would make my heart brim with joy. A painful sense of loss slips below my breastbone until it hurts to breathe. I can never have what the motto promises. I'm not worthy of it.

The wide hall that connects the foyer to the dining room has several windows facing a garden on one side, and displays of earthenware on the other. Each holds an intricate flower arrangement done in a style I've never seen before. The complete opposite of Sherry's preference of placing as many flowers as possible, the ones here have only a few flowers arranged in interesting lines and shapes. But they command a kind of focused attention that Sherry's don't.

The more steps I take, the more my gut twists. Foreboding grows until I feel like I'm about to hyperventilate and faint. *Oh my God, don't faint!* Talk about making a spectacle of myself.

It's just one meal. I can take a few bites and smile and praise the delicious food. That should hopefully make Bryce's stepmom not hate me too much. As for his dad... I'm not sure. He's a lawyer. So is his aunt. Everyone at Harvard has heard about the Huxleys for having been some of the most outstanding alumni. There's even a scholarship in their name for promising prelaw and law students.

Cold sweat slickens my back as Bryce and I reach the long table where seven people are already seated. I recognize Ares, and Josh of course, both of whom are in three-piece suits and regard me like a piece of gum stuck to the bottom of their priceless, hand-stitched Italian leather shoes.

This does not bode well.

At the head of the table sits a surprisingly ageless woman—although from the looks of it, she has to be the grandmother and head of the family, Catalina Huxley. The woman's hair is glossy black and knotted at the base of her head. A bit of blush adds some color to her otherwise smooth, pale skin. Her dress is also black—like she's attending a funeral.

To her left is a man who has to be Bryce's father Prescott. The man's sizable and imposing—I see where the brothers got their height and width. His eyes narrow and his lips purse. *Yup, definitely hoping to rip into me.*

A woman who must be the much-spoken-of Aunt Jeremiah is in a black pantsuit, a lit cigar in her hand and a glass of whiskey in front of her. She puffs out a perfect smoke ring as we enter, her eyes sharp as she scrutinizes me. The only person at the table who merely blinks with mild curiosity is a pretty blonde—Lareina, Ares's wife, in a lovely pastel-green dress. It's nice to have one person who maybe doesn't feel so terrible about our marriage.

An Asian woman in a gorgeous cream-and-pink kimono with intricate sakura embroidery comes over. She's petite with eyes that crinkle when she smiles. Fresh flowers pin her updo, and her spine is straight without looking stiff. Although she isn't a classic beauty, there's feminine charm to her that's irresistible.

"Bryce, you horrible child. You didn't even invite us to your wedding! Is this your lovely wife?"

He nods. "Fiona."

"Fiona?" Akiko gives me a polished smile. "What a lovely name. Mine is Akiko."

"Nice to meet you." The pizza's churning hard in my gut, but I manage an acceptable smile that doesn't scare her away. *Don't throw up, don't throw up.*

"And you. You're so pretty! Welcome to our home," she says sincerely.

Catalina's sharp eyes drop to my rings, then to my face. "Welcome to the family. I'm Catalina Huxley, Bryce's grandmother." She pulls me into a slightly stiff hug, then frowns. "You're shaking. Are you cold? Should we adjust the A/C?"

"Um, no." I hesitate, then opt for the truth with a tremulous laugh. "I'm a little nervous."

Ares and Josh both snort. Bryce shoots them a warning look.

"Oh, no need for any of that." Catalina runs her hands down my arms soothingly, which calms me a little. "We're civilized people."

"Prescott Huxley," Bryce's father says.

I nod hello and shake hands with him. His expression is wary. Does he think I'm going to hurt his son again? Just how does he know about what happened? "Bryce has told me so much about you."

"Really? He hasn't told me much about you." Prescott gives Bryce a look full of rebuke.

"You've been busy," Bryce says.

"I'm always busy, but I've never failed to make time for any of you."

Bryce shifts, clearing his throat. He turns to me. "Fiona, that's my aunt Jeremiah."

The polished redhead laughs softly, lifting her cigar in greeting. "Let's be honest. Bryce hasn't said a word about his new bride. Frankly, I'm shocked he turned up married today. Ares, and now Bryce?" She turns to Josh. "When are you going to elope? Next Tuesday?"

Josh shudders. "Never."

"Oh, that's right. You're searching for your soul mate."

"Yes. And when I find her, I promise I'll hold a grand wedding."

"I look forward to it." Jeremiah's wide smile says she doesn't believe a word.

The blonde next to Ares waves. "I'm Lareina. *Love* that dress! I'm an only child, so I'm excited to have a sister."

"Come. Sit and enjoy the dinner. I'm sorry the food won't be anything special. I didn't have much time," Akiko says.

"I'm sure it'll be fine," I say.

"I told Dad you could've hosted this tomorrow," Bryce adds.

Akiko shakes her head. "Nonsense. A new member of the family ought to be welcomed properly as soon as possible. We wouldn't want her to feel left out."

I just smile, unsure how to respond to such earnestness, especially when I can see Ares and Josh scrunching their faces out of the corner of my eye. Prescott and Jeremiah are difficult to read, and Catalina is too smooth to give away anything.

"Are we getting pizza?" Bryce asks.

His brothers look up with sudden interest. Even Jeremiah's eyes sparkle a little.

"*Pizza?*" Akiko looks horrified. "Takeout, for a formal family dinner?"

The two men visibly deflate. Jeremiah looks away, puffing her cigar.

Bryce and I sit across from Prescott, Akiko and Jeremiah. Bryce pours some sake for me, then leans over. "Akiko has the best sake and plum wine, cold or warm, doesn't matter. The food tonight, though... I'm not sure. I've never seen her demur about it so much."

"It's fine," I whisper back.

"So cute together!" Akiko says brightly. "So lovey-dovey."

I flush. Bryce laughs. "You think we're cute because you know I've been complimenting your alcohol."

"That too." Akiko grins as the first course is served.

I look down at the beautiful, large, white bone china edged with complex fleur-de-lis gold patterns. It's the kind of plate Sherry would be envious of. Some sort of dark purple sauce encircles two bite-sized slices of smoked duck, each topped with caviar and a dot of yellow sauce. I count five green alfalfa sprouts on the right to balance out the colors. On top of the sprouts is a thin line of orange-colored dressing.

If everyone else weren't getting the exact same thing, I might think that Akiko was trying to show how much I don't belong by starving me.

"You've outdone yourself, my love," Prescott says to his wife with a warm glow. Is he used to this kind of portion?

Ares cuts one of the slices in half with his knife and eats the tinier piece. Guess that's one way to stretch it out. *Oh wait.* He's swapping his plate with his wife. Why? Lareina looks at him like he's just single-handedly filled every hungry child's belly with delicious food. I glance at

Prescott and Akiko, wondering if plate swapping is some kind of family custom I'm not aware of, but they don't do that.

"If you want to start a new tradition, give half your food to Bryce," Josh says, his tone less than friendly.

"Don't be a jerk," Lareina says.

"Cut it out, Josh." Bryce turns to me. "Lareina can't eat food that hasn't been sampled first," he explains quietly.

"Seriously?" My eyes widen with shock. "Why? Did Zoe try to get you too?" I ask, then squirm when everyone's eyes focus on me. Maybe I wasn't supposed to mention her, like Voldemort.

Lareina gives me a small, reassuring smile. "No. My aunt and her family tried to poison me because I had an inheritance I was supposed to receive. So it's become a habit. I mean, I know the food here is fine. But it's a mental hangup."

"I understand." My voice softens with sympathy. "I hope your aunt and her family got what's coming to them." If reincarnation really exists like Sherry believes, they might be reborn as slugs.

"Oh yeah, they did." Lareina smiles, then rests her head on Ares's shoulder. "Thanks to my knight in shining armor here."

He kisses her temple. "Queen."

I flush, feeling like a voyeur. There's such emotional intimacy to their interaction.

"They're always like this," Akiko says dreamily. "Isn't that sweet?"

I nod, my throat clogged with longing and loss of my own. I had something close to this with Bryce, and it could've grown into something more if I hadn't shattered it with my own hands. I look down at them resting on the table, wishing I could go back in time. If I'd had the strength of character and experience I do now, I would've chosen differently.

Since most people are done, I pick up a fork and take a bite. *Mmm...* The food is very good—hard to believe she made it just this afternoon after finding out about Bryce and my marriage. Too bad she cooked so little.

The next course comes out: three slices of white fish, topped with a light brown sauce with a hint of freshly ground wasabi. Again, the plate is gorgeous—the kind you have to hand-wash—and enormous. To the right of the fish are little dots of green sauce and tiny blue, purple and pink flower petals laid out to look like a river flowing past a field of wild flowers. Very artistic. It must've taken Akiko so much time to plate this.

"This is a new design," Jeremiah remarks. "And the fish?"

"Suzuki. Japanese sea bream in English." Akiko turns to me. "You can't go wrong, believe me."

"I'm sure." I take a bite. The texture is firm and slightly chewy but delicious.

The rest of the dinner continues in the same vein. How did Akiko make all this? And according to her, what we're eating is a "non-luxurious" version because she didn't have enough time to really prepare. *So what's the fancy version?* I don't think I've ever been to a restaurant that plates this extravagantly.

But Bryce was right about the portions. Even after the tenth and final plate, I'm nowhere near full. No wonder he polished off half a pizza before coming over.

"So is there going to be an actual wedding ceremony?" Catalina asks, as the final plates are cleared.

Bryce says nothing.

I clear my throat. "Maybe in a couple of months..."

"Why the uncertainty?"

"Bryce is busy, and the nice venues are taken, and you know..." I shrug, glancing at Bryce, hoping he cuts in to stop his grandmother from wanting us to have a ceremony.

"A good venue?" Akiko waves a hand. "I'm sure I can pull some strings."

You don't have to be this helpful. "Oh, we couldn't possibly impose—"

"You're family! It's no imposition."

Prescott nods. I haven't seen the man shake his head even once at anything his wife's said. The obvious conclusion would be that he's whipped, but the man is too controlled and cool. He just likes to let his wife do whatever she wants.

For a second, I wonder if he was this indulgent with Zoe as well, and what made her throw that all away.

Suddenly the lights dim. I look around. Akiko is beaming,

although Ares and Josh seem less than thrilled. Whatever the reason, I'm glad for the distraction from all the talk about holding a ceremony.

A beautiful, round cake is brought out and placed in front of me. Flames on numerous candles dance. Swirly writing on the frosting says:

Happy birthday, Fiona Huxley!

I stare at it. Shock that Akiko knew and cared enough to put something like this together is followed by a sweet warmth. This is the first time I'm celebrating my birthday with a family—and it's *my* name on the cake, not Finley's.

Then, on cue, everyone starts singing "Happy Birthday." I look around—from Bryce...all the way to Jeremiah. Everyone is clapping and singing with a smile. Even Josh and Ares manage. It's nothing like the awkward celebrations I had with the Obermans: a forced smile on Zachary's face, desperate happiness radiating from Sherry, who had to believe her daughter was on a blessed path toward good reincarnation, and Aaron, who never bothered to hide how much he despised me for "stealing" his sister's place. And me, sitting there self-consciously and wishing I could sink into the ground, while a ridiculously elaborate and fancy cake with figurines of all the things Finley loved on top said, *Happy Birthday, Finn! We love you!*

Tears well up. I blink hard to keep them at bay, but the skin around my eyes grows hot, the air in my lungs thin. When the song ends and it's time for me to blow out the candles, everyone looks at me expectantly. I try to inhale, but the vise around my chest tightens. I can't.

I cover my face and burst into tears.

A heavy awkward silence descends. *Damn it. Great going, Fiona. You ruined the whole thing.*

I feel like an idiot, but I can't stop the tears. I cover my eyes with my hands, like an ostrich trying to bury its head in the sand.

Bryce's gentle hand strokes my back. I can feel the weight of concerned gazes on me.

Stop crying and show your gratitude. Be the kind of lovable girl who's worthy of such caring and attention.

But no matter how quickly I wipe the tears away, they keep rolling down my cheeks, soaking my face. A sense of failure presses down on me. All I had to do was smile and blow out the candles.

"I knew it." Josh's dark voice makes me tense as I wait for the rest of his uncensored disapproval.

Aaron's constant criticism from my early years rings in my head: *You never act right, you're stupid, you're such a loser, you're—*

"The cake's too small."

The absurdity of his annoyance cuts the flow of my tears. Laughter bubbles in my chest. Ares reaches over and smacks his shoulder. Prescott glares at Josh, then pats Akiko's back.

I shake my head, laughing and crying. "No, no... The cake's fine."

"Did I misspell your name?" Akiko asks. "Or maybe you don't want to take Bryce's last name? I can easily fix it..."

"No, I'm fine. Really. This is a perfect cake." My voice is nasal, and I sniffle. "I'm just so *touched*. That's all."

Bryce holds out a beautifully folded white handkerchief. I stare at it, unsure what to do. He sighs and tenderly runs it over my cheeks and chin, then places it on my nose. "Blow," he orders me.

I hesitate, but he gives me a go-ahead look. I take the soft fabric and blow my nose daintily. It's surreal to be taken care of like this. I realize then that I was never taken care of when I was growing up.

"Are you feeling better now?" Bryce asks.

My face heats with embarrassment. "Yes. Thank you." I turn to everyone. "Thank you so much. I just got so emotional."

"It's just a cake," Josh mutters.

"A perfect cake," I say, then blow out the candles.

"Make a wish," Jeremiah says with a soft smile. "A perfect cake might have more power than others."

Bryce, Ares and Josh look horrified at their aunt's statement.

"When did angels start possessing bodies?" Prescott says, staring at his sister like he doesn't recognize her anymore.

Akiko shakes her head. "Don't be mean, dear. Jeremiah's right." She turns to me with a motherly smile. "Make a wish."

I nod and close my eyes. The desire to belong to the Huxleys forever surges, but I don't dare ask for it. It's too precious. *Please protect and keep this family safe.*

I open my eyes and smile. "Thank you. This is the best birthday celebration ever."

"Better than the one I gave you before?" Bryce asks, eyebrows raised.

"That was different. It was just you and me. This is your family."

His eyes soften. "It's your family, too."

I look at him silently. One heartbeat. Two... Three... I know he's saying this for the sake of his family. He knows better than me that I don't belong, but I desperately want to pretend for the evening. So I smile. "Yes, they are."

31

BRYCE

THE CAKE IS DELICIOUS, but of course Akiko is an excellent baker. She could make a fortune with a bakery, but has zero interest in running a business.

Fiona's *reaction* to the cake was a little shocking. Although... I think back to the belated birthday dinner I gave her while we were dating at Harvard. She didn't cry, but she blinked a lot, and her eyes glistened quite a bit. So maybe she was holding back tears at that time, too...?

It's almost as if her family never celebrated her birthday, but how could that be? Or did Aaron get extra nasty with her on those occasions? It wouldn't surprise me a bit—he's always been a complete asshole.

The way her eyes looked sad even as she smiled and said the Huxleys were her family, too... It made my heart clench, and *I don't like it.* Her impact on my emotions is growing each day, while I'm nowhere near accomplishing my goal of getting her out of my system. Objectively speaking, I'm actually farther away from the target.

Still, damn it, I can't stay unmoved when she sheds tears like that. Not sure why, because when women cry, I usually just look away and pretend I'm not there. Otherwise, I feel like I'm getting a brain tumor.

But now, in the car, Fiona is beautiful with her cheeks glowing, her eyes bright. When we finally arrive back at our place, she sighs. "Thank you. Your family's wonderful."

Her brilliant smile hits me like a wrecking ball. I can't speak, so I do the next best thing—once we go inside, I pull out a box from the small gift bag hidden in a kitchen cabinet. I was going to give it to her before we left, but got distracted when she mentioned meeting Harvey.

She blinks, then flushes. "You didn't have to—"

"It's your birthday." I push the box toward her.

She opens the lid, then gasps, her jaw going slack. It's all I can do to suppress an urge to kiss her. "Oh *wow*..."

"It's..." I shrug. "Whatever."

Her eyes fly to my face. "*Whatever*?"

I shrug again to hide the urge to squirm under her incredulous gaze. I take the diamond choker off the dark velvet and place it around her neck. My fingertips brush her smooth skin, and heat uncurls in my gut. She smells amazing this close, all warm and sweet. A soft, rosy color spreads over her neck and chest. I follow the diffusion with the back of my index finger. A quick inhale, and the delicate veins in her throat work.

I start to lower my head to place a kiss on her neck, but she turns around to stare up at me, running her fingertips over the facets of the impeccably cut gems. The cool stones glitter as brilliantly as stars. The setting holding the large center rock in place has my initial on it, like a collar staking my claim.

A sudden possessive urge overwhelms me as I look into her soft green-gold eyes. The pulse on her throat throbs visibly, and she swallows.

"Thank you," she whispers.

I drop my eyes to her pillowy pink lips. "Thank me with a kiss," I murmur.

Her eyes linger on my mouth briefly before they rise to meet my gaze. Her eyebrows pull together as she hesitates. My heart pounds with anticipation. *She's going to kiss me.*

She lowers her hand from the stones to the dress and starts to unbutton. The outfit slides down her body and pools around her feet.

Reaching back, she unhooks her bra and lets it fall as well. At the sight of her beautiful, soft body, fire burns in my belly, even as bitter disappointment drips into my veins like acid.

She unbuckles my pants, bringing them down my legs along with my underwear. Her hand wraps around my thick shaft, which pulses visibly inside the tight hold.

"I don't have to thank you with a kiss," she says, pumping my dick in her fist.

"I want your mouth on me." *Kiss me, damn you.*

Something dark and unreadable flicks across her stubborn face. "Well then." She drops to her knees, then looks up at me, her eyes challenging. My choker glitters around her throat.

The sight is erotic as hell. Every drop of blood in my veins heats and flows to my cock. It aches so much that I let out a low hiss. At the same time, part of me is vaguely dissatisfied.

Her hot breath caresses the tip, the feathery sensation sizzling along my nerves. She strokes me up and down in smooth motions, brushing her thumb across the top of my cockhead, smearing the precum.

Sorceress. She's trying to bewitch me, and I couldn't stop her even if the world was burning. Her tongue flicks out and licks the clear fluid from my slit. White-hot pleasure streaks along my spine. Her mouth curves into a wicked grin, but I want her lips to smile like that while they're on mine.

She pulls the tip into her mouth. *Fuck.* My eyes roll back at how wet and hot her mouth feels around my dick. She hollows her cheeks to create a delicious suction that leaves me panting with the need for more and starts to bob her head.

Somewhere in the back of my mind is a voice that screams she's manipulating me to deny me what I want. My heart pumps with raw desire and frustration. Her eyes are on me, eager and gauging my reaction. She changes pressure and tempo to maximize my pleasure. If I hadn't asked her for a kiss—hadn't craved it—I'd be enjoying myself. But I can't.

It's impossible to decide if what I want from her right now is just another satisfying orgasm or a kiss on the mouth—an indirect admission that she likes me, even if it's just a little. I can't explain why I'm so obsessed with her kissing me, why I'm so angry and disappointed that she won't do it when she's already sucking me off so beautifully.

I pull out, gently cradle her cheeks and tilt her face up. "Kiss me, Fiona."

Indecision flashes in her green gaze, but then she shakes her head.

"Kiss me," I order her, my voice firmer.

"No." She grips my hips and pulls me back into her mouth.

I tighten my jaw, reveling at how good she feels and hating her for making me beg. *Fine*. I'll give her what she she's asking for.

I loop her long hair around my fist, holding her head still. She raises a questioning eyebrow. Instead of answering, I move my pelvis, thrusting in and out, showing her that her mouth has no use except for mouth fucking for my pleasure only, just like she insisted. She doesn't resist, even though I'm so deep that the head of my cock is bumping against the back of her throat. She merely looks up at me, eyes watery but still stubborn, as her breathing grows rougher.

Air saws in and out of my lungs. An orgasm is fast approaching, crawling along my spine. I tense. A small voice in the back of my head says I should stop, but the part that feels rejected and unwanted doesn't want to. Maybe I want to punish her, or maybe I want to punish myself—even when I get to come inside her mouth, my heart feels hollow.

When the climax comes, I let it go and spill into her throat. She manages to swallow most of it, but toward the end, she chokes a little.

"Swallow it all," I command.

She tries, but some drips from the corner of her mouth and falls on the choker. I hook my index finger between the diamonds and her neck and pull her up. She rises steadily to her feet. I rub the pad of my thumb at the edge of her mouth, spreading the cum. Seeing my mark on her soothes my nerves, but only a little.

"Kiss me."

She shakes her head. "No."

"Why not? Is your kiss that precious?"

"I already told you, I can't."

The anger finally erupts. "You kissed me plenty of times!"

She turns her head away.

Grabbing her chin, I turn her head back to face me. "Don't look away when I'm talking to you."

"That was different. I've changed, and so have *you*. We aren't the same anymore," she says, her voice breaking slightly.

What I hear is, *I have no feelings for you, not like before*. My heart aches unbearably. I steel myself, keeping my tone hard. "Do you honestly believe that nonsense?"

"Don't you?" She wraps her hand around my wrist and lowers it from her chin. "Bryce, we already agreed on what this relationship would be. Even when we do things that blur the baseline rules, the fundamentals don't change. This ends in two years, and I don't want to make things more complicated by crossing the lines. Let's keep our boundaries, okay?"

"Don't you think that, if you're going to thank me, you should thank me the way *I* want?"

"I think pretty much any man would agree that what just happened is worth more than a kiss. Don't you?"

"You don't know what I value." If she did, she wouldn't have gutted me like that when we were in college. *College sweetheart*. How innocuous it sounds, yet how fatal. My eyes drop to her mouth, then to her breasts, noting the pointed tips and the flush on her chest. "Looks like you enjoyed sucking me off."

I push my hand into her panties, stroking my middle finger along the folds from her clit all the way to the opening of her pussy. She's scorching hot and wet. When I push my finger inside, her eyelids flutter shut, and she bites back a moan.

"Let me hear you. If you aren't going to use your mouth to kiss me, use it to moan like the slut that you are."

I slowly pump my fingers in and out of her, stoking her fire without giving her enough to bring her to orgasm. She grips my arms, digging her fingers in, clinging. She rocks her hips to increase the pressure and tempo, but I retreat.

She lets out a frustrated sound. "This isn't going to make me kiss you."

"I don't give a damn anymore," I say, resuming my actions, pushing two fingers inside while the pad of my thumb gently teases her pulsing clit.

"Bryce," she begs. "Now you're being cruel."

I laugh—she's the one who's been heartless. I don't even think she hates me anymore—she did at first, but not anymore. She seems to see me as some kind of outlet for her desires, a fucktoy. I don't know why that makes me so furious when I felt exactly the same way about her and decided to lend her money explicitly so I could fuck her out of my system.

Her knees tremble, then finally buckle. I catch her and roll, minimizing the impact. My fingers invade her again, this time three at once. She lifts her hips off the floor and tries to move them against me, but I hold her pelvis.

"Behave." I rip the lacy panties, revealing the slick, flushed flesh. How can she be this wet and needy and still say no to a simple kiss? I blow on her quivering flesh. Her muscles tense beneath my palms. I lean in to claim her mouth, but she turns her head away. I press my lips on her throat, then trail along the edge of the choker, palming her right breast and pinching the nipple between my index and middle fingers just the way she likes.

Her spine arches. She moves her legs restlessly against me, her scorching core rubbing against my exposed cock, which starts to swell. She pants, tunneling her fingers into my hair. I place kisses along her cheeks, then down at the corner of her mouth. She quivers, but doesn't turn away.

Yes.

Triumphant, I glide my lips over—

An abrupt ringing startles her. She puts a hand on my mouth, then turns away.

What the hell? I glare at her phone, wanting to shatter it into bits of plastic. "Ignore it," I say, but she fumbles for it with the desperation of a person lost in a desert seeking water. *Fuck, fuck, fuck.*

The lusty haze clears from her eyes as she hits the green button without checking who's calling. The violent urge to vent my frustration and fury rages in my heart, and I take a deep breath to control my temper.

"What the fuck is this? You never called to see how I was doing after that fucker hit me! Do you know what happened to me?"

Jude's voice. Fiona turns red, white, then red, her eyes flashing. *Hang up,* I mouth, but she shakes her head. I narrow my eyes and pinch her nipple hard. She bites back a gasp and glares at me.

"Oh, did something happen to you? To your widdle weg?" she coos, but then the coo turns into a snarl. "I hope he *broke your fucking knee*!"

Whoa. The tone cuts through my lust like a laser. I've never heard her talk like that, not even when I got extra nasty with her. Since it's directed at that son of a bitch, I pull her left nipple into my mouth to reward her.

She grips my head. Instead of pulling me away like I half expected, she holds me tight.

"Shut your mouth, you bitch. I can only indulge you so far!"

"Should I be grateful?" She's a bit breathless.

I suck harder and push three fingers into her even wetter pussy.

"Tomorrow's my birthday. I expect you to come to the party with a suitable present. Don't make me lose face this time. The only reason I'm not punishing you for the wedding is because Bryce attacked me and took you away."

"Actually, I took his hand in marriage," she says, panting. "And you don't have to wait until tomorrow for your present. I'm going to give it to you right now. I'm going to let you hear what I sound like when I'm *not faking it*."

I remove my fingers and pull away, wondering what the hell she's saying. Jude never made her come? *In two years?*

"In case it's not clear, I never, ever climaxed with you. Not once. I just faked it so you'd stop grunting over me like a disgusting pig. You're a worthless human being. And about as hot as an ice machine in Antarctica."

Jude shouts expletives, and I snort with mirth. The more furiously he shouts, the more satisfied I become. When she'd just betrayed me, I tormented myself for months thinking about what my shortcomings could've been—wondering if he was better in bed than me.

Scoffing at his tantrum, she puts her own fingers into herself, her eyes on mine, and cups her breast, toying with her nipple, still wet from my mouth.

Defiance and vengeful satisfaction glitter in her eyes, and my dick is harder than stone. I grip my shaft tightly and move my hand up and down, imagining shoving it into her tight pussy as I claim her mouth. "Rub your clit if you want to feel even better."

"What the fuck?" Jude's scream comes from the speaker. "Who the fuck are you with?"

She shifts her hand so she can move her pelvis and grind her clit against her palm. She breathes harder, her mouth slack with rising pleasure. But frustration glitters in her eyes—she can't quite bring herself to an orgasm. Her fingers aren't long enough to hit the most sensitive spot inside her. She's going to need something longer and thicker inside her or need a vibrator.

I push her hand out of the way, then violently drive into her in one hard stroke. She groans. I drive into her relentlessly, gripping her hips and angling her so I'm hitting her G-spot with each thrust. She writhes, her back arching. Her pretty tits rebound with each push, and I take the left nipple into my mouth and suck hard.

She screams as a climax sweeps over her. Her pussy spams around me. Another orgasm barrels toward me. I pull out and pump into my fist. My cum hits her still-quivering belly. Damn, she's infuriating, but when she's flushed and lax with the peak I just gave her, covered in my cum and wearing nothing but my choker and heels, it's like I can almost forgive her for everything.

"That's how she sounds like when she comes with my cock inside her," I say, then end the call. Hopefully Jude just died from blowing a vein or two in his head. "Did you like that?" I jerk my chin at the phone.

"It was satisfying. I should've told him that a long, *long* time ago."

I frown. "You never came with him? Ever?"

"No." She shifts, her eyes unreadable.

"But you guys were together for two years."

"So? That doesn't mean he was good in bed."

I feel utterly confused. I always assumed she left me for him because he was at least decent in bed. I've driven myself crazy thinking about it. "What did you see in him?"

"Nothing."

"But—"

She places a finger over my mouth. "Sometimes a relationship isn't about what you see in the other person. It was just"—she sighs, her shoulders slumping a little—"really complicated."

32

FIONA

AWKWARD, awkward, awkward. Bryce leaves for work at crack of dawn, and doesn't return until well after I fall asleep. The bed's indented next to me, so I know he came back at some point during the night. Otherwise, I might suspect he's sleeping at some hotel.

On the other hand, we agreed to share the same bed each night, and he isn't the type to go back on his word. Is he sulking about the kiss?

When he put the choker around my neck and wished me happy birthday, I could barely stop myself from crying again. The small celebration at his parents' house was his doing. He's the only one who'd remember.

I vowed I'd never care about anybody ever again, but he keeps testing my resolve. Part of me wants to take the leap, but the bigger part—the one that's paranoid about self-preservation—says no. If things go wrong...if my heart is ripped to shreds again after falling for Bryce *again*, I'm never going to recover. The first time was difficult enough. I'm not fully over the ordeal—so many scars still mar my soul.

Is Bryce upset because he believes I used him for my petty revenge against Jude over the phone? Once the highly charged moments passed, logic reasserted itself. I recognize what I did was immature...*albeit sooo satisfying.*

Since the ground rules of our marriage don't say anything about my getting a job, I send out a few résumés for marketing positions. If I'm going to be in L.A. for two years, I need to have a routine, with a job, so I'm not wasting my life sitting at home. Plus, I don't want to use Bryce's money if I can help it. We are technically married, but it feels wrong to touch the credit cards he left out on the kitchen counter.

A week later, I head to a café to meet with Akiko, whom I was hoping to see again. With me is a huge bouquet of pink peonies and hands clammy with nerves. Crimson red roses caught my eyes at the flower shop, but they wouldn't fit the muted, elegant décor of her home. Hopefully Akiko likes them. I gave flowers to Sherry all the time, but she never seemed to really see the bouquets. It wasn't until later that Zachary told me to stop because Finley never gave her flowers, and it made her feel uncomfortable. Since then, I've never bought flowers for anybody. But I didn't want to meet Akiko empty-handed, and I don't know her well enough to pick something else.

Located on the first floor of the Aylster, Merry is an opulent café done with sparkling golden marble and a fresh flower centerpiece on each table covered with a thick white cloth. Crystal chandeliers hang from the high, airy ceiling. Classical music flows from the sound system. Very classy. Very expensive.

I spot Akiko in a booth. She's in a chic sage-green dress and matching jacket. Black pearls hang from her earlobes and circle her neck. I'm glad I put on a cream-colored top and floral apricot skirt. Otherwise, I'd feel underdressed.

She stands and hugs me. "Thanks for coming out to see me, my dear."

"Hello, Akiko." I hug her back, then shift my weight awkwardly and present the flowers. "Here. For you."

Her eyes widen, and she lets out a soft exclamation. "Oh my. They're gorgeous. Thank you!" She buries her nose in the peonies. "They smell so good. I love them."

Some tension in my shoulders loosens. Although in my head I knew she wouldn't openly reject the flowers, deep inside I was braced for it.

She studies my face with concern, then relaxes. "You look well."

"Thank you." I flush as we sit down at the booth. "Sorry I made you worry at dinner the other night. I shouldn't have broken down like that."

"Not at all. You should let it out. It isn't healthy to hold everything inside. Besides, if you can't let go with your family, who *can* you do it with?" She pats the back of my hand.

A server comes over to take our order. Akiko gets green tea, and I opt for milk tea. She purses her lips. "Let's also get some dessert trays. They're so good here." She requests a set of tiered trays with two of everything.

"That's way too much, isn't it?" I ask in surprise. Given how little she served at the dinner, I don't suppose she's going to eat more than a bite or two.

"I like to try what they have on offering. We can split them, so it won't be that much." She gives me a mischievous smile. "Just between you and me, I'm obsessed with desserts. It's just that I try not to overeat because diabetes runs in my father's family. But since it's our first mom-and-daughter date, I believe it's correct to splurge."

A tight, hot knot forms in my throat at the easy way she calls me her daughter. I inhale to regain control of my emotions. *I* refuse *to cry again!*

The waiter returns with our drinks. He places two gorgeous white porcelain pots filigreed with silver on the table, then expertly pours the green tea into the matching cup for Akiko and does the same with the Ceylon tea for me, then sets a miniature jug of fresh organic milk beside my tea. Then comes a huge silver frame holding five trays laden with various mini-desserts.

"Wow." I was here a couple of times before with the Obermans, but never had their desserts. Apparently, Finley never did because Sherry was worried about cavities, so I wasn't allowed to have any either.

Akiko takes a bite of a chocolate mousse. "Mmm. It's good. Have some."

I pick up the other piece. The rich cream fills my mouth, and I close my eyes in bliss. "This is a*ma*zing."

She sighs softly. "If they'd just get their green tea right, the place would be marvelous."

I glance at her teacup. Unlike most green tea, it's actually verdant green. "What's wrong with it?"

"Just a little off. I can see why Bryce complained about it." At my curious gaze, she adds, "He's always disappointed with green tea in America, so he just sticks to coffee. He got spoiled because my mother introduced him to how green tea ought to taste. She was a tea master. In *Kyoto*." Akiko smiles with pride. "A little unusual for a woman, but it was her dream and she achieved it."

"She must have been a lovely woman."

"She was. She doted on the boys, and they were very sweet to her. When she passed away, she included them in her will." Akiko's eyes mist. The affection in her gaze shines. "My cousins joked that she liked her *gaijin* grandsons more than her blood relatives, but I'm glad they had such a loving relationship."

"Your family sounds amazing."

"*Our* family," Akiko says. "You're Mrs. Bryce Huxley. Speaking of which..." She places a glossy black bag on the table. "For you."

I look at the unexpected offering with surprise and pleasure. I pat myself on the back for bringing the flowers.

"Open it," she says, her eyes twinkling.

I pull out a long black velvet box. It bears no logo. Inside are creamy pearls so lustrous they seem to glow from the inside. Studs, a necklace and a bracelet lie on the soft satin bed. My first instinct is to drop it like a hot potato, but I manage to place it gently on the table. "Thank you, but I can't possibly accept these. They're too valuable."

"Nonsense. They're for my daughter-in-law."

"But—"

"I gave a set to Lareina, too."

I'm not your real daughter-in-law. The words get stuck in my throat. The air in my lungs grows thin, and I bite my lower lip. "I...I don't think I should. I mean, Bryce and I—" I abruptly stop. What can I say to her about Bryce and me? The whole complicated and sordid truth? How it was supposed to be about two million and my paying it off with my body? Or that it'll end in two years and there won't be anything between us?

Embarrassment heats my face. The need to hide the real reason for rejecting the gift pulses hard in my skull. At the same time, I can't accept something I don't deserve. I don't want to deceive Akiko when she's been nothing but kind to me. "We're...complicated," I say finally.

Akiko laughs softly. "Fiona, every relationship's complicated. I suspect yours is even more so, with all the history between you."

I freeze for a moment. "Did...Bryce tell you?"

"He didn't have to say anything. I just knew when he told me your name." Akiko sips her tea. "He didn't come home for break his junior year. Josh told me he was busy, but I knew that was a lie. Bryce opted to spend the summer in Japan with his grandmother, and then he came home, looking more haggard than ever. And it wasn't because my mother fed him too little food. He just didn't eat. Then later, when he bought the house he lives in now and redid the backyard, he picked those shrub roses. I'm sure you saw."

I nod.

"When he chose them, I told him they wouldn't look as nice with the other trees and shrubs he had. I recommended calla lilies, hyacinths, daffodils and yellow chrysanthemums."

Her recommendations are on point. They would look prettier in the backyard, more prominent and noticeable.

"But he said he didn't want anything else. Do you know what that particular breed of rose is called?"

I shake my head.

"Fiona. They're called Fionas."

The revelation hits me like a hammer. I'm so dazed, I can't even blink as I try to process. Why did he want anything that would remind him of me in his backyard, which he could see every day from the living room? When I went to Wisconsin, I left everything that would remind me of my past in L.A. and did my best to never look back. If Zachary hadn't died the way he did or Aaron hadn't owed so much to the damn loan sharks, I wouldn't have contacted Bryce again.

"Did he know? About the roses?" My voice is hoarse.

"Yes. The landscaper told him before he finalized the order."

What on earth went through his mind when he made that decision? "Our breakup wasn't pretty." The understatement of the century.

"But he chose to have those roses. Don't you think that might mean your marriage to Bryce might not be as shallow as you imagine?"

I stare at her. "How do you know?"

She smiles warmly. "You didn't want to accept the pearls and said things are 'complicated.' You were so nervous that you were shaking at the dinner. You weren't just anxious about meeting his family, but about the entire marriage itself, right?"

I nod numbly.

"Fiona, if you believe it won't work out, it won't. Your thoughts and beliefs are seeds that sprout. They grow and bear the fruit you imagine them to bear."

The air in my lungs freezes. I've always thought that good things don't last. My life experiences have shown that over and over again since I was little. Not many kids get adopted only to be dumped. Or adopted again only to be told they're a tool so that somebody else can accumulate good karma for a dead girl. Every good thing comes with something equally bad—actually worse, because I've already tasted the sweetness.

But did I add to the problem by bracing for a bad ending? Could I have changed anything in my past by not being so fatalistic?

The notion is frustrating and scary. How can I ever be good enough to be worthy? It's a question I've struggled with for so long. It's disconcerting to hear that I should just *believe* I'm worthy.

My expression must alarm her a bit—she deftly turns the topic to what I'd been doing before I reunited with Bryce. She oohs and aahs over my job at the cheese company, saying how much she loves cheese. Her knowledge of various cheeses and how they're made is pretty impressive. She could easily work at my old company.

When I tell her so, she laughs. "No. I'm just happy being a housewife. It brings me joy to beautify our home, invent new recipes and invite the family over for dinner. I love it when they're well received, and every plate is polished off."

I don't have the heart to tell her that her sons would be licking the plates for the last drop of sauce out of hunger if it weren't considered rude. Besides, her cooking is amazing. Bryce finished every bite even after devouring half a pizza.

"If you want, I can teach you some of my simpler ones. Bryce is fond of kinpira renkon—stir-fried lotus root," she explains when I frown in confusion. "It's just that I rarely make it because it doesn't always go with my dinners."

"Sure. I'd love that."

Shockingly enough, we manage to decimate the desserts on the trays. Akiko sighs with satisfaction. "That was fun." She grins at me. "And delicious. We should do it again. Next time with Lareina. She's a hoot."

"I'd love that."

Akiko insists on picking up the tab, saying it's her prerogative as my mother-in-law. I offer to treat her next time, and we laugh and leave together.

As we spill into the lobby, I stop short. Sherry's there. She seems to have been unaffected by the wedding. The same serene expression, her thumb constantly moving the beads on her japamala. Aaron's debt apparently hasn't affected her—she's still in a designer dress and the Louboutin shoes she loves so much.

Her eyes flick to me, then to Akiko, eyebrows rising a bit at how closely we're standing together. I stiffen, feeling oddly like a man getting caught cheating.

"Hello, Finn."

Akiko tilts her head in curiosity and confusion.

"And this is...?" Sherry trails off, waiting for me to fill in the blank.

I tense as the need to please her and be perfect grips me, like some kind of ingrained conditioning. "Akiko."

"I'm Fiona's mother-in-law," Akiko elaborates, extending her hand smoothly.

Sherry takes a step back. Akiko drops her hand with a puzzled look.

"Mother-in-law?" Sherry turns to me, her voice suddenly taut. "When did you get married?"

"Last week." I clear my throat, then quickly add, "Sorry you weren't invited. It was rather sudden. But literally nobody was invited. It wasn't just you."

"Who's the groom?"

"Bryce."

"That Huxley boy?"

"Yeah." I indicate Akiko with a sideways nod. "This is Akiko *Huxley*."

"I see." Sherry blinks a few times, processing the information. It must be a shock. After all, I was supposed to marry Jude not too long ago. She abruptly spins around and starts to walk away.

"Wait!" I can't let her go like this, when I don't know how upset she is.

She stops, but doesn't turn around. "What is it?"

"Are you...upset with me?"

A moment of silence. "No. I'm fine. We don't have the kind of relationship in which you need my permission to pursue your own happiness. Besides, it's good karma for Finley. You did well, and so did I." She squeezes my hand, then walks away.

I stare at her retreating back. She sometimes says things that don't make much sense, but this is a new height of incomprehensibility. Zachary hated it when I questioned her, so I quit probing. But I wish I could figure out what's going on in her head. What does marrying Bryce have to do with Finley's karma?

"Are you all right?" Akiko says.

"Yes." I turn to her and manage a smile. "I think so."

"Is your mother always so...unique?"

I almost laugh at her word choice. "I guess." Still, I can't shake off the feeling that something's off with Sherry...except I know she won't tell me anything.

33

BRYCE

"Bryce, your uncle is on the line," comes Amélie's voice on the intercom.

I stop in the middle of reviewing a memo one of the junior associates drafted. "My uncle? Who?" There's only one person who calls me at the firm and has the nerve to claim to be my uncle. But Ted Lasker has no business with me. The last I heard, he was busy trying to convince Aunt Jeremiah to sue some rival of his.

"Someone named Harvey Dunkel," Amélie clarifies. "You never told me you had—"

"Five minutes." Normally I'd decline, but it's time to resolve the matter of "the gift" he gave my wife. I put him on speaker and lean back in my chair, my fingers steepled.

"You and Fiona are a stubborn pair," he says, his voice gravelly.

"And you are a persistent pest."

He snorts. "Is that how you speak to your uncle? Show some respect to your elders," he chides me, although there's no heat. He doesn't expect me to give a shit about him or anybody from his side of the family.

"Earn it first," I say flatly. "But first cash the fucking check!" I delivered it international express with tracking to his "official" address in Nesovia, and he sent it back. *Twice*. Bastard.

"Why do you insist on rejecting my gift?"

"Because inside the pretty wrapping is a ticking time bomb."

"I'm not like your mother."

I stiffen. "You want to use me—and Fiona—as much as she does. My wife doesn't need to be indebted to anyone."

"You don't think I can be altruistic?" He sounds hurt, which only makes me want to laugh.

"No. If you had the chance, you would've killed your other brother before Mom could. You're that kind of asshole."

He ignores my jab. "What do you think I'll ask for in return?"

"Don't know and don't care. Neither does my wife. You stay away from us, Harvey."

"And if I don't?"

"I can make things very difficult for you."

He laughs. "You threatening to side with *Zoe*?"

"Don't think that'll be necessary. But maybe I should just go ahead and visit Vincent on my own, and convince him to disown both of you. He's gotta be sick of your antics by now, and I can help him draft the paperwork."

A sharp edge slips underneath Harvey's seeming bonhomie. "You think it's easy to take over an operation as large and complex as what the family controls?"

"Can't be any harder than dealing with you. Accept the check, Harvey, or I'm telling Vincent you abused my wife."

"That's a fucking lie!"

"One of many that have been told in this whole thing." I hang up, then instruct Amélie to block all calls from Harvey.

I finish reviewing the document, then sigh. I don't have anything to do. I should probably go home, but I keep hesitating. I hate it that I begged Fiona to kiss me, begged her for what little crumbs of affection she could spare.

Humiliation burns, and I resist an urge to tunnel my fingers into my hair and scream and kick. Just what the hell was I thinking? This was supposed to be about sex, not about me embarrassing myself. She made herself crystal clear when she dropped to her knees instead.

Too intimate. It's almost like I like you.

I haven't been able to bear facing her since then. How would she look at me? With pity and contempt, most likely. Her eyes would say, *I didn't know you could be so craven*.

At the same time, I can't stay away from her indefinitely. We share a home. We have rules.

Besides, I keep thinking about what she said: *Sometimes a relationship isn't about what you see in the other person. It was just...really complicated.*

What kind of complication would make her stay with a guy who left her dry as a bone for two years? It wasn't like he was good to her *outside* of bed. I wasn't the only one who noticed how badly Jude treated her. The only thing anyone could think of was that he must be a stud in bed for her to stick with him, especially since she didn't even need money.

I stare at the clock on my laptop, then finally close it and stand up. Damn it, it's my house. I shouldn't have to avoid it. As for Fiona's remark, I'll just find a good opportunity to broach the topic and ask her to explain. She probably wasn't in the mood to go into it earlier. We were both overwrought, and I wasn't in the most receptive mode at the time.

My mind made up, I head out. The underground garage is half-full. I spot the red Lamborghini, as usual taking up two spaces rather than one near the elevator. Can never decide if Aunt Jeremiah does it just for giggles or because she's really that terrible at parking. It's incongruent given how capable she is and how much she loves the law.

I stride past it to my Maybach. I left the Ferrari, Lamborghini and Maserati in the garage for Fiona should she need to go out.

"Bryce Emmanuel Huxley!"

I freeze at the nightmarish shriek. *It can't be Mom, it can't—*

The sound of shoes rapidly slapping concrete echoes through the garage. "*How* could you marry that whore? She works for Harvey!"

I turn to see Mom running toward me. Her blue eyes glow with a wildness that chills my blood. I feel like I'm back twenty-two years ago. She radiated the same zealous determination when she tried to kidnap me. I clench my hands to stop the fine tremor from starting. Mom will never see how she affects me, never.

"He's making her do his bidding for two million dollars!" she says shrilly.

"You need better spies." I stand up straight. "And Fiona's not a whore, she's my wife. Show some respect."

"I'm your *mother*!" she says, stopping in front of me.

The reminder makes me want to strangle her. If there weren't any security cameras in the garage, I might actually do it. "I don't give a shit who or what you are. What are you going to do?" My voice shakes with rage and the old guilt that I'm the reason Ares couldn't escape her. "Kidnap me and try to burn me alive, like you did to Ares?"

Mom goes pale. "That was an *accident*!"

"Accident, my ass! He's completely fucked in the head because of you. I'm a mess because of what you've done!"

"*I love you!*" she screams as though saying it louder will make it true and excuse all her madness. "I did it for us—for our family! I thought you'd understand. You've always been a good boy! Understanding and sweet and—"

Familiar fury surges at the tired defense. "Stop trying to manipulate me! I'm not your good-boy puppet anymore! Everything you did *ruined this family*!" I bite out. "You're the worst thing that ever happened to us!"

She staggers like I actually did hit her. But the shock fades almost immediately, replaced by wrath. Her face goes crimson. She slaps me hard enough to turn my head.

My cheek burns, and the corner of my mouth stings. I run the pad of my thumb over the spot and see blood. "So much for love."

"It's *your* fault. I'm doing my job as your mother to discipline you."

"Mother?" I laugh at her. "You haven't been my mother since the day you decided to kidnap us."

She pales. "Bryce—"

"Don't ever approach me again. Or my wife."

"And if I do?"

"I'll kill you," I say quietly.

She sneers. "You wouldn't dare. You and the rest of the goody two-shoes men in the family can't do anything out of the box. Gotta toe the line, don't you? You've always been a rule follower. A perfect child."

"Yeah, you're right. I love rules—know them all by heart, including dozens of ways I can get off on technicalities," I say. "I fantasized about it while studying at Harvard Law. Had a lot of time to think about it, figure out the best way, just like you." I take half a step forward, getting in her face. "You might think you're tough, but that only works with a loser like Aaron. Not me."

Mom's chest heaves as she glares at me. Resentment flashes in her eyes as she realizes she can't control me like she used to. I don't buy into her vision of the family. I'm no longer her "good boy."

"You aren't invincible," she says finally. "You have weaknesses."

The way her mouth twists with bitterness brings forth the image of my wife in shock and pain after meeting my mother. "If you ever appear in front of my wife again, I'll break your legs. If you touch her, I'll break your hands."

"You wouldn't dare—"

"Try me, Mother."

She gives me a hard stare. I meet it squarely, unblinking. As the moments pass, her face scrunches. "Oh my *God*. You have feelings for that bitch, don't you?"

My eyebrow twitches. "What are you talking about?"

"What am I talking about?" Mom lets out a mocking laugh. "You care about your wife so much, you want me to give her respect. Give her *space*." She glares like I just plunged a knife into her heart.

I grimace, not wanting to admit that she's right about anything. But what else explains my reaction to Fiona?

Would it be better if I deluded myself? *No*. I don't believe in living a lie, no matter how pretty and convenient. *Fuck*.

"You have no idea what you're talking about. I'll say it again: stay the hell away from me—*and* Fiona—or next time it won't just end with a warning."

34

FIONA

I ORDER a pepperoni and sausage pizza for dinner and stare out at the crimson roses in the backyard.

What was going through his mind when he chose those roses? Was his reason as romantic as Akiko believes? It's possible I meant so little to him that he didn't care what the roses were called. But if that were the case he wouldn't have been so nasty when I barged into his office to borrow money...

Did I make a mistake in trying to put up a huge shield against Bryce out of fear? Am I acting in ways *right now* that might sabotage my happiness? If I'd opened up a little after meeting him again, would things be different between us?

The door opens, and I turn around. Bryce walks in, holding a pizza. I stare at him. The man is as gorgeous as ever in a dark navy pinstripe three-piece suit that molds to his body perfectly, his mustard tie impeccably knotted. Dark circles underneath his eyes don't take away the beauty of his face, which has to be blessed by the gods, because nobody should be that stunning.

His full mouth quirks in a small smile. "Took it directly from the delivery guy. Hope you don't mind."

He turns and places the pizza on the counter. My heart freezes at the sight of a long red gash on his cheek and a small scab in the corner of his mouth.

"What happened to your *face*?" I shriek, rushing toward him. I rise to my toes to study the wound, but he's too tall. I drag him to one of the stools at the counter and push him down onto it.

"Tilt your head so I can see better." *Not an accidental scratch for sure.* It's too deep and too straight. And the bloodied lip? Has to be intentional. "Who did this to you?"

He pulls back a little. "Whoa, calm down."

"I *am* calm!" I shout, then click my teeth closed. I clear my throat. "Sorry."

"Better now?" he asks.

"Tell me the other guy went to the ER. Or at least that you're going to sue him to death. You're a lawyer. You can do it for free."

Bryce laughs. "It's best not to be your own lawyer. Too close to home."

"Fine. Your father can sue him. Or your aunt."

Warmth softens his eyes. "I appreciate the outrage, but it's okay."

"But look at that scratch! It's all bloody. Well, scabby now, but it must've hurt." I let out an exasperated sigh. Frustration and disapproval pile into my heart, one layer after another until I want to scream. What kind of asshole did this to him? And why hasn't he done something to it? At least put a bandage or something on it. "Let me get something for your cut."

"I'm fine."

"No, you aren't. I need a Band-Aid. Where do you keep them?"

He gives me a half-amused, half-confused look. "The first-aid kit is in the powder room by the staircase."

He starts to move. I put a finger on his chest and push him back into the stool. "Don't even think about it."

"My legs aren't hurt."

I glare at him. "Just *sit*." I go to the bathroom. The cabinet contains only a stainless-steel box with cute anime characters and the Thai Airways logo. I blink at the shockingly adorable box, then pop it open. Inside are some painkillers, individually wrapped rubbing alcohol swaps and Q-tips, cotton balls, Band-Aids, anti-itch cream for bug bites and a small jar of green ointment with a label in some foreign language. I bring the whole thing out. "Very cute," I say, pointing at the box.

"Would be better if you put on a nurse outfit," he says with a grin.

I shake my head. "So you can pounce on me before I can do something for your cheek? I don't think so."

"Priorities."

"Shut up."

"When a woman says, 'Shut up,' like that, it means she agrees."

Ignoring him, I open the box. "So. Which one?"

He points to the jar with the ointment. "This one. It helps heal open cuts." My gaze lingers on the rubbing alcohol. He quickly adds, "It also has some antiseptic properties."

"Okay." I pull out a Q-tip, dip it into the white ointment and dab it gently over the cut. "So. Who did this to you? A client who got mad because you lost a case?"

He shoots me a baleful look. "I don't lose cases." He sobers. "It was Mom."

I tense. "Zoe?"

"Yup. She was upset about our marriage." Taut fury seethes underneath the outwardly careless tone.

I press my lips together. *The woman is a menace.* "Is she going to harass us even though we're married?"

"I don't think so, no."

"But she hit you."

He shrugs. "It's nothing."

I hesitate, trying to find a diplomatic way to ask, but then there's no careful way to talk about it. "Did she...hit you before?" My voice is small.

"No." His eyes grow dim with disgust. "She wouldn't, as long as I was her *good boy*."

He sneers the last two words like he wants to go back in time and beat his younger self for being good. There's a strong urge to hug him and tell him he shouldn't be upset with himself for having been young and sweet, but the familiar fear of making myself too open and vulnerable holds me back.

"Look, I handled her." He lifts his eyes to mine, then points to his cheek. "It didn't hurt that much, and now"—he wraps his warm hand around my wrist—"it's quit hurting altogether."

My mouth dries as his thumb brushes over my pulse point. My belly flutters. I blink, trying to shut out the gush of sweet need and affection—

A loud growl shatters the moment. Bryce's ears turn red. I look at his belly, then his face. "No time for lunch?"

"I was working hard." Although his tone is somber, a bright gleam in his eyes betrays him. "Wanted to come home early to my wife."

I smile softly at his olive branch. "Did you?"

"I'm tired of coming home late." He wraps his arms around me and buries his face carefully on my chest. "I missed my wife."

I run my fingers through his soft, silky hair. "Want to split the pizza? Pepperoni and sausage. Even better than pepperoni alone."

"Sure. I'd love that." He tilts his head to look up at me, his eyes soft. When he's clinging like this, he doesn't look like a mean lawyer, but an adorable puppy wagging his tail, offering playful affection—and asking for it in return.

I bring out plates and some Diet Dr. Pepper. It's a good thing I ordered a large, because Bryce mows through three-quarters of it like he hasn't seen food in ages.

We chat easily, Bryce telling me some gossip from the firm, keeping the conversation light, like he doesn't want the darkness of encountering his mother invading our time. "How about you?" he asks. "What'd you do today?"

"I got together with Akiko. She's lovely."

"Oh. Well, that's nice. Yeah, she's amazing. The best mom we could ask for."

I nod. "She told me a lot of things." I hesitate, but my gut says *this is the opportunity.* If I let it go, I may never get another chance. "Like about the roses outside. That they're called Fionas."

Bryce stops for a second, then resumes chugging down the soda. "Yeah."

"Why did you choose those, knowing their name?" I ask softly.

He opens and closes his mouth a few times as though searching for an acceptable explanation. Finally, he wipes his hands with a napkin, then grabs a bottle of whiskey from his liquor cabinet and pours a glass. "Remember how I told you Mom tried to kidnap me and my brothers—and succeeded with Ares?"

I nod, leaning forward a little and hoping the story isn't going to be too dark and harrowing.

He knocks back the glass, pours another, then drains it too. Air shudders out of him, and he rubs his face. "Grandma and Dad were worried, so they hired a therapist to help us. When the first one didn't seem to work, they hired more. They went through several prominent doctors to heal us. I had Gardy to help me cope, but early on, she wasn't enough. That's when Dr. Wellington—my last therapist—told me I should try to find at least one beautiful thing in my life every day. It could be anything, but it had to be beautiful enough to make me stop and notice.

"Well, I gradually got better, mentally, and quit spending so much of my time trying to look for beautiful things. But the habit must've stuck, because sometimes I just stop in the middle of whatever I'm doing and have to appreciate it if I see something especially lovely.

"When I was younger, I was sometimes invited to Ted Lasker's place. You know, the movie producer? He and Aunt Jeremiah had a thing once, and they have a son together, which is why she still admits he exists. Anyway, he has this unbelievably gaudy house with even more ridiculously gaudy gardens where he likes to throw extravagant parties. At one of those, I was stuffing myself with pastries, trying to pretend I wasn't upset about the fact that my grandfather didn't think I was important enough to deserve justice. It was right after I'd learned the truth about what happened to Mom after the clusterfuck of the kidnapping."

My heart breaks for the young Bryce. I wish I could go back in time and hug him and tell him things were going to be okay. That the pain would pass, he'd heal and become the amazing man I'm blessed to know.

"As I was gorging myself and trying not to seethe with anger, I saw some bright red roses I'd never noticed before. They were so pretty and cheerful that my fury and resentment disappeared, and all I could think about was how nice the flowers were. I asked Ted's assistant what variety they were. And he said, 'Fiona.'"

My breath catches.

"Then, years later at Harvard, when the vet called and said that Gardy had been seriously hurt in a hit-and-run accident, I was devastated. And at his office, he told me you'd saved Gardy, I just couldn't look away from you. You made me feel the same emotions as the roses. It was like time stopped, the world quieted down...and I was okay again."

I press my knuckles against my teeth, feeling a sharp pang in my heart.

"You said your name was Finn, and it just didn't suit you at all. But then you said that was what everyone *called* you. And when your real name turned out to be Fiona, it felt a little bit like fate." He lets out a self-deprecating chuckle. "I know it sounds dumb, but back then...that was honestly what went through my mind. You're like a little rose that careless people might miss, but once somebody notices, they can't look away. The rose that comforted an angry, devastated teenage boy."

"Not dumb," I manage hoarsely. My eyes burn with tears, my heart aching with guilt and love.

I never understood his pain, the reason he fell for me. I thought it was just gratitude at first, then chemistry—because God knows every time we saw each other, the air sizzled. I knew there must've been some affection, but I never knew he put me on the same pedestal as the roses that gave him comfort when he needed it the most.

I should've told him I couldn't be honest about Jude's blackmail because I loved him desperately and wanted him to love me back. Now I'll never know if Bryce would've loved me if I'd told him everything honestly. Would a rose trod on by another man be just as beautiful in his eyes as the day before, when it was still blooming flawlessly?

The wall around my heart crumbles. I've been fighting a losing war all this time.

My hands grip the lapels of his jacket. His eyes go wide as I crush my mouth against his.

35

BRYCE

My heart stops. Every cell in my body freezes.

Am I dreaming? I've been obsessing about her lips for so long. I've fantasized about her taste, and it killed me to lie next to her in bed these last few days, my entire being consumed, burning to kiss her. The need was so great, I'd have traded my soul for it.

She made it clear she would only kiss me if she liked me, but that it would never happen. As much as I pushed her to change her mind, she's impossible to budge once she makes a decision. But if she weren't stubborn, she wouldn't be the girl I fell for at first sight. Or the woman I can't quit thinking about.

Now that the kiss is happening...

My mind disintegrates with her lips on mine. She licks the seam of my mouth, as though seeking permission to enter. I swear my heartbeat skyrockets to two hundred beats a minute. My blood is so hot that it feels like I'm burning from the inside out, my skin melting, my brain turning to mush. I open my mouth to let her in, savoring her bold aggression.

She tastes like our favorite soda, mixed with honey and a fire that's all her—that I adore.

My whole body shudders. My cock is so hard it hurts.

I slant my mouth for a deeper connection, plundering her like my life depends on it. Every nerve zings. The rapid tightening of my balls and the accompanying electric sizzle signal a barreling orgasm approaching.

No fucking way. I'm not coming in my pants like some teenage virgin.

I hang on to what little control remains and wrap my arms around her, pulling her close until we're pressed firmly against each other. My dick pulses against her belly. I rock against her, chanting her name between kisses like she's the center of my universe.

She moans in response, moving against me. She sucks my tongue, strokes it with her own. Her taste fills my senses. It erases every thought in my head. Her soft skin against my solid, much larger body arouses not only lust but protective, possessive instinct.

Mine. My wife. My woman.

I stroke the ring on her, warm from her body heat. Satisfaction swells, but it isn't enough. She pulls back for a second to drag in air, then pushes her mouth against mine again.

Our tongues tangle in another carnal dance. She said kissing was too intimate. An understatement. Kissing her is like baring my soul.

My cock throbs, dying to be inside her hot, welcoming depths. I want to be connected in every way, although I'm certain I'll come undone the moment I become one with her.

"Fiona, baby, I can't wait," I groan, struggling with the desire to drive into her now and the desire to slow the moment and savor it.

"Then don't," she says breathlessly. "Nobody's asking you to."

"Dammit, you're supposed to tell me to control myself or you'll kick my ass."

"Why would I do that when I'm already dripping wet?" she teases, then takes my hand and places it between her legs.

The scorching heat of her flesh nearly undoes me. "Woman. What are you doing to me?"

"Showing you exactly what I want. Is that so wrong?" She gives me a grin full of naked desire. Her eyes glow with heat, but also the gentleness that comforts my soul.

I thrust my fingers into her hair and kiss her endlessly, over and over. What she does with her mouth is criminal—drugging me, turning me into an addict. I grip her ass and pick her up. She wraps her limbs around me.

I carry her upstairs, my erect cock rocking against her with each step.

She moans into my mouth. "Bryce, please," she whispers between kisses.

"Almost there," I say as we reach the bed.

We fall into it together, eagerly shedding our clothes. I resent even the brief separations of our mouths to get naked. But I want to see her beautiful body. I want to see her flushed with the pleasure I give her.

"Bryce," she whispers, spreading her legs, revealing her gorgeous pink flesh, pulsing with need. I didn't believe my blood could get any hotter, but I'm about to spontaneously combust.

I pull out a condom and somehow roll it down my shaft. Supporting my weight on a hand next to her head, I kiss her again. My other hand traces her curves, palming and kneading her breast, thumb teasing the pointed nipple. She twists with need, then opens her legs wider in a silent invitation, her mouth full with my tongue.

I can't wait anymore. Before I completely embarrass myself, I push into her, inch by inch. She groans, clawing at the sheet underneath. Her back arches, pushing her breasts against my chest.

I push into her wet warmth slowly until I'm balls deep, heaving with the effort to cling to control. I kiss her again, enjoying the softness of her lips.

I thrust in and out as we share air. My head spins at her feminine, honeyed taste. Lust and something inexplicably achy course through my veins.

Who would've thought something as mundane as missionary while kissing a woman in your arms could feel like this?

She strokes me with gentle fingertips. Her legs wrap around my waist, like she's holding on to the one thing she can never let go.

I don't know how much of it is wishful thinking and how much is real. But none of that matters as I revel in her heat and sweet warmth. I kiss her greedily while I rock both of us to a peak. Even then, in the throes of climax, I keep kissing her.

36

FIONA

–Bryce: You look adorable.

–Me: I think it's the flowers. (wink-emoji)

–Bryce: What flowers? By the way, the second line of your haiku is missing a syllable. I feel deprived. You should make it up to me by kissing me a lot when I get home.

I laugh softly. Lareina leans over the small, round table at a new café that supposedly serves the best cold brew in the city. She said we had to try it together because we're sisters. Not sure how that logic works, but of course I agreed.

"What are you laughing about?" she asks.

"Bryce." I smile. "He sent me tulips this morning, so I texted a shot of them in a vase in the living room, and this is how he responded." I flip the phone so she can see the photo.

"Where are you?" She frowns as she studies the screen. "I only see the vase on the kitchen counter."

"My reflection's in the stainless-steel fridge." I sip my coffee. It's so creamy and smooth with full-fat milk. I could get addicted to this real fast.

She squints. "Oh..." She chortles. "He's cute."

"He's perfect." Joy laces my sigh. Who would've thought this could ever happen between me and Bryce? But the kiss three weeks ago changed everything. The awkward distance and silence crumbled. Although I still haven't explained what happened with Jude, he hasn't pressed. It's almost like we've agreed to hit the reset button and take each day as it comes without dwelling on the past.

He comes home early enough that we can have dinner together, although I don't cook much, since the only thing I can manage with confidence is cup ramen. Instead, we've hit every restaurant that looks interesting, regardless of the cuisine, and discovered a great little Vietnamese pho place that has the richest broth.

A little gift arrives each day between nine and ten, and I send him a haiku about each one because a simple "thank you" seems too easy. The one about the tulips wasn't simple though. The second line, "waltzing red in the field," is indeed missing a syllable, but I wrote it before finishing my second coffee. I should fix it, though, since I plan to collect all the photos of his gifts and my haikus and print a glossy photo book for our anniversary.

–Me: Change "red" to "crimson" and you've got your missing syllable.

I hit send with a grin, not bothering to add that of course I'd love to kiss him this evening. Haven't I given him kisses every time he comes home from work for the past few weeks?

There's more than just a kiss tonight, though. I want to tell him what happened with Jude. It may not make any difference in how Bryce feels about me, but I keep thinking about it. After all, we broke up, and he harbored a lot of bitterness for a long time. But I feel like he should know. The decision dampens my hands with clammy sweat. I just hope he doesn't react too badly after realizing that I'm not a perfect Fiona rose after all.

"How's job hunting going?" Lareina asks.

I start, then flush, realizing I haven't given our conversation my full attention. "Um, slow. I submitted my résumé to a few places, but with this economy..." I shrug.

"I'm sure you'll find something."

"Hopefully. I want something with flexible hours, but most companies want me nine-to-five." Flexible hours are mostly for my own safety. Bryce acted like Zoe won't be bothering either of us again, but I'd rather be safe—or at least saf*er*—than sorry. If I have regular hours, it'll be easier for her to stalk me. I want to throw her off.

My phone vibrates. I glance at the screen with a grin, which fades rapidly.

–Unknown: You stupid whore! You think you're so clever! I'm going to make you pay for the disrespect!

I block it. I don't know who keeps getting new numbers to send me abusive messages. They started since the evening Bryce told me about his feelings for me. Could be anybody—Jude, Zoe...even Aaron, since there's no way my adoptive brother can stay quiet and civilized for this long. He's lain low since Zoe hit him—probably licking his wounds after being beaten by a gender he considers inferior. He'll need to find a way to reassert his dominance by being nasty to somebody.

"Not Bryce?" Lareina asks, sucking down the last of the coffee.

"Nah. Spam," I say, not wanting to worry her.

"Oh, definite insta-block. I get them too, mostly about investing in a diamond mine in Tanzania. Apparently, I can get a thousand percent return." She rolls her eyes.

I laugh. "I'm building an oceanside resort in Nebraska. You in?"

"Well. If it's *your* resort, sure. Sisters gotta stick together."

I laugh harder. For an heiress worth over sixty billion dollars, she's pretty down to earth and unassuming. Most of the rich kids I met over the years were spoiled rotten and didn't even know it.

"I'm going to pick up some cupcakes from Bobbi's Sweet Things," she says. "Wanna come with me? Ares loves them, and so do Bryce and Josh. We can drop by the office and treat our men."

I nod. "That sounds like a great idea."

"We should pick up an extra for Josh so he doesn't feel left out." Lareina shakes her head. "I told him he should start thinking about settling down, but..." She rolls her eyes again. "Him and his 'soul mate' stuff."

I nearly choke on my coffee. "Soul mate? For real?"

Lareina nods. "Yeah."

"That's unbelievable. He's literally the least romantic guy I've ever met." Josh was a player even back in Harvard, broken female hearts littered everywhere he went.

"That's what he claims." She shrugs. "Apparently he can tell by having sex."

"Uh-huh. Well, I hope whoever sleeps with him doesn't think she actually has a chance."

"At least he's open about it. Much better than the assholes who lie to you about being 'the only one,' and then turn around and screw other women."

"True enough."

We finish our drinks and head for the bakery Lareina can't stop gushing about. I smile, imagining Bryce's reaction when he sees me in his office with a sweet treat he wasn't expecting.

37

BRYCE

JOSH WALKS INTO MY OFFICE. "You're in too good of a mood these days. It's creepy." He hands me a coffee.

"And you're being suspiciously nice to me. What do you want?" I accept the coffee. I'm not stupid enough to reject free caffeine that I don't even have to lift my ass off the chair for.

"I'm thinking about hosting a family dinner," he says, taking the seat on the other side of the desk.

I almost spit out the coffee. "*You?*"

"Yeah, *me*. Why?"

"Who are you? What have you done with my twin brother?"

"Shut up."

Uh-oh. He isn't even trying to come up with a better comeback. This isn't good. "Are you going to prepare the food? Because—no offense—you're really only good at eating it."

"I don't have to cook something to host a get-together. There are plenty of takeout options." He spreads his hands. "Manny's Tacos. I'll even ask for extra jalapeños."

I narrow my eyes. Maybe Josh has a fever. Although we're identical twins, we differ in one thing—jalapeños. I love them; he hates them. Says they taste like spicy vinegar. Besides, when did he start hosting family dinners? Those are usually Akiko's thing. "What do you *really* want?"

His mouth twists. "I just want to make sure you aren't going to get fucked again. That shit-eating grin of yours? I know Fiona put it there, and I don't trust her."

"Josh—"

"You really need to watch your six."

"I know what I'm doing. The only one I'm really worried about is Mom. Maybe Harvey." I don't like it that he still hasn't cashed that check. *Asshole.* "Anyway, none of your worries matter."

"You sure?"

"We'll be fine as long as she doesn't get pregnant." Mom wants a baby badly. She was pissed that the girl I chose wasn't one of hers, enough that she hit me. That's *never* happened before. Even when she tried to kidnap me, she was crying about love.

She might get ideas if she sees Fiona's belly growing. She'll want to my take my wife to Vincent and project a pretty, loving family. *Look what I brought, Daddy! Your great-grandchild to come. Isn't it amazing?* To create the right picture, she'll do anything to get Fiona to cooperate. Kidnapping, drugging, torture—emotional or otherwise... Nothing's off the table. I'd rather die than have anyone harm Fiona.

There's a knock at the door, and it simultaneously starts to swing open. Fiona walks in, carrying a small Bobbi's Sweet Things box. I get up and go around the desk to run my hand along her arm. "Hi. What are you doing here?"

"Maybe she needs to sue somebody," Josh jokes, an almost imperceptible edge beneath his words.

She ignores him and plants a kiss on my cheek. "I was out with Lareina for coffee, then we decided to get some cupcakes to bring over. Except..." She gives Josh a sidelong glance. "Maybe he doesn't want any?"

"Nah. Well, maybe if you've got an extra..." He shrugs, although his eyes linger on the box. He's a sucker for high-end baked goods, and he's addicted to Bobbi's nama-cream cupcakes.

Fiona places the cupcakes on my desk. "I bought four, so we can share."

His hands buried in his pockets, Josh stands next to her and studies the box, probably trying to see what flavor nama cream she bought. He adjusts his jacket and sniffs. "Strawberry. Damn."

I smirk. That's his favorite, but the little sticky labels on the individual cakes show three other flavors as well. I turn to my wife. "Which one do you want?" I ask, hoping she'll stay. "How about the strawberry?"

Josh shoots me a death glare, which I ignore. He can have the blueberry cupcake, which is his second favorite. It won't kill him. He's a big boy.

"I already had one." She smiles, but it doesn't hide a smidgeon of shadow on her face. "And I'm feeling a little tired today. Think I'll head home and nap."

"You can nap here and we can go home together." I start to gesture at a small antechamber where I keep a chaise longue for quick catnaps when I'm exhausted.

"But I brought the Maybach, and I want to drive it back." She runs her hands along my shoulders. "Have these amazing cupcakes, and a more amazing day."

I kiss her on the mouth. "It's already perfect."

38

FIONA

THE SECOND I walk out of the office and pass Amélie, my smile slips.

We'll be fine as long as she doesn't get pregnant.

I initially bought four cupcakes to share with Bryce, but after I overheard that, I knew I wouldn't be able to fake being serene. *Don't overthink it. And for God's sake, don't give it the worst possible interpretation.*

He was probably just thinking about our agreement. A baby would be inconvenient. I'm not sure if I want to start a family right now, and Bryce probably wants a baby even less because his mom is so psychotic about it.

I reach the elevator bank and hit the button. It climbs slowly from the lobby. At least I didn't lie about being tired. For some reason, I'm really sleepy even though I had the largest cold brew on the menu. The cold brew supposedly has more caffeine than regular coffee, so I don't know why I'm still so drowsy. If I didn't know better, I'd suspect that Lareina slipped me some sleeping meds, but she couldn't even drink her own coffee without my sipping it first to make sure it was okay. That poor woman. She told me that she basically starved until she met Ares.

"There you are."

I turn around and face Josh. His voice is as smooth and hard as glass. "Yes? What is it?"

"Games aren't my thing, so I'll be blunt. Don't ever betray or hurt Bryce again."

My spine straightens. Although his criticism is justified, I don't have to like it.

"I hate it that you make him happy, because you're too poisonous. He looks tough outside, but inside he's a big teddy bear. He shouldn't have to suffer for your amusement."

My jaw tightens at the unfairness of his doubts, but I soon realize I haven't given him any reason to know I'm not going to act the way I did back in college. Does Bryce torment himself, wondering about my behavior and motives? Does he believe I might turn my back on him?

I didn't sense anything like it, but Bryce and Josh have always been inseparable. Besides, aren't identical twins supposed to be in tune with each other? What if I missed something?

This reaction from Josh, more than anything else, reaffirms my decision to fess up everything to Bryce tonight. I wouldn't want him to suffer because of my doubts and insecurities. The need to be perfect in order to be worthy of affection has been hammered into me since I was seven. It led me down an exhausting, painful path, and I want to deviate from it, no matter how my belly roils with fear.

I look up at the face so identical to Bryce's, but at the same time so different. "I'm not playing a game. This is my life."

"Your life? Wasn't it your life ten years ago?" Josh scoffs.

"It's different now." My voice is surprisingly firm.

"We'll see about that." He points two fingers at his eyes, then turns them toward me. "I'll be watching, Fiona."

"Watch all you want. I won't ever hurt Bryce again."

The elevator doors open and a woman rushes out of the car, almost bumping into me. "Sorry!" she shouts without turning back and runs off, a plastic bag looped around her wrist.

I frown at her rudeness, then notice a box of tampons in the bag. *Oh...* Nothing like being caught unaware and the bathroom's out of supplies for Aunt Flo.

I turn back. Josh is holding the elevator for me. I shoot him a sidelong glance, unsure why he's suddenly being polite now. "Thank you," I murmur, then step inside the car.

As it descends, I realize *I* haven't bought any tampons in a while—

No. I haven't had a period since Bryce crashed my wedding...

My blood cools, the coffee and cupcake congealing into a nauseating lump in my gut. But there's no way I can be pregnant. Bryce and I were careful. He always used protection. And I'm pretty sure he would have said something if a rubber had ripped or anything...

Stress. It must be the stress. I've skipped periods before when I was in the middle of high-stakes marketing campaigns at work. And my life has been anything but smooth sailing with Zoe and all her insanity.

But things have been calmer since I kissed Bryce three weeks ago. Still, that doesn't mean the effect of the stress disappeared completely, right?

I stop by a pharmacy on the way and pick up a pregnancy test kit and a box of tampons. The former just for reassurance, and the latter for when Aunt Flo decides to visit again.

Back at home, I stash the tampons in the bathroom cabinet under the sink, then tap my palm with the test. I should pee, but can't seem to squeeze out any fluid. I gulp down two glasses of water and start pacing.

We'll be fine as long as she doesn't get pregnant.

The words ring in my head. My feet move faster, but I can't shake off the chilly film of anxiety. *Come on, Fiona.* I'm nervous for nothing. Why would my body produce a baby at the worst possible time?

Because your life is full of absolutely shitty timing? This is the other shoe dropping.

I cover my ears. *No, I'm not listening to negativity. Positivity only, please.*

Finally, I sit down on the toilet and perform the test. The seconds tick by so slowly that I can't help but start pacing again. Finally, I look down at the results box. *Two lines.* What does that mean? I flip the test, but the back doesn't say.

I grab the instruction sheet for an explanation. *Two lines means pregnant.*

I press my knuckles against my mouth, the sharp edges of my teeth digging into my skin. No way am I with child. This has to be a joke. I look at the sheet again. *If there are two lines, it indicates pregnancy.*

Just how reliable is this test? I skim the rest of the paper. It proudly claims the test is ninety-nine percent accurate.

Bullshit. What about the one percent, huh? I could be that. Or this particular test is defective. Could happen. Wait a few weeks and the company will do a huge recall. Bet it was made in some super-sketchy place with no manufacturing standards to speak of.

I drop the test next to the sink. This is a damn lie. I'm going to prove it.

Grabbing my purse, I run out to the Maybach and get in. I'll buy another test, and this time I'm going to hit a different pharmacy, just to be sure. *And* grab a test produced by a different company. Ideally one in the U.S.A. If not, Germany or Japan will do as well.

My teeth cut into my knuckles as I press my hand over my mouth to contain a scream.

We'll be fine as long as she doesn't get pregnant.

But what happens if I *am* pregnant? Are Bryce and I not going to be fine? Will we fight? Argue? Never speak to each other again?

I want to tell Bryce the whole truth about what happened with Jude today, and now *this...*

I rub my forehead. But if I'm really pregnant, it isn't something I can hide. My palms slicken with clammy sweat. What am I going to do?

What's going to happen to my baby?

Bryce doesn't want it. So obviously he won't recognize it as his. Will he bother giving a Huxley family cane to the baby, to let it know it'll be under the family's protection? Or will he turn its back on it?

What about me? I don't want to throw it away the way my birth mother did, even if everyone around me disagrees. My child deserves better. At the same time, I don't know how I'll deal with raising a baby on my own. Zoe's zeal for a grandbaby flashes through my mind, followed by Bryce's story about her kidnapping Ares and leaving him to die in a fire. What if she tries to hurt my baby? Can I protect it?

Can I even be a good mom? I don't know anything about creating a good family environment. The two families that adopted me weren't exactly wholesome and loving examples.

Should I give the baby up for adoption? But what if it meets a family like the Obermans, who provide material benefits but no warmth or love? I didn't realize how much I wanted the latter until I spent time with Akiko. Do I want my child to experience the same kind of lack and pain I've gone through?

I park my car in the corner of a huge lot at a massive strip mall. It has a supermarket, a pharmacy and a few other stores, including a McDonald's. I flex my hands around the steering wheel and drop my forehead on the car horn, lightly enough that the Maybach stays silent. So many questions swirl, all of them unanswerable. But the first step is definitely seeing if I'm really pregnant or if there was a mistake with the previous test. It's possible it isn't even the fault of the manufacturer, but me. I might've peed wrong—I did it without reading the entire instruction sheet first. There might've been a warning that says if you pee for more than two seconds, the test gives a false positive.

I climb out of the car and start toward the pharmacy.

"Finn."

Aaron. I turn and blink at my adoptive brother. Gone is the flamboyant, confident heir. He looks even worse than he did at the hotel. He's unshaven, his bloodshot eyes and cheeks sunken. His skin is dull, his hair messy like it broke up with a comb a while ago. He's in a button-down shirt that's at least a size too big, slacks cinched at the waist with a worn belt. At least he doesn't smell, but he looks like he could use a shower.

"Finally." He smiles. The expression doesn't hold the cockiness it used to. An unholy anticipation glows in his eyes. Did Zoe abuse him more than I realized? Does he blame me for what happened?

"Aaron," I whisper. My throat is too tight to speak louder.

"I'm so glad I ran into you. Aren't you?"

"Were you following me?"

"What if I was? You don't keep regular schedules, and you're around too many people." He sounds baleful.

I shake my head, snapping myself out of the shocked daze. "I don't have time for this."

His hand snakes out, gripping my wrist. "You'll *make* time," he spits out between clenched teeth. "You owe me."

"No. I already took care of your ridiculous debt." I look around, but there isn't anybody in the lot. "Let me go—"

His face contorts with rage. "Shut up, you stupid bitch. It's all your fault. You deserve this."

"No—" My vision goes black.

39

BRYCE

For once, the deposition ends early. I stretch and grab my things. Although I'm not completely done for the day, everything else can be done at home. I want to check on Fiona. Although she was smiling, she looked a little pale and uncomfortable in my office.

Did she sense Josh's dislike? But she didn't react like this at the family dinner, when it was more overt.

I check my phone. She hasn't looked at the photo of the cupcakes or the haiku I wrote to thank her. Maybe she's still napping.

I head out of the office, then stop at the sight of Amélie arguing with a woman. My assistant is on her feet, which means she's less than happy about the situation and feels the need to assert herself.

"What's the problem?" I say, ready to back Amélie up.

"She's insisting on seeing you even though I told her repeatedly there's no appointment."

"I've called repeatedly over the last two weeks, and he's always unavailable. I don't believe that for a second." The woman turns to me. She's familiar—from the auburn hair knotted into a loose chignon to the green-gold eyes. Blue japamala loops around her thin wrist, and a forest-green Dior fits her like a second skin.

Sherry Oberman, in the flesh. How interesting.

If I didn't know Fiona was adopted, I might think Sherry was her biological mother. Except for the eyes—often unfocused and sometimes too soulless. The woman supposedly grieves for losing her real daughter, but underneath it is a little too much calculation. It's as though she tallies everything as a plus or minus, with her being the only arbiter of assigned value.

"Mrs. Oberman," I say coldly. "My assistant doesn't lie. I am extremely busy."

She tilts her chin stubbornly. "You're free now, aren't you?"

"No. I'm about to head out."

"I only need a little bit of your time."

I open my mouth to decline—

"It's about Finn."

My eyebrows twitch a little at the way she says Fiona's name. There's something vaguely obsessive, although I can't put my finger on why. Is Fiona a plus or a minus? Sherry could be upset about the way I stole her daughter away from the wedding—in which case, it's taken her too long to make her complaints known. "Fine." I glance at my watch. "Two minutes, in my office."

Shooting Amélie a triumphant look, she slips inside. Rude old woman. "No refreshment necessary," I inform my assistant before she tries to serve coffee or something. Amélie sticks her tongue out at Mrs. Oberman's back.

I shut the door and lean against it, making it clear I'm impatient to get going. Sherry takes a seat and gives me a blank look. "Do you love Finn?"

"None of your business." I'm not discussing my feelings for Fiona with Sherry, especially when she hasn't given me a single indication *she* cares for Fiona.

Her eyebrows pinch in confusion and disapproval. "But you took her from Jude and married her."

It takes all my self-control to not inform her he would've made a horrible husband because his penis is defective and inferior. "And? Are you intending to sue me?"

She looks taken aback. "Goodness, no. Why would I? It was good karma."

Good karma?

"I was hoping something would happen at the wedding. Jude as her husband would *not* have been good karma for my daughter."

I cock an eyebrow and say nothing. Silence is golden in more ways than one, especially when you're completely lost.

"I've thought about it for a long time. I didn't want to interfere. Finn has her own path to walk. But"—Sherry thumbs the beads—"good karma must be earned. I had to do it to make up for something that happened ten years ago. Something really awful. I heard her crying in her room over breaking up with you when she came home for a break."

My belly tightens. What's Sherry trying to say? Fiona dumped me and reveled in it. Staged the whole scene to make it as painful and humiliating as possible. Is the woman claiming Fiona never wanted to do any of that?

Sherry continues, "I could never ask her why. She wouldn't have told me. She never tells me anything unless it's good news."

"Well, that's helpful," I say. My patience is in short supply. I want to go home and see my wife. "What do you want me to do about it?"

"Nothing, except be kind to her. And Aaron. He's her brother."

Ah. Now I get it. She's here to ask me to keep Aaron off my shitlist. I never liked him—he always bristled with envy and a well-deserved inferiority complex. One of these days, I plan to fuck him up for racking up a two-million-dollar debt with somebody like Harvey and making his sister pay it off.

"I don't need your advice on how to treat my wife." It comes out more harshly than it should. But Sherry gives me a weird vibe, and her continual references to karma creep me out. She doesn't speak about it the way most Americans would. She brings it up in a way that reminds me of my late Japanese grandmother, who was a devout Buddhist.

When I visited her after breaking up with Fiona, she told me to find peace by letting go. If I had no expectations, I would suffer no disappointment or dissatisfaction. By freeing myself from such mortal entanglements and shackles, I could truly experience inner peace and freedom.

I couldn't buy into that or practice it, although intellectually I understood the wisdom of her suggestion. But unlike my grandmother, Sherry displays none of the tranquility. The woman definitely wants something, and wants it so badly it pains her soul. It's just that I don't think what she desires has anything to do with Fiona's wellbeing. The pinched mouth, the zealous glow in her eyes—all indicate it's something personal and selfish. I have no civility left for people like her.

"Perhaps you should take your own counsel and be kind to her, although it looks like it might be too late."

Sherry's cheeks redden with embarrassment and anger at being called out, but she tilts her chin up. "Finn's a good girl. The only thing that anybody could hurt her with is that she was adopted, but why would that matter?"

Is she serious? "It wasn't a normal adoption. She was selected to replace your dead daughter Finley."

Shock slaps Sherry. She stares at me like she can't believe I dare to speak of her dead child.

"Don't look so surprised. What's she supposed to think when you can't even bother to put her name on her birthday cakes?"

"That's—"

"Not interested in your excuses. I'm sure she knew it even before she entered college. Kids always notice things faster than you realize."

Sherry tilts her hardened jaw. "Finn is her *name*."

"If you say so."

"I'm not as oblivious as you think. By the time I realized she had wrong beliefs about the situation, it was too late to do anything about it."

I cock an eyebrow. "Defensive much?"

"I'm not being defensive."

"Of course not. You just let the status quo continue even though you knew it was wrong. It was easier for you to pretend everything was fine rather than reaching out to her and setting things right."

"Don't judge me. You don't know what it was like. What would you have done in my place?"

"I don't know, since I'm not you. But I wouldn't have let her think she's just a substitute. I would've treated her like her own person with her own worth. If you're here to earn points, it's not working. I don't give a damn about your karma math. I won't be used in your weird mental scheme. If you want to know how she's doing, ask her. If you want to apologize, say it to her face. But don't come to me for an easy way out. That's despicable, and I won't do your dirty work."

"I haven't done anything wrong."

"Guess you aren't going to apologize." I glance at my watch. "Your time's up. You can walk out on your own feet or I can have security drag you out."

Sherry stands, her spine stiff. "You're rude. No wonder Finn didn't turn to you back then."

Her jab hits the mark. I hide it with a smile that's all teeth and no warmth. "Her name is Fiona, not Finn or Finley. At least I call her by her real name while you're still using her to soothe your loss." I lever myself up off the door. "A lot of mothers lose children, and I'm sure it's traumatic. But I've never heard of one who'd use an orphan to satisfy her own selfish desires. You're a one-of-a-kind bitch, Sherry. Don't ever come near me or my wife, or I'll expose every dirty little secret you have."

I HEAD HOME, my mind churning as I process what Sherry said. Something happened to Finn ten years ago. She was crying...

The way Sherry tried to link Aaron to Fiona, claiming I should be nice to that subhuman trash, doesn't sit well. Why bring him up at all? He's never been on my radar.

I tap the steering wheel in a steady rhythm. Sherry dropped a few clues, albeit without any order or clarity. I try to process them.

Fiona went from sweet to overwrought, confident to doormat, almost overnight. It was almost like somebody flipped a switch in her brain. She couldn't stand Jude, then all of a sudden acted like she couldn't live without him. But how does Aaron fit into it, if he even fits into it at all? He and Jude were close, but that doesn't mean he had anything to do with Fiona's abrupt change.

Regardless, whatever happened to her must have been awful. I want to give her what comfort I can, let her know that I'll always be on her side, and whenever she's ready to talk, I'll listen. Then I'll take appropriate measures against those responsible for hurting her—behind her back, since she doesn't need to know all the sordid details. I want her to see only beautiful things, hear only pleasing sounds. I don't mind bloodying my hands to give her the sanctuary she deserves.

I park my car and slip inside the house, moving quietly in case Fiona is still napping. She isn't in the living room. I make my way to the bedroom, trying to select the right words to express what's in my heart…and failing. What good is a Harvard Law degree if you can't come up with a decent opening?

The bedroom is empty. The door to the en suite bathroom is wide open. I glance inside. A slim white stick stands out next to the sink on her side of the bathroom. Head cocked, I pick it up. Two lines in a small square box. A pregnancy test.

My mouth dries. When did she take the test? Before or after she stopped by the office? She seemed a little tired, but not overly upset or concerned—

Something crinkles underneath my shoe. An onion-skin-thin piece of paper lies on the floor. I step off and pick it up. An instruction sheet with tiny writing.

Two lines means… *Fiona's pregnant.*

My mind empties for a moment. Heart pounding, I spin around. "Fiona!" We agreed there would be no babies, but my chest swells with emotions that are too hot and special. Fiona and I are creating a life—a precious baby made even more precious because it's half Fiona.

No matter what I've been grousing and deluding myself about, I can't hide the fact that I'm in love with her. I fell in love with her when she rescued Gardy. I was in love with her even after she betrayed me. And in spite of everything, I'm still in love with her.

An overwhelming need to confess to her that *I want this baby* hammers in my heart. I want to nurture this beautiful new life and watch it grow and be the most amazing human being it can be.

"*Fiona!*" I call out again.

Silence.

Did she panic when she found out? I check my phone. She hasn't called. The security system says she left the house in the Maybach about two hours ago. Where did she go?

I text her, but nothing. The message remains unread. She hasn't seen my photo or the haiku about the cupcakes. I try calling. Still no response.

I send her another text.

–Me: I saw the pregnancy test. Don't do anything hasty, and don't make any decisions. Baby, Fiona, let me see you and we can talk about this. We're going to be parents! You have no idea how happy this makes me!

Still nothing.

The phone vibrates in my hand. I glance at the screen eagerly, but it's just Josh.

"Yeah?" I say.

"Fiona's been kidnapped. Aaron nabbed her."

It takes me two beats before my mind processes what my twin's saying—and that he isn't making a very unfunny joke. "How do you know?"

"Because I heard just now." He lets out a breath. "I put a bug and tracker in her purse today in your office."

"*What?*"

"I don't trust her, okay? I wanted to be prepared, just in case."

"You son of a bitch!" Realization hits me in the face. "I should've known something was up when you lingered in my office, wanting to host a family dinner. If Fiona hadn't shown up, you were going to do it at the dinner, weren't you?"

"Yeah, but it was for you."

"How is this for me? I'm your brother, not some kid you have to watch over!"

"I know, but you're too soft."

Rage shoots through my veins. "Says who? Do you think I'm still her good fucking boy who gets his brother kidnapped?"

"Bryce—"

"We're going to talk about this later. Now shut the fuck up and tell me: *where's Fiona?*"

"Hollywood Inn in North Hollywood."

What the hell?

"We gotta hurry. It's Jude and Aaron both."

"Fuck." Jude is never the good news.

"I'm calling 911."

I start to run, pausing at the sight of the Huxley cane gleaming inside the case. I grab it and rush out.

40

FIONA

I SLOWLY SURFACE from the dark, feeling a little fuzzy. What did Aaron do to me? Is the baby okay? Did he use anything that would hurt it?

A soft fabric is wrapped around my head, covering my eyes. The air is cold. A chill spreads over my skin, fueled by terror and despair. I'm propped against something soft on my left—maybe an armchair? My hands are bound behind me, but not my legs. But somehow I can't bring myself to stand up and run. Weakness permeates my muscles.

I move my fingers, trying to feel for clues to my surroundings. The thin carpet is rough—probably cheap and worn. So not in the Obermans' house. Despite the enormous debt Zachary saddled the family with, there are certain things the Obermans would never give up, and creature comforts are among them. Plus, Aaron would never drag me anywhere Sherry might notice.

There's the sound of sirens. And a musty smell, probably from carpet or upholstery. Something creaks above me, and the air stirs. A ceiling fan? A woman yells something I can't make out and a man screams back. Lovely.

Where has my adoptive brother brought me? And for what?

Certain aspects of my current situation mirror what happened in college, the night everything changed. Goosebumps cover my skin, and I shiver.

"Aaron, this isn't funny. Let me go." My voice cracks, but I can't help it. I'm terrified, my mind back to that night ten years ago. This time, it isn't just me in danger, but my baby, too.

Aaron picked me up from a bar after I'd had a few drinks. He offered me a bottle of water, which I took because I was thirsty. Afterward, I passed out, and when I woke up it was in a strange room with Jude on top of me. My memory of the moment is fuzzy. Pain, Jude's grunting in my ear, male laughter and my hazy vision.

If there hadn't been videos and photos, I might've thought it was just a nasty nightmare.

A cold sweat that has nothing to do with the temperature pops out all over me. I squeeze my eyes shut to block the memory. Otherwise, I'll vomit and pass out.

No. NO. I inhale, deliberately slowing my breathing. I'm not that helpless college sophomore anymore. Never going to let myself become a victim again.

"Again, this isn't funny. Did Zoe put you up to this?" She might've promised to let Aaron go in exchange for me, and he'd sell me out in a heartbeat. Still, he isn't a total sociopath, just an irresponsible asshole who has no spine and big dreams he doesn't recognize as impossible. "For once, be a good man. You're my brother, damn it."

"Who are you calling your brother?" Aaron says.

I freeze at his contemptuous tone. "What do you want?"

"What do *I* want? You faked with me? Huh?"

Jude is here? My mouth dries. *Jude*'s the one behind this, not Zoe?

"I'm going to show you how a real man treats a little liar like you," Jude says. "Not just you, but everyone on the planet! You thought you were so fucking clever, deleting all those videos and photos, but I'm not going to let you fuck me over again. This time, the whole thing's gonna be livestreamed from the very beginning."

Terror racks through me, but I grit my teeth. The fact that Jude is here is more reason to focus on the steps I need to take to fight back. He's never, ever going to turn me into that helpless girl again. "You're going to livestream raping me?" Despite my best effort, my voice is too thin.

"It's not rape if you beg for it. And the camera angle won't show my face. But you? Everyone's going to know who you are because I'm going to write your fucking name in all caps on your body with a permanent marker. And I'll make sure to send the link to Bryce so he can see it. After all, that fucker should know what it's like to have something of his violated by me. Again. He should feel the humiliation and helplessness. Publicly cuckolded! How pathetic!"

He laughs maniacally. Isn't he afraid that the neighbors might hear? This place doesn't seem to have much soundproofing.

"Then you're going to sing for me like you did for him! No, better than you did for him!"

If my situation weren't so dire, I'd laugh. Somehow, he found out that I sang for Bryce, but he never knew the circumstances or the tender affection I held for Bryce as I crooned at night to comfort him. So I sang some random songs off the top forty chart, and Jude was satisfied, thinking he'd had from me everything that Bryce had gotten.

He continues to rant, and I start to pick up clues. Jude's upset I told him he was bad in bed, but that actually isn't the main cause for his fury. He's practically spitting with rage at Bryce. He's trying to get under Bryce's skin *by hurting me*. Could this be the real reason he hurt me at Harvard? The unfairness and injustice of it all make my body shake. "Why do you hate him so much?"

"Oh, he acts so high and mighty. Thinks he's *sooo fucking smart*. He's never shown me the respect I deserve! He thinks he's invulnerable. He said I couldn't take anything valuable from him, but I did his most prized toy, and I will again."

My mouth twists. "This is so pathetic. You don't have the balls to go punch him in the face, so you're going to abuse me? Are you going to show the world your tiny penis too?"

"Shut your piehole!"

Pain explodes in my hip. Jude must've kicked me, but he didn't connect where it might hurt the most.

"Shit," he mutters. He probably injured his foot.

"Aaron, be smart. Don't get caught up in Jude's revenge against Bryce. It isn't worth going to prison for."

"Yeah, right." From the way his voice sounds, Aaron isn't standing too close to me. "God, I hate you, flaunting yourself like some whore to be fucked, always faking being good and innocent."

"What? I never flaunted anything!" My clothes were modest because of Sherry, and even when I went to Harvard, I wore similar clothes.

"Don't think I didn't notice," Aaron says tautly.

Oh my God. "That's disgustingly gross, especially for a brother. Or do you have *unbrotherly* feelings for me?"

"Shut up!"

He might as well have screamed, "Yes!" My regard for him drops below zero. "Is this what your hatred and disdain are about? You can't admit your impulses are your problem, so you have to blame the woman?"

"You don't know shit!"

"I still care about Sherry, so if you don't want to get caught up in this crime, let me go. Otherwise I'm reporting you to the police, too."

"You don't think we've planned this whole thing out? The video won't show our faces, just yours. And we're going to be each other's alibis." Jude sounds smug. He's given this a lot of thought. Guess he was furious I ran off with Bryce and then taunted him over the phone the way I did. But I didn't think he'd come after me like this. Much less that he and Aaron would be in it together.

Did they conspire ten years ago, too? Bile rises in my throat. I clench my teeth and count to three. Even though adrenaline spikes through my veins, my head feels cold and numb.

I'm not giving up like I did ten years ago. I'm going to make them pay for everything they've done—and everything that they plan to do.

A rough hand grabs my hair and shoves me down. The back of my skull hits the floor hard, and nausea surges in my gut. A weight on my belly pins me to the floor, and the awkward angle of my shoulders sends pain shooting up my arms and neck. *Shit, my baby.* I try to shift to relieve the pressure on my stomach, but can't.

My hiss turns to a whimper when someone—Jude, probably—grabs my neckline and rips my top. Cold air hits my shoulders, and he curses at my bra.

I can feel his breath on my face. I lever myself, using the direction of his breathing to headbutt him. My skull connects—hopefully with his face. Something cracks.

"*Agh!* Fuck!"

Something warm splatters over my forehead and cheeks. A metallic smell hits my nose. The pain reverberates from my forehead, but it's worth it. The blindfold finally comes loose. I squint at the sudden bright light. Jude clutches his face, blood spurting from his nose. Hopefully I broke it. Standing behind him, Aaron is holding his phone and looks torn. He probably can't decide if he should continue to film or help his best friend.

I bare my teeth. "How'd you like *that*?"

"Bitch!" Jude shouts, and swings.

Pain explodes in my face. Blood gushes from my nose, and I breathe through my mouth, tasting copper and rust. Still I can't stop smiling. He's so pathetic, such a spineless, ball-less snake. I can't believe I gave him so much power over me back then. "Is that the best you can do?" I taunt him. "You sissified, dickless—"

Bang!

The door rattles on its hinges. Jude's eyes flare with frustration and panic.

"Go away!" Aaron screams.

"Help! Two thugs are trying to assault me!" I scream louder.

"Shut up!" Jude tries to stuff the blindfold into my mouth. I bite his fingers hard, and he yanks them out with a curse.

Another loud bang. Jude glances at the quivering door. "Fuck."

"Help! Help!" I start yelling again. "Save me!"

"Shut up!" He grabs a pillow off the bed and shoves it over my face, cutting off the air.

41

BRYCE

SEEDY ISN'T enough to describe the dilapidated motel. The area reeks of pot, urine and food about to go bad. The blaring of TVs and music and every argument of occupants can be heard through the wafer-thin walls and doors.

Where did Aaron and Jude take Fiona? I don't see a car that looks like it would belong to either of them. The lot only contains vehicles that saw better days a decade ago.

A man reeking of alcohol stumbles toward me. "Hey, spare a little change?"

I get my wallet out. "I'm looking for a woman and two guys. All around thirty. They just checked in here, I think."

The man shrugs and looks away. "I dunno... Lotsa young folks around..."

I pull a hundred-dollar bill out. "Try to remember. The girl has reddish-brown hair..."

His eyes light on the money. "Oh, that stoned chick? Pretty girl? And the guys are tall, right? Lanky blond and... I can't remember the other guy. Sort of hard to see from where—"

"That's them." I lean in, but keep the bill out of reach. "Where did they go?"

He points to a unit on the second floor. "That one. Fourth from the end." I give him the money and he shuffles off.

Pumping my arms, I run upstairs. My grip on the cane tightens. The wolf's head glints under the SoCal sun.

I stop in front of the room and kick hard. The door holds. I kick it again. *Fuck.* For a shitty motel, they sure have a sturdy door.

I think I hear somebody yell, "Help," but can't be sure with all the noise around me and my own racing heartbeat.

Fiona, I'm here!

Aaron and Jude couldn't have brought her to this place for anything pleasant. Fury and panic send another surge of adrenaline rushing through me. I kick again with all my might, praying my wife's okay, that I'm not too late.

The door gives in with a splintering crash. I rush inside, and my vision turns red. Jude is sitting on Fiona, pressing a pillow over her face. "Shit," he says, his voice weirdly muffled from a swollen nose and blood.

Good girl. Pride surges at the damage my wife must've inflicted on him. I swing the cane.

The wolf's snarling snout smashes the back of Jude's head. He crumbles as red blooms on his skull and soaks his hair. Aaron rushes toward me, his fists raised awkwardly like a poorly trained boxer. I slash the cane across his face, breaking his nose and taking off a wide layer of skin. He drops like a rock, his scream muffled against his hands as he cradles his face.

"Fiona, baby. I'm here."

I yank away the pillow. My hands shake when I see it's soaked with blood—all of it Fiona's.

"I'm here. I'm here. Let me cover you, okay? You're safe." I rip off my jacket and place it over her ripped blouse, then cradle her face carefully to avoid touching her injuries.

She blinks up at me. Her left cheek has swollen until it looks twice as big as the other side. A killing rage swells, but first things first. I help her sit up and undo the knots around her wrists.

"You fucker!" Jude says from behind me, his breathing uneven and rough. "I'm bleeding."

I put a hand over Fiona's eyes. "It isn't going to be pretty."

"No," she rasps. "I want to see them get punished. I want *justice*."

She doesn't have to tell me twice. I stand up and spin around.

Jude sways on his feet a little, but raises his hands and makes fists. He smirks. "What's it like to see me break your toy again?"

I want to break your face. "She's not a toy, and you didn't break her. You're too weak," I say contemptuously. "I've always wanted to do more than make you bleed."

I raise the cane and bring it down hard on his shoulder. He screams. Aaron comes at me, and I backhand his cheek. He spits out a couple of teeth.

Seeing them in pain doesn't lessen my rage. I want to see them worse than dead. The wolf's head continues to slam into them, one hit after another, until the silver's covered with so much blood that it no longer glints.

Somewhere, sirens wail. A few moments later, the police rush in with guns. "Freeze! Drop your weapon!"

I let go of the cane and raise my hands. Josh runs inside. "He's the husband!" he shouts to the officers. "Those are the kidnappers." He points to Jude and Aaron lying on the ground, unconscious, then hands his business card to an officer and whispers something.

My twin turns to my wife. "Fiona—"

"Needs to go to the hospital." She's on the bed, my jacket wrapped around her and eyes unblinking and focused. "Sweetheart, I'm going to take you to the hospital, okay?" I say in the tenderest voice I can manage.

"Are they going to prison forever?" she asks, tilting her chin at Jude and Aaron.

"I'll do my best," I say, even though I'm certain they won't. They'll be prosecuted, but their defense attorneys will claim they didn't really do enough to be locked up for life. But there are other ways, dark methods that my wife should never know about. I gaze into her beautiful eyes. They should only see beautiful things. "I promise."

"I believe you," she says quietly.

"Good. Can we go to the hospital now?"

She nods. "Okay."

I pick her up and cradle her close as she slumps. The shock of the day must've been too much for her system to bear. I nod at the officer who took Josh's card. "I'll give you my statement as soon as my wife's taken care of." Then I give Josh a cool look. "And you also—later."

It's not a farewell—it's a promise.

42

FIONA

The pungent scent of antiseptic tickles my nose. I sneeze, then wince at the pain radiating all the way down the left side of my face. My shoulders ache, and the skin on my wrists is raw. But other than that, I'm okay.

Better than okay. Smashing my head into Jude's face was liberating. Exhilarating, even. It just felt so...*right* to resist and show him I wasn't afraid of him. Not anymore. And he isn't going to have any blackmail material to manipulate me with. Did he think I was still the college sophomore afraid of getting un-adopted by Sherry?

I used to think she was the only one who could save me from being alone and unwanted. But recently, I've gradually started to realize that might not be the case. What I felt for Sherry wasn't so much gratitude as an overwhelming sense of debt that I needed to be perfect to pay her back. She doesn't feel the kind of love a mother should have for her daughter, either. She just sees me as a tool.

I now understand what love is—not just the romantic love I have with Bryce, but familial love. Although Bryce's brothers haven't warmed up to me, Akiko makes me feel appreciated just the way I am. Lareina treats me like my own person and wants to hang out together just because.

Aaron and Jude should've known that what worked ten years ago when I was young and inexperienced wouldn't work again. Seeing my husband beat them gave me a kind of calm and satisfaction I haven't experienced in forever. It felt like well-deserved justice, even though it's taken so long.

"Fiona. You're awake now," Bryce says, his voice trembling. His warm hand cradles mine, which is like an ice block. "You gave me a scare." He looks at me, his eyes bloodshot, his face unshaven. The hair is messy, like he's run his hands through it endlessly. I've never seen him this haggard.

"What's wrong?" I ask, my voice raspy.

"You were unconscious for three days."

"Three *days*?" I didn't even realize I'd fainted. After the cops showed up and arrested Aaron and Jude, and Bryce promised they'd go to prison, exhaustion overwhelmed me. I only closed my eyes to rest briefly during the ride to the hospital.

He buries his face in my hand. "I was so scared I'd lose you."

"I'm sorry. I didn't mean to worry you."

His head snaps back up. "Sorry? Are you serious? You should be pissed I was too late."

"But you weren't. You crashed into the room like a warrior and saved me, remember?"

His fingers hover over my swollen cheek. "If I'd been in time, you wouldn't be here."

"I'll heal, Bryce." I wrap my hand around his fingers and kiss the tips. "You saved me from another nightmare."

"We," he corrects me. "You did a good job defending yourself. I think you're the one who broke Jude's nose."

Warm satisfaction unfurls through me. "Is it really broken? *Good.* I was hoping for that." I put the other hand over my belly. "And the baby?" I ask, knowing the doctor probably already told Bryce when the hospital examined me in the last three days. Besides, my pregnancy isn't something I can hide. And I don't *want* to hide it, even if he says he doesn't want us pregnant. I'm tired of secrets.

"Healthy. Thank you for protecting our baby," he says softly, kissing the pulse point on my left wrist.

"*We* protected our baby. I couldn't have done it without you."

He shudders and tightens his grip.

I run my hand over his hair, finding comfort in the sensation of the soft, warm strands gliding through my fingers. "How did you know where I was?"

Bryce scowls. "Josh put a tracker in your purse when you stopped by to give me cupcakes."

My jaw drops. *Of all the possibilities...* "Josh put a tracker on me? Seriously?"

"He was in the office to try to invite us for dinner, but I suspect he wanted us over there so he could put that thing in your purse."

"But...*why*?"

Bryce bites his lip, his eyes flicking away briefly. "He doesn't trust you. He thinks you're going to betray me. He thought if he could listen in on what you were doing, he could stop you from hurting me."

I inhale. Although it isn't fair of Josh to distrust me, I've never explained what happened. "It's...understandable. I wasn't exactly the nicest person. The way I hurt you..." I close my eyes briefly, reliving the pain. It was the worst time in my life—even worse than when the first couple who adopted me decided to send me back. At least in that situation I had no choice in the matter. With Bryce... *I* did things that hurt him. I should've trusted him not to shut me out because of the videos Jude and Aaron made. But I was too focused on being perfect, not understanding that I didn't *have* to be perfect to be worthy of love.

I sit up gingerly. This isn't the kind of talk I want to have lying down. "You should know the truth about what happened back in college." I look at him with remorse and regret. His expression shifts to one of quiet patience and openness as he takes my hand and warms it in his.

"Back then..." I trail off and exhale shakily. This isn't easy. He pats my hand, silently communicating I should take my time. "I went out one night with a few friends and got a little tipsy. I'd driven there, but didn't feel comfortable driving back. My other friends were drunk too. I didn't want to call you because you had dinner with your brothers that night, and I knew it was important to you. So I asked Aaron to pick me up, and he said okay and brought me some water to help me sober up. I drank it and sort of passed out. I thought he'd drive me home, but when I woke up..." I put a hand over my mouth, then realize I can't speak like this. I fold my legs, pulling them to my chest and hugging them like I'll be safer this way. "I was naked...and Jude...Jude was on top of me."

"Mother*fucker*." Bryce's voice shakes with suppressed rage.

I hold myself tighter, making myself smaller. "It hurt so much, but the worst part was that he made videos of it. And photos. He threatened to send them to Sherry, and I was so scared of being cast aside." I press my forehead to a knee as hot tears fill my eyes. I don't want Bryce to see them and pity me.

He wraps his arm around my shoulders and holds me comfortingly. "If she'd cast you aside over those photos, she wouldn't deserve to be your mother," he says, his voice breaking.

I blink away the tears and lift my head. His eyes are bloodshot as he gazes at me with heartbreak. I realize his heart is hurting for the girl I was, and turn my hand in his to thread our fingers together. "I understand that now, but back then I was too terrified to think clearly. I never told you, but Sherry and Zachary weren't the first couple to adopt me. There was another who took me in because they couldn't have a baby of their own, but as soon as the wife got pregnant, they sent me back." His fingers tighten. "So in college, although I was legally old enough to be an adult, emotionally I was still really young and immature. I wasn't even sure if anybody would believe me if I went to the police. It'd have been my word against Jude's, but you remember how it was. He was popular in college, in addition to being Aaron's best friend. And Aaron *would* have sided with him. He never liked me. He would've loved to show Zachary and Sherry that they'd made a mistake when they adopted me."

"You were only nineteen." Bryce looks shattered.

I cradle his cheek with my free hand. I wish I could spare him this pain. "I thought I was making the best choice. Jude really hated you. So when you were out studying, he made me take him to your place and staged the entire scene. He actually wanted to have sex with me there, but I told him I was on my period. That grossed him out, but he couldn't let the chance to hurt you go to waste. So he made me fake it."

"Son of a bitch. I should've murdered him," Bryce seethes. "Why didn't you say something?" There's no accusation in his voice, which only serves to make me want to cry for the lost girl I was and the boy who got hurt by the betrayal.

"I was too scared. At first, I was too ashamed at the possibility that you might see the videos and photos Jude took. Then later, I didn't think you would be able to get over seeing me with Jude in your bed. I don't know if I could have, if the situation had been reversed. And what if you didn't love me anymore because I wasn't the perfect girl you'd thought I was?" My voice grows hoarse with unshed tears and old pain. "You said I reminded you of that pretty, cheerful rose you saw, the one that made you forget you were upset. Would you have loved a rose that'd been trampled on?"

"Yes. It's my rose. It's my job to shower it with love and care until it can recover and bloom beautifully again." His eyes grow damp with tears.

Regret wells up and almost chokes me. "I wish I'd *known*. I was so desperate to be loved, I didn't see that what I was doing only made you hate me. I thought you would despise me if you saw the videos and photos."

"I didn't give you the confidence."

I shake my head. "No. You're the best thing that's ever happened to me, Bryce. You just happened to fall for a girl with too much insecurity." I take a moment to gather myself, so I can finish the story. "Anyway... I couldn't see a way out until Jude had that accident. It nearly killed him, and while he was in the coma, I used his fingerprints to get into his computer and phone and delete everything. Everything on his hard drive, the phone and in the cloud. The relief I felt..." I exhale shakily. "It was one of the most liberating moments in my life. I burst into tears. Couldn't stop crying when I realized I was truly *free*, and Jude couldn't control me or hurt me anymore using those videos and photos. I felt so, so safe. But I also had to leave L.A. I didn't trust Aaron anymore. I had no evidence that he was involved, and Jude never mentioned it. But the more I thought about it, the stranger it seemed that I passed out and woke up with Jude that way. My gut told me things weren't adding up."

"I'm glad you listened to your instincts."

"I also selfishly wanted a new start, although that didn't go as well as planned. I was too scared to let anybody get close to me. I never wanted to experience that panic again. I never wanted to *need* someone to love me, or to love anybody. Loving just hurt too much. But in some ways, being away was healing. I found a therapist who helped me get better. I meditated, read and thought about all the ways things could've been different. There were anonymous support groups for rape victims, and they helped me realize I was simply a victim and shouldn't feel ashamed."

"I'm sorry. I should've been there for you."

I brush away the tear trickling down his cheek. "Don't cry, Bryce. It was a long time ago. And I'm okay now. And we found each other again."

His thumb swipes my cheek, and I realize I'm crying, too. "How can you say that? I was such an asshole—"

I put a finger over his mouth to stop him. "No. Didn't you hear what I said? You're the best thing that's happened to me. You saw me for *me*. You made me realize for the first time that I might be lovable the way I was. You're the one I never wanted to disappoint. I was crazy about you back then, and I'm crazy about you now."

"Fiona..."

"I'm telling you I love you. So if you respond by telling me what an asshole you've been, I'm going to be heartbroken."

His chin trembles. "Of course I love you. I love you more than life."

I spread my arms. "Then hug me."

He wraps his arms around me carefully. My tears drench his shirt, but I don't hold back. I want to let it all out. Bryce doesn't hide his heartache, either. As more of his tears soak my neck and shoulder, the old, throbbing pain in my heart seems to lessen until it's just a dull ache, barely noticeable.

We hold each other for a long time, long enough for our tears to dry.

43

BRYCE

When I come out of Fiona's room, Sherry is nowhere to be seen. My family must've driven her away. Good thing, even though part of me hungers for someone to vent my fury on. I don't know what I'd do if she were here. Probably throttle her.

I recall her unannounced visit to my office. That bitch must've known something—and that Aaron was involved. No way she didn't know.

My family comes over, taking in my teary face and growing worried.

Grandma reaches out with a shaky hand and holds my shoulder, digging her fingers in. "What happened to her? Is she..."

"Physically, she's as well as she can be, I guess," I croak. "She just woke up."

"Then why were you crying?" Aunt Jeremiah asks, probably peeved she had to show her emotional side.

"Tears of joy...?" Akiko suggests with an uncertain smile, which crumbles too fast.

I just nod. The family goes in to fuss over Fiona, but Ares and Josh stay back.

"You okay?" Ares peers at me. "You look like you just lost the most important case of your life."

"I just..." I rub my face, then lean against the wall as all the strength drains from my limbs. I rest the back of my head against the concrete and crank my neck. "Fiona told me everything about what happened ten years ago, and I want to kick my own ass."

"What did happen?" Josh asks.

"I can't tell you. It's too private. And don't ask her about it, either."

"Is that why you were crying?" Josh asks quietly.

"The things she told me are just heartbreaking. But she spoke without any expectation of sympathy. It's like everything happened so long ago and she had to figure out how to stand on her own again..." My voice cracks. "If I'd known back then what I know now, I would've gone to prison for two first-degree murders."

"Jesus. Who are they?" Ares demands.

"Jude." My voice is laced with stark hatred and poison. "And Aaron."

Josh's expression darkens. "Fuckers. They're under arrest, but they're going to try posting bail. Want to try to keep them in jail? Maybe we can find a way."

Having Jude and Aaron caged would be satisfying, but I don't want them sitting in jail. They'd be protected there, and I promised justice to my wife. But I realize that isn't all I want.

I want my pound of flesh—and blood—for what they've done. The justice system can't ever make Fiona whole for what she suffered when she was nineteen—or even now. Insufficient evidence. He said, she said. She asked for it. I know all the ways defense attorneys try to spin something like this to their clients off. "No. Let the system do its thing. I'm sure they'll pay the price."

My twin brother clenches his hands. "Why not make things harder for them?"

"We're lawyers, Josh," I say calmly. "We should trust the system and let it carry out justice."

Ares frowns. "Didn't you just say you would've been charged for a double murder?"

"Yeah, but that was for nineteen-year-old Bryce. I'm older now. Seeing the bigger picture," I say with a cool composure I don't feel.

"It's still justice to keep them in jail," Josh argues.

"No. We're *not* going to interfere with this case. And that's final."

44

FIONA

I SLUMP AGAINST THE PILLOWS, my eyes still swollen. The room feels too big and empty without Bryce, but he said he needed to go out and update the family. Maybe Akiko or Lareina dropped by. Everyone else is probably busy with work.

I look at the pretty flowers—fresh Fiona roses in the vases along with stunning pink orchids. I smile a little, knowing exactly who brought the roses.

The door opens, and Catalina walks in, followed by Prescott, Akiko, Lareina and Jeremiah, who shuts it firmly. Before I can say hello, Akiko cries, "Oh my God, you poor child."

"I'm okay," I say quickly.

Lareina rushes over and hovers. "I..." She struggles to find words to express her outrage.

I reach over and squeeze her hand. *I understand.*

She turns her hand in mine and holds tight.

"'Okay'? Look at the bruises on your face." Anger and concern burn in Prescott's eyes. "I'm going to do everything I can to make those two pay."

"I'm disappointed Bryce went easy on them," Jeremiah says with a scowl, then glances at Prescott. "Look what they did to her. They not only hurt her, but the baby as well. That's double kidnapping and assault."

Prescott purses his mouth. "We should add spikes to the cane design. That way it'll hurt more."

"Don't be ridiculous. I'm not degrading the design just for that." Catalina sniffs. "There are other things the family can do to punish those who hurt one of our own."

"Two," Lareina says. "They hurt *two* of our own."

Catalina's eyes chill. "True. Two." She studies me, her eyes brimming with worry. "Do you need anything for the pain, my dear?"

I shake my head.

"If you need anything for any reason, you let me know."

I'm stunned at how quickly Catalina's entire demeanor shifts, but I'm glad she considers me worthy. "Thank you."

"Bryce already gave a statement, but the police will need yours as well."

"When?" I ask, my mouth going dry. How much do I have to tell them? Just what happened three days ago or everything—like what happened at Harvard?

Jeremiah rolls her shoulders. "Whenever it's convenient for you. If they contact you directly, tell them to talk to your lawyer." She stands even taller in her heels. "Me."

"*You*'re my lawyer?" I glance at Prescott then back at her. Behind them, the door opens and Bryce, Ares and Josh slip inside.

She cocks an eyebrow. "Am I not good enough for you?"

"Nonononononono." I even shake my head, my eyes flicking to Bryce.

He moves over and puts a protective arm around my shoulders, lending me strength and comfort. "I just thought *Bryce* might want to be my lawyer," I say, patting his hand.

"This isn't his specialty. You want the very best—*me*." Jeremiah smiles, her eyes flashing murder. If she were a prosecutor, Jude and Aaron wouldn't get out of prison alive.

Akiko sighs. "Must we discuss unpleasant things right now? She should be allowed to rest. And get fed. What do you say to some fruit salad? I made some."

"Sure." I'm a little hungry, but since I haven't eaten in a while, I probably shouldn't eat anything too heavy. And her portions are tiny.

"Great. I made a large salad. You should eat extra. For the baby." She hands me a regular-sized bowl from the mini-fridge in the room.

Bryce, Ares and Josh stare, then glance at each other with *are you kidding me* looks.

I smile. At least it's not a shot glass. "Thank you." I take a bite of pineapple—juicy and sweet without any tartness.

"So when is the baby due?" Akiko asks after I swallow the first chunk.

"I don't know yet. I haven't had a chance to see an OB-GYN."

Catalina tsks. "What is that boy doing, not taking you to see a doctor?"

"We just found out!" Bryce says. "But the doc who checked Fiona over said she's about six weeks along."

She nods. "Let me know the date. We need to make sure we have a cane for the baby."

Tears surge, and I wipe my eyes before they can drip down. "A cane? *The* cane? My baby's worthy of the family cane?"

Catalina frowns. "Of course. Every Huxley gets one."

"Pietas et unitas," Lareina says.

Bryce nods. "You're family, Fiona. It's about time you get used to what that means."

45

FIONA

The next day, Josh visits me in the hospital. He comes alone, while Bryce is away preparing for a hearing. I give him a long look, unsure what he wants. I haven't forgotten what Bryce told me about the bug/tracker he placed in my purse. Although it ended up saving my life, I'm still unsure how I feel about his attempt to spy on me.

He clears his throat, shifts, then clears his throat again and sighs.

"Hi, Josh," I say.

"Hey." He shoves a huge bouquet of lilies in my face. "Here."

"Thanks?" I take the flowers and look at him with a mix of confusion and amusement. "So...?"

"I'm sorry."

I raise an eyebrow.

"About putting the bug in your purse. I shouldn't have, but I just didn't trust you."

"Well. Bryce and I didn't exactly have the best history, and I wasn't exactly forthcoming."

"Bryce warned me yesterday. He said..." Josh exhales and looks away.

I wait with bated breath. *Did Bryce tell his brother everything?* I don't really want it to be public knowledge. It took enormous courage to share with Bryce, and I'm not ready to do it with others. I may never be ready.

"He said you explained what happened back at school, and he basically said you were a victim. Wouldn't elaborate, but I trust his judgment."

My shoulders sag with relief and gratitude, glad that Bryce tried to resolve the bad feelings Josh and Ares might have for me without giving away the specifics of my past pain. "Thank you."

"So I'm going to trust you, too."

"That's all I want, Josh."

He looks at me steadily for several very long moments. Then, finally: "Yeah. Well. Guess we're good?"

I smile. "Yes. Thank you. Although I don't necessarily approve of the tracker, I'm glad you and Bryce found me when you did."

Pain and fury twist his face. "That should never have happened. They should've never had an opportunity to touch you."

I give him a helpless look. "I know, but people like Aaron and Jude only go after those weaker than them. They're cowards." I bury my nose in the flowers and breathe in the sweet fragrance. "But I'm glad to have a brother like you, Josh—loyal, brave and honest. Thank you."

His expression softens. He rocks his weight back and forth on his feet, then mutters, "What the hell," and comes over to hug me.

I embrace him back, so like Bryce and yet so different. "I'm glad we got to clear the air. And by the way, next time, bring me a box of truffles. The baby is craving chocolate so bad."

He laughs. "Got it."

Later that evening, a box of German chocolate arrives and I gorge on it with gusto. Bryce complains he could've gotten it for me, but I shake my head.

"It's not the same. Besides, this doesn't mean you can shirk *your* duties as my husband to bring me chocolate. I have a separate stomach just for that."

He laughs, then sends me two boxes the next morning. I text him a haiku and lots of heart emojis.

After two long days, I finally leave the hospital and come home.

Bryce wants me to stay longer—maybe until I deliver the baby, from the way he's acting—but I really don't like the place.

A week later, the bruises on my face have subsided enough to be hidden by makeup. However, Bryce continues to act like I'm about to shatter at any second. He won't let me touch anything heavier than a fork if he can help it.

"You know I'm not going to break, right?" I say over dinner of beef and cheese burritos at Manny's Tacos.

"Doesn't matter. Don't move. Just let me get you the guacamole."

I give him a look. "It's literally right in front of me."

"Exactly." He reaches all the way across the table, scoops it up from the bowl and places it on my plate.

When I whine to Lareina, she says it's just the way it is. "Ares was the same when my cousin nearly killed me. And I was hurt less than you. And I wasn't pregnant. Bryce will get over it once he realizes you're okay. It's just that...you know, with the baby, it may take longer."

I sigh, half exasperated and half affectionate. I know he means well, but does he have to be *this* impossible?

"He was devastated when you wouldn't wake up at the hospital. I've never seen a man look so lost. I mean, I was scared too when you didn't wake up for days. I can't imagine how Bryce must've felt," Lareina says. "Just indulge him for a bit."

I sigh again, but she makes sense. Unlike his family, he learned the truth about what happened ten years ago, and that must be weighing on him, too. Just like I needed time to heal, he's going to need time to sort through his emotions. If he wants to work it out by being overprotective... Well, I can deal with it.

Jeremiah visits me at the house and tells me Jude and Aaron got out on bail. Disappointing, but not shocking—they both must've hired top lawyers. Although Bryce promised they'd go to prison for life, it isn't something he can control.

Sherry seems to be siding with Aaron. She hasn't contacted me since we ran into each other outside Merry. It should hurt, but the pain is a barely perceptible throb. The old panic, the sheer terror that I might not be wanted, doesn't circle in my head like a vulture anymore.

I look at Jeremiah. The woman wears a cool, detached expression, but she speaks with patience, her eyes studying me from time to time to gauge my reaction.

"There's a restraining order, but those don't do much good. If I were you, I'd get bodyguards. Or at least don't go anywhere without the cane. It's perfectly weighed for swinging. As good as a golf club. If you want, I can teach you. Or Bryce can."

I realize this is her being family—no hugs, just solutions. I smile. "Thank you, Auntie."

The tips of her ears redden. "It's nothing." She stands, clearing her throat. "I need to get going. Deposition."

"Thanks again." I hug her.

She stiffens, then pats me awkwardly. "Take care of yourself. And don't forget: we stand with you. Always."

After she's gone, I look at my phone. The police want to talk and are coordinating a time with Jeremiah. She hates it that I have to relive the trauma, but I told her I'd do whatever necessary to make the two pay for their crimes.

My phone buzzes. I look at the screen and frown.

–Unknown: Finally. I can't believe you blocked me. How could you?

I lick my suddenly dry lips, my gut churning. The only people I blocked were Jude, Zoe and Aaron.

–Me: Who is this?

–Unknown: Me! Your mother!

–Me: Sherry?

–Unknown: Of course. Do you know how many times I had to text you and call? None of them connected. I had no idea until Aaron told me.

I don't remember blocking her, but my phone broke during the kidnapping incident, and Bryce replaced it. Did *he* block Sherry?

Annoyance fleets through me at his high-handedness, but I focus on how she said Aaron told her she got blocked. So she's with him now. That explains why Bryce didn't want her to be able to reach me. I also note she hasn't said a word of concern for me. She has to have heard what happened. After all, it isn't something Aaron can hide.

She didn't visit me at the hospital, didn't even send flowers. Nobody from the Huxley family brought her up, either. Maybe Bryce's family—no, *my* family—already knows she doesn't really care about me and wants to keep her away.

–Me: What do you want?

–Unknown: How are you?

Now she's asking?

–Me: Fine.

–Unknown: Glad to hear it. Can you forgive Aaron?

–Me: FORGIVE HIM???

–Unknown: Do you have to send him to prison? He's your family, your brother.

I start to shake. She waited all this time, got a new number and finally reached out *only to save her son's ass*?

I call the unknown number. Sherry picks up immediately.

"Do you know he gave me to Jude *to be raped?* Do you know it wasn't his first time?

"He's remorseful," Sherry says. Her calm voice is anathema to my ears. "He didn't mean to. He's your brother, Finn."

"And how about me? What am I to you? Do I mean anything except as a tool for better reincarnation for Finley? Do I get to be treated with some respect and dignity?"

"I've always treated you as my own child. You know that."

"If Finley were alive and Aaron did to her what he did to me, would you ask her to forgive him?"

Two beats, and no response.

"Exactly," I say. "*Never fucking call me again.*"

I hang up and block Sherry, resisting the urge to hurl the phone against the wall. There's no need for an answer. I know where she stands.

When it really matters, she abandons me with ease.

I clung to her so hard for so long, hoping and praying that she could be the family I desperately wanted, even though deep inside I knew it would never be. Why did I waste so much of my life trying to be perfect for her? Why did I sacrifice so much for someone who wasn't worthy?

I feel stupid and ridiculous, but I don't let myself cry. Sherry doesn't deserve my tears. After being around Bryce's family, I've realized that *family* loves you unconditionally—*family* backs you up without question. I don't have to be perfect to be worthy.

46

BRYCE

"Gotta say, I'm a little surprised you wanted to see me."

I take the seat opposite Harvey at Merry. He already has a steaming coffee in front of him. I order an iced Americano and ask the server to prepare a box of desserts. Fiona's been craving a lot of sweets.

"How's your wife doing?" he says, crossing his legs. His expression is relaxed, but his eyes are sharp.

Just thinking about how she looked when I found her makes my blood boil, but I maintain a cool, indifferent smile. "Could be better."

He makes a small noise in the back of his throat. "In case you're wondering, it wasn't me."

"I'm not." Harvey's too methodical and rational to go after Fiona. Mom, on the other hand, is another matter. When it comes to family, she's unable to think straight because she's so hung up on how she isn't part of it anymore—how she was robbed of her children. "Did Mom have anything to do with it?"

"Not sure, but..." He shakes his head. "Nah, probably not. Idiots like those two? She would've picked somebody more capable."

I take a sip of the icy coffee placed in front of me. "Don't you have spies?"

"Sure. But I can't have her watched twenty-four seven."

Doubtful. He just doesn't want to show all his cards yet. "Fiona's pregnant."

He uncrosses his legs and sits up, but there's no surprise in his eyes. He probably heard already. Likely has spies at the hospital too. Not that I'm upset about that. You can't hide a pregnancy, and sooner or later, Harvey would've found out anyway.

"Is she, now?" he says.

I nod, trying to decide how I'm going to use him to fulfill my promise to Fiona. I vowed that Jude and Aaron would stay in prison for life, but that isn't likely based on the state penal code. And in any case, it's not enough.

I'd take care of them myself, except I need to stay pristine for my wife and our unborn baby. But there are other ways to get what I want.

"Yup. Got a sonogram." I pull it out of my pocket and show it to him.

Greed flares in his gaze. I'm a little surprised he hasn't tried to break into the doctor's office to grab a copy. I thought he'd read over the OB-GYN's files already. He reaches for it.

I pull it back. I was going to show him the sonogram, then throw in a handwritten note as a bonus, but I guess that won't be necessary.

His eyebrows snap together. "What's this supposed to be?"

"You know what it is. Want it?"

"You offering it?"

"Aren't you planning to steal it?"

He sits up straight. "You think I'm a common criminal?"

"Don't answer my question with another question, Harvey."

"Of course I want it. It's my first grandnephew."

"Might be a grandniece." My heart is already melting at the idea of having a baby girl with Fiona's eyes and spirit.

"Whichever. Children are precious. Yours in particular." His eyes flash with calculation.

"Vincent would be thrilled to...you know." I wave the black-and-white photo.

A corner of Harvey's mouth quirks. "Do tell."

I study my uncle. He's so happy, it's disgusting. It reminds me of Mom, professing love for me and my brothers as she tried to kidnap us.

In some ways, Harvey and Mom are too much alike—nothing but self-interest at heart.

It irritates me that I have to use my unborn child as a lever, but if I don't seize the opportunity, the Dunkels will take matters into their own hands. I doubt it'll end with just breaking into the doctor's office and stealing medical records. Harvey and Mom can't remain civilized for long, not while half of Nesovia's organized crime is at stake. This way, I'm in charge of what happens and can extract concessions from Harvey.

Aaron and Jude *will* pay for what they did.

Harvey sticks his hand out, palm up. "I answered your question."

"You can have the sonogram. And a signed affidavit from me saying it's real. But there's a quid pro quo."

He leans back, his eyes narrowing. Now I'm speaking his language. "Aren't you doing this to fuck your mom over?"

"No. But even if I were, you hate her more. I'm giving you a chance, Harvey. Vincent probably needs something to cheer him up in his old age. Just imagine if you could present him a sonogram of his first great-grandchild. What it would do for your prospects?"

His eyes are fully hooded now. "You know what it would do."

I nod. "We both do. So earn it. Be a dutiful son to your father, taking care of the family. Be a good uncle to me and Fiona." I hold his eyes. "*Twice.*" I chug down the rest of the coffee and stand. "Thanks for the Americano."

I leave the café behind. Harvey's a smart man. He'll figure out what he has to do.

I stop by Sebastian Jewelry on the way home, but don't see anything appealing. Irritating. Harry Winston doesn't have anything that screams Fiona's name either. It shouldn't be this hard to get something sparkly for my wife, should it?

I head to Peery Diamonds, hoping the store has something. The clerk smiles at me. "Good afternoon. Anything special in mind?"

"No. I just feel like my wife deserves something pretty." A small grin tugs at my mouth as I think about Fiona.

The clerk obviously approves. "Mmm, romantic."

"Well, she deserves it." I smile. "How about a marquise- or princess-cut diamond, ideally ten carats or bigger?"

"Certainly. This way." She leads me to one of the private rooms. It's cozy without appearing small, and the leather couch is quite comfy. I stretch my legs out as she places a dark velvet tray with several rings on the glass-top table in front of me. "These are some of our best items."

My eyes skim over the rings—pretty, but nothing exceptional...

Wait...!

My heart pounds. *This is it!* I lean forward. "That one." I point to a gorgeous marquise-cut red stone.

"An excellent choice. Red is the rarest of the colored diamonds." She picks it up with a gloved hand and lifts it to the light, letting the exquisitely cut stone sparkle. The shade matches the roses in the garden. "It's a little small, however. Slightly under eight, but I thought you might appreciate the quality and rarity." She turns the piece slowly, showing me the whole ring. "The stones on the French pavé band are clear diamonds, round brilliant, 1.1 millimeter in diameter each."

"Perfect. I'll take it."

She smiles, then prepares a purchase agreement. A little over eight million. Not too bad for a ring this perfect for my wife.

I have my banker deal with the payment with the clerk and leave with the ring, then pick up a case of the sparkling pear and peach juice Fiona has been addicted to since getting pregnant.

When I get home, she greets me lying prone on the couch, eyes hazy with sleep. "Did you nap?" I ask, then place a kiss on her soft mouth.

She nods. "I'm *constantly* sleepy."

"Good. You need the rest."

She shakes her head. "I'm sleeping my life away. I'm pregnant, not a hibernating bear."

"Who cares? Do what you like."

She looks at the glossy bags hanging from my wrist. "Are those for me?"

"Desserts from Merry, along with your sparkling pear and peach juice."

Her eyes wide, she sits up and hugs me. "You're the best. How did you know I was craving them?"

I laugh. "Because you crave them every day." I kiss her forehead tenderly.

"The *baby* craves them," she says, even as she greedily eyes my gifts.

I chuckle. "Of course. How thoughtless of me."

Grinning, she starts to pull out the miniature sweets. Before she opens the box, I gently grasp her left hand and drop to one knee. The smile on her lips fades slowly as she looks at me.

"Fiona. You're the rose that makes my heart sing. The beautiful thing I've been searching all my life to brighten every day I live. I love you more than I can express. Will you marry me?" I open the lid.

Her gaze drops to the ring, then back to my face, her jaw slack. "Thank you...? But... We're already married... Aren't we?"

I smile. "Yes...but you deserved a better proposal. I want to replace that old, ugly memory with a beautiful new one. Will you let me?"

She cups the back of my neck and presses her forehead on mine. "Every time I don't think I can love you more, you prove me wrong. Yes. And yes." She kisses me. "Yes forever."

47

BRYCE

My phone vibrates on my desk. I take a quick break from reviewing a motion I need to file, in case it's Fiona needing something. She says she doesn't want to bother me during the day, but I love it when she texts me with food she's craving. She's gotten over chocolate, but now she can't get enough of Korean glass noodles. Apparently, a friend of Lareina's fed her some and now she's obsessed.

–Unknown: I deserve more than one. I should get three. I'm your uncle, damn it.

I frown at the message. *Harvey*. It's been two weeks since we spoke, and I thought he wasn't going to bother.

Still… What does he mean *three*? He doesn't explain further, probably to avoid implicating himself. He trusts me as much as I trust him. I don't ask for clarification, since I don't want anything to come back to haunt me later.

However, Harvey knows if I don't see how he "earned" it, I won't give him anything. I Google Jude's name to see what pops up. Several articles, all of them less than an hour old.

I click on the top one, skimming. Two males. Out on bail after allegedly kidnapping and attempting to rape a local woman. Apparently were drunk and got into a bar fight the night before. Likely beaten to death by somebody holding a grudge, because the bodies were bruised and mutilated. Discovered by a YouTuber who put it on his channel.

I pull up YouTube. The guy is breathlessly recounting the condition of the bodies, his face pale. "Genital mutilation. Holy shit. Their mouths held the missing dicks. Guys, I almost threw up," he says wild-eyed, sweat beads under his nose.

I turn off the video and drop the phone on the desk with a soft sigh. I honestly don't know what I expected when I asked Harvey to "earn it." But I wanted Jude and Aaron punished for *all* that they'd done, and the state of California would only have meted out justice for the kidnapping and attempted rape...and even that would have been plea-bargained down. I was never going to get the kind of justice *I* wanted, where all their crimes were listed for the world to see, so that everyone could condemn and spit on those two pathetic excuses for men.

Is this heaviness in my heart remorse? No. I'm not sorry they're dead. Just frustrated that the legal system's justice will always be incomplete.

When a couple of detectives drop by to ask about my whereabouts last night, I tell them I was home, with my pregnant wife, to help her get over the trauma, and I'd be more than happy to provide security footage of my being inside with her the entire night.

They have nothing. Harvey's annoying as hell, but his men do good work, which is why he's been able to expand into the U.S. despite the criminal organizations already established here.

I have a special courier deliver three sonograms in an envelope for Harvey.

–Me: I'm sending you the last three sonograms. You're staying at the Aylster, right? I'll leave them with reception.

–Unknown: I'll have them picked up tonight

–Me: Enjoy them. Quid pro quo.

I block the number. He'll understand the subtext: *stay the hell away.*

48

FIONA

The strains of "Here Comes the Bride" soar to the sky. My heart flutters, full of anticipation and joy.

The groom—my husband—stands on the other side of our gorgeous yard, surrounded by Fiona roses in full bloom, their aroma sweetening the air.

Next to him as his groomsmen are his brothers. Lareina is my maid of honor—the only one. I don't have any friends and no one from the Obermans is here. But that's okay, because I'm surrounded by people who want the best for me.

I wanted the ceremony small and intimate, just family. Catalina sighs with a huge smile. Prescott and Akiko sit together, watching me get ready to march to their son. Jeremiah nods, but she isn't the most emotive type. Bryce's cousin came also with his wife.

Isn't this perfect?

Bryce smiles brilliantly, waiting for me. I smile back and take a step, then another. My pulse races. When I told him I wanted a husband who loved me and a family I could belong to—my heart might've known I was talking about him.

My strides get faster, and then I'm running toward him. His smile grows wider and brighter. Laughter and cheers rise from our family.

He spreads his arms, and I wrap my arms around his neck, holding on to my love, my husband, my future.

49

JOSH

Am I doing the right thing?

Neutrality isn't going to work in the war between Mom and Harvey. They're going to do whatever it takes to pull me and my brothers into their power struggle. And both of them will do whatever it takes to win. Although Vincent disapproves of their hurting family, I don't trust them to heed his warning. I'll never forget how he sided with Mom, not us, when she nearly killed Ares.

Still, there are so many things that I don't care for about what Vincent is doing. He has to have an heir in mind, but he's letting his children fight it out, with us as little more than pawns. It's almost like he's taunting them—*neither of you is good enough, so fight it out for my amusement.*

"This way," a nondescript man in a crisp black suit says. He'd be a great companion to keep around if you didn't want to be noticed.

He opens the door and gestures me inside. I walk into the suite and see an elderly man in a leather armchair.

Was he always this small? He used to be so big and thick, like a tree. But now thin skin hangs off his bony face and rather slim body. If he didn't have the respect of—and dirt on—everyone, somebody might've eliminated him a long time ago.

"Josh," he says in a reedy voice.

"Hello."

"Come closer." He gestures. "Let me see you."

The old resentment and fury over the injustices my brothers and I have suffered start to simmer, but I hide them with a smooth smile, the kind I wear to court before I fuck the other side over. "Yes, Grandfather."

He gives me a long look up and down. "As I expected. Sharp. Ruthless. A true Dunkel." Vincent's eyes shine with pride. "There's someone I want you to meet."

A man steps out of the shadows behind Vincent. He towers like a century-old oak, much like Grandfather did in his prime. A small white scar by his left eye stands out against his tanned complexion. Other than that, he's a carbon copy of Vincent. Too old to be some hidden love child gotten late in his life.

Bryce's mention of the other brother Mom allegedly killed flashes in my mind.

The man smiles. "Hello, nephew."

TITLES BY NADIA LEE

Standalone Titles

Beauty and the Assassin

Oops, I Married a Rock Star

The Billionaire and the Runaway Bride

Flirting with the Rock Star Next Door

Mister Fake Fiancé

Marrying My Billionaire Hookup

Faking It with the Frenemy

Marrying My Billionaire Boss

Stealing the Bride

The Huxley's

The Accidental Marriage

Her Wicked Husband

The Lasker Brothers

Baby for the Bosshole

My Grumpy Billionaire

The Ex I'd Love to Hate

Contractually Yours

Finally Forever

Still Mine

The Unwanted Bride

The Sins Trilogy

Sins

Secrets

Mercy

The Billionaire's Claim Duet

Obsession

Redemption

Sweet Darlings Inc.

That Man Next Door

That Sexy Stranger

That Wild Player

Billionaires' Brides of Convenience

A Hollywood Deal

A Hollywood Bride

An Improper Deal

An Improper Bride

An Improper Ever After

An Unlikely Deal

An Unlikely Bride

A Final Deal

The Pryce Family

The Billionaire's Counterfeit Girlfriend

The Billionaire's Inconvenient Obsession

The Billionaire's Secret Wife

The Billionaire's Forgotten Fiancée

The Billionaire's Forbidden Desire

The Billionaire's Holiday Bride

Seduced by the Billionaire

Taken by Her Unforgiving Billionaire Boss

Pursued by Her Billionaire Hook-Up

Pregnant with Her Billionaire Ex's Baby

Romanced by Her Illicit Millionaire Crush

Wanted by Her Scandalous Billionaire

Loving Her Best Friend's Billionaire Brother

ABOUT NADIA LEE

New York Times and *USA Today* bestselling author Nadia Lee writes sexy contemporary romance. Born with a love for excellent food, travel and adventure, she has lived in four different countries, kissed stingrays, been bitten by a shark, fed an elephant and petted tigers.

Currently, she shares a condo overlooking a small river and sakura trees in Japan with her husband and son. When she's not writing, she can be found reading books by her favorite authors or planning another trip.

To learn more about Nadia and her projects, please visit http://www.nadialee.net. To receive updates about upcoming works, sneak peeks and bonus epilogues featuring some of your favorite couples from Nadia, please visit http://www.nadialee.net/vip to join her VIP List.

Printed in Dunstable, United Kingdom

68639028R00180